UNCLEAN HANDS

UNCLEAN HANDS

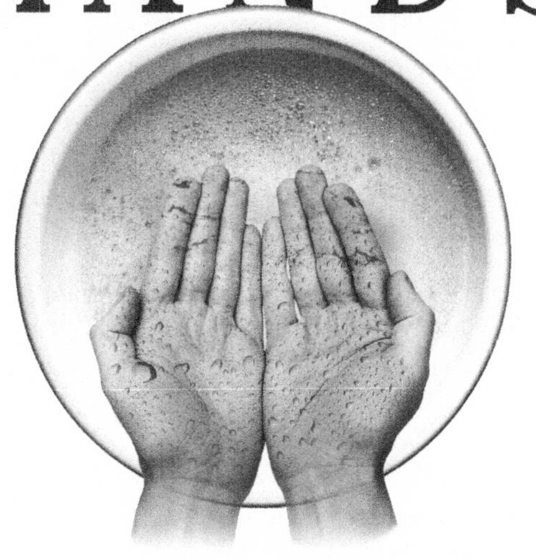

ANDREW SCHAFER, M.D.

Unclean Hands

For information about this title or to order other books and/or electronic media, contact the publisher:

Andrew Schafer
ais2007@med.cornell.edu

ISBNs:
978-0-9999036-1-2 (hardcover)
978-0-9999036-3-6 (softcover)
978-0-9999036-4-3 (eBook)

Printed in the United States of America

To Pauline

and

In memory of my parents, Stephen and Lili

PROLOGUE

AUGUST 15, 1865

Five men in black frock coats and a young priest encircled the freshly dug grave. They acknowledged each other with slight nods. Barely a word was exchanged. The sultry summer afternoon quickly turned ominously dark. Gusts of moisture-laden wind whipped in to announce the arrival of a storm. As the priest began the burial ritual, the skies opened. Struggling to open their umbrellas against the downpour, the men stared down at the rain-pelted casket in the ground. The first flashes of lightning appeared in the distance, so the priest hurried the rest of the rites: "*requiem aeternam dona ai, Domine, et lux perpetae luceat ei.*"

The driving rain now obscured the bleakness of the Schmelz cemetery, located in a godforsaken suburb of Vienna.[1] Patches of brown grass overrun by weeds sprung from the bare earth that was quickly turning into mud, creating gullies of streaming rainwater. The men standing around the priest were all doctors. They knew each other well, but avoided each other's eyes. Joseph Spath, along with the brothers Carl and Gustav Braun, were well-known Viennese obstetricians. Lajos Markusovszky was a Hungarian surgeon who had traveled here by the new train from Budapest. Karl von Rokitansky was a world-renowned pathologist at Vienna's medical school.[2]

The men were attending the funeral of a colleague. Ignác Semmelweis had died suddenly, unexpectedly, at the age of forty-seven.

"Shall we wait for his family before we continue?" The priest raised his voice to be heard over the roar of the pummeling rain.

"They're not coming!" shouted one of the mourners.

As soon as the service was over, the men scurried off in different directions, leaving a drenched cemetery worker to hurriedly fill the grave with mucky earth.

CHAPTER 1

AUGUST 1837

For the first time since the boat departed from Budapest, the two young men sat silently, spellbound by the majesty of the Danube Bend. Atop the Basilica of Esztergom they could make out only the base of its dome under construction. The river beneath the blazing summer sun was congested with vessels of all kind, including crude box-like boats, ferries, barges, cargo ships, and paddle streamers spewing smoke. Nineteen-year-old Ignác Semmelweis was on his way to begin law school in Vienna, accompanied by a young man he called Marko. They were aboard the single-chimney steamboat *SS Franz* of the First Danube Steamboat Company.[3] Marko was Lajos Markusovszky, now an advanced medical student. Ignác looked to Marko to be his savvy roommate and guide to Vienna and its renowned university.

Ignác's cheeks were flushed with the excitement of adventure. Even as the sun was setting on the hot day, he could barely contain his restlessness as the ship approached the port of Nussdorf, just outside Vienna. Young Hungarians, like others within the vast territories of Vienna's Habsburg Empire, were mostly considered too unrefined to merit a place amongst Austria's elite students, so he had never dreamed of being admitted to the glamorous capital's renowned university.

Finally docked in port, the two students jostled down the gangplank with their bulging suitcases, swept along by the disembarking mass of mostly well-dressed, German-speaking passengers. Before long they were in a carriage, teetering and rattling along the rough dirt roads toward their student apartment just outside the ancient walls of Vienna's Inner City. Lugging their hefty, beat-up trunks of leather, wood, and heavy iron up three flights of narrow steps, they barged through their apartment door and collapsed onto their beds.

Ignác was jolted awake late the next morning, overcome by an alarmed sense of dislocation. Sitting up in bed, he squinted at the beam of midday sunshine streaming through a small window. Marko was gone, and Ignac's eyes fell on a card on the nightstand they shared:

"Didn't want to wake you. Had to go to the hospital to work. Coffee this afternoon at 4 at the little shop next door? M."

Ignác would have to find his way to the university to register for his first year of law school classes and to buy the required books. He dressed quickly and skipped down the steps of their third-floor corner apartment at Wickenburggasse 2, in the Josefstadt district, where most students lived. He passed by the main entrance to the general hospital, the *Allgemeine Krankenhaus*, on Alserstrasse, stopping to ask the guard to let him glance inside its enormous oak door. He got a glimpse of a vast campus of interconnected buildings separated by grassy courtyards, not at all the bleak bastion he envisioned a hospital would look like. He wondered for a moment where Marko might be working in there.

He walked briskly through a gate in the wall surrounding the outer city, into Vienna's Inner City. He was awestruck by the magnificent buildings. Nothing like Budapest, with its unplanned hodgepodge of low-slung, dilapidated structures, described as Ignác remembered reading by the Hungarian statesman of the time, István Széchenyi, as "*pór és sár*" (a city of "dust and mud"). There were mansions, small palaces, and grand structures with massive granite steps leading up to column-lined porticos. There were ornate Gothic churches and cathedrals. And all around there were well-groomed gardens with flowers in full bloom and larger-than-life statues everywhere. On one street, he came across a small battalion of street sweepers with brooms, shovels, and dustpans, cleaning off litter and horse waste. One was washing the street with a water hose attached to the nozzle of a hydrant. No wonder the pavements and roadways were pristine. To Ignác there was something impossibly splendid about this panorama of Vienna.

He found his way to the university's main building, which housed the offices of the "Juridicum," the Faculty of Law. Bounding up the white marble staircase, his heart pounding, he became aware of the echoes of his own footsteps. He walked through spacious hallways with gilded walls and marble floors until he encountered other students streaming toward the registration area. Most wore monochromatic frock-coats with upstanding collars encircled by neckties. Ignác self-consciously stood out wearing his finest Hungarian folk clothing, ablaze with a riot of colors. Mortified, Ignác slinked away as quickly as possible after registering and got directions to the used-book store, which sold the required textbooks. He had to buy five very big, very heavy tomes. They were titled *Ancient Roman Law*, *Bailments*, *Equity Contracts*, *Parliamentary Law*, and *Lex Mercatoria*. He then lugged them for several blocks to the café where he was supposed to meet Marko.

Marko was already there, smoking a cigar. Panting and perspiring, Ignác dropped his armload of books onto the table in front of him.

"You look a little flustered, my friend," said Marko, crossing his legs and leaning back in a feigned pose of relaxation.

"Goddamn it, look at these!" stammered Ignác. "What the hell am I supposed to do with them?"

"Well, I suppose you have to read them," Marko said, impishly twitching his eyebrows. "And you had better read them *fast*."

"Why fast?"

"Because you must have thousands of pages there," he replied, pointing to the heap of books on the table. "And you have to memorize it all. Didn't you know that?"

"Go to hell, Marko," snapped Ignác as he slumped into his chair. "I don't even understand the *titles* of these fucking books."

"Well, it's not just reading and memorizing." Marko sent up a puff of smoke toward the ceiling. "There is also a lot of writing to do in law school."

"How would you know all that?" the exasperated Ignác challenged his roommate.

"Well, what do you think lawyers *do*? They have to read and write all day."

Dead silence followed. Ignác was by now so discomposed that he couldn't tell if his friend was mocking him or being dead serious about what lay ahead.

"So tell me, my friend. I never asked you this, but what made you choose law for a career?" continued Marko.

"My father thought I could become a military judge. Even if not, he said, a legal career would open all sorts of doors for me to pursue civil service, move up in society."

"Is that what you want, Ignác? To move up in society? Is that your goal?"

"No," Ignác snapped. "That was his goal, not mine. I just want to make a difference. I want to be recognized as someone who has contributed something important to society. In any case, I did very well in school in Buda, except maybe in writing."

"Aha!" interrupted Marko. "But that's what lawyers have to do *especially* well. Writing! If you don't like to do that, it's like a doctor saying he doesn't like to be around sick people."

As the friends finished their *Kaffee mit Schlag* in silence, the dismayed Ignác stared ahead blankly, the pile of books on the table blocking his view of the amused Marko.

Over the next few weeks, the drudgery of law school deepened in Ignác's mind. To break the tedium, he took Marko up on his offer to take him to a medical school lecture.

On the walk to the medical school, Marko explained to Ignác what they were going to attend.

"It's a class in anatomical and forensic pathology," said Marko.

"Forensic sounds like just law school!"

"We examine the organs and tissues of someone who has just died to try to understand the mechanisms of whatever disease killed him."

"An autopsy?"

"Well, it's much more than that. It's a very detailed investigation. An autopsy is just seeking the cause of death. Here we want to understand the disease that caused the death. One of our younger faculty members, named Rokitansky, brought these ideas here."

Ignác perked up. "So, he will be lecturing?"

"No," replied Marko, "it will be one of his colleagues, Joseph Berres.[4] He is a physician who is also an expert microscopist."

As Professor Berres entered the lecture room, the clamor of medical students talking with each other immediately subsided. He spoke forcefully and eloquently.

"Gentlemen, we have developed a new field of 'photomicrography.' We have found a way to adapt the process of taking photographs through the lens of a microscope, using an iodine-sensitized plate and mercury vapor."

Berres turned on his ponderous contraption on a table at the front of the room. It was an opaque projector that he had modified from the megascope to enable him to show images on the white wall behind him.

"This process allows us to project pictures taken through the microscope. We can create these images using a photographic process called daguerreotype."

The first image appeared on the wall in the darkened lecture room.

"This is a common leaf. Here you see the midrib, the veins," said Berres, pointing to each structure of the leaf that could be identified by the naked eye upon very close inspection. "But what can we *not* see without the power of a microscope?"

Fumbling, he exchanged the photomicrograph being projected for another one as some students giggled.

"Here is the leaf's cuticle, its epidermis," and he pointed to each of the microscopic layers of the leaf that had been dissected.

"Next, we are looking at something else. What is it?" There was silence in the room. "Anyone?"

"A spider," shouted out one student.

"An ant," shouted another.

"Brilliant!" Berres shot back. "And you can see very clearly each part of this ant's anatomy as viewed through a microscope. The antennae, the mandible, the compound eyes, the propodium, and, of course, the sting at the back. But what's inside, beneath the surface?"

He changed to the next slide.

"These are things *none* of you have probably ever seen before. The ant's inner organs. This is its digestive tract, this is its hind gut, and here, very prominently, is its nervous system running along the back."

There were murmurs of impressed acknowledgment throughout the room. Ignác leaned forward.

"But, gentlemen, I am a doctor," continued Berres. "And you will be doctors. Nothing could be of more interest to us than to use this new method of photomicrography to discover the microscopic structure of human organs. Human organs in health. And human organs in disease. Side by side. To see exactly how they differ in those conditions. Pathological *anatomy* will be critical for us to be able to discover what aberrant *physiological* changes are responsible for various diseases. Now look at this."

Professor Berres fiddled with his opaque projector.

"Now what is this?" Professor Berres paused, hands in his pockets, proudly thrusting out his chest. There was no response.

"Aha! You can see these beautifully organized, elongated bubbles, called 'cells,' one stacked on top of another. Like we would have in a neatly piled stack of books," he continued. "Except these are cells that can be seen only through a microscope."

Marko turned to Ignác with a devious smile in the darkened auditorium. But Ignác was transfixed.

"So *these*, gentlemen, are called cardiomyocytes. They are the cells of heart muscle. I have prepared this photomicrograph from the heart of a healthy young man who was killed in an accident. This is how cardiac muscle cells should look *normally*."

Berres left the slide on for a full minute, saying nothing, allowing the students to fully assimilate the image. He had one more slide to show.

"And these cells are *also* cardiomyocytes. But they don't look normal, do they? There are big gaps in the layers of cells in this case. You can also see," he said as he pointed to it, "the amorphous material that has accumulated between the heart cells. This is a preparation I recently made from the heart muscle of a sixty-year-old man who died in our hospital from heart failure."

All the students were now sitting forward in their seats.

"*This*," Professor Berres declared, "is what will give us the critical clues to understanding why and how heart failure occurs. Without this knowledge of basic structure, we can have little idea about function. And, without understanding the relationship between structure and function in health and disease, we cannot hope to find effective, rational treatments."

While other students rapped their knuckles on their desktops in acclamation, Marko noticed that Ignác looked dazed.

On the way down the staircase from the lecture room, Marko had to ask.

"Is there something wrong, my friend?"

"Hell no, Marko. I had never thought of doctors also being able to study things like this, doing research. How exciting it must be for a physician to discover something big, something that will change the care of patients for the better. Do they really do that?"

"Well who else would do it?" Marko asked with a self-satisfied smile ear to ear.

Several days later, Ignác was returning to his apartment after a long day of law classes, one arm weighed down by textbooks, and distracted by far-away thoughts about his uncertain future, when he suddenly found himself lost. He had wandered off his usual path and into a wretched neighborhood of dilapidated houses, crumbling shacks, and seedy-looking tenements outside the city walls. Nothing like the Vienna inside the city wall that he'd beheld on his first day there. Pavements had disappeared, and the dirt roads were strewn with trash. A nauseating stench emanated from cesspits behind houses and open sewers that ran along the roads, clogged with human waste. There were emaciated, stray dogs walking around, but no people to point the way back toward his apartment. From some distance ahead, he suddenly heard what sounded like a protracted, deep moan. And each time it subsided, it started up again, louder than before. As he approached, he could make out that the grunting was followed by rapid, frantic panting before it completely stopped again.

In the alley he was passing, he saw the form of a woman, crumpled on the dirt roadway, looking up toward him with an expression of terror on her face. As he hurried to come to her aid, he noticed that the ground around her was soaked with a clear fluid that was seeping away from her, and her half-raised skirt was stained with blood. She tried to crawl away as he approached, but Ignác reassured her that he was just passing by and only wanted to help. Standing over her, he now saw that she was just a girl, no older than perhaps fifteen or sixteen, holding her big belly with both hands. She began to emit another sustained spasm of full-throated moaning interspersed with panting. Although he had never seen anything like this before, Ignác knew she was in labor.

He squatted down next to the girl and stroked her perspiring and dirt-smudged forehead. She confirmed that she was about to have a baby. Feeling unnerved and helpless, Ignác told her he was going to run to get some help to take her to the hospital as fast as possible. But as he got up to do that, the girl screamed.

"*Ich möchte nicht! Noch nie!* I am not going to the hospital. I am going to have my baby right here. Mothers are murdered in the hospital!"

She must be delirious from her agony, Ignác thought, so he bent down again and asked her hesitantly if he could look under her skirt at the area she was clutching with both hands. She nodded. Then another wave of the excruciating spasms began, and her face turned red from straining. Between her legs, Ignác could barely make out the moldy crown of a baby's head. He sat down on the ground across from her and instinctively held the emerging baby's head. At this moment, a pudgy, elderly woman wearing work clothes and an apron came waddling out of the house next door, as fast as she could.

"Oh, my God, Johanna. You are having the baby right here and now?" she yelled, holding a hand to her mouth.

"Are you her mother?" Ignác asked, now kneeling on the ground, supporting the girl's shoulders.

"I am her grandmother. Her mother died after giving birth to her. And who are you? Are you a medical student, dearie?" she asked hopefully.

"No, I am a law student," replied Ignác just as Johanna started another noisy contraction.

"Oh, Jesus Christ!" the grandmother shouted, slapping her forehead in horrified disbelief.

But this contraction was finally expelling the baby, head first. The woman exhorted her granddaughter. "Push! Push! Push!"

The baby emerged slippery, slimy, silent, and very blue. Ignác reflexively reached for his handkerchief and wiped the baby's face, cleared out his mouth, and vigorously rubbed his back along his rib cage. And suddenly the newborn burst forth with his first agonizingly forceful cry, turned to a purplish hue, and then a deep pink. The grandmother gently placed the baby onto Johanna's chest, and it wasn't long before the newborn sought to nurse. Meanwhile, the afterbirth was delivered, attached to the cord, and Johanna began to bleed. Her grandmother turned to run back into the house to get a pan and some cloths, she said. By the time she returned, Ignác had already covered the baby with his jacket. The placenta was placed into the pan, still attached to the baby, and the grandmother asked Ignác to find a carriage to take her to the hospital to get it cut. Johanna screamed again:

"Not the hospital! We are not going to the hospital! Never!"

But her grandmother reassured her that it was just to have the cord cut and the placenta separated, nothing more. A neighbor ran to hail a carriage, and when it finally arrived Ignác accompanied them with the girl's newborn to the hospital, through the main entrance and all the way up to the closed gate to the maternity wing, where they were received by an attendant and a nurse to take them to the ward upstairs. It was the same *Allgemeine Krankenhaus* Ignác had peeked at on the way to his law school registration, the hospital where Marko was a student.

Johanna was quiet now, content and smiling, with her son nursing. The older woman was silently weeping with joy. She kissed her own hand and touched it to Ignác's forehead in a gesture of gratitude.

"You are going to make a very good lawyer, young man," she said, laughing through the tears.[5]

The following week, Ignác was able to find his way back to Johanna's house in the suburban slums. The grandmother opened the door, hugged him, and asked him to come in for a few minutes to "see what you did!" In the darkness of the small, run-down room, another child, maybe two years old, was stumbling around the floor. Johanna was sitting on a broken-down couch, holding her baby. When she saw Ignác, she sprang to her feet, handed the baby to her grandmother, and embraced him.

"My Grandma says you were my savior," she sobbed. And then she carefully handed him the baby to hold for a while.

When Ignác returned to his apartment, Marko looked up at him from his armchair with an expression of concern. Ignác was disheveled, covered with encrusted dirt and blood, and beaming from ear to ear as if he had lost his mind.

"What the hell . . ."

"Say hello to a new godfather," Ignác said to his now utterly bewildered, speechless friend. "I will be a godfather; can you believe it? And I think I have found a new calling."

CHAPTER 2

FALL 1837

Ignác wrote a long letter to his father explaining his wish to switch his studies from law to medicine. He said he hoped his father wouldn't be too disappointed. A terse reply followed, simply giving his assent, which gladdened Ignác. It then took only a few days for Ignác to complete the university's paperwork to transfer.

Many of Ignác's new medical school classmates came from working-class families and often very poor backgrounds. Nonetheless, those who grew up in Austria effortlessly adopted the ersatz mannerisms, bearing, and speech of their more privileged classmates and the Viennese aristocracy. But young Ignác Semmelweis couldn't simulate those same affectations, and he became increasingly self-conscious about his social and ethnic roots. He had descended from generations of illiterate peasant farmers on his father's side. His ambitious father, Jozsef, was able to extricate himself from that ancestral pedigree and became a successful grocer in their village of Kismarton in Fejer megye, an agragrian county in central Hungary on the west bank of the Danube. And then Jozsef married "up" to Teresia, the daughter of a wealthy Bavarian coach manufacturer. The now *nouveau riche* family moved to Buda during his childhood, yet Ignác was not well schooled in language. His greatest handicap was his lifelong spoken dialect, which was a mongrel Germanic Danube-Swabian. He was fluent in both German and Hungarian, but when he spoke German, it didn't sound authentically Austrian, and when he spoke Hungarian, it didn't sound authentically Magyar. So, whether he was in Vienna or in Budapest, Ignác's accent constantly betrayed him as a foreigner.

And young Ignác never lost his rustic persona. He was socially old-fashioned and maladroit. He had the chubby, plethoric appearance of a farmer. He was amiable and jovial, but also uninhibited, passionate, and spontaneous. His very Magyar temperament, alternately fiery and melancholy, chafed in contrast to the staid and often haughty manners of the Viennese aristocracy and medical establishment.

Despite these mostly self-perceived handicaps, Ignác actually navigated the social circles of the medical school and university community effortlessly, right from the outset. His classmates spontaneously aggregated themselves into cliques which rarely violated their boundaries. The majority of the class was Austrian, but even they created separations amongst themselves along social strata and regional origins. The others self-segregated mostly by ethnic origins: not only Magyars, but also Germans, Czechs, Poles, Italians, Croats, Slavs, ethnic Jews, and so on. But Ignác seemed to be able to transcend these factions, and he did it unwittingly. Because of his indiscriminatingly gregarious nature and his irrepressible good humor, profane as it was at times, Ignác became an agreeable social companion to them all.

The curriculum of the medical school at that time was dictated by the politically appointed head of the Vienna Medical School, a man named Joseph Andreas von Stifft. It was no coincidence that he also happened to be the Emperor's personal physician. Ignác learned that Stifft was regarded by many as a despotic reactionary who was a true embodiment of the age of Restoration. As a result, the first three years of medical school were filled with mostly mind-numbing lectures in courses like anatomy, botany, chemistry, pharmacology and materia medica, and even one in the "Study of Diseases and Epidemics of Domestic Animals."[6] The standing of students was based on their performance on frequent examinations that were tests of verbatim memorization. Ignác often wondered how this was any more intellectually satisfying than the law school he had fled.

"I don't know about medical school, Marko" he said one evening in their apartment. "It's not what I thought it might be. It's been real drudgery. Goddamned memorizing facts. And all of it just to prepare us for one examination after another, it seems. We speak only when called on, and questioning is forbidden."

"It's beginning to change, my friend," replied Marko. "We have a whole new generation of very smart young professors coming in, like Rokitansky and Hebra and Skoda. They are already bringing with them their fresh ideas and passion for research."

"I'll believe change when I see it," replied the unconsoled Ignác with a big sigh, turning back to his textbooks.

But change it did, and Ignác didn't have to wait long. He began his clinical studies at the start of the fourth year with a course called "Practical Medical Instruction and Exercises at the Bedside," under the tutelage of Professor Josef Skoda, one of the rising stars Marko had told him about.[7] Skoda was already considered to be Vienna's most astute diagnostician. He had long, unruly hair covering his ears and wore circular, rimless glasses to compensate for his severe near-sightedness. Even from his first encounter with him, Ignác understood why he had a reputation for being a peculiar man. He dressed carelessly and displayed no pretense of having any social graces. And his demeanor was perpetually cheerless. But he was also a reformer who risked his own faculty position by encouraging free thinking about alternative theories of disease causation and treatment. He had already paid a price for his insubordination. Because of his insistence on unconventional diagnostic techniques, he'd been banished by the authorities for a year from the university and assigned to serve in a mental hospital. He had just now been allowed to return, presumably rehabilitated. The chastened Skoda not only taught Ignác and his classmates from his lectern but also took them in groups to the bedsides of patients to demonstrate how to take a history and do a physical examination.

"We have here a fifty-two-year-old man with syphilis and severe heart failure," said Skoda to his students, who now surrounded the patient's bed one afternoon. The man looked much older than that, and he was sitting up in bed, laboring for every breath and alarmed by all the visitors.

Skoda drew up a chair to sit next to the patient.

"Gentlemen, I didn't sit down here because I am tired," Skoda said, struggling to adjust his diminutive but corpulent body to the much-undersized chair. When situated as well as he could, he pushed his rimless spectacles all the way to the top of his nose and turned to the patient.

"Herr Weiss, these are my medical students."

Then pivoting back to face his students again, Skoda continued. "I sat down here because I want to let my patient know that he has my undivided attention and that I have whatever time he needs to tell me his complaints. It's also a way to meet him at his eye level and not have to speak down to him from the foot of his bed as if you were his superior."

Arrayed on a small stand in front of Skoda were several wooden cylinders of different lengths and widths.

"These are the stethoscopes I had crafted for me to conduct my examinations," he explained. "They are made from cedar wood. The earpiece and the chest piece are made of ivory. Professor Laennec in Paris was the first to use hollow tubes to listen to the internal organs of patients. Actually, he first used just a rolled-up piece of paper. I have adapted his idea to enable me to auscultate different sounds with a high level of discrimination. Why the hollow tubes?" he abruptly asked, looking around at the students.

There was no response. So he asked again, insistently. "Come on, gentlemen. What do we want to accomplish using these instruments?

Again there was no response.

"Sound waves that travel through a solid tube," Skoda finally said, lifting high one of his stethoscopes, "will bounce off its inside surface. And the *length* of the tube will determine the frequencies that flow and reflect off of it. So this is a way to amplify and finely distinguish between different sounds from inside the body to make a diagnosis."

Skoda shook his head in disappointment at the students, and stood up to begin his auscultation of the patient's heart with the biggest one, firmly placing the orifice of its wide end to the patient's anterior chest, just below the left nipple, and its narrow end to his own ear as he bent over the bed to make contact. He spent what seemed like minutes listening intently to the same spot, holding the cylinder in place with one hand and counting beats of the heart with the forefinger of his free hand, like an orchestra conductor. Then he moved the chest piece of the stethoscope slightly toward the breastbone in the middle and repeated the same routine. As the standing students began to fidget, Skoda relocated the trumpet end of the cylinder to adjacent spots, listening and conducting at each site, until he was up to almost the level of the collarbones. When he finished, he removed the stethoscope and stood up straight, much to the relief of the students. But then he picked up another stethoscope, a different-sized one, and repeated the same maneuvers with it. He pointed to the spot he had just examined, calling one of the students forward to listen for himself at exactly the point where he kept his forefinger pressed to the patient's chest.

"Right here!" Skoda exclaimed. "I want you to listen right at this point."

The hapless student who was selected tried his best to imitate Skoda's movements. He listened so intently at the spot Skoda had marked that his face contorted into all kinds of expressions of effort. But the poor soul had no idea about what he was hearing. He was all but frozen in place, bent over the patient, to whom he now appeared to be physically appended by the wooden cylinder. Finally, Skoda tapped him on the shoulder to disunite the hapless student from his patient.

"So, what did you hear?"

"Well, Herr Professor, I was trying to listen for the 'lub-dub-lub-dub' beats of the heart, but . . ."

"But you couldn't hear them?"

"I don't think I heard them . . ."

"Good for you," Skoda exclaimed. "You could have easily said you heard them, but you are being honest."

"I guess the lub-dub was drowned out by this noise I heard with every beat."

"Aha! What kind of noise?" asked Skoda. "Low-pitched, high-pitched?"

"I would say high-pitched," replied the student.

"Good. But what did the high-pitched noise sound like?" Skoda said insistently.

"I don't know how to describe it."

"Well, try! Did it sound like anything you have ever heard in nature?"

"Maybe a bird," said the student.

His classmates chuckled, but Skoda urged him on. "What kind of bird?"

"Maybe a seagull. Like a crying seagull?"

"He has found a crying seagull inside this man's chest," giggled one of the students, and the others followed.

Skoda frowned. He called on another student to listen, and this one thought it sounded more like a cooing dove.

Finally, Skoda was satisfied. "Good descriptions. Laennec himself used those very terms. And the sound is loudest at *that* spot in his chest, I will give you that. So, what is the anatomic correlate of that sound? What's wrong with the patient?"

There was silence around the bedside. Now the alarmed patient whispered as loudly as he could through his heavy breathing: "Why am I becoming a bird?"

"Don't you worry," Skoda reassured him with a pat on his shoulder. "We won't let that happen. You will still very much be Herr Weiss." Then, turning back to the students, he said, "That's the sound of aortic insufficiency. His aortic valve is incompetent."

All the students nodded in agreement.

"Why are you all nodding?" prodded Skoda, frowning again. "How do I *know* it's aortic insufficiency?"

"The textbooks say that's what it is, and you are the professor," said one of the students, proudly smiling.

"No! That's not the reason. I don't presumably believe everything the textbooks say. Neither should you. I have to see for myself," Skoda declared. "And I have been able to see that this kind of heart murmur is actually caused by aortic insufficiency because I myself have done many autopsies of patients who have died from it. In Professor Rokitansky's morgue."

"But the . . ." a student started meekly.

"But what?" snapped Skoda, now visibly annoyed. "The textbook? You can memorize all you want, but you won't know anything until you *understand* it!"

Skoda turned back to the patient, patted him on the shoulder, and quietly reassured him. "Don't worry, Her Weiss, this was just technical jargon. We are all here to help you."

Ignác shook his bowed head in silent admiration.

What really impressed him was not so much the professor's clinical acumen and uncanny skills in physical examination. He had heard about those before. It was Skoda's constant questioning. Yes, he had an unjustified reputation for being a grumpy, humorless curmudgeon with a constantly dour demeanor. Yet it was his insatiable inquisitiveness that Ignác admired, even when he himself didn't know the answer. *Especially* when he didn't know the answer. This was not the way professors were supposed to conduct themselves.

Foremost amongst the younger professors from whom Semmelweis drew special inspiration was Carl von Rokitansky.[8] Like Skoda, Rokitansky came from the Bohemian–Moravian region of the empire. So they, too, were considered "outsiders" within the elite medical community of Vienna. However, for them, the stigma of being alien immigrants had been mitigated many years earlier by the sterling reputations each of them had earned as brilliant medical scholars.

Ignác had caught the attention of Rokitansky. All medical students were required to spend assigned time in Rokitansky's morgue and autopsy room doing dissections under supervision.[9] But Ignác stood out because of his curiosity and eagerness to work on autopsies at other times, whenever he could, inspired by Skoda's teaching about the importance of relating clinical manifestations of disease in living patients with their autopsy findings after they died.

"Tell me, Semmelweis, why are you so interested in anatomical pathology? I don't think I have ever seen a medical student so engaged in it." Rokitansky told him one afternoon.

"I don't really know, Herr Professor," Ignác hesitated. "I suppose there is no better way to learn about what causes a disease then by anatomical dissection of ones who have died at different stages of that disease."

"What a remarkable observation, young man!" exclaimed the astonished Rokitansky.

On a late Saturday afternoon, while expecting guests at home, Rokitansky sent a messenger to the morgue, hoping that Ignác might be there, to ask him to bring to his house a file he had left behind on his desk. Ignác picked it up and ran back to his apartment with it to scrub his hands and put on clean clothes; then he hurried to Rokitansky's home at the address he was given by the messenger

Ignác arrived wearing his only suit. It was almost comically oversized for him. Led into the dining room, he saw the professor already engaged in animated conversation with a short, corpulent man who was seated with his back to the door. They both stood as Ignác cautiously approached, his hands clasped uselessly in front of him, an apparition of terror frozen in place. The man with Rokitansky was Skoda.

"Come, come," exhorted Rokitansky, heartily waving his arm toward the table. "Come *in* my boy. Josef, this is Ignác Semmelweis, the Hungarian medical student I talked to you about. Semmelweis, I want you to meet Professor Skoda, one of our most accomplished faculty members in internal medicine."

"Yes, yes, of course. Professor Skoda," stammered Ignác, bowing very deeply.

"Sit," said Rokitansky, motioning to the empty chair between the two professors. "Have some of this wine with us." The host poured, ignoring a feeble gesture of no thanks by Ignác. "Dinner will be brought shortly, so why don't you stay for it if you can."

Rokitansky turned back to Skoda.

"It's really too bad you can't join us for the opera, Josef."

"My regrets, Professor," replied Skoda. "You know I have little patience for such lengthy amusements."

"I must disagree with you, Josef. I don't think they are idle pleasures at all . . ." Rokitansky momentarily stopped pouring the wine.

"Oh, I beg your pardon. I didn't mean . . ."

". . . Not idle in any way," continued Rokitansky. "I think a good opera or a good play teaches us about the human condition like no textbook of philosophy can."

Ignác sat silently transfixed, wondering to himself how or why a simple, ordinary medical student like himself, of no special distinction, had earned this privilege of sitting with these two famous physicians. He was starstruck. And he was sitting between them right here in Vienna, the capital of the Habsburg Empire and the mecca of medicine in the world. What could he possibly contribute to their conversation that wouldn't sound ridiculously uninformed?

His reverie was interrupted when Rokitansky abruptly turned to him.

"Semmelweis! Why don't you join my family and me at the opera? I have an extra ticket, now that my dear colleague here has declined to go to . . . such a lengthy amusement."

Rendered speechless, Ignác could only nod vigorously.

"Ignác, Professor Skoda and I were just arguing before you came about the political situation we are finding ourselves in today," said Rokitansky.

After a pause to see if Ignác had something to say, Skoda picked up the thread of the dialogue.

"Shutting down the students' newspaper yesterday is really the last straw. Metternich has gone too far this time. The problem with that insane dictator is that he is not accountable to anyone other than our poor, feeble-minded emperor, who hasn't the slightest idea what's happening around him. Metternich can get him to do whatever he damned well wants."

"Government censorship is not a new problem, you know," said Rokitansky.

"But people are angrier now than ever," argued Skoda. "When free speech is completely stifled, when popular assembly is essentially banned, and when police spying to root out so-called dissidents and subversives is institutionalized, as it is now, *rebellion* becomes inevitable in any civilized society. Don't you think so, Herr Professor?"

"Perhaps," conceded Rokitansky, "but let's be realistic. The Habsburg Empire has never been more powerful than it is today. Never in its . . . what is it now . . . its almost six centuries of existence. The Habsburg territories encompass practically half of all continental Europe now."

"Yes, but those territories are the homelands of so many disparate ethnic groups that they have become virtually impossible to govern. They are all divided by language, history, religion, and culture. My God, Professor," continued Skoda, "look at them all! Croats, Serbs, Slovaks, Czechs, Italians, Poles, Germans, Slovenes, Ukrainians, Romanians . . ."

"And Hungarians," Ignác blurted out, immediately reproaching himself. *Stupid, you idiot!*

"Right, Hungarians," conceded Skoda, flashing a passing glance at Ignác.

"And even Austria itself isn't completely united," Skoda continued. "How can it all possibly survive as a single power?"

"I don't know," replied Ignác, thinking the question was directed to him. But he clammed up when he realized it wasn't.

"In exactly the fashion it is surviving right now," replied Rokitansky. "*And* thriving, mind you!" he added, hoisting his glass of wine. "By ever-increasing authoritarian and autocratic rule from Vienna. By an iron-fisted monarch." The sly smile of a devil's advocate now appeared on his face.

"Surely, you don't believe that," Skoda protested. "There is a limit to the oppression people will bear. Look at our university, for instance. It's now completely controlled by the imperial government. We have no freedom to make even the smallest changes in our educational system without those ignorant bureaucrats interfering."

Ignác was feeling embarrassed by his inability to contribute anything to this conversation. The issues were unfamiliar to him.

"I can't argue with that, Skoda," replied Rokitansky.

"So I don't understand," said Skoda. "Then why don't you think it's reasonable to conclude that we're on the brink of rebellion in this land? In fact, I would dare say the Empire is on the brink of dismemberment."

"Because *rebellion*, my dear Skoda, is very different from *dissent*. And what you are talking about is *rebellion*, I believe. Armed insurrection. Revolution. Aren't you?"

"Indeed, I am."

"And *how* do you suggest that a few hundred rag-tag students and underpaid faculty members might accomplish that against one of the greatest military forces in the world?"

"Because," replied Skoda with conviction, "our power is much greater than that. You haven't considered the workers."

"The *workers*?" Rokitansky guffawed with mock incredulity.

"Yes, the workers, the unemployed, the poor people, the disenfranchised, impoverished masses that are literally starving out there," Skoda replied pointing toward the dining room window, "in squalor. Just outside the gates of that wall surrounding Vienna."

"Hah!" Rokitansky shot back. His squint intimated that he was provoking Skoda for the sake of argument. "So those miserable souls are going to storm the gates of the city wall to come in here to fight alongside some snot-nosed students . . . for the sake of the university's academic freedom?"

"It's a necessity, Herr Professor," concluded Skoda. "Necessity creates strange bedfellows."

The spirited conversation was interrupted by Frau Rokitansky, who arrived with soup and exhorted the Rokitansky sons—seven-year-old Victor and eight-year-old Hans—to take their seats at the dinner table.[10]

"Serve yourselves quickly," she said. "Our carriage will be here in one hour."

After bolting down a hearty dinner of *Sauerbraten* and walnut strudel, the Rokitansky family and a wide-eyed Ignác Semmelweis went to a performance of Mozart's *Zauberflote* ("Magic Flute") at the *Theater an der Wien*, Vienna's glamorous venue for grand opera. As they filed in with the elegantly dressed audience, Ignác was mesmerized by the opulence of the building's interior. Settling into their seats near the back of the theatre, Rokitansky leaned across his wife to tap Ignác on his knee and point up to an older man sitting mostly in the shadows at the back of one of the private boxes.

"Metternich," he said in a loud whisper, "the chancellor himself!"

A blue-uniformed police officer, called a *gendarme,* with a sword at his side, stood at attention next to Metternich. The policeman had a thick, black, tightly twisted and waxed, extravagantly long handlebar mustache, which Ignác thought looked quite menacing.

The sparkling chandeliers and gaslights darkened, the doors were closed, and a hush descended over the audience as the orchestra began the overture. The airless theatre grew stiflingly hot, and the smell of perfumes and cigar smoke intensified. Ignác was at first spellbound, but by the end of the first act he found his head nodding, barely able to keep his eyes open.

Jolted awake by the thunderous applause for the Queen of the Night's high F in "*Der Hölle Rache*," Ignác instinctively jumped to his feet with the others, ready to leave. But Frau Rokitansky pulled him back into his seat with a firm tug of his sleeve, and, much to Ignác's disappointment, reassured him that most of the second act was still to come.

Ignác studied hard and for long hours, but whenever he could, he also relished the lively and spirited university life of Vienna. Many uproarious evenings were spent with his expanding circle of friends in cafés and their favored neighborhood beer hall, the *Gösser Bierklinik* on Steindlgasse. They would swap bawdy stories and jokes, local gossip, but hardly ever anything of substance like world affairs. Ignác was a most affable and jovial companion. His appetite for life was matched only by his appetite for food, and by the time he turned twenty-three he had become a little portly. His blonde hairline had begun to recede, but his thick, proudly groomed "Magyar" mustache was more elegant than ever.

The unabashedly cheerful and down-to-earth Ignác was becoming quite a ladies' man. They found his unpretentious nature and social awkwardness endearing. Some of his Viennese professors may have sneered at his lack of culture and unrefined manners, but young women considered him charmingly unassuming. Life in the Inner City of Vienna and around the university seemed comfortable, even prosperous, and the mood carefree and festive.

During Ignác's last year in medical school, he attended a series of memorable lectures given by Professor Ferdinand Ritter von Hebra, a young physician who specialized in an area not pursued by any others at the time. The study of diseases of the skin, dermatology, was in its infancy. When he delivered these lectures to Ignác's class, Ferdinand Ritter von Hebra was already writing his treatise on the classification of skin diseases, *Hautkrankheiten,* and was clearly on the fast track to a distinguished career.

During one case presentation, Hebra brought to the amphitheater one of his patients who he had recently diagnosed with scabies, and demonstrated to the students what mites scraped from the patient's skin and pillow looked like through a magnifying glass and, with even higher magnification through a microscope. This demonstration of transmission of disease had a profound influence on Ignác. And thereafter Hebra became a personal mentor, advocate, and even confidante of the impressionable young Hungarian.[11]

Toward the end of medical school, Ignác became increasingly worried about what he would do after graduation. It was tacitly understood that most of those who were not native Austrians would be expected to return to their homelands to practice medicine after graduation. Therefore, the choice of career opportunities in Vienna was closed to Semmelweis. He was even rejected for student research positions to which he applied at the university.

Given the limited options made available to him, Semmelweis took the course in obstetrics.[12] This was actually not a consolation prize to him, despite its lack of prestige. After all, it was his experience of delivering that young woman in the street a few years earlier that had ignited his love of medicine. Here he encountered Johann Baptist Chiari, who was serving a two-year term as apprentice to the chief of obstetrics, Professor Klein. As the appointed assistant to Klein, Chairi was essentially in charge of the day-to-day running of the hospital's maternity teaching service and was entrusted with the bedside training of all medical students on their obstetrics clerkships.

A native of Salzburg, Chiari was only one year older than Semmelweis, and was clearly designated by the Vienna faculty to be on the fast track to professorship.[13] Chiari was unlike any clinical teacher Semmelweis had previously encountered. He was brilliant and intellectually inquisitive, as well as polished and confident. But unlike so many other clinical professors he had seen, who preferred to remain empathetically distant from their patients, Chiari was adored by them. He was a dedicated doctor. With time, Ignác and Johann developed an enduring friendship. It was Chiari who persistently encouraged and inspired Semmelweis to pursue a career in obstetrics.

CHAPTER 3

JUNE 1844

As Semmelweis's studies came to a close in 1844, his mother, Teresia, became ill, and he hurried home to Buda. It would be another three decades before the now freestanding municipalities of Buda and Pest, separated by the Danube, would become united as Budapest, the capital city of Hungary: ancient Buda built on steep-sloped hills and topped by the royal castle on one side of the river, and the commercial hub situated on the flatlands of Pest on the other.

Ignác and his siblings were born and raised by their parents in the Tabán district of Buda, a fast-growing, commercially vibrant neighborhood along the banks of the river, at the foot of the steep hills. Its strategic location for trading made the Tabán district not only quite affluent but also uniquely cosmopolitan. It was a polyglot community of hard-working and upwardly mobile Hungarian Magyars, Germans, Serbs, Macedonians, Croatians, Galicians, Italians, and Greeks. There was a spirit of religious and ethnic tolerance that was born of practical necessity. The Semmelweis children grew up in the same house on Apród Street where their father had opened his first successful variety store, the White Elephant. It sold high-quality groceries, wines, fabrics, cosmetics, paints, and whatever else was in demand in the extended neighborhood. The profits the elder József Semmelweis earned from this venture, together with his marriage to Teresia, the daughter of an even wealthier businessman named Fülöp Müller, allowed Ignác's father to make sound real estate deals and purchase other houses on both sides of the Danube.

By the time Ignác hurried home to see his ailing mother in 1844, his parents had relocated their home to a grand house at 15 Dísz Square in the Buda Castle District. Literally moving up to the Castle Hill was, in many ways, a validation of upward social mobility.

So, after disembarking on the Buda bank of the river upon his arrival from Vienna, Ignác had to make the long trek to the top of the hill to his parents' new home. He paused to rest periodically, turning toward the river below to take in the panoramic view of a monumental Pest under construction on the other side of the Danube.

As he approached the newly cobble-stoned streets of the Castle District, something made Ignác suddenly stop. He unexpectedly caught the faint whiff of a long-forgotten fragrance. It was the lilacs. Lilacs in the fresh, warm breeze instantly transported him back to his carefree summer days as a young boy, playing with his friends in the Buda hills, where they wildly flowered. He inhaled slowly and deeply several times, as if that would capture and bottle this sweet, wistful scent of childhood.

When Ignác arrived at his parents' home, he learned that his mother had died earlier in the day. He had worried that he would be too late to kiss her goodbye, and now he was even more heartbroken. He stayed there for the funeral and afterwards to help his father take care of family affairs, and this gave him a chance to get reacquainted with the city. He was unprepared for the things he saw and experienced during those few days, and he was enthralled by them. A fresh atmosphere of unrest and youthful political energy had emerged in the city.

Shop signs everywhere were now frequently in Hungarian, not German. The streets, parks, and cafés buzzed with life, filled with people from all social strata. He saw men and women wearing traditional Hungarian attire representing different regions of the country. Especially on warm days like these, the people would appear together like an animated pastiche of vivid colors.

A revival of Magyar nationalism and patriotism was in full swing. The people had won demands for restoration of Magyar as their country's official language. The primacy of Hungarian culture had risen to the surface. The new national colors of red-white-and-green were proudly displayed everywhere.[14]

The evening before Ignác returned to Vienna, his sister Júlia[15] and her husband Péter wanted to take Ignác out to a farewell dinner. But Péter's supervisor, Béla Esterházy, insisted on joining them and picking up the bill. On the way to the restaurant, Júlia and Péter explained to Ignác that Esterházy came from a poor Hungarian farming family, but one would never know that when first meeting him. Béla Esterházy had made it big. He became a successful pharmacist and an even more successful businessman. He shrewdly gained part ownership of three apothecaries in rapid succession, including the famous Holy Ghost Pharmacy on Király Street in Pest.

So Esterházy chose his favorite restaurant, *Das Unendlich Kaiserreich*, in the Castle Hill district of Buda. Elegantly dressed in a charcoal frock coat, stiff-collared shirt, and top hat, waving a walking stick with an elaborately gilded head, Esterházy greeted his three younger guests at the door with theatrical flair: a sweeping bow and delicate kiss of Júlia's hand, an extravagant hug for his protégé Péter, and a stentorian greeting with a gripping handshake for Ignác.

"*Guten Abend, Herr Esterházy, wie geht es Ihnen?*" greeted the maître d', clicking his heels and lowering his head as Béla's party entered through the heavy, glass doors. The ornate restaurant was dominated by a fabulous chandelier hanging from the center of the ceiling, and the cherry-red walls were lined with gilded mirrors. The expansive, tiered room was heavily carpeted and furnished with plushly upholstered armchairs and curved banquettes arranged around tables covered with sparkling white tablecloths. The clinking of glass and clanking of silverware on china was sharply audible over the murmur of subdued conversations and occasional bursts of laughter. Waiters in tails, wearing white gloves, nimbly scurried amongst the tables to serve the patrons unobtrusively. *So this,* thought Ignác, *is Vienna's ostentatious presence in its primitive neighbor colony of Hungary.*

They were led to a table in a quiet corner. The restaurant was strictly old-world Habsburg Empire; everything written and spoken in German, and nary a Magyar dish on the menu. Ignác went along with Béla's selection of *Schweinebraten* (roast pork), while Júlia and Péter ordered the *Wiener Schnitzel.* And, to the wine steward's demonstrative approval, Béla ordered a bottle of *Chateau Lafite.* The renowned 1818 vintage.

Júlia, Péter, and Ignác chatted about how Budapest seemed to be changing so quickly while Béla sat in stony silence, slouched in his armchair, legs stretched and crossed, scanning the room. His expression of overt disinterest in the conversation was met with Júia's visible annoyance. Ignác surmised that she didn't like her husband's colleague but tolerated him for pragmatic reasons. Finally, after ordering their meals, Béla turned his head toward Ignác without changing his posture. He daintily dangled a glass of aperitif, twirling it between two fingers in a gesture of bored disdain.

"So, Ignác," sighed Béla, "tell me about your famous Josef Sko-da." Béla articulated the last name slowly. "Have you met him? I've heard a lot about him from my pharmacist friends in Vienna."

"Yes, I think Professor Skoda is a brilliant clinician," replied Semmelweis. "The students admire him tremendously."

"Well, frankly, Ignác," said Béla, glancing up toward the ceiling, "my friends think the man is a buffoon!"

"How so?" replied the bewildered Ignác.

"Skoda is what we call a 'therapeutic nihilist,' a man who doesn't believe any treatments are worth anything. Anything, I suppose, except for the divine powers of the human body to heal itself."

Semmelweis didn't respond.

"Skoda is putting all the pharmacists of Vienna out of business, you know!" said Béla.

"Well, Professor Skoda does teach us to prescribe medicines only when we know they will work for the patient's disease. And, frankly, there aren't a hell of a lot of those."

"My boy, you don't understand. When someone is ill, he looks to his doctor to give him something—*anything*—to at least try to make him feel better," replied Béla. "Don't you think so, Péter?"

Péter nodded sheepishly.

"But what if it makes the patient even worse?" Ignác took up the challenge.

"You will learn," sighed Béla again, "to take what Professor Skoda teaches . . . with a grain of salt. He is one of those subversive revolutionaries, you know."

There was a long pause, and then Béla grabbed Ignác's forearm as it rested on the table, not letting him pull it away. He leaned into Ignác and looked directly into his eyes.

"Listen to me," Béla began, darting glances around the room to make sure he wasn't being overheard. "Be very, very careful! Don't let yourself get caught up in this madness. These young people don't even know what they want. They are wide-eyed idealists. They are dreaming of fantasies in a very harsh world they don't even know yet. And as for the older ones, who should know better, . . . well, they are agitators . . . anarchists . . . or worse."

"Worse?" said Ignác incredulously.

"Yes, some of them are probably even . . . traitors."

"But they are all Hungarians, like us. Aren't they?"

“Never mind. You have been too far away, cloistered in your medical school,” responded the exasperated Béla with a dismissive wave of his hand. “You know we Hungarians have thrived and prospered in the Habsburg Empire for more than three centuries, and don’t think for a moment that this . . . this little breeze of unrest can blow it all away now. Mark my words, what you are seeing now is only a brief moment of childish rebelliousness, something that has happened many times in the past with our people. And, as before, nothing will come of it now. But many people *will* get hurt.”

“What are you saying?” Ignác demanded, yanking his arm out of Béla’s grasp.

“I am trying to tell you,” said Béla, “that you are my dear protégé Péter’s brother-in-law, and I don’t want to see you harmed. You have a promising career ahead of you. Don’t throw it away. Work hard and keep your nose out of politics. You can become a well-to-do, respectable doctor, maybe even a wealthy one if you find a lucrative practice. You can live out your life in peace and comfort. Same for your family. What more could you possibly ask for?”

As he bid farewell to his guests in the restaurant’s foyer, Béla shook Ignác’s hand firmly, clasped his left shoulder, and smiled for an instant. “Take care of yourself, Ignác.” And out the door he went.

“I am sorry,” said Júlia, affectionately taking hold of her brother’s arm. “We couldn’t refuse his invitation, you know.”

“Of course not. But he *is* quite a fox, isn’t he?” replied Ignác.

“Yes, he is a bit eccentric,” said Péter, “but he is a very influential man. I have managed to stay on Béla’s good side, now that I am on my own. I must say he has always been very supportive of my career. But heaven help those who cross him.”

The next morning Ignác returned to Vienna by boat. This time, though, he could have taken the new steam train at least part of the way. The world was changing fast.

CHAPTER 4

FALL 1844

Upon his return to Vienna, Ignác temporarily resumed his lodging in Alservorstadt with his good Hungarian friend, Marko Markusovszky.[16] He received his medical diploma without ceremony, having missed the formal commencement exercises due to his mother's death. And he immediately plunged headlong into a brief but intense course in midwifery in preparation for a previously arranged apprenticeship with the powerful professor and chief of obstetrics at the University of Vienna, Johann Klein. The position that had been promised to him was that of a so-called "Aspirant," the lowest position for doctors at the university. If his performance as aspirant was deemed satisfactory by Klein, he would be elevated to the position of his "Assistant" after two years.

Ignác came back to Vienna with a renewed seriousness of purpose. The images of a revitalized and emboldened homeland stuck in Ignác's mind. In many ways he was a changed man; a more mature person, one with a social conscience, a worldview, and a serious sense of priorities. And now, starting his career as a physician, Ignác would come face-to-face with the shocking circumstances of an unfolding medical tragedy that was to change the rest of his life.

To his friends, however, Ignác still appeared to be the same jovial, good-natured young man whose company they had come to enjoy so much. He had the same *joie de vivre,* the same ardor for good food, beer, and more than an occasional flirt with a comely young *mädchen.* The night before Ignác was to begin his apprenticeship to Klein on the obstetrical wards, Marko decided to take him out for one final celebration.

The two friends set out on foot for Grinzing, just outside the city, to a well-known wine tavern that was popular with the Viennese university students. On the way they walked through the magnificent *Volksgarten.* The lovely park had been recently opened to the public. They passed by the pavilion, well lit by lanterns, where a string trio played the waltzes and polkas of the day surrounded by dancing couples whirling around the bandstand counterclockwise. Marko pointed out to Ignác a local celebrity who was conducting, a young man named Johann Strauss.

Vienna was bustling with life on this warm Saturday night. Finally arriving at the *Heuriger,* Ignác and Marko met up with their medical student friends and their pretty sweethearts of the moment sitting on crowded wooden benches, already more than a bit drunk. An accordion and a violin played in the background. As the night wore on, Ignác tried to dance with as many of the girls as he could. Eventually the warm breezes and fragrance of wines in the garden became displaced by the stifling crush of young people. The roar of the crowd made the music barely audible in the background. For Ignác, now giddy and dizzy from the wine, the forms of the many people became gradually indistinguishable. Sense of time faded, and all he seemed to hear now above the festive buzz were the shrill outbursts of the women.

Ignác didn't remember much else as he found himself walking unsteadily up the warped marble steps of the darkened building, holding onto the railing. He had walked there in the pitch-dark silence of the city before dawn. Only a few gas lamplights along Alserstrasse indicated that he was near the hospital. Walking through its main entrance into the sparsely lit courtyards, he found his way to the maternity building. Instinctively knowing where to go, he reached the building's second floor. Then approaching the maternity ward down the long, empty corridor, accompanied only by the echoes of his steps, he could hear the occasional screams of a woman in the distance. But they were very unlike the boisterous screams of the inebriated women in the *Heuriger* that had filled his head only hours earlier. These were screams of agony.

Ignác arrived at the closed main entrance to the obstetrical ward. Removing his top hat, he cautiously opened the massive door, and immediately his breath was taken away by the stale, sweltering hot air emanating from within. Even in the darkness, the enormity of the cavernous ward could be appreciated, filled with the forms of women lying in beds arrayed in closely situated rows along the lengths of both long walls. He hesitantly stepped inside. A nauseating stench permeated the heat; some unholy combination of human sweat, decay, and waste. Muffled groans and the sounds of tossing and turning disturbed the silence. Intermittently illuminated by a few flickering candles, he saw some women writhing in agony, while others were lying utterly still on their backs but breathing loudly and fast. He was then startled by a blood-curdling scream coming from somewhere at the far end of the ward. It was the one he had heard from far away when he first stepped into the hospital. The assaults on his senses jolted Ignác into a state of total alertness. He was reassured to find that, in his shamefully besotted state, he still had the presence of mind to stop by his apartment after the night of merriment to get dressed in his black morning coat and cravat, properly attaching a starched white collar to his shirt, before finding his way to the hospital.

Marko is to blame for this, he thought, but he was angry with himself.

An elderly nurse approached him carrying a candle-lit lantern.

"*Herr Doktor,*" she said, holding the light up to his face. "You must be Doktor Semmelweis."

Ignác nodded. He had been here many times before as a medical student, but never like this, in the pre-dawn hours. And never before, it now struck him, with any of the responsibility that he now carried as a doctor.

"You are early, Doktor Semmelweis," she continued. "Doktor Breit[17] is still asleep in the *Dienstzimmer.* It was such a difficult night for him. One delivery, and we lost two other new mothers."

"Don't awaken him," said Ignác. "I am here now. How can I help?"

The *Allgemeine Krankenhaus*, also known as the Vienna General Hospital, was originally planned by the Empress Maria Theresa during the previous century. It was a massive, sprawling hospital complex composed of interconnected, uniformly laid out, barracks-like buildings, two or three stories in height, all with uniformly sloped red roofs punctured by chimneys. The lengthy buildings formed quadrangles, the interiors of which were grassy courtyards. And in 1844, when Ignác began his two-year trial period as Aspirant to Klein, the hospital housed the largest inpatient obstetrical service in the imperial city, perhaps the world. There were eight intercommunicating wards of twenty or more beds each, all under Klein's autocratic control. The wards had high windows placed ten feet above floor level, which were kept open at all times to permit cross-ventilation. The still air of a hot summer night made this function useless. Open doors connected the wards. Common lavatories were situated at the back of each ward, separated from the patient beds only by barred partitions through which the women could be constantly observed. One area was reserved for women in active labor. Mothers with their newborns were expected to walk back to the wards right after delivery. This system efficiently allowed more than 6,000 deliveries to take place in 1844.

The great majority of those who delivered here were indigent, even destitute. Many were prostitutes, unmarried or abandoned women, and women from the most impoverished working classes. In exchange for free care, these women resigned themselves to becoming involuntary teaching subjects for the institution's numerous medical students and visiting foreign trainees.

There was a small, special area that was separated from the wards and reserved for Klein to admit his own wealthy private patients who had complications. Most women of some means delivered at home, however. But for the women in labor on the general teaching floors and those who survived postpartum, the conditions were wretchedly crowded, noisy, and foul-smelling. Doctors, midwives, and medical students subjected their patients in labor to frequent, almost indiscriminate vaginal examinations that were repeated for teaching purposes by other inexperienced students. The newborns were delivered in rapid succession, with used instruments and dressings. The doctors and medical students often didn't even wipe their hands between procedures, much less wash them. After the women had delivered in a separate, cramped delivery room, they might return to the wards to occupy different beds that had been previously vacated, covered with bed sheets that were soiled with the blood and lochia of their previous occupants.

Johann Klein, now fifty-six years old, whose assistant Ignác aspired to become, was by no means a physician of any great distinction. He had climbed to his current lofty position through a combination of good fortune, mere seniority, and extraordinary political connections in the imperial government. Klein was particularly close to Baron Landolf, Metternich's Minister of Education, under whose control fell the Vienna medical school as well as its teaching hospital, the *Allgemeine Krankenhaus.*

In 1823, Klein had wrested the directorship position in obstetrics from the elderly Dr. Johann Boër, who had been director of the lying-in hospital since its opening. Boër had established its preeminent reputation in the world of medicine. But Boër's style was very different from Klein's. Whereas Boër had very little use for official rules and regulations, Klein was a bureaucrat and stern disciplinarian who followed directives to the letter and demanded the same from those who worked for him. A strict dogmatist, he insisted on unyielding adherence to established clinical practice and frowned on any attempt at innovation. Although Klein spent a lot of time away from the hospital, pursuing his lucrative private practice, his overbearing presence was constantly felt by his subordinates.

Ignác was now a graduate physician, usually preoccupied with his hectic clinical duties. Yet he remained insatiably curious. So he scheduled himself to spend one or two hours in the early mornings of each day in Rokitansky's morgue.[18] Here Ignác honed the skills in autopsy pathology he had learned during medical school under Rokitansky's tutelage. Klein didn't object as long as it didn't cut into his responsibilities on the obstetrics ward. Some of these autopsies were dissections of the bodies of women who had died in the hospital during the previous day from obstetrical complications. There were ample cadavers to go around to everyone, including the students. Once Rokitansky knew that Ignác would begin training as an obstetrician and gynecologist, he wanted to ensure that his pupil wouldn't become just technically proficient in his specialty. He wanted Ignác to really learn the mechanisms of disease in women, to become a keen observer, an astute diagnostician, and an inquisitive thinker who could perhaps one day become an innovator and trailblazer. Like Rokitansky himself.

So Ignác's typical day would begin in the morgue at the crack of dawn, and by eight o'clock, he would have to wrap up his dissections to start his duties on Klein's hospital wards. The dreary, stuffy, noxious-smelling dissection room was located in an old, single-story building that had been previously used as a rifle factory. Barn doors to the mortuary provided entry for wagons bearing new corpses from the hospital on most days. There were many of them. Gas lamps were suspended from the ceiling, lowered as much as possible to situate them above the dissection tables. These provided adequate light to begin preparing the cadavers even while it was still dark outside, but the actual dissection of internal viscera had to await sunrise. There was no refrigeration available to store the corpses, and the preservative properties of formaldehyde were yet to be discovered. The dissection room was kept as cold as possible to slow decomposition of the bodies. But their putrefaction would create an unbearable stench, so the prosectors worked as swiftly as they could to complete the examinations. It was a short outdoor walk across the hospital courtyards, across a gate, to the building that housed the maternity wards.

Ignác was often the first to arrive in the morgue, eager to do as much dissection as he could before he had to begin the day's clinical activities on the maternity wards. But he was usually joined by an older man who had been one of his instructors in medical school, Jakob Kolletschka.[19] Kolletschka had also been a student of Rokitansky, and for many years he had been assisting the great professor in performing autopsies on every patient who had died during the previous day at the *Allgemeine Krankenhaus.* Kolletschka had recently been appointed a professor. He was a most amiable, good-natured, unassuming man with a round face, round glasses, black hair neatly parted in the middle, and a twirled black moustache. Ignác took an instant liking to him. Over the course of weeks and months, often working only by themselves in the otherwise empty morgue of the cold early-morning hours, they became fast friends. Despite their age difference, they even became mutual confidants.

CHAPTER 5

DECEMBER 1844

In 1844, women on Professor Klein's maternity wards were dying at an alarming rate, often along with their newborns. During some periods, almost one-third of all women who delivered on these wards did not leave the hospital alive. They were succumbing to "puerperal fever" or "childbed fever," so called because death would occur while the victims were nursing their newborns. The reasons for this carnage were completely unknown. However, careful statistics had been kept at the hospital for many years. And these data showed a marked increase in mortality beginning about two decades earlier.

For women who were struck with the fever, death came swiftly and in a predictably horrific manner. It would usually begin on the second or third day after delivery with the sudden onset of high, spiking fevers, shaking chills and rigors. This was followed by sensations of extreme heat and thirst accompanied by profuse sweating. And then came the dreaded pain in the abdomen, mild at first but then quickly becoming so unbearable that the new mothers often lapsed into delirium and mania. The belly became distended and hard. Attempts at treatment, like bloodletting and purging, were not only futile but often actually hastened death.

This was the situation that the young Doktor Semmelweis encountered when he began his period as Aspirant to Klein in 1844.

And this would be his virtual home for the next several years. He was assigned a tiny room around the corner from the maternity ward, overlooking courtyard Number 8. It was furnished with nothing more than a simple bed, a small desk, a chair, and a stove. This *Dienstzimmer* combined to serve as his ward office and on-call bedroom. On days he was assigned to admit patients, Ignác spent all night in the hospital in order to be immediately available to the nurses for deliveries and emergencies. He used his bed for brief periods of sleep at night, which often never came.

It wasn't long before a routine was established. Ignác would begin before sunrise in the morgue, regardless of how fatigued he felt from the previous day's work. The medical students began to file into the dissection room at eight o'clock. They would noisily assume their stations in small groups around their assigned dissecting tables. While Ignác finished up his own work to hurry across the courtyards to the maternity wards, Kolletschka stayed to teach anatomy to the students.

The first hours of the morning's activities on the wards were consumed by catching up on the previous night's problems with whoever had stayed on call overnight. Then, with Klein's assistant and the nurses, Ignác would make work rounds on all the women in labor and those who were postpartum, internally examining each in turn. He frequently had to break away from these rounds to admit and deliver a seemingly steady stream of patients, attend to emergencies, and write progress notes. Most importantly, Ignác tried to devote the morning hours to help Klein's current assistant, Franz Breit, prepare for the ceremonial professor's rounds.

Klein would appear on the ward at precisely eleven o'clock, arriving by coach from his private practice office. By this time, the dozens of medical students had streamed into the wards from their dissecting session in the morgue. They hardly had to introduce themselves; the young men wore the unmistakable stink of cadavers.

All would fall silent, practically stopping in their tracks. Even the nurses, in their full-length, long-sleeved dark blue serge dresses with clean white aprons tied to their waist, and frilly bonnets neatly tied under their chins, would stop attending to their patients as Herr Professor Klein walked in. He leaned on a carved ivory and silver mounted walking stick. An elegantly dressed, stiff, and humorless man with an imperious carriage, Klein habitually addressed people by raising his chin so that he could look at them through a fixed downward gaze.

The hush that greeted Herr Professor's arrival would be disturbed only by moans and howls of pain emanating from different beds and by patients having to be rolled in and out of delivery. But during the professor's rounds newborns were temporarily taken away by the nurses so their cries wouldn't interrupt and incur Klein's ire.

Professor Klein began to move with his retinue from patient to patient at a brisk pace, stopping at least briefly at each bed and often pointing with his cane at a medical student to summarize the case at hand.

"You there," Klein picked out a tall young man at the back of the group gathered around the first bed. "Yes, you. What's your name?"

"Luka Dragovich, Herr Professor," the student replied, squeezing his way to the front. The bed was occupied by a mature woman, overweight, writhing in obvious pain.

"Go on, go on, Dragich," Klein said tapping his cane on the floor.

"Dragovich, sir."

"Yes, whatever," Klein mumbled under his breath.

"This is Mathilde. She states that she is thirty-eight years old. Multigravida..."

"How many?"

"She thinks eight, sir. Two live ones for sure," replied Luka.

Klein finally turned to the patient and asked her what was the matter, as if he didn't know. Mathilde was perspiring, groaning, grimacing, and periodically clutching her lower abdomen.

"When did labor begin?" Klein turned back to the student.

"During the night."

"When precisely? Be precise!" Klein raised his voice, sounding very annoyed.

"Approximately four o'clock," replied the student. "I mean *at* four o'clock, Herr Professor."

"Well, then" Klein pronounced, scanning his entourage. "There is no time to waste, is there? A multigravida with contractions every two minutes. Time to move her to delivery, I should think. But first," he continued, now glancing at the distressed patient. "She is a good case! A very good case. I will examine her . . ."

As he began his own nimble internal exam, he looked up at the patient and said, addressing the group behind him, "I want Drag, what's your name, to do it next. And then just three others."

"I will organize them with Semmelweis, Herr Professor," said Klein's Assistant, Franz Breit, stepping forward. The rest of the group moved on to the next bed.

They now converged on a young woman who was lying completely still, panting, sweating profusely, and letting out frequent strangled screams that could be heard throughout the ward. Klein waved his cane toward a short, round, young man in the front. "What's your name?"

"Jaroslaw Prochazka, Herr Professor."

"Oh, good Lord. Your names used to be so much simpler," sighed Klein, not even trying to repeat this one.

Nobody knew exactly why Klein asked each student's name, because he never seemed to remember any of them anyway, even a few minutes later.

"So," Klein said, gently poking the cherubic Czech student in the chest. "What's going on here?"

The student stepped to the patient's bedside to take a closer look. He touched her forehead with the back of his hand.

"She has a high fever, sir." And then examining her face close up, he continued, "Her lips are very dry; her eyes are rolled up in their sockets." Looking up at the chalkboard above her bed, he called out her name, gently rubbing her breast bone with his closed fist. "Klara," he whispered, and then more loudly when there was no response. "Klara. Klara, can you talk to us?"

The only response was a weak moan. Klara was lying flat on her bed, legs drawn up with knees flexed, and motionless except for her rapid, shallow breathing. Jaroslaw gently lifted her woolen cover to reveal a grotesquely distended abdomen, well beyond what a gravid abdomen at term should look like. Instantly, a nauseating stench emanated from the bed, causing one student to cup his hand to his nose and turn his back to the patient.

"Palpate it," said Klein.

"But sir . . ."

"Didn't you hear me, young man? Push on it!"

Jaroslaw now hesitantly laid a hand gently on the woman's swollen abdomen and ever-so-gradually exerted increasing pressure.

"It's like a rock, sir," he said turning to Klein. "I don't think I should . . ."

At this moment, the woman let out an almost inhuman, blood-curdling shriek. Nurses working with other patients stopped and turned to look.

"Diagnosis?" asked the satisfied Klein from his students as a group.

Several said, "Puerperal fever," almost in unison. One added, "Peritonitis." Klein acknowledged them with a hearty, "Good!"

As they moved to the next bed, Klein grabbed Jaroslaw by the arm to stop him.

"What's your name again?"

"Jaroslaw Prochazka, sir."

"Yes, well, you must stay behind and do an internal exam. Then you can rejoin us."

"But Herr Professor, should I be subjecting this poor woman . . ."

Klein's face turned red and his pursed lips curled downward with barely contained rage as he pushed the reluctant student back to the patient's bedside.

"How the hell will you learn anything?" he sputtered and walked away. Turning back for a moment, he then ordered the student to just do it a little more slowly than usual. "And then get the nurse to do the usual routine."

"Well, what have we here?" Klein asked the group as they gathered around the bed of a lovely, pale girl. She was diminutive and appeared terrified. Her wide-open eyes darted around to take in all the strange people who now arrayed themselves in a semicircle around her bed. Yet, despite the girl's overt anxiety, a faint but beguiling smile soon settled on her face. Even Klein seemed charmed.

"What's your name, my dear?" Klein asked. He glanced at the board over her bed, which identified her as Mókus.

There was no answer.

"I have never heard of that name before," Klein continued. "How do you pronounce it?"

The girl remained silent, staring at Klein.

"Herr Professor," called out one of the students. "She was admitted yesterday, and she hasn't said a word to anybody. The nurses and attendants think she is mute."

"So, in that case, how was it decided to admit her?" Klein asked. "And what's *your* name, since you are obviously not also mute."

"Friedrich Bauer, Herr Professor," he said, standing up straight.

"Finally a name I can pronounce! Go on, Bauer."

"She was in false labor. We estimate at seven months from our initial exam. And look . . ."

Friedrich whipped off the girl's blanket and pointed to her feet, which were strikingly swollen.

"She also keeps pointing to her head and grimacing at the same time," Friedrich added, "so I think she is trying to tell us she has headaches."

"Toxemia of pregnancy?" Klein asked, addressing his Assistant, Breit.

"Perhaps," said Breit. "We could test her urine to see if it contains protein."

"Bah!" Klein dismissed the suggestion with a wave of his hand.

"You know, Professor Rayer in France has recently reported that women with toxemia of pregnancy, or eclampsia, have proteinuria," Breit continued.

"Yes," Ignác interjected, "and just last year there was an article about the same finding from Guy's Hospital in London. Why don't we send a sample of her urine to our chemistry laboratory?"

"Nonsense!" exclaimed Klein. "I have never heard of this poppycock. Just confine her for observation. She will be good teaching material, but not yet. No need for any of the students to be examining her now."

As Klein was about to move on to the next patient, he turned to the young girl again and asked, "Where are you from, my dear?"

When there was again no response, Friedrich exclaimed with a giggle, "She is a *Prodahure*!" This brought on some restrained snickering among the medical students.

"What did you say?" Ignác now turned on Friedrich with furious indignation. "What was that word?"

For the first time, a little smirk appeared on Klein's face.

"*Proda-hure*," Friedrich enunciated slowly. "Our Hungarian Aspirant obviously hasn't been around here long enough. It means she is a 'Prater whore'! A whore who walks the streets around the Prater."

"I know what it means," Ignác shot back, summoning all the reserves of self-restraint he could muster to stop himself from belting the insolent smart-ass.

Later that evening, after the chaotic activity of the ward had subsided, Ignác came back to the bedside of the mysterious young girl named Mókus.

A nurse told him that Mókus had registered her age as eighteen but they agreed that she looked much younger than that.

The girl was still wide awake, propped up with her pillow, and a sunny smile greeted Ignác as he approached and pulled up a chair to sit down beside her bed.

"Mókus can't be your real name," he said, surprising her by speaking Hungarian. "Mókus means 'squirrel' and I've never heard any girl called that in Hungary."

The girl's lips parted in wonderment. This time Ignác just waited for her to respond.

"But Mókus *is* my name," she finally said extremely quietly in Hungarian.

Ignác shook his head and laughed. "All right, Mókus, what was your name when you were growing up, the one your parents gave you?"

"Erzsike," she said.

"That's more like it . . . Erzsike." Ignác was fascinated.

"My family and friends always called me Erzsike," she continued.

"So what is Mókus then?"

"Mókus is my Vienna name. Csaba named me Mókus when he brought me here." The smile on her face faded.

"Well, then, I will call you Erzsike," said Ignác, "because that's a dignified, beautiful name. It comes from Erzsébet."

Erzsike, who spoke haltingly at first, was now ready to open up to Ignác in Hungarian. She talked about growing up in the village of Poroszló, near Lake Tisza. Her father was a fisherman who drowned on the job, or so she had been told when she was much younger. Her mother tried her best to work and raise her and her three younger brothers in a poor peasant hut. But then her mother became very ill, and, in a matter of just a couple of years, she gradually lost all function of her extremities, mostly lost her vision, and became confined to bed, where she had to be cared for by the children and kind neighbors.

"Then, one day when I was told I had turned thirteen, an older, well-dressed man with a handsome mustache came to our house. His name was Csaba."

"A relative?" Ignác asked.

"I don't think so. He said he had been my father's friend."

At this point Erzsike looked instantly exhausted and closed her eyes. Ignác said nothing more and just waited for her to fall asleep.

The next evening, Erzsike was visibly eager to resume her story.

"Csaba brought us presents. And he gave me this," she said, sitting up and proudly displaying the full circumference of the shiny necklace she was wearing.

After Ignác admired it, she continued.

"My mother then told me that Csaba had become a wealthy merchant in Vienna and he was willing to take me there to give me a start to the kind of comfortable life I deserved and could never get if I stayed in Porszoló. But I was so sad . . ."

Tears welled up in Erzsike's eyes.

". . . sad to leave my family. But Csaba told me he would take care of them, too. The journey to Vienna was a long one, but Csaba treated me like a princess. When a cold rain started to fall during our carriage ride, he tucked me in warm and dry inside while he went up above and got drenched and frozen."

Erzsike's expressive face now turned forlorn.

"When we arrived in Vienna, he took me to an apartment in Leopoldstadt, near the Prater. I was dreaming about a palace, but instead he took me up some dark stairs to a smelly little room that I was to share with four other women. Just for a while, he said."

But the days and weeks turned to months. And, as Erzsike described it, the older women spoke to each other in some other foreign tongue.

"It didn't much matter," she said, "because they didn't like me, and I didn't really care for them."

"So how did you manage?" Ignác asked.

"There were these men," replied Erzsike. "These older men who spoke German. And one or another of them would come by every day to bring us food and other necessities."

"They kept you in that room?"

"Not always," replied Erzsike. She now looked away from Ignác. "They took us out, one at a time. They taught me a trade, they called it, which was to entertain other men. But I didn't like it because they were all strangers. Many of the men were quite old. And some of them were disgusting. They made me do . . ."

Erzsike put a hand on her mouth and began to sob silently, still averting her eyes from Ignác.

"What?"

"They made me do things I didn't like."

"And what happened to Casaba? Did you ever see him again?"

"Oh, yes," she said, wiping her cheeks and composing herself. "He would come to visit. He would always bring me marzipan. I loved marzipan. It was the most delicious thing I ever tasted. Casaba was always nice to me. We spoke in Hungarian. He would tell me my family was well. He told me he was proud of 'his Mókus' because I was well liked in Vienna. And he would always care for me. But then he stopped coming one day."

"Did he say why?" Ignác asked.

"No. He just stopped coming after I became pregnant. I haven't seen him or heard from him since then. Not even a letter. But I do hope . . ."

Ignác now signaled for her to speak no more for now, putting his forefinger to his closed lips. He instructed a nurse to cover her with a blanket.

Ignác was becoming increasingly tormented by the high death rate. But what disturbed him even more was the apparent indifference of everyone around him, especially Klein's. It was as if all this was inevitable and routine. Ignác frequently talked about it with the dismayed Kolletschka, his old partner in the autopsy room. And he regularly tried to get the attention of Klein's Assistant, Franz Breit, about the matter. But Breit was a harried and distracted young man whose main priority seemed to be to please Klein. And indeed, Klein was an intimidating man. It took Ignác weeks to organize his thoughts and mount sufficient nerve to approach him. He finally did it one afternoon after rounds.

"Herr Professor Klein," Ignác said as he drew Klein aside, "may I have a few minutes of your time?"

"All right, but I will have to return to my private patients shortly."

Nobody had ever seen Klein smile, and his lips seemed perpetually pursed. He firmly took Ignác's arm and led him out of the ward and into the quieter corridor. Klein surprised him:

"How have you found the experience so far?"

Ignác thought he actually detected a sincere expression of personal interest and even warmth from Klein. But his nervousness didn't dissipate. He had rehearsed how to begin.

"Herr Professor, I know that you are very aware of our . . . regrettable . . . problem with puerperal fever on the wards. But I have to ask, most respectfully, what is being done to reduce the mortality rate, and what may I be able to do in service to you in this regard?"

"Semmelweis, I share your concern," replied Klein with authoritative slowness, "and I have been personally struggling with this problem for many years, young man. I was working on it even before you became a medical student . . ."

"I can imagine," interrupted Ignác. He instantly wished he hadn't been so openly sarcastic.

Klein paused and poked his forefinger into Ignác's chest. "We now know that there are *many* possible causes!" resumed Klein. "My former students and I have been systematically compiling lists of likely causes. We must approach such kinds of problems in medicine analytically, scientifically. You understand? It's much more complicated than you might think. It has baffled the best doctors in Europe. You see, puerperal fever is by no means limited to our great hospital in Vienna. It's even rampant in your own home city in Hungary."

"But with all due respect, Herr Professor, hasn't the mortality rate in the Vienna General Hospital risen greatly in recent years? Isn't it much higher here than other hospitals in Europe?"

Klein frowned and his lower lip curled down.

"You can be assured that I am on top of the problem. You needn't concern yourself with such things. Just work hard and keep your nose to the grindstone. You have some potential. That's why I selected you to be my future Assistant. Now I must go to see my office patients." Klein lightly tapped Ignác on the shoulder, but his demeanor had instantly chilled. He flashed a forced smile, turned, and hurried away.

Ignác was silently infuriated. *How am I ever going to convince this sonofabitch to open his eyes? What do I have to do to break through his inaction? It can't be just indifference. It's bloody arrogance!*

Erzsike, who was still called Mókus by the ward staff, had passed her estimated due date. Ignác still stopped by her bedside every day. She'd had had no visitors since admission, but she hardly lacked for attention since the ward staff had by this time essentially adopted her.

"Are you still determined to give up the baby as soon as you deliver?" Semmelweis asked her now, not for the first time.

"What choice do I have?" she replied. "What kind of future can I possible offer it?"

"Probably better than the foundling home could.[20] The baby would have a better chance. And even if you don't think you could give it the amount of time you think it needs, you are, after all, this child's mother."

The next morning, active labor began. Semmelweis decided to perform the delivery himself. After all that she had been through, he couldn't trust the medical students. By mid-afternoon, Erzsike had delivered a healthy, very pink, bawling baby boy.

She was overjoyed, held him close, and rarely took her eyes off him.

"How could I have ever even thought about giving him up?" she said, beaming, to Ignác. "Just look at him, Doctor. Isn't he the most beautiful baby you've ever seen?"

A problem arose in the evening when the boy appeared to have some intermittent respiratory distress, sometimes even turning temporarily blue. He had diarrhea and refused to suck vigorously. His skin became mottled. And later that night he had a seizure that lasted only a few seconds. But then he finally went to sleep peacefully in Erzsike's arms. Erzsike herself drifted into a contented slumber.

A nurse shook her awake in the morning. The baby was lying by her side, facing his mother, but motionless, cold, and dusky blue. The nurse had to pry the dead newborn from her grasp. Erzsike was frantic. Semmelweis was called to her bedside and examined her. He found that she had no fever and, except for her understandably fast heart rate and heavy breathing, she was in no physical distress.

Ignác sat down beside her bed, as before, but this time, the hysterically sobbing girl abruptly turned her back to him, and curled up with knees up against her chest.

The next morning, Ignác found Erzsike lying in bed on her back, lifeless and blankly staring at the ceiling. She didn't resist being examined. She just lay there in a limp state of apathetic helplessness. Fortunately, she had no fever. But an internal exam indicated that her uterus had unexpectedly failed to retract to its normal size after the delivery, and a small amount of foul-smelling discharge issued from her cervical opening. She had not touched her breakfast or lunch.

Ignác felt suddenly hollow. *Oh, God! Not her!*

At dinner that night, in a small, dimly lit café they frequented near the university, Ignác told Kolletschka about his encounter with Klein. Kolletschka listened intently and then wondered, "Why do you have any reason to doubt Klein? How do you know he isn't pursuing the matter conscientiously, just like he said?"

Ignác retrieved a neatly folded but creased piece of paper from his pocket. "I don't have a really good reason. But look at this." He unfolded the paper and held it up to the candlelight on the table so that he could read his own handwritten notes. "I was able to get some statistics about mortality rates in the lying-in division of the Vienna General Hospital over the past several years. And they show something very disturbing."

"Where did you get this?" Kolletschka asked.

"I just went to the hospital director's office, Jakob. The registrar gave me the information. I don't think there is anything secret about it."

"But you should have asked Klein first," replied Kolletschka.

Ignác continued without responding, reading from his notes. *Overall deaths in all the lying-in wards of the hospital generally occurred at rates of less than one percent per year before Klein took charge. For example, in 1822, which was Professor Boër's last year as head, the mortality rate was only 0.84 percent. Then, almost immediately after Klein replaced Boër, the mortality rate jumped to 7.5 percent!* [21] *And, taking into account the expected month-to-month fluctuations, it has continued to increase every year since then.*

Kolletschka shook his head, looking incredulous. "How can that be? I understand that our Professor Rokitansky doesn't have the highest opinion of Professor Klein, but surely he must be competent as an obstetrician. And I can't imagine that the midwives and trainees on his service have suddenly declined in quality."

"Neither can I. Nor has there been any obvious change in the kinds of patients who come to the hospital," added Ignác. "I can't think of what might have changed since Klein took over, but the numbers are the numbers. What really troubles me is that nobody seems to be looking at this. And women just continue to die of puerperal fever at ever-increasing rates."

Kolletschka fell into deep thought, distractedly picking at the food on his plate.

Finally, he looked up and said, "I can see why you are so upset. But you must be careful about the political implications. I want to make sure this doesn't derail your career. Perhaps we should go to Professor Rokitansky for his advice. I know he will be most discreet." Ignác was skeptical.

Rokitansky could see them the next day. His office perfectly reflected his austere personality. It was small and cramped. Even though it was midday, the heavy drapes over the window were drawn, and the room was dimly lit by just a kerosene desk lamp. Rokitansky's shelves were overflowing with a jumble of books; his desk was almost completely covered with messy piles of paper. He was obviously in the midst of writing a manuscript.

The professor arose from his chair as Kolletschka and Semmelweis entered and smiled warmly. They sat in the plain wooden chairs in front of his desk while Rokitansky sank back into his cushioned armchair.

Ignác related his concerns to Rokitansky. He had re-transcribed the figures he'd previously shown to Kolletschka onto a clean sheet of paper. His handwriting was bold and elegant.

Rokitansky took the paper and silently perused the data Ignác had obtained from the hospital registrar. Every now and then, he removed his glasses, sat back in his chair, and contemplatively looked up to the ceiling. The mortality rates were neatly displayed for each month, beginning in 1818, some five years before Klein's ascent to his current position as chief of obstetrics. Rokitansky handed back the sheet to Ignác. "Well, there is no question about the significant upswing in postpartum mortality rates within the first six months after Professor Klein took charge of the lying-in division. Do you gentlemen have any ideas?"

"We are completely baffled, Herr Professor," said Ignác. Kolletschka nodded in agreement.

"So am I . . . at least for the moment," replied Rokitansky, now intently leaning forward across his desk and glancing back and forth between the two men. "But there *must* be a reason. There is always an explanation when the data are so unambiguous. You must find it." He pointed right at Ignác.

"But where should I begin?"

There was an awkward pause.

"You must begin where you should always begin," continued Rokitansky. "The first step has to be careful, meticulous, detailed, and *thoughtful* observation. You must *look,*" he said, pointing to his own eyes, "and at the same time *think,*" now pointing to his temple. "At least this first step shouldn't create any problems for you with Professor Klein. You should make sure that you yourself do every single autopsy you possibly can on any woman or newborn who dies of this syndrome, this so-called puerperal fever. I will instruct my staff to give you all such autopsies you can handle. And, Kolletschka, you should back up Semmelweis and perform any that he doesn't have the time to do. This way, there will be only two observers, variability will be minimized, and the two of you can easily compare detailed notes."

Kolletschka nodded in assent.

"As a courtesy, Semmelweis, you should inform Professor Klein," continued Rokitansky, "otherwise, you might antagonize him even more when he found out. Take detailed notes, do you understand? Gentlemen, we are scientific detectives first and foremost. We can't allow ourselves to become satisfied with guesswork about something we don't understand."

"Certainly," replied Ignác, "but, with all due respect, how long can we wait? The problem is urgent . . ."

Rokitansky raised his hand to gently cut him off. "There are no shortcuts if you seek the truth. We cannot effectively prevent something we don't understand or prescribe treatments for such a disease without the risk of doing the patient more harm than good. Ask our Professor Skoda about it."

They stood, shook hands, and agreed to meet again when progress had been made.

In the weeks following Semmelweis's hallway confrontation with Klein, there was an influx of additional medical students assigned to the maternity service. It made conditions even more crammed than they were before. The fetid, stagnant air in the wards was suffocating. It was made worse by the administrative decision to begin heating the wards even though the late autumn days were unseasonably warm. At the same time, deaths seemed to be on the rise. On some days, there were as many as three or four, one after another.

The pain began in the evening. At first, it was just a gnawing discomfort in the lower abdomen. But it gradually turned into waves of agonizing cramps, accompanied by low-pitched moans. The nurse summoned Dr. Breit, who came to her bedside, with Ignác hurrying along behind him. Erzsike's breathing was now rapid and shallow. Her pulse had greatly quickened, and it was thready. She was ghostly pale, with her mouth slightly open, nostrils flared, and her saucer-eyed stare expressed alarm. Soon she became flushed with fever and began to shake violently with chills. Rigors. The nurse wiped her face with a wet cloth, and Ignác held her hand, squeezing it with each rush of tormenting pain and chills. Breit stood at the foot of the bed, arms folded, shaking his head.

Ignác, Breit, and the nurse were each called to different areas and had to leave Erzsike's bedside. Three of the women in the ward were in the late stages of labor, another was having severe late pregnancy bleeding from the vagina, a fourth was vomiting unremittingly, while several others were in different states of suffering. There wasn't sufficient staff to take care of all this.

Suddenly, a spine-chilling shriek drowned out the din of the room. It was a jarring scream that was of an almost inhuman, otherworldly quality. It came from Erzsike it was repeated in rapid succession. Ignác dropped what he was doing and rushed to her bedside, but Erzsike was now delirious and didn't even recognize him. Her abdomen had become grossly distended, her body was fixed in place, and her legs were drawn up at the knees. Even the slightest motion made her cry out in agony. Blood trickled from her nose and mouth. As Ignác was called to an emergency breech delivery, life slowly ebbed away from the girl he now had to leave in solitude.

After a mostly sleepless night, a drained Ignác managed to drag himself to his scheduled dissecting time in the morgue. He finished examining his first cadaver without paying much attention. The protocol had become quite routine. He was still alone in the room. Then he unwrapped the next cadaver that had been placed on his dissecting table. It was just the bloodless, alabaster corpse of what must have been yet another young woman. Without further thought, he made his initial, deep incision all the way down from the sternum to the pubis, laying open the abdominopelvic cavity effortlessly. As he exposed the internal organs of the abdomen, the familiar stink of pus arose, but he no longer recoiled from it. Ignác absentmindedly glimpsed at the head. And it was then that he was suddenly overcome with lightheadedness and the rapid pounding of his heart. He dropped his scalpel. Realizing that he was about to faint, Ignác lowered himself to the floor, holding onto the dissecting table. And there he sat, on the cold, stone floor, practically immobilized, his head hung low between his knees.

He had just slit open Erzsike!

Kolletschka and a couple of medical students arrived, and Ignác was jolted into somehow being able to stand up, holding onto the autopsy slab, so they wouldn't see him in this condition.

"Good morning, Ignác!" Kolletschka proclaimed cheerfully. "How are you doing?"

"Not so well," Ignác mumbled. "I feel rather ill and have to get some fresh air. Would you mind finishing this autopsy?" He pointed to it, his head turned away.

"Of course," replied Kolletschka. "Take a walk, and get some rest. If you feel better by this evening, maybe we can have dinner together."

"Sure," Ignác said as he hurried out of the morgue with his head bowed. He made it to the first tree in the courtyard, held onto it, and vomited.

CHAPTER 6

JANUARY 1845

Klein had repeatedly put off responding to Ignác's increasingly urgent requests to meet with him. Finally, on a snowy February afternoon in 1845, Ignác walked to Klein's private practice office for his long-awaited meeting to request his chief's permission to continue to work early in the mornings under Rokitansky's supervision to autopsy women who had died the previous day from puerperal fever. Now that Ignác was officially a full-time Aspirant on Klein's service, both Rokitansky and Ignác were worried that Klein would ban Ignác from the morgue if he found out that he was working there behind his back. Klein's office was located on the elegant Rotenturmstrasse. To get there, Ignác passed through the Stephansplatz in the center of the old city, with its magnificent gothic cathedral. The steep, tiled roof of St. Stephen's was decorated by enormous mosaics of the double-headed eagle, the imperial emblem of the Habsburg Empire. They remained visible even in the midst of the heavy, falling snow. He shivered in the freezing cold during the brisk walk to Klein's office. Or maybe he was shivering in dread of Klein's expected rebuke.

The doorbell was answered by Klein's landlady, a short, chubby woman with rosy cheeks. She escorted Ignác up the staircase into the small anteroom to Klein's office. Cigar smoke emanated from behind the closed office door, and he could make out voices from within. Klein must have been finishing a previous meeting. The landlady waited for a response to her knock and then waved for Ignác to follow her in. He could barely make out Klein sitting at his desk behind thick smoke. Sitting next to Klein were two younger men. Ignác recognized one as Eduard Lumpe, who had served as Klein's assistant just a few years earlier.[22]

"Hello, Semmelweis," greeted Lumpe, standing to shake hands.

Klein remained seated. He motioned for Ignác to sit on an armless chair across the desk from him.

"Bring us some coffee," said Klein, vigorously rubbing his hands and turning to the landlady. "I've just returned from house calls in this wretched weather, and the damned fireplace has been out." He was visibly annoyed with Frau Schlank.

Glancing to the side, Ignác wondered if he was supposed to know the silent young man with thick, curly, black hair who had remained stiffly seated next to Lumpe, staring intently at Ignác.

"Oh, yes" said Klein, extending his arm toward the stranger, "I want you to meet Carl Braun." The dour young man stood up, momentarily bowed his head toward Ignác, and then sat down again before Ignác could shake his hand.

"Braun will be finishing his medical studies this year. He has taken a great interest in obstetrics," continued Klein, "so he has been working with Lumpe in all his spare time. I can only wish that our other medical students could show his kind of . . . ambition." He pumped a fist in the air to underscore that last word. "We expect great things from young Braun. Don't we, Lumpe?"

"Absolutely, Herr Professor," snapped Lumpe in response.

As the men chatted about the weather and sipped coffee *mit schlag* from porcelain cups which Mrs. Schlank had promptly brought in, Ignác scanned the grand study. The bright white light of falling snow flooded into the room through the large window behind Klein. The professor's huge desk was almost entirely bare, with only a few papers arranged in a neat pile to his right. The bookshelves were occupied mostly by figurines, memorabilia, honorary medals, and other knickknacks. There were very few books.

"So, Semmelweis, tell us what's on your mind," said Klein, leaning back in his swivel chair, savoring his cigar.

"I wish to help if I can, Herr Professor, in any research you are doing into finding the cause of this infernal puerperal fever that's been plaguing our patients," replied Ignác.

"But I told you before that we already know a lot about it!" interrupted Klein. He was now leaning forward, elbows on the desk, fingertips touching in a raised steeple.

Before Ignác could regain his train of thought, Klein continued. "It's not as simple as you seem to think. Puerperal fever is caused by many factors. Lumpe here," Klein said, turning toward his former assistant, "has studied the problem with me extensively, and he has just written a treatise on the subject. Have you seen it, Semmelweis?"

"No, sir."

"Too busy with your work, are you?" Klein paused for some uncomfortable seconds, lower lip curled in obvious displeasure. "Well, we have now engaged our eager young student Braun to help us with the project. I had a hunch that this was the matter you wanted to see me about, and that's why I asked both of them to join us today. What do you say, Lumpe?"

Lumpe sat up straight and cleared his throat. "Yes, indeed. I have to date identified almost thirty different causes of puerperal fever. And Carl over here is now looking into a couple of other real possibilities. They are quite diverse."

"Like what?" interrupted Ignác, momentarily seeming to forget that he was in Klein's presence.

"Like general deprivation and malnutrition, emotional stresses like fear—yes, merely the fear of dying after giving birth—as well as the shame many of these pitiful, abandoned young women must surely feel when they are in labor. We are now quite certain, however, that the *predominant* etiology is related to miasma."

"Miasma?" Ignác asked.

"Yes, miasma. Those atmospheric changes which in these cases are undoubtedly exacerbated by overcrowding in the wards."

"Pardon me, Lumpe, but what possible evidence do you have that *any* of these factors can cause puerperal fever?" pressed Ignác.

"Evidence?" Klein felt impelled to interrupt. "How does one find evidence but by reasoning? Reasoning by systematically examining all possible variables that might be implicated. And then ruling them out individually, one by one—" Klein pressed a forefinger into his temple "—through rational deduction!"

"And that's what we have done," added Lumpe.

"Really?" muttered Ignác with feigned approval.

"And I have my own theories," added Klein after exhaling another big puff of cigar smoke. "They are based on my considerable experience. I have always said that only intelligent, educated, and meticulous physicians and their well-supervised medical students should be performing deliveries. I can't take responsibility for what those midwives do, but we have been required to accept them into our profession since they were foisted on us by that antiquated edict of Empress Maria Theresa decades ago. And that's exactly why I decided to separate them to do their deliveries on a different ward in the lying-in division."

Four years earlier, in October 1840, under orders from Klein and by imperial decree, the maternity wards of the hospital had been formally separated into two divisions. The so-called First Division (*Erste Abteilung*) was to be housed in the more modern wards, directly under Klein's supervision.

This service was to be entirely dedicated to teaching medical students and postgraduate physicians. It was the service to which Ignác was now exclusively assigned. Klein appointed one of his former assistants, Dr. Franz Bartsch,[23] to run the Second Division, where only midwives performed the deliveries. Bartsch was a reserved, dutiful, reclusive man who was not often seen and seemed to be more interested in Byzantine architecture than in medicine. The First and Second Divisions were located in adjacent wards, and they shared a single anteroom. However, Ignác practically never set foot in the midwives' Second Division wards. Nor did the medical students, whose work was also restricted to the doctors' teaching service in the First Division. By early 1845, as he neared the end of his first year as an Aspirant, Ignác knew that the mortality rate was gradually increasing, at least for the women delivering on Klein's First Division.

"But, with all due respect, Herr Professor," Ignác continued, facing Klein, who now sat behind a swirling haze of cigar smoke, "it seems to me that wouldn't have solved the overall problem. It would have just shifted it to the midwives."

"No, but my intent was to allow us to place blame where blame should be placed, and that's the first step to any solution," replied Klein, smugly repositioning himself in his chair. "Eventually, the obvious outcome of separating the wards should get the attention of the newspapers. And only that will move those imbecile bureaucrats in the imperial government to place strict limits on the work midwives are allowed to do."

"But the problem appears to me to be getting worse, not better, even in our own First Division." Ignác immediately caught himself veering into an area where he hadn't planned on going to this meeting. *This will really infuriate him,* he thought to himself. *Watch your words, goddamn it.*

"Nonsense!" thundered Klein, leaning across his desk toward Ignác. Quickly composing himself, he slumped back into his arm chair. "Puerperal fever is an old problem. It comes and goes over time. It is epidemic. One year the miasma in the air creates bad statistics, and other years things are good. But look here," he said pausing to inhale deeply and then exhale a generous puff of cigar smoke, "it will sort itself out."

"Yes, it will sort itself out," echoed Lumpe.

"Well, what about learning something about it by thoroughly analyzing the autopsies of those unfortunate women who have succumbed?" Ignác persisted, trying to get to the point of the meeting.

"Autopsies?" blasted Klein. "Autopsies tell you about dead people. We are in the business of living people. Concentrate on examining your living patients! As I told you last year, don't concern yourself with these matters. As you can see, we are studying the problem. Isn't that right, Lumpe?"

"Yes, Herr Professor, we are working hard on it."

Ignác thought the heat from the roaring fireplace was more than sufficient now, sensing beads of perspiration forming on his forehead.

"Well that's it, then," proclaimed Klein, slapping the palms of both hands on his desk.

The conversation was obviously over. Ignác rose to take his coat as Klein and Lumpe also stood up simultaneously. So did the earnest student, Braun, who hadn't spoken a word. Without further ado, Ignác left, descended the stairs, and walked out into the drifting snow.

Back in the office, Klein sat at his desk, scribbling a note on a sheet of paper, while Lumpe and Carl Braun remained standing. It wasn't a long note—just three lines. He then neatly folded it, sealed it with a personalized wafer, and handed it to Lumpe.

"Please take this to Schiffner at your earliest convenience. Today."

Lumpe nodded and gleefully slipped the letter into the inside pocket of his jacket. He and Braun collected their overcoats and left.

Ignác ambled vacantly through the frigid, windy streets of Vienna, the snow now only gently falling. There were many people walking about purposefully in the late afternoon light, lots of carriages and horses in the streets, but their sounds were now muffled as he trudged through the freshly fallen snow. Ignác felt strangely disconnected from the street scene, and everything seemed to him to move in slow motion. He soon found himself on side streets he didn't recognize. Numb with cold, his mind in a haze, he wandered into a small café.

Sitting by himself at a small, marble-top table, sipping a coffee he didn't really need and toying with a pastry for which he had no appetite, Ignác felt waves of indignation welling up. He hadn't gotten anything accomplished. He hadn't even managed to clearly articulate the purpose of his visit, to inform Klein about Rokitansky's recommendation that Ignác concentrate his morning autopsy sessions on dissections of the recently deceased women from the maternity ward, and to document his findings meticulously. He felt he had been stonewalled. The more he replayed the scene in his mind, the more his exasperation turned into a mix of anger and, for the first time, a vague sense of fear.

Ignác ruminated. *Why didn't Klein share my sense of outrage at the virtual carnage of women in the lying-in wards? Didn't he care? Didn't patients like Erzsike matter to him at all? Was he just too preoccupied with his affluent private practice and his political activities? Was he worried that the state of affairs on the maternity wards would reflect badly on him and damage his own reputation? And what were Lumpe and that medical student Braun doing there? Am I to be marginalized?*

Suddenly, Ignác sat bolt upright in his chair. He had to remind himself *where* he was and *who* he was. As Marko and others had so often said, this was, after all, the mecca of medicine in the entire world. All his professors, yes, surely including Klein, were accomplished, preeminent medical scholars. And he—Ignác Semmelweis, son of a Swabian merchant—was a nothing! His indignation *had* to be misguided. And it was certainly disrespectful. His position here was a privilege for which countless other medical school graduates would envy him. *How could someone so fortunate be so ungrateful?* he reprimanded himself.

By the time he'd pulled himself together, the sun had set, and he had to hurry back to the hospital for his night shift. He had lost track of time. He was late, and he was freezing.

Ignác's clinical workload on the First Division was becoming overwhelming. And there were now so many autopsies to be performed on some mornings that he had to ask Kolletschka to do some of them. Nevertheless, Ignác performed his dissections with more attention to detail than ever. He took copious notes of his findings, just as Rokitansky had recommended. Since many of the autopsies he had to perform were on women who had been previously under his own personal care before they died, he also began to keep detailed notes on the clinical courses of all the patients in the First Division. As infuriated as he was with Klein's obstinacy, he didn't forget Klein's admonition to Ignác to "concentrate on examining your living patients." This way he could eventually try to make connections between the clinical events leading to death and what he found on autopsy in the same women. *What was different about the ones who died from those who survived?*

CHAPTER 7

MAY 1845

Spring arrived before Ignác was suddenly shaken out of his busy routine. It occurred one night on call, while he was trying to catch some sleep in his tiny *Dienstzimmer*. Ignác was rudely awakened by the shrieks of a woman outside his door in the corridor. He sprang from his cot and, flinging open his door, he could make out in the darkness a young pregnant woman crumpled on the floor nearby, being dragged by two attendants toward the maternity ward. She was sobbing hysterically, and he could barely make out what she was wailing.

"Please, I beg you . . . in the name of God . . . I don't want to go there. Don't take me to *that* ward. I will die. I don't want to leave my baby an orphan! Please!" And then, as she was forcibly placed on a gurney and strapped in, she screamed out, "I want to be delivered by the midwives!"

She was quickly wheeled out of sight, her calls of distress fading as the doors to the ward closed behind her. One of the attendants remained behind in the corridor, straightening his uniform after the struggle. Ignác ran up to ask him what the commotion was all about.

"Oh, don't worry about that, sir. That was just another young woman who didn't want to come to this ward for her delivery," said the burly attendant in a Slavic accent.

"Why not?" demanded Ignác.

"We see that all the time these days, sir. But it usually doesn't happen up here on the floor. We deal with them downstairs at the admitting gate . . . and sometimes even outside the hospital main entrance when they try to run off. We have to make sure they don't do anything foolish to themselves, like delivering their babies in the street. They've been known to do that, you know, sir."

"And these things happen only when the women are assigned to the First Division?"

"That's right, sir. There is talk all over the city now that women die in childbirth much more frequently here than in the Second Division. Ever since them two separate wards were made. So they all want to be delivered by the midwives in the Second. Well they can't all bloody well choose to do that. Depends on the day of the week, as you know. It's the luck of the draw."

Ignác returned to his call room in utter bewilderment. As dog-tired as he was, he couldn't go back to sleep. so he lay on his cot in the darkness of the room, eyes wide open, staring at the ceiling. He had suspected that the overall death rate must have increased, but how could he have not known that it was so different in the two divisions? Anyway, was it really true, or was it just a rumor? And, if it were true, how many people here knew about it, and what on earth could be the reason? Wasn't this exactly the opposite of what Klein had expected and indeed wanted to disprove when he separated the services?

The next morning Ignác asked Franz Breit, Klein's current Assistant, what he knew. Breit replied that he knew the postpartum mortality rate on the First Division was rising and that he had heard about stories of women begging to be admitted to the Second Division.[24] But he was just too busy and he hadn't made all that much of it.

"Anyway," Breit told Ignác, "irrespective of statistics, rules are rules, and the workload requires that there be a strict rotation of all admissions, going to only one or the other division on alternate days."

Ignác mumbled a crude Hungarian curse under his breath.

Now he suddenly felt impelled to see the actual statistics. As soon as there was a break in the clinical activity that afternoon, he returned to the registrar's office, which was in a separate administration building inside courtyard Number One. There he recognized the helpful young man who had several months ago given him the annual total mortality rates in the hospital's lying-in division.

"I am Doctor Semmelweis, Professor Klein's Aspirant. Professor Klein and I have become increasingly concerned about the rising death rate, and we need some more detailed information. We want to look at a *breakdown* of deaths in the two divisions. I told Professor Klein that I wanted to help him track down the possible cause of the problem."

Ignác felt self-conscious about being deliberately misleading, but he was desperate to get the information. The registrar's clerk remained seated and looked up at Ignác over his glasses, trying to remember the face.

"Semmelweis, you say?"

"Yes, Doctor Ignác Semmelweis. Professor Klein's Aspirant."

There was silence as the clerk reached for a piece of paper on his desk, looked at it, carefully folded it, and then slowly rose to his feet. "Wait here, Doctor. Let me see what I can do."

With that, the clerk walked down the hall to an ornate door, which he entered after knocking. Ignác moved over to see the sign on the door: 'Professor Johann Schiffner, Krankenhausdirektor.'

Within minutes, a tall, elegantly attired man with a high forehead stepped out, holding his hands firmly behind his back. His expression was not welcoming.

"Dr. Semmelweis, my name is Professor Schiffner. I am the director of the hospital. May I have a word with you, if you would kindly come into my office?" he said with an outstretched arm, bidding him to enter. The young clerk quietly slipped past them to scurry back to his desk. Ignác was gripped by a sense of foreboding.

The director's office was spacious, with antique furniture arranged on a vast Persian rug. An enormous desk was situated in front of a large window, overlooking the hospital's main courtyard. The walls of the office were covered with diplomas of various kinds. Ignác glanced at the one that was the largest and most prominently displayed just inside the door. It read: "*Ehrenburgerrect der Stadt Wien, Johann Christian Schiffner, 22 September 1834*" and was topped by a large seal of the Habsburg Empire. Damn it: he was speaking with an "Honorary Citizen of Vienna," Ignác deduced, now rather shaken.[25] Schiffner pointed Ignác to a chair in front of his desk while he took his seat in the high leather chair behind it. Leaning forward intently, with his elbows on the desk and hands clasped to support his upturned chin, he began in a low, gravelly voice.

"Semmelweis, I have heard from Professor Klein about your concerns. He sent me a note—did you know? He doesn't completely share them . . . as you very well know. So I can't imagine why you would even suggest to my registrar's clerk that the esteemed professor might have assigned you to look into these statistics. You *know* he didn't."

A distinct chill instantly descended over the encounter.

Startled, Ignác could only stammer a few words in response. "I didn't mean to take . . . I mean I didn't mean to say . . . I certainly didn't say I was assigned . . ." He suddenly felt himself again reduced to his old self: the stumbling, inarticulate, Hungarian foreigner.

"We take unauthorized intrusion into the hospital's files with the utmost seriousness," continued Schiffner. "What exactly are you trying to do?"

"Sir, I want to help figure out what's causing the rising rate of puerperal fever, and I thought we could learn something important from the pattern . . ."

"I know," interrupted Schiffner, impatiently holding up a hand to stop Ignác, "I know all about your . . . what shall I call it . . . your curiosity. But this is simply not public information." Schiffner paused and sat back in his chair, mulling over the situation. Changing his tone, he continued, "What specific kind of information are you looking for?"

"I want to know the comparative trends in mortality between the First and Second Divisions."

"I am afraid I don't have those numbers. But I can tell you generally that the death rate in the First Division has become significantly higher than in the Second Division. We are all frankly disappointed because Professor Klein had predicted that the outcomes of deliveries by midwives would be inferior to those performed by doctors and their students. And now we seem to be finding the opposite."

Ignác was bewildered by the director's candor. *He must have a reason for telling me all this!*

Schiffner rose from his chair, signaling that the conversation was over. He had nothing more to say. Schiffner walked Ignác to the door. Then, taking a deep sigh, as if to brace himself for the need to part on a conciliatory note, he met Ignác's gaze.

"That's probably more than you should know, Semmelweis. But we need all of your skills and your hard work to help us turn this problem around. Can I ask you to redouble your efforts with the care of these patients?"

The crafty old fox is planning to use me for something disingenuous. He impressed himself with how he was beginning to understand the underhanded workings of academic medicine.

"You can count on it, Herr Direktor," replied Ignác as they shook hands. On his walk back to the First Division, Ignác couldn't help reflecting on the menacing tone of much of his conversation with the hospital director. He decidedly didn't like Schiffner at all. *A bullying bureaucrat prick*, he thought. At the same time, however, Ignác felt buoyant. He had been provided with a piece of information that he sensed would become a vital piece of the puzzle.

Returning to his residence in the evening, Ignác related what had transpired that day to his trusted roommate and compatriot, Markusovzky. The two friends' available time together had become increasingly limited by their busy and dissimilar clinical duties. But Ignác had managed to keep Marko sporadically apprised of his experiences. Marko's reaction to the meeting with Schiffner was one of deep concern, almost alarm.

"I hope you realize who you were speaking with. Schiffner is not only the hospital's director, but he is also one of the most powerful men in Vienna. He is a personal friend of Metternich, and his political connections have supposedly destroyed the careers of many who have crossed him."

Ignác had clearly underestimated the impact of the confrontation. "Shit, what can I do at this point, Marko? I guess I am screwed! But I am still very earnest about my need to intervene—somehow, any possible way. I can't bear to just accept and ignore such tacit institutional disregard for all the deaths and suffering going on in front of my nose. But I'll be of little value if I lose my position."

"Exactly," responded Marko. "At least you have kept *some* of your precious few Magyar senses."

The two friends sat in silence in the well-worn armchairs of their anteroom. Then Marko abruptly sat forward, struck with an idea.

"Schiffner needs your help, Ignác. He as much as told you so at the end of your conversation. Don't you see? Regardless of his political status, he can't afford to have this kind of hospital scandal on his watch without doing something about it. After all, he *does* report to the Imperial Ministry. Even Metternich wouldn't tolerate this kind of bad press. It will be all over the newspapers."

"What the hell are you talking about?"

"What I am saying is that you must write a letter to Schiffner right away. You should express your deepest appreciation for his valued advice, blah, blah, blah, and pledge to work as hard as possible for the patients of the First Division. You must say you want to help *him* and the institution. He will like that. It will show your allegiance and dependability."

Ignác squirmed with an odd feeling of both gratification and apprehension.

"But I must carry on," he replied.

"Carry on with care. *Great* care!" offered Marko. "You are treading on ground that's filled with land mines."

The next day, Ignác reiterated the events to Kolletschka, who took much the same position as Marko. "Just remember that you are due to be appointed Klein's Assistant starting next July. Don't risk that now. If Klein retracts his offer, you will have achieved nothing. Plug away at the problem privately, and keep a very low profile. Be cautious about who you talk to about it."

CHAPTER 8

SEPTEMBER 1845

In the ensuing months of 1845, Ignác applied himself to his work with more intensity than ever. The daily routine remained unchanged, and his relationship with Klein seemed no less cordial. But the sobering events of the past winter made Ignác mindful of being watched. For the first time, thoughts of who he could or couldn't trust had crept into his head. During ward rounds, he periodically ran into Carl Braun, the enigmatic medical student he had met in Klein's office in February. They would acknowledge each other with only a silent glance and a nod.

But Ignác didn't stop stockpiling his daily frustrations. His indignation and rage grew in surges with each tragedy he witnessed. He just couldn't dissociate the personal stories of the patients he cared for from the statistics. Like Erzsike, each of these women had a name. But, with continued encouragement from his friends and supporters, he was somehow able to muzzle himself from outbursts. As they all advised, he carried out his clinical duties more conscientiously than ever, kept his head down, and continued to silently observe and take careful notes. He used every minute of free time to think systematically about how the pieces of the puzzle might fit together to get to the bottom of the cause of puerperal fever, a crisis which, apparently, only *he* viewed with alarm.

As serious and often dejected as Ignác was during his long hours at the hospital, he retained the ability to transform himself into his old, buoyant, charming self at nights and weekends. But these occasions were now few and far between. He could still be a devil-may-care *bon vivant*. He still patronized Vienna's beer gardens and dance halls with his friends and acquaintances, but it took more and more coaxing by them to get him to go. During these times, he was the same amiable, irreverent Ignác who'd arrived in Vienna eight years ago. In their company, he seemed to be completely uninhibited and detached from his growingly arduous and dispiriting clinical responsibilities. He drank and ate in excess, smoked incessantly like most Hungarians, cussed profusely, and flirted with the girls.

But unlike his Austrian medical student friends who often became indiscriminately vulgar as the beer flowed, Ignác at all times kept his wits and treated the young women as ladies, addressing them with the utmost respect and deference, regardless of their social standing. However inebriated he might become, he never lost that exaggerated, almost comical sense of obsolete courtliness that stereotyped the traditional Magyar man. Others would snicker and giggle at Ignác good-naturedly. But his flamboyant gestures of graciousness, his constant bowing to the ladies, and his kissing of their hands never ceased to charm them.

His most endearing practice with the ladies he really liked was to regularly present them with a nosegay of freshly cut flowers. He would vary the flowers in those sweet-smelling small bouquets by the feelings he had toward each one at the time, using the cryptic "language of flowers." Like the rose meaning love, the orchid for exotic beauty, carnations for admiration, and purple lilacs for the first emotions of love . . . yes, Ignác liked the lilacs most of all. He didn't know why. But maybe their entrancing fragrance reminded him of the lilacs blossoming on the bushes and trees that covered the hills of Buda, where he used to romp as a careless boy with his friends on those warm, breezy days.

Ignác became paunchier around the middle, and he lost more hair, but he danced better than ever. His Magyar persona was much more attracted to the spirited spontaneity of his native *ciganyzene* (gypsy music), like the *csárdás* and the *verbunkos*, than to the staid formality of the new Viennese waltzes. But he became agile with those as well. Ignác was never one to remain seated when lively dance music was being played and a lovely young lady was available to partner.

But as the mounting tragedy of his work increasingly burdened him, his interludes of social time became progressively more infrequent and limited.

Ignác neatly compiled the notes from his clinical and autopsy observations. He had been regularly updating them in tabular form on reams of paper that he stored in folders in his *Dienstzimmer* desk. Reviewing them over and over again, he searched for those crucial links that might uncover the real cause of puerperal fever. But the more data he amassed, the further away he seemed to get from finding the elusive answer Rokitansky had assured him was there, under his nose, just waiting to be discovered.

By the fall of 1845, more than 300 autopsies of women who had died of puerperal fever had been performed, most by Ignác and some by Kolletschka. Ignác's diligence and productivity had been extraordinary, especially since he did all this before his regular work days began. A few common threads were becoming clearly apparent.

Many of the corpses, especially those from the First Division, had evidence of some trauma to the birth canal. These women had been obviously subjected to frequent and inexperienced pelvic examinations by the medical students. Especially striking was that every one of the corpses from both divisions had endometritis, an extensive swelling and inflammation of the inner lining of the uterus. The great majority of corpses also exhibited evidence of peritonitis, inflammation that had spread to the membrane linings of the abdomen, in many cases accompanied by large pockets of pus. This was the reason why incisions into the abdomens at autopsy immediately released that most awful stench.

But the other autopsy findings in these women were more variable. Some had meningitis, inflammation of the linings of the spinal cord. Many, but not all, had collections of pus along the linings of the lungs in the chest cavity. Abscesses were found in other organs throughout the body—some within the lungs, others within the spleen or liver or the brain, yet others within the bones or subcutaneous tissues at various sites.

And then there were the findings in the dead babies. Remarkably, their autopsies revealed exactly the same kinds of widespread inflammation and abscesses their mothers had.

The conclusions were becoming clearer. The disease in the mothers must have always started in the birth canal and uterus, because this was found in every single autopsy case. It then spread to adjacent structures, finally entering the circulation through the uterine veins and traveling through the bloodstream to different organs, where it formed abscesses at distant sites. The dead newborns must have had the same kind of blood-borne process, but where was the entry point in them? It was definitely not the birth canal. The deadly disease struck girls and boys equally. They must have acquired it from their mothers somewhere during the birth process. *Maybe transmitted through the umbilical cord that joined their circulations before birth*, he thought.

So now Ignác finally understood how puerperal fever started, spread, and eventually killed the mothers and some of their newborns. Kolletschka and Rokitansky agreed with his conclusions. But were there really more cases from the First Division than from the Second Division, as he suspected, and as the hospital director, Schiffner, had hesitantly affirmed? And, if so, why? The answer to the first question came soon enough.

CHAPTER 9

DECEMBER 1845

One winter evening, Ignác needed a break and went with some friends to a local tavern that was frequented by medical students, especially the "privileged Austrian" ones. It was smoke-filled and noisy, but a lively gypsy orchestra was playing spirited *csárdás* numbers that lifted his spirits for a while. But just as the rowdiness was beginning to peak, Ignác decided to go home much earlier than he would have done in his student days. He bid good night to his inebriated friends, but as he got up, he noticed a commotion in a back corner of the tavern. A couple he had seen there before, at the same table, were in the midst of a heated argument. Their features were difficult to make out across the room through the thick smoke and haze, and he certainly couldn't hear anything they were shouting at each other through the deafening noise of the boisterous crowd. Suddenly, they both sprang to their feet. The man grabbed the woman's shoulders with both hands and shook her violently; then he shoved her backward onto the bench where they had been sitting. Others around them pulled him away, but the man freed himself and, with a grand flourish, turned on his heels and stalked out of the tavern. The small crowd that had formed around them dispersed, but Ignác remained standing, appalled, his eyes riveted on the young woman, who gathered herself, straightened her dress, and slumped back onto her seat on the bench.

Ignác weaved his way through the mass of people to see if the young woman needed help. Her head was buried in her arms on the tabletop, and she was silently sobbing and heaving.

"Excuse me, Fraulein. Are you hurt?" Ignác said, leaning forward with his hands clasped behind his back. She didn't seem to hear him. So he leaned lower, tapped her arm, and asked again louder. At this, the young woman abruptly raised her head. Ignác was struck by her special beauty, even with her face covered with tears and her eyes almost swollen shut from crying. She just kept staring at him quizzically.

"May I sit here? I mean . . . *there*, across from you?" Ignác asked timidly.

She didn't say anything, so he did.

After sitting across from her in silence for a while, he introduced himself. "My name is Ignác. Semmelweis. Ignác Semmelweis."

She muttered something he couldn't hear, her lips barely parting. He leaned forward.

"Caroline," she said, inaudibly, but, this time, he could read her lips.

Ignác sat across from Caroline for a long time, just looking at her and wondering what he should do. He wanted to be helpful, but he also wanted to make sure she didn't think he was taking advantage of her misfortune to make advances to her. The crowd around them in the tavern was getting increasingly raucous, mostly drowning out the Romani musicians. Then a scuffle broke out. Caroline looked up.

"May I escort you home?" Ignác asked. "This is no place for you to be now by yourself, and, anyway, I'm going home myself."

Caroline nodded.

"I promise I will not touch you at all. I just want to get you home safely."

She nodded again. Ignác went back toward where the fight was taking place to get his coat and then helped Caroline put hers on. As they approached the door to exit, a full-scale riot was breaking out. The musicians stopped playing and scattered. Above the clamor of breaking glass, overturning tables and benches, and crashing bodies was a cacophony of vulgar curses shouted in German, Hungarian, and other languages he didn't recognize. It looked like some of the students were hurling anatomic body parts at the townspeople who were regulars at the tavern. As Ignác opened the door for Caroline, he turned to take a final glance at what had become a pitched battle incited by the intoxicated medical students. He shook his head.

On the way to Caroline's home in Leopolstadt, the 2nd district of Vienna, the cold, fresh air invigorated them. Caroline told the story of her short-lived fling with the handsome young cadet in the imperial military.

"We were attracted to each other," she said, "but it was never meant to last. We came from very different backgrounds and had practically no interests in common."

"But that's no reason for him to be physically abusive toward you," protested Ignác as they walked through the moonless dark of the city, Caroline leading the way. "I mean, did he ever beat you before?"

"Beat me?" Caroline repeated. "I guess you can say that."

"My God, why on earth did you put up with that?"

"I didn't. I fought back," said Caroline, "even more ferociously. That's why the bastard left."

"But you are a young woman . . ."

"We don't know each other," she interrupted. She stopped walking and gently caught Ignác's arm, turning to face him. "But I am not one of those sad, helpless creatures who assume they have no choice. Don't you worry about me," Caroline said with a smile, looking straight into his eyes and patting his cheek before resuming their long walk.

"I knew I couldn't best him physically. But I could most definitely outwit the stupid scoundrel."

As Ignác walked back by himself to his apartment, he couldn't stop thinking of Caroline.

What a remarkable young woman. What strange ideas, he said to himself, shaking his head with a smile of admiration. *But how bloody marvelous!*

CHAPTER 10
SPRING 1846

Caroline's father was a shopkeeper. Her mother came from a large, well-to-do Jewish family. While the family was far from impoverished, it had to work hard to make ends meet. So, in addition to her domestic chores starting at dawn, Caroline was accustomed from her childhood to spending long, dreary hours at home, doing contracted needlework like cutting buttonholes, making ribbons, and stitching gloves and garments. With time, Caroline became a skilled seamstress and began to earn good wages.

But Caroline's father also encouraged her to get as much schooling as was permissible for girls at that time. Admission to the university was barred to women,[26] but Caroline attended a Haskalah-run school, where a Jewish girl could study progressive, secular subjects, learn German as well as Hebrew, and develop the skills and habits to assimilate into mainstream Austrian society.[27] Caroline had a special gift for the written word. And she had been recently engaged by the Jewish underground press of Vienna to write for one of the growing number of new, liberal newspapers.

With each meeting, Ignác increasingly appreciated Caroline's keen intelligence. He also saw in her a temperamental reflection of himself. She was assertive, passionate, tempestuous, and witty, he thought. He was beginning to feel like she was his soul mate. Soon Ignác found himself beginning to spend all of his free time with Caroline. He began to call her by her affectionate nickname, "Charlinchen."[28]

When the early winter winds and snow made it impossible to be outdoors, Ignác and Caroline were content to sit by the fireside in his apartment. Marko had returned to Hungary, so Ignác was living alone now in a third-floor corner apartment at Wickenburggasse 2, in the cheerful student quarter of Alservorstadt. It was during their first winter together that conversations there would often turn to serious subjects. Caroline would launch into impassioned, breathless tirades about the imperial government's indifference to the plight of the miserable working class.

"The people are desperate," she asserted. "They are herded like cattle into tenements outside the city walls and beyond the glacis. They are kept out of sight of the upper classes in the Inner City. Peasants, laborers, immigrants. We don't want our rich people to see all that squalor. It's very unpleasant, you know, quite disturbing to the privileged. Have you ever been in the suburbs?" asked Caroline rhetorically.

"Well, of course, my patients . . ."

"Yes, prostitutes, the unemployed, the sick," continued Caroline. "All the undesirables, living on the margins of existence, crowded into filthy, miserable lodgings. I've seen and smelled the open sewers running down the alleys. People are dying of typhoid and famine. Countless numbers in mass graves. And did you know about all the unemployment?"

"Not . . ."

"It's shameful. Thousands of laborers lost their jobs in Vienna just this year. And those of us who try to call attention to it? There is Metternich's ever-increasing, oppressive censorship and his secret police. The people will rise up, mark my words! It's only a question of time."

When Caroline became whipped up like this, it became difficult for her to engage in real conversation. All Ignác could do was to lean back in silent admiration. And when she became exhausted with talk of revolution, Ignác tried to tell her again about the conditions on the maternity wards at the Allgemeine Krankenhaus.

"I am conducting my own revolution, Charlinchen," said Ignác. "I must figure out why all these poor mothers are dying, and I must fix it! The injustices of our society are glaringly on display in our maternity wards. I see it every hour of every day. The nameless rubble of our population. Despairing women, many brought to the hospital with unwanted pregnancies and literally led to slaughter there. The ones who survive take with them often fatherless babies with no one to help raise them. The rich aristocrats who are supposed to be these wretched women's supervising doctors see them as just 'good teaching material.' They lackadaisically order the medical students to crudely examine them, over and over again, and then butcher them at delivery."

Caroline was aghast, holding her hand to her mouth.

"And then I sometimes get to see the other side," Ignác continued. "The wives of the rich are delivered at home by the society obstetrician of their choice, surrounded by sumptuous furniture, housemaids, cooks, and servants. And then I do wonder, like you, how long this inequity can be allowed to go on."

As he carried on, Ignác again became distracted by his plight at the hospital. He was increasingly discouraged and pessimistic about the prospects of solving the problem with so many powerful people blocking his way. But he was about to get a big break from unexpected sources.

CHAPTER 11

NOVEMBER 1846

Finally, in November of 1846, the imperial ministry could no longer ignore the growing public outrage fueled by newspaper articles about the scandalous conditions in Vienna General Hospital's obstetrics wards. A commission was appointed by Metternich's ministry to investigate the situation.

Klein assembled his team to greet the visitors. He reluctantly included Ignác. A hospital administrator was assigned by Schiffner to escort the visitors around the hospital. The commission was a motley group of characters. Only one of them, a retired obstetrician, could have been considered an expert, though even that was open to debate. There were two grim civil servants from the ministry who were dressed in dark, well-worn suits, and whose ashen complexions suggested that they hadn't seen the sun in a very long time. The group included the young, flamboyant and amiable Count Leopold von Thun, who had earned much public praise for his charitable work with the prostitutes of Vienna but had no experience in medical affairs. There was also a general practitioner from the country who appeared quite overwhelmed by the crowded wards, stuffy air, and noise level. And they were joined by the Cardinal's representative, a canon of St. Stephen's

Cathedral, who was dressed in a white surplice tunic with wide sleeves over his ankle-length, violet-trimmed black cassock robe. He walked around ever so slowly with his hands clasped in front of him.

During the tour of the wards, Klein and his assistant made their rounds with the commission members to show them the patients, a few of whom were exhibiting signs of puerperal fever at different stages. At each bedside, Klein spoke in an imperious, professorial manner, giving highly technical explanations of the women's medical conditions. He often demonstrated physical findings to the visiting dignitaries. Ignác was revolted by Klein's show of phony deference to these people he must have considered to be of vastly inferior backgrounds. But after a while, most of them seemed to lose interest in viewing these messy exhibits.

The demonstrably bored Count Thun finally drew up a chair to sit next to a patient he had recognized from the streets, and engaged in familiar conversation with her. As he held her hand, the new mother's spirits were visibly raised. Then, from the corners of his eyes, the Count spotted Ignác. He had been cursorily introduced to Semmelweis at the beginning of the visit and knew the young man was an obstetrician in training. But now the Count was impressed by the personal attention the young doctor was paying to a patient who was delirious with fever, offering her encouraging words, and dabbing her forehead with a cold, damp cloth. Ignác instantly stood as the Count approached and shook his hand.

"Herr Doktor, what is wrong with this young woman?"

Ignác ushered the Count away from the bedside.

"She has the childbed fever, and she will die shortly," replied Ignác.

"Is there nothing you can do?"

"Only to comfort her. She is alone and frightened."

"I am quite amazed that you are spending time like this with a dying woman. I am very impressed, young man. But how can we stop these deaths?"

"I am working on that problem day and night, sir," said Ignác. "I am determined to get to the bottom of its cause and then to hopefully find a rational way to prevent it."

"Good for you," said the Count, slapping Ignác on the shoulder. "You seem to be the only one who is really concerned about it around here." He smiled warmly and even seemed to bow ever so slightly as he left Ignác with his patient.[29]

When the tour was over, the visitors were led into an ornate boardroom in the administrative building inside courtyard Number One to meet with high-level hospital officials. Klein sat next to Schiffner at the head of the U-shaped table. They faced the members of the commission, who were seated at a long table at the front of the room. Others connected to the obstetrics service were seated on wooden chairs lined along the walls. Ignác was there, along with Klein's Assistant, and the seemingly omnipresent medical student, Carl Braun. Ignác scanned the room for people he could recognize. Sitting at the board table were Anton von Rosas, the ophthalmologist, and von Hildebrand, the professor of internal medicine; they were friends of Klein who, like him, were politically well-connected, senior Viennese physicians of the medical school's conservative old guard. He didn't see Rokitansky, Skoda, or Hebra.

Standing at attention in one corner of the room was a mustachioed *gendarme,* ornate sword placed securely into the sheath attached to his belt. Ignác thought he looked ominously familiar. *Could he be the one who was guarding that dictator Metternich in his box at the opera?*

Klein ran the show. He called on Schiffner to make introductory comments. And now, finally, Ignác heard the data he had been seeking. Sheets were passed out that tabulated the numbers. Schiffner said that the mortality rates reported in the newspapers were a sensationalist exaggeration. But he admitted that he and Klein were indeed concerned by the higher rate of deaths in the First Division.

"For the year 1844," Schiffner said, straining to read from his notes, "8.2 percent, or 260 of the 3157 patients admitted to the First Division, died of puerperal fever. This is compared to 2.3 percent, or 68 of 2956 who died in the Second Division. Then last year, in 1845, the mortality rates were 6.8% and 2.0% in the First and Second Divisions, respectively."

"We are now at the end of November, Dr. Schiffner. So, do you have any updated figures for the current year?" asked Count Thun.

"Yes, I am afraid the trends have continued. So far in 1846," continued Schiffner, "422 of 3665, that is 11.5 percent, on the First Division have died. And this compares with 2.8 percent on the Second Division: 96 of 3440 dead."

Count Thun leaned forward. "Are you saying, Doctor Schiffner, that more than four times as many women are dying in the First Division as in the Second? More than *four* times?" He sounded incredulous. "Why, these are much higher mortality rates than we know about for women who give birth at home, or even in the streets!"

Ignác was stunned by the differences in numbers. Even as he quickly wrote them down on a piece of paper, he was simmering with outrage at the indifferent, matter-of-fact way the statistics were being presented. He glanced at Count Thun, who had a fixed frown on his face. At one point, Klein asked Lumpe to stand to recite the thirty different possible explanations they had considered. Count Thun interrupted to ask Lumpe what he meant by "atmospheric cosmic-telluric changes."

"Miasma, your honor. Noxious forms of bad air," replied the flustered Lumpe.

"Ah, yes!" Miasma, of course," responded the Count with feigned satisfaction as he sat back in his chair.

Klein had to explain to the committee why the differences in mortality between the two divisions were exactly the opposite of what he had expected when he separated them. But, Klein asserted, therein may be a key clue. Blame for the higher death rate on his service could be squarely placed on the ever-increasing number of visiting foreign medical students who were allowed to work here.

"These foreign students bring with them a much cruder approach to examining patients than we teach our own students," declared Klein. "Even the visiting students from other lands within the Empire—the Slavs, Magyars, Serbs, Italians—they are brought up differently. They have, frankly, less sophisticated standards of conduct."

"I have to agree with the esteemed professor." The cardinal's representative sniffed into his handkerchief. "But what can be done? Immigrants in general just keep coming in larger and larger numbers. And they multiply like rats."

"I am sad to conclude that there is only one solution to our problem," responded Klein. "For now, until these young people assimilate to the cultural expectations of our Viennese medical community, we must severely curtail their admission to study at the *Allgemeine Krankenhaus*."[30]

Carl Braun now raised his hand and spoke up. "If I may be permitted to say, honored gentlemen, having recently been a student myself, I can confirm Herr Professor's astute insights from my own, firsthand experiences working with these foreigners day to day." And then, pausing to nod towards Ignác with an ever-so-subtle smirk, he added, "Present company excluded, of course."

Ignác left the room in a daze and wandered off by himself through the hospital courtyards to clear his head. He finally had the information in hand, confirming that he was on the right track. His autopsy findings showed that all the women died the same way, regardless of the division in which they had been hospitalized. But the death rates were strikingly different between the two divisions. Why? Ignác now finally had the affirmation in hand to be able to hone his analysis of the cause of puerperal fever.

Ignác neatly tabulated the two sets of statistics he had obtained, the first from his initial sojourn to Schiffner's office and the second from the recent review team visit, as follows.[31]

Overall Combined Mortality:

Year	Births	Deaths	Rate
1816	2410	12	0.49
1817	2735	25	0.91
1818	2568	56	2.18
1819	3089	154	4.98
1820	2998	75	2.50
1821	3294	55	1.66
1822	3066	26	0.84
1823	2872	214	7.45
1824	2911	144	4.94
1825	2594	229	4.82
1826	2359	192	8.12
1827	2367	51	2.15
1828	2833	101	3.56
1829	3012	140	4.64
1830	2797	111	3.97
1831	3353	222	6.62
1832	3331	105	3.15
1833	3907	205	5.25
1834	4218	355	8.41
1835	4040	227	5.61
1836	4144	331	7.98
1837	4363	375	8.59
1838	4560	179	3.92

1839	4992	248	4.96
1840	5166	328	6.44
1841	5454	330	6.05
1842	6024	730	12.11
1843	5914	457	7.72
1844	6244	336	5.38
1845	6756	313	4.63
1846	7027	567	8.06

Mortality Differences Between the 2 Wards Since Separation of Doctors' and Midwives' Services:

	1st Clinic			2nd Clinic		
	Births	**Deaths**	**Rate**	**Births**	**Deaths**	**Rate**
1844	3157	260	8.2	2956	68	2.3
1845	3492	241	6.8	3241	66	2.0
1846	4010	459	11.4	3754	105	2.7

Actual mortality data, as recorded by Semmelweis

A meeting was quickly arranged by Kolletschka. He, Hebra, Skoda, and Ignác sat around Rokitansky's desk. Skoda was fidgety, pulling his pocket watch attached by a chain through his waistcoat buttonhole, and opening and closing its cover to look at the time. Ignác passed out to each of them the mortality trends he had painstakingly copied five times over the night before. They sat in silence as they perused the numbers. Rokitansky scribbled some notes on the papers with his quill pen. Skoda used his pencil to emphatically circle some of the numbers. He was the first to finish. Flipping open his pocket watch again, impatiently tapping the arm of his chair, he finally spoke up.

"Well, gentlemen, we don't have all day. The numbers speak for themselves," he said.

"But wait a minute," Hebra said, looking up from the papers he was holding. "Something just doesn't seem to add up here."

"Hebra is right," added Rokitansky, removing his glasses. "There is something wrong with the numbers."

"What do you mean, Herr Professor?" the unnerved Ignác asked. "They come directly from the hospital records."

"I see the problem," said Kolletschka. "The sum total of deaths for the two clinics doesn't exactly correspond to the overall combined mortality numbers for any given year. For last year, the sum of the two clinics adds up to 307, but it's noted as 313 in the combined mortality table. For 1844, it's 328 versus 336 in the two tables. The discrepancies . . ."

"No, I am talking about something much bigger," said Rokitansky, holding up his hand. "It's a requirement to do autopsies on every single patient who dies in this hospital. Correct?" Everyone nodded. "Well, it seems to me that we do a lot more than the 300 or so autopsies per year reported here for 1845 on women who die of puerperal fever. What do you say, Kolletschka?"

"That's what I was thinking also," interjected Hebra.

Kolletschka was looking up to the ceiling. "Yes," he finally replied. "If we only did 307, it would be less than one a day for the year. That's absurd! We must do at least two a day"

Rokitansky slowly rose from his chair and went to his bookshelf, from which he pulled a file and turned to the page he was seeking.

"521, exactly, in 1845," he said. "There were 521 autopsy-documented deaths from puerperal fever in this hospital last year. And for 1844, the total was . . ." he ran his finger down a column ". . . 476."

"And Semmelweis's report indicates only 328 for 1844. So the numbers have to be all wrong," said Hebra.

"Not at all, my dear Hebra," replied Rokitansky, still standing by his bookcase, with the file open in his hands. "The hospital records state that there was a total of 307 deaths on the obstetrical wards last year, but we have records here that there were 521 autopsies performed on women who died from puerperal fever during the same year. It must mean that more than 200 women died of puerperal fever somewhere else in the hospital. And then look here: for 1844, there were 476 puerperal fever autopsies but only 307 deaths reported in maternity. Where in hell are all these women dying?"

They all turned to Ignác, who now looked ashen.

"God damn it, Klein *disposed* of them!" Ignác exclaimed.

"What are you talking about, Semmelweis?" asked the exasperated Skoda.

"The missing numbers are the women Professor Klein has been transferring out of the obstetrical wards to the general medical services," Ignác declared, in disbelief himself.

"You mean . . ." Kolletschka began.

"Yes, of course, this has been happening routinely in the First Division for many years," Skoda interrupted, "but we never thought there were that many."

"Whenever a patient on our service comes down with the fever, Dr. Klein wants her transferred off our wards as quickly as possible. He says such a patient's condition requires expertise in internal medicine at that point, not obstetrics. He has claimed that these women receive better care on the general medical wards, so it's the policy," Ignác said.

The men now sat in stunned silence.

"So the mortality rates reported for the obstetrics wards in only the First Division are an underestimate of the women who die of puerperal fever overall in the hospital."

"A *crucial* underestimate," added Hebra. "Maybe in his eagerness to suppress the publicly reported mortality rate in the First Division, Klein has been actually transferring women out of maternity into the general hospital as soon as they begin to develop symptoms of puerperal fever. While they are still alive. That way, their deaths elsewhere in the hospital wouldn't be counted in the First Division statistics. Instead, they would be attributed to the general hospital's census. He sure as hell wouldn't be transferring them in order to save their lives, since they all inevitably die, regardless of where they are."

"Sonofabitch, he is cooking the books to make his service look better," Kolletschka added.

As the men started to stand up to leave, Skoda, who had been the most impatient of all of them at the beginning, said, "Wait a minute, gentlemen. There is something else that's interesting in these numbers."

They sat back down. Skoda continued. "Look at the annual total mortality rates over the years on Semmelweis's sheet. Do any of you see a trend? Something that sticks out?"

They all began to scrutinize the numbers again. They were previously fixated on the differences between the First and Second Divisions. The totals had seemed less important.

"I don't know what this means," Hebra was the first to speak. "But there is a spike in the overall mortality rate after 1822. In fact, look here, it jumped from 0.84% in 1822 to 7.45% in 1823."

"Precisely!" exclaimed Skoda.

"So what happened in 1823?"

Rokitansky slowly removed his glasses again and loudly exhaled through pursed lips. They all looked at him.

"Klein became chief of obstetrics in 1823," he quietly said. "That was the year he took over from Professor Boër. I wasn't here then, but I understand it was quite an acrimonious transition. Professor Boër was getting along in years, but he was still a revered physician and teacher. It is said that he was essentially forced out, and Klein was behind it."

The key to the solution obviously lay in some fundamental difference between the two wards. Ignác also knew that the death rates of women delivering at home or even in the streets were, if anything, even lower than those seen in the Second Division. That was why increasing numbers of destitute women were waiting to deliver in the streets and back alleys of the city, like the woman Ignác had helped shortly after his arrival in Vienna. They would then bring their newborns and afterbirths to the hospital rather than risk the much-talked-about prospect of death if they delivered in the dreaded wards of the First Division.

So, Ignác reasoned, the difference between the two divisions had to be due to some adverse condition that was present specifically only in the First Division, not in the Second Division, and not outside the hospital. Just in the First Division. But what was it? Surely it couldn't be some combination of the thirty or more different things that Lumpe, Klein, and Braun had conjectured. There was hardly a shred of rational evidence for any one of them. There had to be *a single cause.*

Every waking hour that he wasn't working was now consumed by thinking and scribbling down on paper the *possible* differences between the divisions. Ignác filled sheets with lists of every variable he could think of, however trivial or inconceivable. Then, next to each entry, he wrote notes about why or why not that variable might be important. He kept these notes neatly organized in his files in the *Dienstzimmer,* but he also copied them on separate sheets that were kept in his apartment. He couldn't risk losing them, by accident or otherwise. Ignác narrowed his list to the most reasonable possibilities.

Possible Differences in the First Division:

1. Doctors and medical students delivering in First Division; midwives in Second Division. **YES**.
2. Differences in medical practices, treatments. **NO:** same in both divisions.
3. Differences in diet. **NO:** same kitchen.

4. Overcrowding. **NO:** more overcrowding, if anything, in Second Division.
5. Clusters of disease only in First Division. **YES:** Clusters of death in adjacent beds *do* occur in the First Division, but cases are entirely sporadic and random in Second Division. Why?
6. Differences in location of the two divisions. **NO:** they are located next to each other and even share a single anteroom.
7. Older facilities in First Division. **NO:** First Division is similarly designed and is actually a newer building.
8. Differences in ventilation. **NO:** In both divisions, the main source of ventilation is opening of windows, even in winter months.
9. Differences in cleaning, laundry. **NO:** Divisions share common laundry and maintenance personnel.
10. First Division patients older, sicker, more malnourished, have more failed induced abortions, longer periods of labor, are often unmarried. **NO:** Patients have same characteristics. They are admitted to one or the other division on alternate twenty-four-hour periods, so they are randomly assigned.
11. Seasonal variation in mortality rate. **NO,** except lower in the summer for the First Division only. Why? (There is no seasonal variation in deaths from street births.)
12. First Division mortality no different from that found outside the hospital. **NO:** Mortality outside hospital is more like that found in Second Division.

The first three items related to possible differences in obstetrical practices and medical management. Items 4, 5, and 6 were possible factors that might be related to contagious mechanisms that would involve the disease being directly passed from one patient to another. Items 7, 8, and 9 were possible differences in physical conditions between the First and Second

Divisions. And the last three items, Ignác speculated, might account for epidemic causes restricted to the First Division.

Exhausted, Ignác pulled his chair away from the desk, stretched out his legs, and clasped his hands behind this head. *Only the first possibility is likely*, he thought, staring at the ceiling. *Holy Mary! Am I really closing in?*

To reward his fine performance during the commission review, Klein named Carl Braun to the position of Aspirant.[32] Braun thus became next in line of succession to follow Ignác as Klein's Assistant at the end of Ignác's two-year appointment. During December, January, and February, the number of foreign students permitted to work in the First Division was radically reduced by Klein, as he had promised the review commission. But the deaths from puerperal fever continued unabated.

Ignác was now obsessively arranging and rearranging his lists and adding to them any other variables he could think of—however far-fetched they might be—that might explain the striking difference in death rates between the two divisions. For example, the possibility of "fear" was included in Lumpe's list. He thought back to that episode last spring when he awoke to the screams of a woman in labor as she was dragged by attendants through the hospital corridors. He never forgot the look of sheer terror on her face. Ignác had at first dismissed this possibility as absurd, but now he was determined to keep a completely open mind and leave no stone unturned.

He went through all the steps that took place before a patient died on the maternity wards. When there was an impending death, the hospital summoned a priest to administer last rites at the patient's bedside. The priest would appear in ornate vestments, preceded by a sacristan, whose job was to ring a loud bell during the procession. The ominous toll of the sacristan's bell was a chilling sound even to Ignác himself, and he could just imagine the dread it created among the patients lying in their beds. Yet another impending death!

When Ignác traced the route of the religious procession, it struck him that patients in the Second Division might not notice it at all. When a Second Division patient became acutely ill, she would be promptly transferred from the open ward to a small room that was located next to the chapel. In this way, the priest and the sacristan could go directly there, bypassing the Second Division wards. However, when a First Division patient became ill, the room to which she would be routinely transferred was at the far end of the rows of beds. So all the patients in the First Division were subjected to the sight and sound of this foreboding procession for last rites; even when they were asleep, they would be surely awakened by the tolling of the bell. It was hardly likely to be a cause of the higher death rate in the First Division, Ignác thought, but it *was* a variable between the two wards, and there was only one way to eliminate it from consideration.

Ignác therefore went to the chapel to explain his concerns to the priest. At first the priest wouldn't even consider violating such an old ritual. But finally, he responded to Ignác's appeal to him to place patient welfare ahead of all else.

"It is a time-honored rite of the church, young doctor, but surely it would not be the will of Christ to continue it if it endangered his daughters."

With that, the procession to administer last rites became a silent one.

Klein found out about the change a few days later from Braun. Enraged, he hurried to confront Ignác, with Braun in tow. When they found Ignác in the corridor, Klein tore into him.

"Semmelweis, must I remind you who you are and who I am?" shouted Klein, his face flushed, veins bulging on his neck. "You are not even my Assistant yet. You are just an Aspirant. I make the rules here, and you are not to deviate from them even *one millimeter* without my permission! Do you understand, Semmelweis?"

"But Herr Professor, with all due respect, it was you yourself, with Lumpe, who brought up the possibility of fear as a cause of childbed fever. I was just trying to . . ."

Klein had now menacingly closed in on Ignác, whose back was against the wall, and was poking him in the chest with the end of his cane as he continued to vent his fury. "I have a good mind to terminate you immediately for insubordination! Your job depends on me, and me alone. You are unnecessary to me—do you understand?"

"Yes, Herr Professor," mumbled the recoiling Ignác.

"You could be dismissed now, and I could just replace you with Braun," continued Klein. "You are in a bad situation, Doktor Semmelweis!"

Klein whipped around and stormed off, with the silent but apparently satisfied Braun following closely behind him. Ignác was frozen in place for a minute, but when he collected his thoughts, he realized that several days had passed without the death bell tolling, and, yet, the mortality rate in the First Division hadn't decreased; it was actually even higher. He hurried to his *Dienstzimmer,* took the notes from his desk and added to his list: "Number 13. Greater fear in First Division patients. **NO**."

Caroline's newspaper was becoming the target of a different kind of harassment. It was publishing increasingly strident reports about the miserable condition of the tenements in the suburbs, along with the rising poverty, unemployment, crime, and disease there. Finally, the imperial ministry's police censors shut down the newspaper and arrested its editor.

The following day, the newspaper's underground printshop was found vandalized, the printing machines and duplicating equipment destroyed, the lithographic stones smashed, and the remaining papers turned into a smoldering pile of ashes in the fireplace. Caroline's own articles were among them.

That evening, Ignác sought out Caroline to try to cheer her up, but she was inconsolable.

"The newspaper is gone. I must find other ways to help the people," Caroline said. Ignác sensed her despondency but at the same time her resolve.

"There will be time," he said.

"No. No, there is no time," snapped Caroline, looking with fire into Ignác's eyes. "The condition of our people is deteriorating by the day. People are literally starving to death in the streets."

"I understand."

"So," continued Caroline, "I have contacted a Frau Karoline von Perin-Gradenstein,[33] who has been a customer in my father's shop. Frau Perin has started to organize meetings in her home with some ladies who are interested in forming a women's association. It would be a democratic women's organization devoted to charitable work. I know I could help. What with my personal understanding of the poor and my journalistic experiences with the people in the tenements, I could do a lot, don't you think?"[27]

"Yes, you certainly could. You are indefatigable." Ignác smiled.

"I am telling you Ignác," Caroline said, still in tears. "This society is about to explode. Metternich's authoritarian rule, his secret police, his spy network, and everything else. We just can't take it anymore."

"What gave Metternich so much power?" Ignác asked. "We have an emperor, don't we?"

"Not really. Emperor Ferdinand is a hydrocephalic, epileptic, mentally incompetent monarch. Yes, he is beloved by many people because of his childishness, but he is completely incapacitated. He is incapable of ruling. So Prince Klemens von Metternich," she said, slowly enunciating his full name with stinging sarcasm, "has become, in effect, the governor of the entire empire. That damned opportunist."

"But I still don't understand why you think there's going to be an uprising," replied Ignác. "Surely there has been horrible poverty in the past. So why now?"

"Ah, my dear, you have been too occupied by your work as a doctor to see what's happening in the world around you." Caroline said, affectionately patting his knee. "The feudal system of past centuries is dissolving. And at the same time, Vienna is nearly bankrupt . . ."

"How can that be?" Ignác interrupted. "I see nothing but wealth and opulence around the Inner City."

"It's a mirage," Caroline said. "And, in any case, the real numbers are outside the city wall's gates, not within it. Metternich has spent outrageous amounts of money putting down revolts all over the Habsburg Empire. So Vienna's finances are in very bad shape. That and the terrible harvests of the past couple of years have driven those already downtrodden to the verge of famine."

"And you really think these poor, starving people have the strength to fight a mighty empire?"

"Ignác, it's about to happen in France, we hear. The monarchy is about to be overthrown there. And do you know about the peasant uprising in our territory of Galicia just a few months ago?"

Ignác shook his head at his own ignorance.

"The land-owning nobles of Galicia revolted against Vienna's rule. They wanted independence. And you know what Metternich did?"

"No, I don't," Ignác replied sheepishly.

"He got all the peasants, the serfs of Galicia, to rise up against the nobility of their own land. And the peasants crushed the insurrection of their compatriot nobles who were so hated. There has been an awakening of nationalism. You know very well what's been happening in Hungary," said Caroline.

"Oh, yes, I've seen it with my own eyes."

"Well then, there. This is the time. We have the coming together of our own starving and unemployed people, who are at their breaking point, and the boiling desire for independence by other territories, all at the same time. It's all going to come crashing down on Vienna."[34]

Ignác was glad to see the color back in Caroline's face and to hear that breathless passion in her voice.

CHAPTER 12

JANUARY 1847

With the beginning of the new year of 1847, an advanced medical student named Joseph Späth appeared with some regularity on the maternity wards. He was assigned by Klein to be apprenticed to Johann Baptist Chiari, who had completed his assistantship to Klein just before Ignác began his Aspirant position in 1844. Späth was born in the Alpine foothills to a noble Austrian family, and he had the bearing to go with his distinctly aristocratic pedigree.[35]

Ignác took an immediate dislike to him. He found Späth's seemingly constant smirk and loud voice to be inappropriate and insufferable affectations. And he thought his cockiness was entirely unmerited. Späth appeared to be unabashedly ambitious, obsequious, and politically motivated, without any real interest in taking care of obstetric patients. In the midst of an increasingly hectic and tense environment, Ignác found himself not infrequently snapping at Späth's irritating behavior and stupid comments, only to be repeatedly reminded by the grinning young man that he was assigned by Professor Klein to be Chiari's student, not his. Ignác, in turn, felt an obligation to protect his patients from this bombastic ignoramus.

Matters came to a head in a bristling confrontation between them. It occurred after Ignác overheard Späth ridiculing his rustic Magyar mannerisms and poor diction to a group of fellow students. Späth promptly reported Ignác's outburst to Klein. This convinced Klein that his young aspirant was becoming unhinged and was in dire need of a break before he took on his responsibilities as his assistant in March.[36] His friends, Chiari and Kolletschka, and even Caroline, told Ignác that they actually agreed with Klein and encouraged him to get away for a restorative holiday in Venice.

After two restful weeks in Venice with some friends, Ignác arrived back in Vienna late at night on March 20, 1847. He immediately resumed his routine the next morning. As usual, he arrived in the dissection room at the break of dawn. He was surprised that Kolletschka wasn't there yet but began without him to prepare his first corpse for her autopsy. Across the room, he spotted some sheets of paper on Rokitansky's usually clear desk and walked over to glance at them. Across the top was written: "*Pathologischen Institut, Wien. 17. März, 1847. Autopsiebefund über Jacob Kolletschka.*" Was this a practical joke? Ignác grabbed the papers and held them close to his darting eyes. His heart suddenly pounding and breaking out into a cold sweat, he scanned the words, but his mind didn't follow. He was tremulous. He kept seeing the word "pyemia," and terms like "pericarditis," and "fibroserous inflammation," and "pelvic cavity," and "membranes surrounding the brain."[37] He suddenly felt faint and had to sit down. From the corners of his eyes, he spotted a figure emerging from the darkness at the end of the room, approaching him. It was Rokitansky. Rokitansky never came early in the morning.

Without even greeting him, Rokitansky put a hand gently on Ignác's shoulder, pulled up another chair and sat down beside him. "I didn't want you to be here alone when you found out about this," he said, looking straight into Ignác's eyes.

"Kolletschka is dead?" were the only words Ignác could muster.

"Yes," responded Rokitansky in a barely audible voice.

"But I saw him the day I left—just two weeks ago—and he was completely well!"

"It was a terrible accident," began Rokitansky. "Our dear friend was helping a medical student with his dissection. They were doing an autopsy of another woman who had died of puerperal fever. Nothing out of the ordinary, just another routine case. And as they were exploring the inflamed pelvic organs, the student accidentally stuck Kolletschka's index finger with his scalpel. The wound wasn't big, but it was deep. It drew blood and Kolletschka had to bandage it up. He didn't tell anybody about it, and he was all right for a while, but then the next day he began to experience fevers. I saw him, and so did Skoda and Hebra. The redness around the cut on his finger had begun to spread. Red streaks extended from the wound all the way up his finger toward his hand and forearm. We diagnosed lymphangitis."

Ignác was still in a daze, but he tried very hard to listen.

"By the third day," continued Rokitansky, "his fevers were spiking, he was perspiring, and he looked very ill and short of breath. Skoda had him admitted to the hospital. He was given lots of fluids, but his kidneys stopped working. He wasn't making any urine. And by the fourth day, poor Kolletschka was delirious. He didn't even seem to recognize us, his arms and legs became ice cold, and then purpura appeared all over his skin. Hebra said he had seen this previously in patients who had overwhelming pyemia. And then . . ."

"Yes, I understand," mumbled Ignác.

"You know this has happened before. Just last year, one of our medical students stuck himself while dissecting a cadaver and developed the same symptoms Kolletschka had. Fortunately, he survived after a long illness but required amputation of one of his fingers. We've had other deaths in the past, but these things occur extremely rarely. As you know, Semmelweis, we take great care to instruct our students about the proper techniques of dissection and how to do it safely."

"But, Herr Professor, why Kolletschka, of all people? I don't understand!"

"I don't, either," sighed Rokitansky, gently patting Ignác on the back of his head. And then they both sat in complete silence until they were finally interrupted by the commotion of medical students entering the room.

CHAPTER 13

MARCH 1847

Upon his return from Venice, Ignác officially started his position as Assistant to Klein. He was assigned to his regular turn on call as the house obstetrician that night. Despite his agitated state of mind, he insisted on carrying out his clinical assignments. But he couldn't sleep, even during long periods of quiet. He obsessively read and re-read Kolletschka's autopsy report, the same passages, countless times. He scribbled notes in the margins and wrote lists on a clean sheet. And he looked over all the notes he had written and collected from his own autopsy observations over the past two years.

After a while, Ignác became convinced that most of the postmortem findings in Kolletschka, except for the urogenital tracts, of course, were exactly the same as the ones he had noted so many times before in the mothers who had died of puerperal fever. And those, in turn, were quite similar to what was found in their newborns who had also succumbed. Kolletschka's autopsy showed evidence of meningitis, collections of pus in the pleural cavities, and pockets of pus widely spread throughout many organs, including the lungs, liver, spleen, and the brain. Just like in the women who had died of puerperal fever. The disease always started and spread from the female organs of the postpartum women. But in Kolletschka's case, the portal of entry of the disease, the pyemia, must have been the cut on his finger. And it was from the open wound on his finger that it spread into his veins and then disseminated through his bloodstream to the same organs as in the mothers. Ignác startled himself with his own flash of insight.

But exactly how could he tie Kolletschka's fatal accident to the puerperal fever that was ravaging the First Division at such a higher rate than the Second Division? Ignác tossed and turned on his hard, lumpy bed until he finally fell asleep.

He awoke to a noisy commotion outside his room and immediately realized he had overslept. Bright sunlight was pouring through the *Dienstzimmer* window. This had never happened to him before, so he now quickly got dressed and walked out to find the noise emanating from dozens of medical students who were loitering around in clusters in the corridor, each holding his own personal wooden box of dissecting instruments. They were engaged in animated conversation, talking and laughing loudly. Ignác realized that it must have been after ten o'clock because the students were already finished with their dissecting exercises for the morning and were waiting to begin their clinical duties on the maternity ward.

He was angry at himself for oversleeping, but there was something else. What now struck Ignác was not so much the clamor, but the overwhelming putrid stench of all the students gathered together in one place. Ignác had gotten used to the distinctively fetid smell of the cadavers and the same malodor that clung to his own hands and clothes after dissections. They no longer bothered him. But he was now taken aback by the collective stench that emanated from the large congregation of students.

Those who noticed him acknowledged Ignác's silent and unexpected appearance in the hallway with perplexed giggles. And now, as they filed in through the door to the maternity ward, on their way to examine patients, they were carrying with them the rotten stink of the decomposing cadavers on which they had just worked. Ignác froze where he stood.

The pieces of the puzzle that had been tormenting him for so long suddenly fell into place in his mind.

All at once, it seemed so simple! It was the putrid cadaveric particles that were transmitting the disease. They were picked up by the students on their bare hands from inside the bodies of women they had been dissecting who recently died of puerperal fever. Then, not having cleansed their hands before leaving the morgue, in some cases not even having wiped them, the particles were introduced directly by the same contaminated, unclean hands into the vagina and uterus of living mothers on the wards. The idea percolated in his mind all day as he distractedly went about his daily clinical responsibilities. And he tried very hard to not allow the excitement of this epiphany interfere with caring for his patients. But flights of ideas were inevitable, and one in particular horrified him. It struck him that, if his theory was correct, then not only the medical students, but *he himself* was also responsible for contaminating the patients. He had been unwittingly complicit in the murders of countless women.

As soon as he got a break from the work, Ignác sought out Skoda. He could barely contain his excitement as he explained his ideas to the most eminent internist and diagnostician at the university. Surely if there was a flaw in his logic, Skoda would be the one to point it out. Ignác took his notes with him.

"I could see clearly that the disease from which Kolletschka died was identical to that from which so many hundred maternity patients had also died," began Ignác. "The only difference was that the cadaveric particles were introduced into women in labor through the uncleaned hands of those who repeatedly examined them internally, while they entered Kolletschka's system through the cut on his hand made by a contaminated scalpel. Otherwise they caused the same fatal disease, don't you see?"

"But I have seen students sometimes wash their hands after dissections, before they go to the wards," interrupted Skoda.

"That must mean that washing with soap is not sufficient to remove all the adhering cadaveric particles. This is proven by the cadaverous smell that the hands retain for a longer time," responded Ignác. "In any case, sir, I can tell you that most of our students, and even our obstetricians, don't wash their hands at all! They will barely wipe them on their coats."

"And why does this only happen in the First Division?" asked Skoda.

"That's quite simple. As you know, midwives are not allowed to dissect actual cadavers or perform autopsies. That's been the policy for a very long time, I believe. They are taught pelvic anatomy using only phantoms, those authentic-appearing, painted, wax models. So their hands don't become contaminated with cadaveric particles before they examine their patients or deliver the babies."

"Interesting," Skoda thought aloud. He slowly removed his glasses, rubbed his eyes, and then continued, "I think you are onto something, but you have to tie up all the loose ends. I remember when you first showed the mortality data to several of us, I became curious about the abrupt increase in deaths that occurred in 1823. Professor Rokitansky pointed out that the year coincided with Klein taking over the directorship of obstetrics from Professor Boër. You now need to find out if anything different—anything special—happened during that year in practice routines on the maternity wards. I have a feeling that this will uncover another important part of the puzzle."

Of course, the most obvious person to ask about any change in practice that might have occurred between the years Boër was in charge and after Klein took over would be Klein himself. But that was out of the question. Ignác was already unnerved about the prospect of having to tell Klein about his theory. To ask him something so provocative might spell the end of Ignác's career. But who would have been there at that time? Even Rokitansky was just a medical student in Prague in 1822. And then it struck him: Bartsch! Bartsch had been Klein's pupil, and he seemed to recall somebody mentioning that Klein brought Bartsch with him from Salzburg when he became head of the obstetrical service in Vienna. But Ignác barely knew Bartsch. Even though he was director of the Second Division, he was virtually invisible.[23]

Ignác hurried over to the Second Division wards, and, when he couldn't find Bartsch even in his office, he asked one of the midwifery students working there.

"Why, Herr Professor is drawing!" said the student as if Ignác should have known.

"Drawing what?"

"He is in the *Karlskirche*, drawing the church! He's been there every day for the past two weeks. It's a big project for him, you know!" explained the midwifery student.

"But who has been supervising all the deliveries here in the Second Division," wondered Ignác, "while Professor Bartsch has been doing his . . . what did you call it? His 'big project.'"

The student broke out in a big grin. "Aaaah, Herr Doktor, there's no need for that, you know. The midwives are doing perfectly well by themselves."

Ignác thanked him. He then walked the long distance from the hospital to Karlsplatz inside the city walls, where the imposing church of St. Charles was situated. With its Byzantine dome and minaret-like columns flanking it, Karlskirche was an impressive edifice. Walking around the church's cavernous interior, he searched for Bartsch until, finally, he spotted him sitting behind a column near the high altar. He was busily sketching it on an easel.

"Professor Bartsch," Ignác's voice carried like an amplified echo across the church.

"Ssshhh!" said Bartsch without interrupting his drawing. He put down his pencil and slowly turned toward Ignác. "Semmelweis, what are you doing here?"

"I must speak to you about an urgent matter. I have to ask you some questions that might help me figure out why the First Division has such a high mortality rate," continued Ignác.

"Well, not now! We can't talk here, and I can't just pack up my equipment in the middle of everything. It can't possibly be that urgent. Why don't you meet me in my office tomorrow morning at nine o'clock?"

Ignác sighed in frustration.

When they met the next morning, Bartsch started to ramble about Byzantine art, but then he finally got around to something more meaningful.

"Professor Boër was a very lax and permissive chief. He had a reputation for not caring much about rules and policies. When Professor Klein replaced him," Bartsch stumbled, "I mean *succeeded* him, it took him a lot of work to change the culture, bring some discipline onto the service, and really shape things up."

"How do you mean?" Ignác asked.

"Well, Boër trained in London, you know. And in London he was taught to minimize the 'intrusiveness,' as he would put it, of physicians on women during labor. So when he came to Vienna as chief, he taught his students to perform pelvic exams on the women only when absolutely needed and then to do them only with the utmost gentleness, preferably without the use of any instruments."

"And Professor Klein?" continued Ignác.

"Like night and day," responded Bartsch. "Professor Klein insisted on discipline. He demanded—yes, demanded—that his students gain as much experience as they possibly could, by frequent and thorough physical exams of the women in labor. That would take precedence over *any* other consideration! This is after all, as Professor Klein has said repeatedly, a teaching hospital. A *teaching* hospital, first and foremost, and there was to be no relaxation of Klein's directives."

"Were there other differences in their practices?"

"Well, another big one was how they followed hospital and university policies," added Bartsch. "The medical school curriculum long ago began to require trainees to practice deliveries on recently deceased corpses and then to dissect the bodies of every woman who had died of an obstetrical complication."

"Including puerperal fever."

"Certainly including puerperal fever. But Boër thought these practices were 'inhumane.' That's what he called them—'inhumane'—can you imagine that? How can you be 'inhumane' with a dead person, I ask you. Anyway, Boër defied the directives of the curriculum and substituted the use of those phantom models the midwives now use to learn female anatomy. *Well*," Bartsch huffed in righteous disbelief, "Professor Klein immediately fixed *that* when he took over."

"Fixed it?" asked Ignác.

"He promptly reinstituted the requirement for students to dissect the cadavers of women who had died in childbirth. He would permit absolutely *no* deviation from the written curriculum of the university!"

"Thank you for your time, Professor Bartsch," concluded Ignác. "You have been so helpful." They shook hands. Ignác inhaled deeply, and turned to walk away with a sense of satisfaction. Skoda's missing piece was now in place.

CHAPTER 14

APRIL 1847

Ignác had barely spoken with Caroline since he had returned from Venice in March. So much had happened. He sensed that she was annoyed with him for not finding time for her. That evening, when he returned to his apartment, Ignác found a note from her under his door.

"If you can get away, meet me tomorrow at 6 o'clock at our bierstube at the Brünnenmarkt.

Love, Caroline"

The next afternoon, Ignác hurriedly made his way to the Neulerchenfeld district, one of the most miserably crowded working-class slums of the suburbs. He found Caroline in the tavern surrounded by a boisterous cluster of women; some were just girls. Dressed in tawdry and tattered attire, heavily made up and perfumed, they appeared to be preparing for a long night of work. Caroline jumped up to greet Ignác and clutched him in a lingering embrace.

"They are my friends," she said into his ear as they hugged. "Our women's association has started to reach out to the less fortunate women of Vienna. Come on, let's take a walk."

Ignác and Caroline strolled arm-in-arm through the litter-strewn outdoor marketplace as shopkeepers scurried to close their stalls. The sun was beginning to set on a raw, overcast April day. Older women wandered about, picking up pieces of discarded vegetables and bread from the street, stuffing them into bags. Passing the brewery, Ignác and Caroline entered a densely packed maze of dark alleys and winding streets that were narrow enough to support laundry hung on rows of strings between buildings across from each other. Dilapidated houses and shacks were blackened with soot and grime. Acrid smoke pouring from surrounding factory chimneys filled the air. The nauseating stench of sewage and human waste was unmistakable. It was quite unlike the less noxious smell of horse manure that Ignác was more accustomed to in the streets of the elegant Inner City.

The clamor of late afternoon activity turned into a cacophony of swarming humanity as Ignác and Caroline entered the heart of the neighborhood. They were now bumping up against people walking in every direction, older men and women squatting or sitting on the dirt-covered streets, pressed against doorways, barefoot street urchins hawking all manner of goods, and mangy dogs running around aimlessly. A filthy little boy with a snotty nose and a girl in tattered clothes sat huddled together on the step of another doorway, begging in a whimper. The boy couldn't have been more than five years old, and the girl beside him perhaps even younger. But their skeletal faces and sunken eyes were like those of grownups.

A young man in front of them was staggering wildly, stumbling and weaving from side to side.

"Drunk. How pathetic," commented Ignác.

"And him too," said Caroline, pointing to another young man lying in the gutter as they turned a corner.

"How can they be in such a condition when it's not even sunset yet?"

"They don't work," responded Caroline. "These streets outside the city walls are filled with them. All day. By nightfall, most of them can't stand straight."

"Idle youth," sighed Ignác.

"Not idle," said Caroline, "desperate. There's no work to be had for even our most able-bodied young men."

Ignác was taken aback by all this. The squalor, the cesspits and open sewers, the wretched people jostling for public water spigots, the vacant apathy in the hollow faces of hungry children and adults of all ages. Ignác's mind suddenly flashed back to the pitiful girl he'd helped deliver in the street shortly after his arrival in Vienna. He momentarily imagined that baby now grown up and blending anonymously into this crowd of hopeless people. Yes, he had seen beggars in the streets of the Inner City. He had heard the increasingly strident talk about restless masses of the poor. And, of course, he had treated the pregnant prostitutes and abandoned women in the hospital. But they were just patients who needed only a few days of care, weren't they? Or not even that, if they died in their hospital beds. Until now, he had never quite thought about them coming from the extreme conditions he now saw. As they walked, he listened to Caroline expound on how this was the powder keg for revolution.

Caroline abruptly stopped and turned to clutch Ignác by both arms.

"Join us, Ignác. We must help these people rise with one voice. There is no other way anymore."

"But Charlinchen, I *am* fighting for them. I've been working for them day and night, trying so hard to save them. And I think I've made a breakthrough. I haven't even had a chance to tell you about it yet."

But Caroline wasn't listening.

She drew him closer and gazed directly into his eyes. "We will take up arms if we must. *This,*" she said, pointing toward the crush of pathetic people jostling past them while holding Ignác even tighter with the other, "this can't go on."

Spent by their seemingly futile efforts to get through to each other, Ignác accompanied Caroline back to her apartment with barely another word. As they strolled through the darkening streets, each was lost in separate private thoughts.

Ignác could now answer Skoda's question about why the major uptick in mortality rates coincided with Klein's ascent to the directorship twenty-five years earlier. By his dictatorial insistence on strictly enforcing the university's requirement for medical students to practice dissections and autopsies on an ongoing basis, following Boër's long period of permissiveness and laxity, Klein had unwittingly unleashed a virtual epidemic of puerperal fever on the maternity wards. But now Ignác had to confront Klein with his theory, with all its incriminating implications.

The next morning Ignác tried to catch Klein's attention immediately after the teaching rounds were finished. He told him he had some important things to tell him but needed to explain them to him in some detail.

"I don't have time to sit now. My private patients are waiting for me," said Klein abruptly.

So Ignác spoke as hurriedly as he possibly could. Barely pausing to breathe, he rattled off all the arguments and data he had accumulated to support his argument that puerperal fever was introduced into the maternity patients through hands contaminated with cadaveric particles.

What Ignác now thought might be his triumphant discovery was met by dead silence. Klein's expression didn't change.

"You have a lot of work to do to try to convince us," Klein finally muttered.

"Yes, sir, but I believe I know how to prove it. I mean, we now just have to figure out the best way to prevent it. To eradicate puerperal fever," responded Ignác.

And as Klein turned to leave without saying anything further, Ignác thought he heard him mutter "arrogant peasant" under his breath.

His path to proof now seemed clear. Ignác would require every student to cleanse his hands after completing his morning dissections and before examining his first patient. And not by just a casual rinse with water and maybe a little soap, as a few of them actually did bother to do. He meant thoroughly scrubbing them with the most powerful disinfectant solution available and for as long as it took to expunge all traces of the smell of cadavers. He now set about single-mindedly researching what would be the most effective antiseptic.[38]

Ignác devoured everything he could find to read about disinfectants and antiseptics in the university library. He consulted the faculty members who had been his supporters, like Rokitansky and Hebra, both of whom had already heard about Ignác's new ideas from Skoda and encouraged him to push on.

In fact, word that Klein's Hungarian assistant may have found something interesting had already spread to other departments of the hospital. At a regular meeting of the leaders of the medical faculty, known as the Collegium of Professors, Hebra had overheard Klein muttering something about it to his good friend, the fifty-six-year old ophthalmologist Anton von Rosas, Klein's ideological and political ally. Both Klein and Rosas appeared to be cantankerously dismissive, and Hebra even heard Rosas grouse about "that upstart Jew."[39]

Skoda, Hebra, and Rokitansky gave Ignác their own suggestions about disinfectants. But they also connected him with some of the experts in pharmacology, pharmacy, and medicinal chemistry at the university. Ignác eagerly sought out each of them: Franz Schneider, a scientist widely admired for his groundbreaking research that integrated the fields of medicine and chemistry[40]; Wenzel Bernatzik, a rising star in pharmacology; Joseph Redtenbacher, a noted professor of chemistry at the Faculty of Philosophy, and several others.

Ignác was in a hurry. He viewed each day that passed without action as adding to the toll of human suffering. So, at the end of this brief but intensive immersion into studying the state-of-the-art of antisepsis in 1847,

Ignác came down to a choice of two compounds that would be most effective for hand scrubbing.

The two best disinfectant solutions would be liquid chlorine (referred to as *chlorina liquida*) and bichloride of mercury (referred to as *corrosive sublimate*).[41] Chlorine dioxide gas and its ability to be dissolved in water had been discovered only about thirty-five years earlier, so Ignác knew that experience with its use as a disinfectant was relatively new. As for mercury, its antiseptic properties were very much part of Viennese medical history: Ignác learned about it in medical school. The great physician, Gerard van Swieten, founder of the University of Vienna's medical school a century earlier,[42] had developed a treatment for syphilis using an oral solution of corrosive sublimate (bichloride of mercury), which was still used in practice a century later. In fact, it was known as *liquor Swietenii* (*Liquor Van Swieten*).[43] Similarly, the so-called "Van Swieten's solution" (consisting of one gram of bichloride of mercury dissolved in one liter of water) was widely used as a topical antiseptic. It was said that some practitioners at the Paris Maternity were even beginning to use Van Swieten's solution to rinse their hands when they were too dirty.[44]

So Ignác considered that a combination of both liquid chlorine and bichloride of mercury might be a particularly effective antiseptic solution.[45] After carefully writing out a prescription for such a solution, he walked out of the building and through the hospital's courtyards, into the basement of another building, where the main pharmacy was located. He knew it would be important not to just drop off the script but to personally explain what was needed to the most senior apothecary he could find there.

After pulling a string to ring the bell at the entrance, the door's peephole cover slid open, and Ignác identified himself. A young man wearing a laboratory apron pulled open the heavy wooden door that had been locked and bolted. A tall, handsome man with blond hair and a well-groomed mustache, he welcomed Ignác with a bright smile.

"Come in, Herr Doktor. My name is Franz Siebert." Siebert was in the second year of his required five-year apprenticeship to qualify for an apothecary license.[46]

The large front room of the pharmacy was well lit with gas lights. Near the ceiling, there was a horizontal series of clerestory window slits that presumably opened to the outside at street level for ventilation. The familiar and not unpleasant medicinal scent of pharmaceuticals, herbs, and solvents permeated the air. Covering the entirety of three walls of the main room were ornate, dark wood shelves, lined in near perfect order with colorful apothecary vessels made of glazed pottery, china, glass, and wood. All the containers were topped with lids and labeled with the names of the medicinals they contained.

Ignác saw three other young men, surely other pharmacy apprentices or journeymen, intently working behind laboratory benches that were cluttered with glassware of all sizes and shapes, two-pan balances and scales, mortars with pestles, distillation retorts, evaporation vessels, and charcoal burners. Books and pamphlets lay open on a separate table. Ignác asked Franz to see the pharmacy director about a special new prescription.

"I'll get Herr Schuster right away," said Franz, and hurried to a side door.

It seemed like an eternity before Franz reappeared, now followed by Herr Direktor der Apotheker Dietrich Schuster, who was frantically trying to straighten his stiff collar as he shuffled toward Ignác. The elderly, gaunt man had a full head of disheveled white hair, a plethoric face, and a big, bulbous nose. And, as he approached, Ignác saw that his red cheeks were really networks of spider veins, and his black suit was frayed and stained. The director had alcohol on his breath, and he reeked of body odor.

"I presume Professor Klein knows about this," Schuster mumbled as he took the prescription from Ignác and held it up to his eyes with a tremulous hand.

"I have most certainly spoken to him about this on several occasions," responded Ignác, summoning the most authoritative tone of voice he could muster. He again had to be cagey but not untruthful about Klein's involvement.

"We will need two well-cleaned basins, each containing two liters of fresh solution, placed just outside the entrance to the First Division wards every weekday morning," continued Ignác, "no later than eight o'clock in the morning. They have to be available in time for the students to use them on their way from the morgue into maternity. One of the basins will be exclusively for my personal use so that I can repeatedly demonstrate to all who enter how the hands must be washed. So, please label one of the two basins for 'Dr. Semmelweis.' And, oh, yes, we will also need small brushes we can use to scrub hands, fingers, and around the fingernails."

Herr Schuster nodded in assent and shuffled back to his office. Ignác shook hands with Franz as he walked out. "We must begin tomorrow," he reminded Franz as the door was closed behind him.

Early the next morning, Ignác placed a prominent sign on the wall just outside the entrance to the First Division, where antiseptic-solution-filled basins had been placed on two tables: *"ALLE ARTZE MÜSSEN IHRE HANDE MIT CHLORKALK WASSEN"* (*"All medical practitioners must wash hands with chlorine."*) Hand brushes for scrubbing and towels were placed next to the basins. Ignác stationed himself there, arms folded over his chest, awaiting the arrival of the students from the morgue.

The first to appear, well ahead of the students, was Carl Braun. Although Braun didn't regularly do dissections in the mornings, on this day, he had just completed an autopsy on one of his former patients. Ignác had briefed Braun earlier about his findings, and Braun's response was to just shrug his shoulders and say that he would "suspend judgement." But now, as Braun hurried past Ignác into the ward, acknowledging him with a curt "Morning," Ignác stopped him cold in his tracks. "You must wash," ordered Ignác, reaching out to lightly grab Braun's arm.

Braun turned to look incredulously at the wash basins and towels that he hadn't noticed before, one of them on a special table conspicuously labeled for Semmelweis only.[47] "What are you talking about? Have you lost your mind?"

"Not at all. This is the logical next step to proving my theory," responded Ignác.

Still holding onto his arm, Ignác led Braun to one of the wash basins while he himself demonstrated the procedure to him using the other one.

"Who the hell do you think we are? Pig farmers? Peasants? Butchers?" Braun's face was turning beet red.

"No, we are doctors," responded Ignác, stifling his ire, "and if there is any possibility of protecting our patients from diseases we unknowingly carry, we must do whatever it takes."

Braun scrubbed alongside Ignác, fuming in silence. He dried his hands with a towel, and shouted "Goddamnit, Semmelweis, you've gone too far this time with this humiliating exercise." Then Braun stalked into the ward to start his own rounds.

As the students began to stream out of their morning dissections and into the main hall outside the maternity ward, Ignác raised a hand to hold them up.

"Gentlemen," he began, "I want to announce that the cause of puerperal fever has been now conclusively demonstrated. The disease is transmitted to the patients by our own hands, which are contaminated with cadaveric particles picked up by those who have just completed dissections of the dead."

He had their rapt attention now. He heard murmurs of incredulity.

"Yes," he continued, "we have been unwittingly contributing to the deaths of these unfortunate women. I myself feel unspeakable guilt. But shame must be replaced by scientific solutions to prevent future occurrences. So," he turned to point to the new wash basins, "from this moment on, all who come here from the morgue will be required to thoroughly scrub their hands in this antiseptic solution before entering this maternity ward. There will be no exceptions. Now I shall demonstrate!"

Ignác rolled up his shirtsleeves and began scrubbing his forearms, hands, and individual fingers. The area around each fingernail was scrubbed to the point of bleeding. He scoured for several minutes, narrating each step of the ritual. But soon he began to sense some agitation amongst the students, and he heard muttering and chuckling. Ignác abruptly stopped and turned, hands and forearms shiny red, slippery, and dripping. He glared at the amused students. "And in case any of you don't think I will be seriously enforcing this new policy," he announced, "let me *assure* you that I will be standing here every morning to smell your hands after you think you have washed adequately."

"Smell our hands?" The ridicule came from one of the students. "Smell our bloody hands, did you say?"

"You! Dorfmeister!" Ignác bellowed, pointing to the student who was mocking him. "Come here now, and start scrubbing next to me. We shall *both* demonstrate!"

The student shuffled meekly to the other basin. When they were both finished, Ignác ordered him to wipe his hands with the clean towel. Then forcefully grabbing them by the wrists, he held the young man's hands up to his nose. "Not enough, Dorfmeister—there is still a faint smell. Two more minutes of scrubbing!"

Dorfmeister complied while Ignác observed in stern silence. A line soon formed, and Ignác intently supervised them all, closely smelling the hands of each before allowing entry into the ward.

All the students filed into the maternity ward, one by one, as soon as they had obtained Ignác's approval. All but Späth, that privileged new student from the Austrian Alps.

Späth decided to hurry directly to Klein to report this extraordinary occurrence. Frau Schlank recognized Späth from previous visits to Klein's office and let him in.

"Go ahead upstairs, Herr Späth. Doktor Braun just arrived a few minutes ago, and he is upstairs talking with the professor." Späth bounded up the steps.

When Späth entered the office, Klein and Braun were in the midst of an animated conversation about Semmelweis's findings and his new protocol for hand washing. Klein waved to the panting Späth to take a seat. "So what brings you here in such a hurry?"

"Did you know about the outrageous orders Semmelweis is enforcing this morning before allowing anyone to enter the First Division?"

"Braun has just started to tell me about it," replied the increasingly agitated Klein. After he had heard enough, Klein stood and motioned to Braun and Späth to follow him. Down the stairs they bounded, sweeping past a gaping Frau Schlank, out the front door and into a waiting carriage. Arriving at the hospital's main entrance on Alser Strasse, Klein jumped out before the carriage had even come to a full stop and hurried, propelled by his quick little steps, through the passageways that connected several courtyards, up the stairs into the First Division, waving his walking stick ahead of him as if to clear the way. There he confronted Ignác at the ward entrance, still supervising the hand washing of a couple of stragglers.

"What in hell do you think entitles you, Semmelweis, to simply make up your own rules like this on *my* service? You are *nothing* . . . nothing but a starting Assistant, for Christ's sake!

"But Herr Professor, I tried to tell you last week . . ."

Klein wasn't listening. "Your impudence is becoming intolerable!"

Klein was almost beside himself with rage, poking and prodding one of the wash basins with his cane until it came crashing down from its stand, spilling its liquid contents onto the floor. Then he glared at the remaining wash basin, labeled "*for Dr. Semmelweis only*," placed on a different table.

"And look at this!" he bellowed. "He has his own special set-up! He is not even a trained obstetrician yet, but he thinks he is a damned professor!"

Ignác's protests were to no avail. He had no choice but to let Klein's long tirade expire. Then, mustering all the tact he could, Ignác tried to explain how he had tried earlier to present his data to Klein and had wanted to discuss with him the intervention that would be needed to provide final proof.

"It's a great breakthrough, Herr Professor, and the hand washing intervention is nothing more than a harmless nuisance," Ignác began, surprised by his ability to string those words together under such hostile circumstances. "What could be the risk, and *think*," Ignác paused to swallow hard, "just think of the credit you will receive . . . *your* triumph, Professor Klein, if it is successful!"

The placated but still scowling Klein was now ready to listen to Ignác's story. And at the end, he reluctantly gave his approval for a one-month trial. "Do you understand, Semmelweis? *One month* is all you have to show me if this crackpot idea of yours has any merit. Then I will shut it down."

As the sulking Klein turned to march away, he abruptly turned back to Ignác. "And one more thing: this antiseptic solution of yours is much too expensive! You must find a cheaper substitute for the chlorinated water. I have to stick to my budget from the ministry. Is that clear?"

CHAPTER 15

MAY 1847

Klein had kept his colleague, the ophthalmologist Anton von Rosas, informed about his increasingly troublesome Assistant. Klein and Rosas were good friends and fellow guardians of the status quo of Viennese medicine. Klein also knew that Rosas, an elegant, handsomely aging, earnest man, was highly regarded in the Hofburg. In fact, Rosas' powerful court contacts made him a good bet to succeed Schiffner as the hospital's next director. He was a good man to keep at his side.

Ignác knew about Rosas and his reputation. He was actually born in Hungary, a fact he never talked about. He lived as a dyed-in-the-wool Austrian chauvinist. But now, for the first time, he began to fleetingly see him from afar, sometimes talking to physicians and nurses of the First Division. It struck Ignác as odd to see an ophthalmologist around a maternity service. He began to worry that Rosas was now becoming curious about him, this young Magyar upstart. They crossed paths one day in a hospital corridor. When Rosas paused, Ignác ran up to him eagerly to introduce himself to the eminent ophthalmologist.

"Herr Professor," began Ignác breathlessly, shaking Rosas' hand, "it is such an honor to finally meet you. I am Ignác Semmelweis."

"I know who you are," replied Rosas curtly.

"Your fame is known even back in your homeland. *Én is Magyar vagyok!*" beamed Ignác.

"I am not Magyar, Semmelweis, I am an Austrian. And we speak only German here. I strongly advise you to assimilate quickly if you wish for a career in our capital city."

As Rosas turned to continue on his way, he looked back at the chastised Ignác. "In any case," Rosas continued, "aren't you Jewish?"

"No, sir. I was born and raised a Roman Catholic."

"Oh, I think you are Jewish, young man. Your name is Jewish.[48] You look like a Jew, and," grabbing the lapel of Ignác's jacket, pulling it to his nose and theatrically sniffing it, "by God, you smell like a Jew!"

"I am afraid it smells of the cadavers I was dissecting earlier this morning. I haven't scrubbed yet."

"Difficult to distinguish," exclaimed Rosas, letting go of Ignác's jacket. There was a long, tense pause. One side of Rosas's mouth was twisted in a rictus of condescension. Finally, without changing expression, he patted Ignác on the chest. "Keep working, Semmelweis," he said, and without further ado turned to leave. Ignác was dumbstruck about what had caused this show of animosity.

Among the experts Ignác had reached out to in formulating the best possible antiseptic solution was the great German chemist, Justus von Liebig, professor at the University of Giessen. Much to his surprise, von Liebig's letter of response had just arrived the day before, advising him that liquid chlorine or the much less expensive chlorinated lime would be equally effective in removing cadaveric material. So Ignác quickly wrote a new prescription and hurried back down to the pharmacy to deliver it. Franz let him in.

"I hope Professor Klein has been happy with our disinfectant solution?" he asked.

"Oh, yes," said Ignác, "he was very . . . *excited* . . . by it! He suggested that we make a minor substitution, so I brought a new prescription."

"I'll get Herr Direktor. He will be so pleased," responded the beaming apprentice.

Schuster was just as disheveled as last time. His eyes were watery, and he was holding a handkerchief to his runny nose. He appeared to be even more tremulous than before.

"Professor Klein would like to substitute chlorinated lime for the liquid chlorine because he wants to keep the costs down," said Ignác as he handed the Direktor the new prescription.

Schuster yawned.

"The corrosive sublimate remains the same," Ignác added, pointing to where it was written on the sheet.

Schuster yawned again and turned to shuffle away.

"What a peculiar man," exclaimed Ignác to Franz.

"Yes, he is quite a character," replied Franz.

"How did he get to become the pharmacy director?"

"The story we've heard is that Herr Schuster had a very promising career here in his younger days," explained Franz, "and then he fell into addictions. First it was alcohol, and then opium elixir, which he stole from the pharmacy. Then when morphine became available, around 1820, he started using that as well. When he was found out, he was fired by one of the previous hospital directors," explained Franz.

"It looks to me like he still has some problems," noted Ignác.

"Yes, I am afraid he still does. But no one is allowed to talk about it," Franz replied in a whisper. "Sometime in the past, nobody knows exactly when, he was rehabilitated . . . I guess . . . and the hospital director was ordered by someone high up in the imperial ministry to hire him back. Well, Herr Schuster was so grateful to get a second chance that he endeared himself to Schiffner and many of the older doctors in the hospital by working hard, day and night, following orders without fail, never asking questions, and always providing prompt service."

"And he was promoted to pharmacy director?" asked Ignác incredulously.

"Yes. But I can tell you, there is just nothing Herr Schuster wouldn't do for Schiffner and the older doctors around here! His loyalty to the men who took him back is boundless."

The antiseptic scrubbing protocol was introduced in the middle of May 1847.[49] And then the women stopped dying. Only on occasional days in the last two weeks of May did a single patient succumb. The abrupt drop in the mortality rate was plain to see, and practically miraculous. Every morning Ignác zealously guarded entry to the maternity ward, allowing no one to pass without his personal visual and olfactory inspection to ensure that the hand-scrubbing routine had been completed. He ignored the snickering and snide remarks of the medical students. He pretended not to hear even their most derisive quips about the irony of a Hungarian peasant teaching the Viennese about cleanliness.

One morning at the end of May, as Ignác was embroiled in a confrontation with a rebellious student, he was startled by a firm hand grabbing his shoulder from behind. He turned to face a shaken Hebra. Ignác's usually jolly friend was pale and perspiring profusely.

"Hebra, what the hell . . ."

"Come quickly, Semmelweis," stammered the young dermatology professor. "I need you right away."

Without a further word, Hebra pulled Ignác by the arm through the main hallway toward the front doors of the maternity building and across the courtyards to the hospital's main entrance. And as they hurriedly brushed past doctors, nurses, patients, and visitors, Hebra explained breathlessly, "It's my wife, Semmelweis. Johanna is at home, in labor. You must deliver her."

"Me?" protested the bewildered Ignác. "Why me?"

"You are the only one I trust to do it safely," responded the frantic Hebra, "and it's our first child."

Ignác suddenly stopped, pulled out of Hebra's grasp and started to run back toward the maternity ward. "Stay right here," shouted Ignác without breaking stride. "I'll be right back!"

Back outside the First Division, Ignác pushed a student aside and subjected himself to an accelerated hand-scrubbing routine with the antiseptic solution. Rushing back to where he had left Hebra nervously waiting, Ignác's arms and hands were still dripping and red.

Frau Hebra was clearly in labor, but her contractions were still only several minutes apart. So Ignác calmed down his young colleague and asked for soap and a bowl of water so that he could complete his handwashing regimen before examining her. He ordered clean bed sheets to be placed under his new patient.

And then, around noon on May 24, 1847, Ignác Semmelweis delivered Frau Hebra of a healthy boy, whom they named Johannes.[50] A beaming Professor Hebra was summoned to be introduced to his beautiful son, sleeping snugly in the arms of his mother.

As the proud parents admired their new baby, the perspiring, disheveled Semmelweis stepped out into the living room and took from his black bag a slightly squashed nosegay of lilacs which he had intended to give to Caroline. He brought it back into the bedroom to present to Frau Hebra.

"Why Ignác," she said, "what an incredibly kind gesture. And after all you've just done! They haven't extinguished that Magyar chivalry in you yet, have they!"

Over the next few weeks, the impressive improvement in statistics confirmed the impressions of those who worked in the First Division. The mortality rate had declined dramatically, from 14.5% in May to 2.4% in June. And then in July, it dropped further, to 1.2%.

Professor Klein didn't dispute the striking results, but he attributed them more to a newly installed ventilation system in the First Division than to Ignác's hand washing ritual. With the start of summer vacations and his private practice burgeoning, he began to spend less and less time in the hospital. This allowed Ignác to assume increasing oversight. Despite his public skepticism, when Klein did appear, he discreetly washed his own hands before entering.

Braun and Späth, on the other hand, were utterly unconvinced. They promoted Klein's theory about ventilation even more vocally than Klein himself, working to undermine Ignác at every step. Their hostility toward Ignác was plain to see.

In the middle of the summer, a couple of young physicians came as observers to the Obstetrics service of the *Allgemeine Krankenhaus.* The first was Hans-Hermann Schwartz, an assistant obstetrician in Kiel in northern Germany. Schwartz had been sent to Vienna by his chief, Gustav Adolf Michaelis, who had heard about some remarkable progress being made there in the prevention of puerperal fever.[51] The problem had been plaguing Michaelis's own clinic for many years despite some radical preventive measures he'd attempted to implement, like temporary closure of the wards whenever a spike in deaths was noted. It greatly troubled Michaelis. Not long after his arrival in Vienna, Schwartz wrote an exuberant letter to his chief, providing him with some impressive results Ignác was getting. Professor Michaelis tried the Viennese regimen in Kiel and then responded to his assistant Schwartz as follows:

> *"Your letter has excited my highest interest. I have also sent a copy of your letter to Copenhagen. I can recommend very emphatically the security gained through chlorine washing. The hands retain the [bad] smell for several days in spite of repeated washing; but this*

is not the case with chlorine washing. Since adopting this practice, no one delivered by me or by my pupils has contracted the slightest degree of fever. I extend congratulations to Dr. Semmelweis for what is probably a great discovery."

But Michaelis also added some poignant personal comments to this same letter:

"I cannot refrain from communicating something to you that is obviously connected with these matters. Last summer my cousin died of puerperal fever. I had examined her after delivery at a time when I had autopsied patients who had died of puerperal fever. From that time, I was convinced of communicability."

And he ended the letter:

"You know that puerperal fever has been with us since 1834. That is also about the time when I began to occupy myself actively in teaching and when I instituted vaginal examinations by students. This fact may also be related."[52]

The other young German physician to arrive in the summer of 1847 was named Adolf Kussmaul.[53] He came to enroll for several months of advanced clinical study at the University of Vienna, including a clerkship and lectures in obstetrics taught by Ignác. Kussmaul was a recent graduate of the renowned medical school in Heidelberg, and he had served as assistant to the noted German obstetrician, Franz Karl Naegele, a man Ignác revered by reputation. A strapping young man of sharp wit and keen intellect, Kussmaul had a virtually encyclopedic fund of medical knowledge for a physician of his young age.

Kussmaul eagerly began to follow Ignác on maternity ward teaching rounds, even when Klein was absent. Some mornings he would join Ignác to assist him with autopsies. And after he did, he would emulate Ignác's fervent hand washing routine to reinforce its importance in front of the medical students. Kussmaul and Semmelweis became fast friends.

"You are doing amazing work here," Kussmaul said during a less hectic moment. "Word is already spreading about your discovery."

"There are still a lot of skeptics. Even here, in my own hospital."

"But surely the facts speak for themselves! I mentioned your findings to Professor Naegele in my last letter to him, and he immediately wrote back to say how impressed he was with you."

"I don't know what to say. I am . . ." Ignác hesitated. "I'm so honored he would even mention my name. But please be sure you tell him I am doing all this under Professor Klein's supervision. Without giving credit to Klein, I am afraid I won't have his support for much longer."

"All right, all right. I understand why you feel a need to be deferential to Klein. But I also see how detached he is and how terribly hard you are working. It seems like you are here all the time. It just doesn't make sense to me that he would be antagonistic to you!"

Rather than being comforted by Kussmaul's support, Ignác's inner indignation flared again at hearing an outsider's affirmation of his plight.

"But he is, and I don't know why, either," Ignác responded. "Believe me, I've lost sleep over it. Maybe it's because I am not as polished as all the others around him. I get easily flustered. My German isn't crisp, I don't have the proper accent, and I'm certainly not very articulate. Maybe it's because I'm not . . ." said Ignác, looking down.

"Not what?"

"Not *Austrian*."

Ignác's students and young colleagues, who had so much enjoyed his joviality and exuberance in the past, were now growing concerned about his bouts of petulance. He had begun to appear gaunt and frequently distracted. They couldn't remember the last time they saw him leave the premises to take a full meal. By the end of the summer, Ignác had essentially moved into the hospital, as if on continuous vigil. There was talk about his staying awake for much of every night, just sitting in the darkness of the ward with a vacant gaze, his face illuminated only by a few flickering candles next to the patients' beds. He paced the dark, empty corridors of the hospital, even wandering into the Second Division at times, and only occasionally disappearing into his little *Dienstzimmer* for short intervals, presumably to take naps.

Then, in the weeks ahead, Ignác became more and more preoccupied by the thought that just about anyone around him, even including the medical students, could sabotage his work, to do something malicious to disprove his findings. As a result, he was now often morose, withdrawn, and non-communicative. At the same time, whenever he suspected anyone was violating his rules, he erupted with contemptuous rage. These explosions were all the more terrifying to those around him who were so accustomed to his congeniality, especially in contrast to his ever-punctilious and officious Austrian counterparts. But for most of the time this once ebullient man didn't want to talk to anyone.

As the summer months passed, he would rant and rave, often incoherently or even in Hungarian when he was really beside himself, his face turning beet red, spewing spittle. Physicians, students, and staff had all accepted Ignác's frequently colorful cursing, but in the past, it was all so good-natured. It was part of his Magyar charm. But now his outbursts were laced with malicious, accusatory profanity. Ignác's explosions occurred ever more frequently and unpredictably. And they were interspersed with long periods of sullen solitude.

The only exceptions were his patients. He never lost his temper with them, and he remained immensely generous with his time whenever they needed him.

Hebra had been dropping in to see Ignác in the First Division wards to give him joyful updates about how well his little Hans was thriving, and to thank him for his expert delivery of his baby son. But he was also growing concerned about Ignác's appearance and outright change in personality. Although neither Skoda nor Rokitansky had seen Ignác for much of the summer, they were getting word of the miraculous decline in mortality rates in the First Division, and they were eager to talk to him. Ignác was summoned to a meeting in Rokitansky's office.

After praising their young colleague, they spoke of their worry about Ignác s own well-being.

"You are running yourself into the ground, Ignác," began Hebra. "People say you are working day and night. They never see you go home, they rarely see you sleep, and they don't think you eat much."

"You've got to conserve your energy," added Skoda. "You may be on to something quite momentous, but you've got to maintain your composure. Otherwise your credibility will be questioned."

"*Credibility?*" Ignác snapped with eyebrows raised, his face suddenly flushed. "What the hell are you talking about my . . . my credibility?" Leaning forward in his chair and grasping its arms as if preparing to stand to challenge them, Ignác suddenly appeared menacing. He glared directly at Skoda and Hebra but seemed oblivious to Rokitansky, who sat across from them, silently scowling. "Are *you* questioning my goddamn credibility?"

"Calm down, old boy," said Hebra with a nervous smile, gently motioning to Ignác to sit back. "We're all on your side!"

"Frankly, you do look like hell," Rokitansky finally chimed in. He had been observing Ignác in a sadly contemplative way.

Ignác looked at them in stony silence, dabbing some saliva that had settled in the corners of his downturned lips with his handkerchief. He was concentrating on collecting his composure after his outburst.

"And what about writing up your findings for publication?" asked Skoda, changing the subject. "The world needs to know what you have found. There are already rumblings about it, even outside the Empire."

"Are you saying that I should write an article *by myself*?"

"Well, who else would write it?" snapped Skoda. "Klein has never published a goddamned paper in his life!"

"I can't write," replied Ignác.

"Can't *write*?" Skoda's tone of voice turned incredulous.

"I mean I can't write *it* . . . without Professor Klein's help. After all, he *is* my professor and mentor. *He* is the one with the name to get it published. I am a nobody. Whatever else we might say, I just can't violate . . ."

"Violate what? Academic protocol?" Skoda interrupted in an exasperated tone. "For Christ's sake, when are you finally going to give up your damned idealism?"

Skoda caught himself glancing at Rokitansky, who frowned. "Excuse me . . . your darned idealism," Skoda continued. "Things just don't work this way in the real world."

"Well, I can ask him, but I'm sure he won't help," Ignác replied.

"*We* can help you," said Hebra. "I know I can work with you to organize at least a first draft, Ignác. Don't forget, I am a medical editor."[54]

"Aha!" Ignác exploded again. "So you just want to take some credit for my work by writing it up *for* me!"

"Not at all. It's all yours, of course. But I'd like to publish it in my journal."

"Gentlemen," Rokitansky injected, "I think Semmelweis should first go to Klein and get his approval to begin writing. Otherwise Klein will eventually find out about it from someone else. And then he could become even more antagonistic."

"He won't approve," said Ignác. "He simply won't. It's out of the question."

"Yes, he will," replied Rokitansky, "but first you must win him over. Give him credit for the discovery. Swallow your pride, and tell him you owe it all to him. Tell him he was your inspiration!"

"He certainly was," snickered Hebra under his breath.

Rokitansky continued. "Tell him the world will know this discovery was made on the great Johannes Klein's service. And you were merely his *instrument*!"

Ignác remained silent, his brow furrowed and lips tightly pursed.

Leaving Rokitansky's office, Hebra pulled Ignác aside for a private word.

"Listen, you just can't speak to people like you did in there. I don't mind personally because we are such good friends, and I do understand your frustration. But you've got to control your temper. I'm just giving you some collegial advice. This is Vienna, you know."

"Ah, yes, of course, Vienna, the epitome of civilization and refinement," Ignác sneered with sarcasm. "And here is this barbaric Magyar, misplaced in its midst!"

"Oh, Christ—don't be such an ass. You take offense at everything," replied Hebra. "I am not one of them, either, you know. I worked my way up, just like you're doing. You just have to learn a different *decorum* here. *Equanimitas*, my friend!"

"*Equanimitas?*"

"Yes, *equanimitas*. Latin for "equanimity." Being calm, collected, cool, and dispassionate. Especially under stress. Unperturbed even in the face of provocation. It's a good thing for any physician to learn, but especially a Viennese one," continued Hebra.

"Well, to hell with your 'equanimity'!" bellowed Ignác. Hebra was startled. But then Ignác's face dissolved into a broad, warm grin, and he laughed out loud with his old hearty Magyar guffaw.

CHAPTER 16

LATE OCTOBER 1847

Ignác was now aware that something was wrong with himself. He had no idea what it was, but he despaired for a clear-thinking yet sympathetic ear. Only Caroline could provide that here. But he knew he hadn't been good to her. He had been so completely absorbed in his work that he'd essentially excluded her from his life. He'd even lost track of how long it had been since he last saw her. At least a season had passed, he figured, and maybe more.

"But that means you didn't really miss me. Don't you see that?" Caroline said holding his hand, her head on his shoulder, as they sat together on a bench in the Volksgarten on this unusually warm afternoon in the late fall.

"Of course, I must have missed you," Ignác tried to explain. "That's exactly the problem. I've been so preoccupied by what has been happening in the hospital that I feel like I have lost all human contact with the outside world."

Ignác now stared blankly into the distance. A chill wind passed, and he pressed Caroline closer to himself, but he seemed to tune out all the surrounding bustle and noise in the park.

They sat in silence for what seemed like a very long time.

And then Ignác started to wistfully relate to her some sundry stories of his childhood, his old friends, his teachers, and whatever came to his mind.

"We all had to be tolerant and respectful, even if we didn't really like someone. My neighborhood in Buda, my school, my parents, and their friends. We all came from a multitude of cultures and religions. It didn't seem to matter much what we looked like or what our accents were. We didn't have reputations to live up to because there were constantly people, families moving in and moving out. So pedigree didn't count for anything: only what your character was like."

"I think we are both rather like that, don't you see?" Caroline said. "When we met—do you remember—neither of us thought for even a moment whether the other was Austrian or Magyar, working class or well-to-do, Jewish or Catholic."

Ignác had a sudden inspiration. He jumped up, grabbed Caroline's hand firmly, and pulled her along as he sprinted through the park. Caroline giggled in amused befuddlement as she tried to keep up. Exiting the Volksgarten and running through the narrow streets of the Inner City, Caroline in tow but occasionally stumbling on the cobblestones, Ignác spotted a flower shop and dragged her inside. After frantically looking around the shop to find exactly what he wanted, Ignác picked up a big bouquet of fully bloomed red roses and handed it to Caroline with a kiss on her cheek. He then asked the bewildered shopkeeper if he had any inexpensive bunches of lilacs. The man returned from the back of the shop, shaking his head, carrying several nosegays of pathetically drooping lilacs.

"This is all we have, sir," he apologized.

Ignác grabbed them all from him in delight. "They are *perfect.* I'll take them all, and also those roses. How much is all this?"

Back outside on the street, Caroline held the roses and embraced Ignác in a tight hug. She kissed him passionately on the lips and then flashed a devious sideways glance at him.

"All right," she said with a twinkle in her eyes. "So who are all those other flowers for?"

"I am afraid you are not the only one, Charlinchen," he said with a feigned downcast face that slowly transformed into a mischievous smile. "There are so many other young ladies I have been ignoring. Fixating on them only as numbers but neglecting them as people."

"Your patients?"

"Yes."

"And why lilacs?"

"In the language of flowers," replied Ignác, "they signify innocence and new beginnings."

"I am impressed with your botanical literacy." They both laughed.

"I don't know why, but they also somehow remind me of playing with my friends as a young boy," he said.

Ignác escorted Caroline home. But after he dropped her off, with a big hug, he raced back to the hospital with a spring in his steps.

The next morning two of the women were discharged with their babies in their arms. Neither of them had any problems postpartum. No family or friends had come to pick up either one of them. As heartbreaking as this scene was, it was more common than not in the maternity ward of the *Allgemeine Krankenhaus*. The women smiled bravely as the nurse led them out through the door of the maternity ward and down the long corridor to the main staircase.

The echoing sound of running footsteps materialized behind them, and they all stopped. A disheveled and panting Ignác caught up to them and presented each of the new mothers with a nosegay of lilacs; then he bowed slightly to both and wished them Godspeed. The women were overcome and carefully handed their babies to the nurse to hold for a moment, one at a time, and clumsily held out a hand to their young obstetrician. Ignác took their hands but also pulled each of them close for a strong hug. As he hurried back to the ward, he could hear them sobbing right where he had left them in the corridor. It sounded like the nurse was also sniveling. He cursed to himself in Hungarian as he jogged back. "Damn it, I should have bought more!" he said to himself, beaming from ear to ear.

For his upcoming presentation to Klein, Ignác meticulously prepared the data from his hand-scrubbing intervention, He tabulated the unembellished numbers as plainly and simply as he could. He had learned that Klein had no patience for details. The data were compelling. The results were incontrovertible. How could Klein not be pleased? Klein would somehow take credit for the discovery, no doubt, but Ignác didn't mind as long as he finally gained the chief's confidence and was allowed to continue his work.

Regaining his old enthusiasm, Ignác now bounded through the streets of the old city with great expectations. He appeared in Klein's office with an armful of papers he had accumulated in the course of his work in the First Division. He was eager to explain all his data to Klein. But before he could even begin, Klein brusquely waved for him to take a seat. Dispensing with any preliminary niceties, Klein now launched into a litany of complaints he had received about Ignác's conduct.

"Your behavior has become entirely unacceptable, Semmelweis. Your co-workers find you impossible to deal with. It's not just the nurses, orderlies, and students, you understand. Even your closest colleagues are complaining to me. Braun, Chiari, Lumpe, and especially Späth. They are all reporting to me your increasingly erratic comportment. They say you have irrational outbursts and that your tone of voice has become supercilious, offensive, and even downright insulting. What have you to say for yourself?"

This is most certainly not what I came to talk about, Ignác thought to himself. His heart started to pound, and his face became flushed with dread. He had to remain composed.

"Herr Professor, this has been an arduous period . . ."

Klein just sat there in stony silence, scowling at Ignác. This just heightened Ignác's sense of panic about what might be coming.

"But I think I am recovering my composure after all the difficulties," he blurted out.

"What are your . . . what did you call them . . . 'difficulties'?" Klein interrupted caustically.

"They have to do with what I came to discuss with you, sir. The hand washing regimen is working very well. We are cutting the mortality rate substantially. But sometimes there is a problem with enforcing it. And then I have no choice but to crack down on those who refuse to comply," explained Ignác. "I want to show you all the data we have accumulated so far that demonstrate the effectiveness of hand washing."

Ignác stood up and carefully placed the sheets of paper he'd brought with him on Klein's desk.

"If you would look at the top two pages," continued Ignác, leaning across the desk to point to them, "they summarize the data. All the detailed information is on the papers underneath."

Klein lifted the first two pages, held them close to his eyes, and scanned them. He became agitated, hands beginning to tremble and eyes darting up and down and across both sheets, as if searching for something.

"The first column of numbers on the first page, . . ." began Ignác.

"What is all this scribbling?" Klein was exploding with impatience. "I can't even read some of your writing! At least you used to have readable handwriting. What are these things in parentheses? And these notes at the bottom of the second page?" fumed Klein, his voice now quavering with barely contained annoyance. "It looks like some kind of Magyar gibberish." Klein looked up at Ignác, his face red. "What's wrong with you, Semmelweis?"

Before Ignác could continue his explanation, Klein threw the papers back on his desk with utter disdain.

"Well, they are just my notes," said Ignác, "I thought you should see the originals, and I tried to summarize them in the front." He now felt lightheaded. "They are certainly not ready for publication in this form."

"*Publication?*" Klein thundered. "Never! Not without my permission! Do you understand? In any case, you couldn't even write a proper scientific manuscript if you wanted to."

And, as if he hadn't already made himself amply clear, Klein shoved the pile of papers on his desk back toward Ignác, causing a couple of them to float to the floor. Ignác scurried to pick them up.

Leaving Klein's office, Ignác felt utterly humiliated. As he crossed the Stephansplatz on his way back to the hospital, it suddenly occurred to him that Hebra, Skoda, and Rokitansky might not be the allies he presumed them to be. After all, hadn't they just given him misguided advice? Hadn't they just directed him straight into the lion's den? Was it possible that they had set him up? Maybe they were, after all, in collusion with Klein and his cronies. Was there *anyone* he could really trust? He picked up his pace to return to work.

Kussmaul had likewise become troubled about Ignác's deteriorating behavior, even in the short time he had known him. He was determined to take his young teacher and new friend out of the hospital for a conversation.

They made the long walk through the Schottentor gate of the walls into the Inner City. Arriving at Gerstner,[55] they were seated at a small marble-topped table by one of the tall windows. The overheated inside was thick with the aroma of freshly roasted coffee and tobacco smoke. The neat but tiny room, made to look larger only by a mirror covering its back wall, was buzzing with conversation.

"Herr Ober," Kussmaul called to the waiter, "we'll both have *schwarzer* cafes—make them strong—and your *kipfel* pastry."

They took off their coats and rolled up their shirtsleeves. Ignác sat back in his bentwood chair and started to ask Kussmaul about his experience in Vienna. The sun shining in on Ignác through the window accentuated his sallow complexion. But what struck Kussmaul most were Ignác's hands and arms. They appeared raw red and the skin was peeling in patches.

"What's happening to your hands and arms?" Kussmaul interrupted Ignác.

Ignác paused and examined them outstretched. "Oh, that's nothing," he said with a dismissive smile, "just washing and scrubbing them so frequently, they tend to get chafed."

"They don't look to me like they're just chafed," replied the frowning Kussmaul. "It's like some kind of skin disease. Have you shown them to Hebra?" Kussmaul pulled Ignác's hands closer to him by the wrists as he intently inspected them. "After all, he *is* an expert in diseases of the skin!"[56]

"I'm sure he has seen them. Nothing to worry about," replied Ignác as he withdrew his hands from Kussmaul's examination.

"But have you actually *shown* them to him?" insisted Kussmaul.

Ignác tried to ignore the question and resumed his chatter about Kussmaul's life in Vienna, but the young man from Heidelberg would have none of it. "Tell me again, Ignác, what exactly does your disinfectant solution contain?"

"It's a combination of chlorinated lime and bichloride of mercury.[43] I recently substituted the chlorinated lime for liquid chlorine because it's much less expensive. And anyway, Professor von Liebig from Giessen recommended it."

"But who recommended the bichloride of mercury? That might be the culprit. After all, that's why we commonly call it 'corrosive sublimate.'"

"Yes, Adolf," replied Ignác, "but it's also well known to be as powerful as liquid chlorine as a disinfectant. I have researched the subject, and they are the two most effective antiseptics used in practice. Surely their combination has to be better than either one alone."

"Not necessarily," countered Kussmaul. "And corrosive sublimate can cause all kinds of other problems when it's absorbed through the skin. Maybe that's why you've lost your appetite. Maybe that's why you have become so damned irritable, Ignác. And as you were holding out your hands just now, did I not detect a fine tremor in them?"

Ignác laughed out loud. "Ha!" he exploded. "Look at the young Doktor Adolf Kussmaul, *master diagnostician*, just graduated from medical school!" Ignác exclaimed in good-natured mockery. "As you know, topical mercury has long been used as a treatment for syphilis. The symptoms you are attributing to corrosive sublimate are actually the symptoms of the syphilis for which it's used, not the mercury itself. And I can assure you, my dear Adolf, that I most certainly don't have syphilis!" [57]

Kussmaul wasn't laughing. "There is plenty of evidence . . ."

"And in any case," Ignác interrupted, "I surely wouldn't be able to absorb all that damned mercury through the skin into my system. So I suppose it could be contributing to the rash on my hands and arms, but I can't imagine how it would be causing all the other problems you're talking about."

"I wouldn't say that," cautioned Kussmaul. "I'll never forget an experiment my great Professor Tiedemann at Heidelberg once demonstrated to our medical school class. It left quite an impression on me. He had his assistant rub turpentine on his hands in front of us and then sent him out of the lecture amphitheater with an empty glass container. The assistant came back ten minutes later with a sample of his own urine in the flask, which he passed around to the students. Well, don't you know it, that urine sample had the strong smell of turpentine. It proved that he had absorbed the turpentine from his skin and had excreted it through his kidneys."[58]

"Anyway, it's the results that matter," said Ignác, "and the results have been amazingly good. Why should we argue with that?"

"But if the good results are coming at the expense of putting mercury into your own system, as well as the bodies of your students and your staff, and maybe even into your patients by examining them with mercury-coated hands, then more harm than good can come from it in the long run," suggested Kussmaul.

Ignác suddenly looked stricken; he was still remorseful about his unintended complicity in transmitting contaminants from cadavers to his patients and, thereby, causing the deaths of a countless number of them.[59]

"Why don't you try for at least a few days to use only chlorinated lime, just as Professor von Liebig recommended to you, and then follow the mortality rate closely," continued Kussmaul. "Any uptick in deaths, and you can immediately go back to adding the mercury."

Early in the morning the day after his conversation with Kussmaul, Ignác brought a new prescription to the pharmacy. He handed it to Franz.

"We have to delete the corrosive sublimate, Franz," he explained. "There is some concern that it might be causing some side effects. So, just pure chlorinated lime starting today. Same strength."

"Of course," Franz replied, taking the prescription. "I'll get Herr Schuster's approval right away. We can deliver the new formula to your ward this morning."

Ignác was all business this time, and turned to leave in a hurry. Franz was struck by his odd abruptness, so he tapped him on the shoulder. "Are you all right, Doctor Semmelweis?" he asked. Ignác pivoted back to face Franz again.

"Am I all right?" he snapped indignantly.

Then Ignác just stood there, glowering at the now-unnerved Franz.

"What exactly did you mean by that? Is there some reason I shouldn't be all right? Why do you want to know? Who told you to ask me that? How am I supposed to be feeling?" Ignác rattled off the questions in a crazed tone.

"No . . . nobody . . ." Franz stammered, as Ignác stepped closer to him. "I am just glad to see you are all right, sir."

"Good!" Ignác declared as he turned and hurried out.

When he returned to the First Division, Ignác found Johann Chiari waiting for him. Only a year older, Chiari was the one who had introduced Ignác to the practice of obstetrics during his own assistantship to Klein four years earlier.[13] So, Ignác now viewed Chiari as both mentor and friend. To everyone's amused surprise, Chiari had recently become engaged to Klein's oldest daughter. Despite Klein's growing hostility toward Ignác, Chiari's new relationship with Klein didn't seem in any way to get in the way of his friendship with Ignác. Or so Ignác hoped.

Chiari warmly shook his hand and clasped his other shoulder. "How are you holding up, old boy?" I know how stressful things have been for you these days. But what a remarkable discovery! What a triumph! We are so proud of you."

"I'm not so sure your future father-in-law shares that same sentiment," chuckled Ignác.

"But, of course, he does," roared back Chiari. "How can he not? He just doesn't express it directly. Old school, you know. In any case, that has to do with why I dropped by to see you. My bride-to-be and I have persuaded the old man to host a gathering in his home as a sort of belated welcome reception for Kussmaul. It's tomorrow evening. And we want you to come, of course."

Ignác's face dropped. He looked down at the floor and suddenly appeared ill at ease. "I don't know, Johann . . ." he said, head shaking.

"But everyone will be there! All of Klein's former assistants, many of our friends," said Chiari, smiling broadly. "And just so the old man can entertain himself, we told him to invite some of his own cronies. That way, the rest of us can have a merry old time!

"Oh, and why don't you bring that gorgeous sweetheart of yours?" Chiari added after there was no response.

"I've been here in the hospital almost all the time, you know, and I don't think I can get away tomorrow night. In any case, I don't do very well in social circles like that."

"Nonsense. You've always been the life of the party! I have such great memories of all the fun we had together in medical school."

"All right, I'll try to come," Ignác mumbled.

Head bowed, Ignác started to shuffle back to his work on the ward.

"Seven o'clock," shouted Chiari down the hall, as Ignác raised his arm without turning back.

The next evening Ignác felt increasing butterflies in his stomach as the time approached for Klein's reception. He got dressed for it but desperately didn't want to go. This surge of insecurity and shyness was new to him, and it made him all the more frightened. He thought of all kinds of untruthful excuses for why he couldn't go at the last minute. But finally he summoned the courage to set out for Klein's home on Rotenturmstrasse. It was twilight, and the gas lamps on the streets were being lit. He knew the way well because it was in the same building that housed his private office. He gave himself plenty of time to get there but felt more and more lightheaded as he approached. He got there before St. Stephen's bell rang seven. So he nervously waited outside on the street, partly hidden, a few houses further down, to see who was arriving. Most of the guests were older men, and he didn't think he recognized any friends. And now Ignác became terrified, frozen with a kind of apprehension he had never felt before. He walked up to the familiar front door, which was opened for him by a butler.

Under chandeliers, surrounded by paintings and tapestries on the walls, standing on colorful Persian rugs or sitting on the finest Biedermeyer chairs and sofas in the Kleins' spacious living room, several young physicians were sampling Viennese hors d'oeuvres and pastries. They became increasingly animated in conversation as others they knew arrived to join them and glasses of wine and champagne were filled and refilled. Ignác stood rooted in one position next to the fireplace, surveying the scene but mostly looking down at the glass of champagne he was holding. He knew most of the people there, but suddenly they all seemed like strangers to him. Some came over to say hello but soon left when Ignác couldn't think of anything to say to them. It was like he was on the outside looking in. Klein came in to greet some of the young people. For a moment, Ignác thought about going over to him to thank him for the invitation, but then his heart began to pound so fast and hard that he stayed where he was. Klein left the room.

Maybe he saw me and just didn't want to greet me, Ignác thought to himself. He spied some small groups of young physicians with their lady friends who were laughing, drinking, and eating. He was sure some of them were staring at him across the room and talking about him.

Overcome by nervousness and the sense of not belonging here, he abruptly hurried out of the room as inconspicuously as he could, using servers as cover, until he was back outside in the fresh fall air. Feeling liberated, he didn't stop walking fast until he was back within the safe confines of the hospital.

Ignác stayed alone in the hospital for the rest of the night, repeatedly reproaching himself for his inexplicable social cowardice. It was something he had never experienced before.

Meanwhile, the affair in Klein's posh home was, indeed, cheerful. After Klein offered a toast to Kussmaul as the guest of honor, he and his old chums retired into the quiet sanctuary of Klein's ornate study. They included some of the elite of Viennese medicine, including the ophthalmologist, Rosas, and the hospital director, Schiffner. Puffing on cigars, swirling and savoring apricot brandy from Kecskeme, their conversation centered more on the increasingly unsettled political situation throughout the Empire than on any medical issues. A little later, the group was joined by Carl Braun, accompanied by his younger brother Gustav, as well as Lumpe, Chiari, and Chiari's ever-present student, Späth.

As the young physicians in the living room began to leave at the end of the evening, Kussmaul knocked on the study door and entered to thank Klein for his family's gracious hospitality.

"Come in for a minute before you leave, Kussmaul," summoned the uncommonly expansive Klein. "Tell us what you think of our medical school. Is it anything like your Heidelberg?"

"I love Heidelberg. It's my home," responded Kussmaul, "but Vienna! Well, Vienna must be the greatest medical center in the world today."

"So you have learned a lot from your experience with us?" asked Schiffner, who hadn't met Kussmaul before this evening.

"Oh, yes, especially on Professor Klein's obstetrics service. What an incredibly exciting time for me to be here!"

"Are you referring to the drop in cases of puerperal fever?"

"Yes, sir—it's great progress, isn't it?" replied Kussmaul.

"Do you have any suggestions for us about what else we could be doing about that problem?" asked Klein.

"Well, in fact I spent quite a bit of time talking with Ignác . . . I mean Doktor Semmelweis . . . just yesterday about his preventive solutions. I suggested to him that he would get just as good results if he left the corrosive sublimate out of the chlorine disinfectant solution. It seems to be causing him some skin problems, and, of course, you never know what kinds of systemic effects the mercury might have if it was repeatedly absorbed into the bloodstream."

"What did Semmelweis say to that?" asked Rosas.

"He agreed that the mercury should be removed immediately, at least for a trial period."

"Good idea!" said Klein.

"Maybe that's why Semmelweis is going crazy," exclaimed Rosas with a hearty laugh, exhaling a large puff of cigar smoke.

"I think Professor Rosas may have an interesting point there," Carl Braun interjected as he moved his chair closer to the inner circle, leaning forward to catch all the words.

Klein continued, "You're absolutely right, Kussmaul. We are very pleased with the progress Semmelweis is making. It was so wonderful of you to come tonight, and we're all looking forward to continuing to work with you for your remaining time here. It's too bad it has to be so short." And with that, Klein stood to shake Kussmaul's hand and escort him out the front door to make sure he had a carriage waiting for him.

By the time Klein returned, most of the young people had left the living room to go home, and a maid was cleaning up under Mrs. Klein's supervision. The study, however, was still filled with smoke, and a heated political conversation was in progress. Klein closed the door behind him, sat back down in his armchair, slowly scanned the people in the room, and was satisfied to note that the group hadn't changed while he was out to send off Kussmaul. He waited for a pause in the discussion and then spoke up.

"Gentlemen, I don't think it's a secret among those of you here that I have had deep concerns about Semmelweis," he began slowly and softly. The others leaned forward to hear him. "Kussmaul is a very fine young man with a promising future. So I didn't want to taint his brief experience in Vienna by appearing to publicly contradict his favorable opinion of my brash young Hungarian assistant. But, just between us, I believe Semmelweis has become a disruptive force."

"I can't agree with you more, Johann," chimed in Schiffner. "I have known it since my first encounter with him when I caught him lying to get unauthorized access to hospital data. If you want my opinion, I think he is downright dangerous."

"Oh, come now, Dr. Schiffner," said Chiari. But there was already a murmur of agreement around the room.

"He must be stopped," said Rosas. "We have to take down that young Jew before he contaminates our noble medical community. But how? It won't look good if you just summarily fire him right in the middle of a streak of good outcomes in the maternity ward. But I don't see any alternatives."

Klein sat deep in thought, staring up at the ceiling, absentmindedly puffing away on his cigar and taking sips of brandy. Nobody said another word, waiting for Klein's response. And then it came.

"We must find a way to *discredit* him."

Over the next several weeks, the mortality rate in the First Division remained low, giving Ignác reassurance that the change in antiseptic solution recommended by Kussmaul was still effective. In fact, Ignác's habit of giving posies of lilacs to all the new mothers who were being discharged with their newborns was happily costing him more and more money as the number of healthy discharges kept increasing. He was handing out up to ten a day. So Ignác began to keep a constant supply of fresh lilacs in a glass of water on his desk, and handed them out just two single ones at a time, one for the mother and one for the baby, or two in the case of twins, when they were being discharged. When mothers asked why they were getting them, Ignác would explain that the flower symbolized both motherhood and childhood, purity and innocence. But to Ignác, each pair of lilacs represented a triumph. He would pin them on the mother's and baby's dresses as they left the ward. It was a gesture that almost invariably provoked a tearful hug from the grateful mother. Everybody, even including many of the nurses, thought this was a ridiculous ritual, and much fun was made of it by the medical students. But they all dismissed it as a harmless eccentricity on the part of an eccentric young doctor.

But then disaster struck.

At the beginning of November, within a span of just two days, eleven patients came down with puerperal fever and died in rapid succession. Curiously, all the stricken patients were in beds adjacent to each other on one side of the ward. The large, open ward was designed to accommodate twelve beds against its northern wall and the same number along the southern wall. So only one of the patients along the northern wall was spared.

Ever since becoming chief, one of Klein's idiosyncratic orders had been to demand that adjacent beds be precisely equidistant from each other. To avoid incurring Klein's wrath, the ward staff routinely measured the distance between beds every morning before the professor's rounds and made whatever slight adjustments were needed to comply. No questions were asked. So the one thing Ignác could be sure of now was that this outbreak couldn't be blamed on some kind of new crowding problem. Otherwise he was utterly baffled.

As one after the next patient died in sequential beds, Ignác became frantic about getting to the bottom of the crisis. At first he was sure the cause must be some breach in his hand washing protocol. So Ignác now stationed himself at the entrance to the ward at the customary time every morning and loudly reproached anyone coming from the morgue who he felt was taking any shortcuts to his prescribed scrubbing routine.

By the second day of the outbreak, as the women continued to fall ill despite his nearly manic scrutiny, Ignác felt he had to get outside to think clearly. He walked briskly through the Schottentor of the city wall to the Volksgarten. But on his way, passing through the old city's familiar narrow streets, his mind became flooded with thoughts of sabotage and conspiracy. He tried to banish them, unconsciously uttering Hungarian dismissals: "*Nem! Nem!*" But the images kept rushing back.

It must be Klein himself. He couldn't bear the thought of being upstaged. Klein and maybe his old cronies, like Rosas and Schiffner. Maybe in cahoots?

The humiliated Viennese "establishment," he thought, and a little smirk flashed over his face. *Or maybe it was one of Klein's young disciples. Those damned sycophants. Braun, that pretender to his position. Yes, definitely Braun. Or Lumpe? That bastard Lumpe would do anything to please Klein, wouldn't he?* But then he shook his head vigorously as if to rule him out. *Späth, of course! Yes, Späth—that slimy, obsequious reptile.*

But what if it was someone less obvious? Someone like Chiari. Was Chiari really his good friend? Or was he now a spy as Klein's future son-in-law? Was it possible that Chiari was now taking instructions from the old man? Surely it couldn't be his supporters, like Skoda, Hebra, and Rokitansky. But no one can be beyond suspicion at this point.

And then he blurted out a final "*Nem!*" Passersby turned to look at him as if he were crazy. Impossible! Preposterous! Ignác finally arrived at the park. Finding a familiar bench to sit on, his mind going blank with confusion and rage, he dozed off.

On this occasion, he awoke to the chill of the late afternoon, in a daze. He realized how exhausted he must have been. A *gendarme* was standing a short distance away, looking at Ignác suspiciously. It was him again, the one with the long handlebar mustache from Metternich's box at the opera. Ignác turned his head away for a moment, and, when he looked again, the policeman had disappeared. Ignác took a walk around the park to shake the cobwebs and then returned to his bench. The celebrated roses of the Volksgarten were no longer in bloom, and the trees were almost bare of leaves. But Ignác felt reenergized.

Eleven of the twelve beds on only one side of the ward, he reminded himself. *What are the other facts? You must think like Rokitansky*, he thought to himself. The women in those beds had been stricken one by one, all within a day or two. The only one who survived was the first one: the one nearest the entrance to the ward.

But why?

Ignác was staring blankly into the distance. "What was different about her? Patient Number One had cancer. Cancer of the uterus. But why would that have helped her survive when the others didn't? If anything," Ignác reasoned, "you would think a mother sick with cancer would be more, not less, likely to come down with the fatal fever. Or maybe the cancer had nothing to do with it. Maybe it was just the fact that she was first in line!"

As Ignác repeated to himself "first in line," he willed his mind to be transported to ward rounds. He tried to replay them. "We scrub our hands before we enter. And then we go to the first patient to do a pelvic exam on her. The one nearest the entrance. Our one survivor in this case. And then we . . ." Ignác's reenactment of rounds jolted him to an abrupt stop.

"And then we go to the second bed's occupant to do a pelvic exam. *But we don't scrub our hands again between the first and second patient!* Nor between the others thereafter."

Everything suddenly fell into place in his mind. *If the first patient had a diseased organ that we touched during our exam—like cancer of the inner lining of the uterus—then we might carry its particles right into the internal organs of the next patient. In this case, the first patient's cancer was so invasive and advanced that it was discharging foul-smelling pus!* Ignác recalled how all the ward staff had been complaining for days about the putrid malodor emanating from the first bed.

He sprung to his feet, overcome with his moment of breathtaking insight. Maybe puerperal fever wasn't caused *only* by the transmission of material from cadavers. Maybe it could also be transmitted from one *live* person to another.

But there was no time to ruminate more about this now. There were new mothers to be saved.

Flushed with the excitement of possibly solving the cause of this most recent outbreak, Ignác dashed back to the hospital. Now that he knew what to do, there wasn't a minute to lose. As he ran through the streets, he somehow intuitively recognized that he had done much more than just solve a single problem. His new insight had fundamentally embellished and advanced his theory about the origins of puerperal fever.

Ignác was breathless, sweating, and disheveled when he got back to the maternity ward. New patients were already arriving to occupy the beds of those who had just died. And only Ignác knew that they were in immediate danger. So his first priority was to order the nurses to isolate the patient with uterine cancer in a separate room. When they asked why, he barked at them: "Don't ask questions now. Just do it, goddamnit!" And then he ordered disinfection of hands between every examination, not just before the first one. The students and staff fumed and grumbled about these further inconveniences.

But the outbreak was immediately terminated.

CHAPTER 17

DECEMBER 1847

By the first of December, more wash basins had been placed around the ward. There was growing opposition to Ignác's new order to wash hands with chlorinated lime before examining every single patient, not just upon entering the ward. Students, physicians, and even nursing staff railed at what they considered Ignác's irrational, bureaucratic rules.

The resistance to repeated hand washing was compounded by Ignác's increasingly bizarre behavior and his outbursts of utter rage when he even imagined that someone might be questioning him. Nobody dared to approach him anymore when he sat by himself for long periods at the back of the ward. From a distance, he was sometimes seen talking to himself, even arguing with himself. Ignác now felt he was assuming the role of a righteous lone warrior in combat against the forces of an ignorant establishment, the solitary protector of the defenseless mothers under his care. Whenever a thoughtful student would approach him with even a polite request to explain the rationale of the hand washing protocol, Ignác would rebuff him with a curt "It saves lives—don't you understand?" And he would sometimes even shake the poor inquirer by his coat lapels.

The time came for Kussmaul to leave Vienna and return to Heidelberg. Ignác bade him a dejected farewell. Firmly shaking hands, simultaneously grabbing each other's shoulders, they expressed their mutual admiration for each other. A valued friend and confidant was now gone.[60]

Ignác's sullen withdrawal now became punctuated by shattering headaches. He didn't know what was happening.

He continued to have uncontrolled explosions of temper, ever more frequent and unpredictable, ever more ferocious. Spittle formed around the corners of his mouth during these fits of rage, and he sprayed his perceived offenders with saliva. Students started to refer to him as a rabid dog.

It was at this low point that he received news that completely gutted him. It came in the form of a brief letter from Hans-Hermann Schwartz, the young physician from Kiel who was sent to observe the program in Vienna the previous year by his chief in Kiel, Gustav Adolf Michaelis.

Schwartz informed Ignác of the sudden tragic death of Professor Michaelis. Ever since the Kiel clinic had adopted Ignác's hand-scrubbing protocol a year earlier, the mortality rate from puerperal fever plummeted and remained at almost zero. But instead of being elated by it, Professor Michaelis fell into a deep depression, wracked by guilt for his beloved cousin's postpartum death, which he was now certain he had directly caused by his own careless examinations with unclean hands. He remained inconsolable. He also assumed total blame for countless other puerperal deaths he felt he could have prevented on his service. So, the good outcomes now only proved his culpability in the past. In despair, Professor Michaelis threw himself in front of an oncoming train approaching the station in Hamburg.[61]

The bitter irony of Michaelis's suicide was inescapable to Ignác. Here was a good man who did all the right things, yet conscience killed him. At the same time, all around him, he saw obstinate, arrogant men with the power to do the right things yet lacking the conscience to do so.

Late in the afternoon of New Year's Eve, an orderly came to tell Ignác that a young woman was waiting to see him at the front gate of the hospital on Alserstrasse. She had not been permitted entry. The visitor wouldn't give her name but was insistent that she would stay there for as long as it took for Ignác to come out to talk to her.

Indignant at the boldness of this intrusion, Ignác bolted from the ward, down the long corridor. He bounded down the staircase and through the outside courtyards in the freezing drizzle of the late afternoon to the hospital entrance. He had a guard unlock the heavy wooden doors and pull them open. On the street, he saw the back of a shivering, lone woman huddled in the corner against the biting cold wind. She was wearing a shabby overcoat, and her head was bundled in a heavy scarf.

"What the hell?" Ignác thundered.

She turned with a start, and their eyes met. Ignác now approached Caroline, his arms outstretched in joy.

"What's the matter, Charlinchen?" Ignác started, keeping his distance as she had gestured.

"I have been leaving notes under your apartment door, wondering where you were."

"I have hardly gone home in the past few weeks. But let's step inside the door, or we'll both freeze to death," said Ignác.

"I've come to realize that our relationship was never meant to work from the start. And I have to move on. There is so much to be done."

"But I have tried to tell you before that, in many ways, we have the same goals . . ."

"Yes, yes," she said, "I have my revolution and you have yours. We have talked about it many times. And, of course, we are both right. We are like two ships sailing in the same direction but so far apart that we can't see each other."

In the blistering cold, windy twilight of day, the freezing drizzle stopped, and the swelling sounds of crowds of people could be heard in the distance.

They could see more and more people even on the Alserstrasse, right outside the hospital gates, all heading in the same direction, singing, laughing, and producing a din.

Caroline took Ignác's hands.

"All right, let's be together tonight, and we'll talk afterwards. Just for tonight. Let's celebrate the New Year together."

By nightfall, Vienna's old city center was filled with revelers to celebrate *Silvester,* Vienna's New Year's Eve. Caroline and Ignác were soon swept along by the swelling crowds toward the Hoher *Markt.* It was still freezing cold, but at least the sharp wind was buffered by the crush of people.

As midnight approached, Caroline and Ignác met Caroline's friends and worked their way to St. Stephen's. Firecrackers exploded all around them. The crowd, made up of people of all social strata, rich and poor, cheered together deliriously at the sound of the booming bells of the cathedral chiming midnight. As they shouted "*Prosit Neujahr!*" and "*Einen guten Rutsch!*" friends and strangers embraced and kissed each other indiscriminately. They shared and swigged from each other's bottles of champagne and wine.

"Look at the camaraderie," beamed Caroline. "It's the spirit of the people . . . united and energized!"

"I am worried about what the New Year will bring, Charlinchen," said Ignác, suddenly subdued.

"Look!" hollered Caroline, tipsy from the wine. "There's an old gypsy woman over there doing *das Bleigiessen.*" She grabbed Ignác's hand and pulled him toward the open fire nearby. People were milling around the fortune teller, waiting for their turns to participate in the old *Silvester* tradition of pouring molten lead, as Caroline explained it to the puzzled Ignác.

After pocketing their tip of two coins, the old woman handed Caroline and Ignác each a spoonful of lead she had just melted over the fire. Caroline went first, quickly dumping the contents of her spoon into a basin of cold water. The lead solidified, and the gypsy fished out a piece of metal roughly in the shape of an anchor.

"Das ist *ein Anker*," she said. "It means you will be in need of help." Caroline's smile vanished, but the old woman quickly added, "Don't fret, Fräulein. You will soon get it, and it will make you very happy."

Then Ignác poured his spoonful of molten lead into the cold water. As the old woman scooped it out, her eyes suddenly widened in fright. "*Das Kreuz*! It's a cross," she exclaimed. Caroline gasped and put her hand to her mouth.

"A cross. Why I must be blessed!" Ignác wondered with a tenuous smile.

"Not blessed, sir. It signifies death."

Ignác and Caroline spent much of the rest of the night in his apartment, candidly talking about their relationship. They talked through the night, drank wine, cried, and laughed. And they greeted the dawn of the first day of 1848 with a new appreciation that they would have to part with a deep mutual affection and respect for each other's different life priorities, yet would be forever in love. Ignác escorted her home, as he had on that first night. And when they got there, they embraced, sobbing and smiling.

CHAPTER 18

THE NEW YEAR, 1848

Hebra could no longer contemplate the prospect of anyone other than his good friend Ignác being given credit for this major medical advance. He finally used his position as editor of the prominent Viennese medical journal, *Übertagungen der Kaiserlichen und Königlichen Gesellschafet der Ärtze zu Wein* to publish his own editorial in its January 1848 issue, announcing "the great breakthrough made by Ignác Semmelweis." [62]

But the tumultuous political and social events of 1848 throughout Europe, and particularly in Vienna, completely overshadowed all that was going on at the Vienna General Hospital. The chain reaction of upheavals began in Paris on the night of February 22, 1848. Barricades went up, and the first shots were fired when workers revolted over the failure of electoral reform that had been promised but never granted by King Louis Philippe. Within just two days, the king abdicated, effectively ending the French monarchy and giving birth to the Second Republic.

Word of the swift success of the popular uprising in France spread like wildfire throughout Europe. In Vienna, it emboldened students and academics who had been increasingly agitating for the reform of university government and the end of censorship, as well as other repressive practices of Metternich's regime. And it also buoyed the hopes of urban workers, peasants, and the growing ranks of the unemployed for major social reform. At the same time, there were burgeoning nationalist sentiments within the non-Austrian ethnic populations of the Habsburg Empire. Some extreme factions even advocated for full separation and independence.

Nowhere was this movement more manifest than in Hungary. On March 3, the charismatic radical Magyar reformer, Kossuth, delivered the first of a series of stirring, revolutionary speeches in front of the Hungarian parliament in Bratislava, the country's capital at the time. Kossuth addressed the assembly of legislators with his demands for a new constitution that would create an essentially autonomous Hungarian state.

Unlike his colleagues and students, who were much more engaged in current affairs, Ignác caught only bits and pieces of all this news. He was too preoccupied by his work in the hospital. He was mostly oblivious to the escalation of restlessness that was simmering outside the walls of the Allgemeine Krankenhaus.

Sunday, March 12, 1848, was a cold, overcast day with on-and-off drizzles, but Ignác had to get some fresh air after his morning patient rounds. He wandered around the nearby university campus and arrived at the Jesuitenkirche, the Baroque-style University Church, just as Sunday morning mass was letting out. He sensed from the high noise level of conversations among the exiting students that something was up. And instead of dispersing after mass as they usually did, all the students were streaming into the adjacent Alte Aula, the great hall of the university, on Ignaz Seipel-Platz. In the emerging crowd, he recognized one of his medical students, who was engaged in an animated debate with a group of friends. Ignác pulled him aside.

"What's going on here?" Ignác shouted to his student above the din.

"Haven't you heard, Dr. Semmelweis? The students are up in arms. We are ready to take on Metternich's oppressive government. Professor Füster just gave us a very inspiring sermon on freedom and human rights."

"What did he say?"

"He told us that Lent was a time of hope, and that truth would be victorious if the students were courageous."

Just then, Ignác spotted the imposingly large and charismatic theologian, Anton Füster, coming out of the church, mobbed by a large cluster of students. Füster was a familiar figure around the university, well known as a liberal, activist cleric.[63]

But Ignác didn't even bother to ask his student what they were planning to do in the university's great meeting hall.[64] Instead, he hurried back to the hospital. The next morning, Monday, March 13, Ignác wondered why none of the medical students came to work. They hadn't shown up for their required autopsy session in the morgue, either. So, after rounds, Ignác went out to explore the situation. Braun and Chiari agreed to cover for him for deliveries; they told Ignác they frankly didn't have much patience for irresponsible medical students and couldn't care less what kind of mischief they were up to this time.

Ignác came upon a crowd of thousands who had gathered in front of the *Ständehaus*, the house of estates in *Herrengasse,* to press their demands to the *Landtage,* Lower Austria's legislature. It wasn't just students, however. There were quite a few university faculty members, doctors, lawyers, and businessmen among the protesters. A small delegation of them were admitted to present their petition. As the hours passed with no word from inside, the crowd became restless, and some walked away.

Ignác pushed his way to the front of the crowd, which packed the building's courtyard, where he spotted an old friend. Adolf Fischhof had been a classmate of his in medical school and was a Hungarian compatriot. A slightly built, unassuming man with a sickly pale complexion and thick, black beard, Fischhof was a Jew who had always been more interested in politics than medicine. Like Ignác, Fischhof had done postgraduate training in obstetrics, so the two of them had become quite close, despite their very different career priorities.

"Adolf!" Ignác shouted over the heads of those who separated them. Fischhof waved, and the two friends squirmed their ways to each other.

"I figured you would be at something like this. What's going to happen here?" Ignác asked.

"Just wait and see," beamed Fischhof.

"Do you support them?"

"Of course!" Fischhof snapped back. "You know how I feel about the situation. It's intolerable. You must be supporting them, too."

"To be honest, Adolf, I've been so immersed in my work that I've lost track of daily events in the world. I don't even know exactly what the issues are here."

"But my friend," exclaimed Fischhof in disbelief. "We are on the very brink of revolution! A glorious revolution. Freedom of expression, workers' rights, the end of government oppression and censorship, no more poverty, a new tolerance for nationalist sentiments."

Fischhof suddenly heard his name shouted out from a distance and stopped. The excitement of the crowd was dissipating. Fischhof shook Ignác's hand with great vigor, embraced him, and as quickly as possible pushed his way up to the front. He shouted back to Ignác, "Just listen!"

Ignác started to leave but bumped into Hebra, who seemed quite excited, talking with someone Ignác didn't know.

"Lot of young doctors and medical students here today, eh?" Hebra asked. "But I wouldn't have expected you to be out here, too, Ignác. I am glad you could get away and see this historic moment."

There was a roar in the crowd coming from the courtyard. People in front of them were craning their necks, standing on tiptoes, and shifting positions to get a glance at what the commotion was about. A man was being hoisted onto the shoulders of others.

"Christ!" Ignác yelled. "Isn't that Fischhof?"

"Who?" Hebra asked as the crowd noise swelled.

"Adolf Fischhof. An obstetrician. He was my classmate in medical school, and we are friends from Hungary. We were talking to each other just a few minutes ago when he was called away, but he didn't tell me he was . . ."

After several shouts for quiet and some applause in unison up in the front, Fischhof spoke up. To Ignác's amazement, his voice was loud and powerful.

> *"Today we have a serious mission to fulfill. We must take heart, be decisive and hold out bravely. Those who have no courage on this day belong in the political nursery. Ill-advised statecraft has kept the peoples of Austria apart. They must now come together as brothers and increase their strength through unity."*[65]

The end of the oration was met with thunderous applause, and Ignác joined in, proud of his friend, as did Hebra. As a makeshift platform was now being assembled in the courtyard for other speakers, a journalist named Franz Putz climbed onto the drained fountain in the middle of the square. He held in his hand a German translation of Kossuth's stirring speech to the Hungarian Diet, the country's parliamentary assembly, on March 3. In the days since Kossuth's oration, word of its power had spread throughout Vienna, but this would be the first public reading of it in German. Putz recited it passionately.

> *. . ."From the charnel-house of the Viennese system a poison-laden atmosphere steals over us, which paralyzes our nerves and bows us when we would soar. The future of Hungary can never be secure while in the other provinces there exists a system of government in*

> *direct antagonism to every constitutional principle. Our task is to found a happier future on the brotherhood of all the Austrian races, and to substitute for the union enforced by bayonets and police the enduring bond of a free constitution . . . The dynasty must choose between its own welfare and the preservation of a rotten system."* [66]

With that final ultimatum to Vienna, the crowd erupted in a frenzy of cheering and hurrahs. It was now galvanized and soon grew greatly in size as word of insurgency spread rapidly through the city. As the impoverished people outside the city walls received reports of uprising, a huge number of workers and the unemployed stampeded through the previously closed city gates and flooded the Inner City. People now packed the adjacent streets, all the way to the heavily guarded Hofburg imperial palace. At about noon, a massive roar spread through the crowd, and there was a sudden surge of the masses toward the doors of the *Ständenhaus.*

"What's going on here?" shouted Ignác as he was swept along with the others.

"There! Look over there!" someone cried out, pointing frantically to the side of the building, where a man was seen locking the doors.

"They are locking our delegates inside!" came another howl, repeated by others. "They are arresting them! They are going to keep them as hostages!"

Before anyone could explain that the locking of the side doors of the *Ständenhaus* was nothing more than a daily, noontime routine, the mob had turned ugly. The front doors were broken down, the building was stormed, and the meeting chambers invaded.

Behind the surging mob, the imperial court in the Hofburg called out its military forces from the barracks to restore order. Lines of grenadiers with fixed bayonets now marched toward the back of the crowd, led on horseback by Archduke Albert, the commandant of the city. They were met with curses and pelted with stones and other flying objects. As the grenadiers tried to clear a path through the unmoving, enraged mob, shots rang out, and several people fell to the ground. Mass panic ensued as thousands scattered for their lives in every direction, running down the narrow streets of the old city and into houses and shops along the way. The first to die that afternoon was an eighteen-year-old mathematician at the university. Three others were shot to death by the soldiers, a young woman was trampled to death by the fleeing crowd, and countless others were badly injured.[67]

The dazed Ignác, now separated from Hebra, wandered aimlessly around the emptying square. He thought about going back to the hospital but then decided to stay behind to help tend to the wounded. The revolution so many others, like Caroline, had been talking to him about for months, but he never thought would actually happen, had started.

The next evening, one of the medical students who had been absent all day burst through the doors of the obstetrics ward. Seeing Semmelweis writing notes at the back of the room, he ran to him without hesitation and whispered excitedly, "Dr. Semmelweis. You won't believe this, but the student uprising has already spread to the workers in the suburbs. They tried to march to the Inner City, but the gates of the wall have remained locked. So, they stopped working and began to riot in the suburbs, burning buildings, looting stores, and smashing machines in the factories."

"Was their riot put down?" Ignác asked.

"No. And a couple of hours ago, Emperor Ferdinand made concessions on virtually all our demands. And listen to this: Metternich has resigned!"

An older nurse marched to where they were now talking loudly and angrily hissed, "Shhhh!"

Ignác nodded his acknowledgment, but turned back to the student. "Where is Metternich now?"

"No one knows for sure," replied the wild-eyed student, "but there are rumors that he fled to London in disguise.[68] In any case, the order was given for the troops to withdraw. And listen to this! We have been granted authority to arm ourselves and form an academic legion."[69]

"Are you sure?" Semmelweis demanded. "An academic legion? My God, it's a full-scale revolution!"

The events of March 1848 roused in Ignác a measure of latent Magyar patriotism. Perhaps it was fueled by his growing antipathy for Viennese elitism. In any case, Ignác proudly joined the academic legion and had himself fitted for a uniform. And he took to sometimes actually wearing the uniform when giving lectures at the medical school.

Klein deeply resented his ostentatious show of nationalism. Klein also undoubtedly viewed this outfit as subversive and perhaps even treasonous—even though many native Austrian students and university colleagues also wore it. This greatly inflamed Klein's already fractured relationship with Ignác, particularly because the costume represented such a public display of partisanship.

Work went on the best it could at the hospital. Most of the medical students, like the undergraduates at the university, all but abandoned their studies to participate in the demonstrations and street fighting. Student attendance on ward rounds and lectures was sporadic at best. Caught up in the excitement of the day and drawn to the action in the streets, Ignác sometimes relaxed his own stringent standards of supervision. Remarkably, statistics at the end of March showed not a single death (out of 276 births) on the wards for the first time in the recorded history of the Vienna General Hospital. By contrast, for the same month in 1846, there were 48 deaths for 311 births. These results were not merely fortuitous. Although unintended, they actually provided confirmation of Ignác's theory because they reflected the complete absence of students doing dissections in the morgue during that month in 1848.

After a lull in the demonstrations and riots, the revolution was reignited in mid-May, when Emperor Ferdinand and the imperial family fled to Innsbruck, and plans were announced to abolish the academic legion. New demands for social reform were made. With the official closure of the university for the summer, street fighting intensified on May 24.

Ignác walked to one particularly serious clash at sunset on May 28 on Michaeler Platz, fronting the Hofburg palace.[70] As he approached, he saw students frantically building barricades. Anything they could find was piled high to block one of the streets. Furniture, mattresses, and planks of wood were thrown out of windows. Overturned carts, chopped-down trees, wooden wheels, barrels, beams, and all sorts of lumber were brought to the site and indiscriminately heaped onto the barricade by the clamorous young men. The barrier was built up to the level of the first-floor windows of the abutting buildings. Women brought supplies, food, water, and bottles of wine. So he sat on the ledge of a non-functioning fountain in the middle of the square to just watch the unfolding events.[71]

He recognized one of his former students dragging a large, broken cart wheel. And then his eyes fell on a handsome, blond, mustachioed young man standing atop the mounting pile, shouting orders and appearing to be very much in charge. He looked familiar.

My God, realized the transfixed Ignác, *that looks like Franz, the hospital pharmacy apprentice.*

He checked his pocket watch; it was past five o'clock. Then he looked back up at Franz. *I can't believe it,* he mused. *Who would have thought of that polite and reserved young man as a revolutionary!*

Franz was yelling up to someone in a third-story window. A young woman leaned out, shouted something, and tossed Franz what looked like a bag. Ignác stood up in disbelief.

Can it be possible? Is that really Caroline?

Getting over his initial bewilderment, Ignác gave a little nod and expressed a knowing smile.

The distant tumult of an approaching mob could be heard. The uproar became ever louder and more boisterous as yet more young men could be seen streaming forward to the ramparts, some carrying muskets and rifles, some bearing the large red-white-green flags of Hungary, and others the Pan-Slavic blue-white-red tricolor. In the square, in front of the barricades, some of the men were setting fires. Others began to hurl stones at the windows of the stately government buildings facing the square. Ignác scurried to the safety of an alleyway leading out of the square, positioning himself next to two squatting men who appeared to be newspaper reporters.

Approaching from the opposite side of the square, imperial troops came into view, marching in formation. The thunderous clip-clopping of boots stomping in unison on the cobblestones echoed across the square as the infantry led the way, resplendent in white uniforms with red trim. They were followed by white-coated cavalry, including horses pulling cannons. Black-and-yellow Habsburg flags flew alongside red-white-red Austrian flags with the familiar double-headed black eagle seals at their center.

Now in the open square, the order to the troops was shouted to halt. In response to another series of orders, the soldiers assumed firing formation, front row on one knee. Rifles were aimed at the barricades, cannons were pulled up to the front line, and the dragoons on horseback drew their swords. And then all movement on both sides stopped cold, and a tense silence descended over the Michaeler Platz.

The stillness was broken by a rock thrown by someone from atop the barricades. Then came another, followed by a barrage of rocks pelting the troops. The soldiers moved back to the opposite edge of the square, out of range of the projectiles. The retreat was greeted by whoops and yelps from the insurgents.

Now emboldened, several young men ran from the barricades toward the troops, picking up more stones and hurling them in their direction. But this time, the artillery responded by moving to the front, more orders were thundered, and the troops resumed their slow forward march. Howitzer cannons launched a barrage of shells that exploded in mid-air, raining down their fragments on the men behind the barricades. Some atop the barricades were hit, but most of the screaming came from behind them as the air filled with smoke.

Ignác strolled aimlessly to absorb the thrilling atmosphere. In the distance he heard volleys of gunfire and the shouting of crowds coming from different directions. And he caught glimpses of other barricade skirmishes down the narrow streets of the old city. He was energized by what he was seeing. He even fantasized about joining the rebels. But then thoughts of his patients in the hospital disrupted his reverie. *What if I am arrested and imprisoned? Or badly injured or killed. Who is there in the hospital to take my place? Who would pick up my work to make sure the wholesale murder of those helpless mothers doesn't start all over again? Isn't that just as important as all this?*

The air in Vienna in the following months was filled with excitement, even euphoria. But it was also tinged with an undercurrent of anxiety about how this would all end. Workers and the unemployed poor were now seen in ever-increasing numbers vocally participating in meetings and rallies organized by the students. But many amongst the well-to-do middle class fled the city for prolonged summer vacations, out of harm's way. Klein was one of them. He went to Innsbruck, where the Emperor and his court also happened to be hiding out.

Fearing for Caroline's safety since spotting her at the barricades, Ignác regularly checked the general hospital admissions register. All wounded in the street fighting were routinely brought to the *Allgemeine Krankenhaus* for treatment. With even more dread, he looked likewise at the daily list of those killed. This was especially easy to do, because the bodies of all persons found dead, killed accidentally or by violence anywhere in the city of Vienna had to be brought to the hospital's Dead House for autopsies supervised by Rokitansky himself. But there were virtually no further violent confrontations through the summer and into fall. The medical students returned to their ward assignments.

Ignác went to the pharmacy to check on supplies. Franz wasn't there, and he was informed by the apprentice who let him in that they hadn't seen him for weeks. Ignác asked to see Direktor Schuster, who shuffled out of his office.

"No, Franz is no longer here. I really don't think pharmacy will be the career for him."

Ignác couldn't get Schuster to say anything more about it, so he asked if everything was all right with the antiseptic solution supply.

"Yes, of course," said Schuster, still not looking up. "Let me show you. Wait right here." And he shuffled back into his office, returning after quite a while holding a piece of paper.

"This is it," Schuster continued, tremulously holding up to his eyes what appeared to be a handwritten note. "Strict instructions to me about making up the solution for Dr. Semmelweis's basin."

Ignác wondered who and why anyone would have written those strict instructions.

"But there are now several basins every day," he said.

"Yes, yes," Schuster replied, roughly folding the note with his shaking hands and stuffing it into his coat pocket after missing its opening a couple of times. "Six basins. One labeled for Dr. Semmelweis—prepared separately—and the others for everybody else, just like you ordered."

And, without once making eye contact, the old man turned back.

CHAPTER 19

AUGUST 1848

As the sun began to set on Monday, August 28, 1848, Ignác took one of his customary getaway walks to the Volksgarten during a lull in activity in the maternity ward. There he happened on a large gathering. They were raptly listening to a speech being given by a young man. The speaker was no orator, but what he had to say was frequently interrupted by bursts of applause. Ignác had been to some of the rousing political rallies that were held in the park in the months following the March uprising, but this assembly seemed different. The atmosphere was less celebratory, less raucous. As Ignác ambled toward the front, he got a close look at the stocky young man speaking on the podium. He had luxuriant but unkempt black hair that hung over his ears, just beginning to prematurely grey in the front, and the features of his face were practically buried under a bushy, coal-black beard and moustache. All the hair made his perpetual frown and stern, piercing eyes stand out even more.

Ignác listened for a while as this bear-like man spoke about social revolution, class struggle, the scourge of capitalism, and kept referring to terms Ignác had heard before but never bothered to understand, like the *bourgeoisie* and the *proletariat*.

"Who is this angry fellow?" he whispered to a man standing next to him.

"Karl Marx," the man replied without looking at Ignác.[72]

"What the hell is he really talking about?" wondered Ignác.

"Ssshhh!" the other man whispered, glaring at him. "If you don't know, you shouldn't be here."

Intrigued, Ignác stayed for the rest of the speech and the one that followed by a man named Julius Fröbel, who hit on similar themes. "Workers of all countries, unite!" both men exhorted. But a comment that Marx made about the necessity for revolution resonated with Ignác. "Violence is the midwife of every old society pregnant with a new one."

As the buzzing crowd began to disperse at the end of the program, a student dressed in the uniform of the academic legion hurriedly approached Ignác. He stood out because very few were still wearing the uniform that had been so omnipresent in the streets in those early, more bellicose spring days of the revolution.

"Herr Professor," the student said breathlessly, "what are *you* doing here?"

"I am sorry," replied Ignác, bending backwards at the waist to scan the young man from head to foot. "I don't think I know you."

"Sure you do!" said the student grinning from ear to ear, "I am Dorfmeister."

"Dorfmeister?"

"Yes, Hans Dorfmeister. The medical student you scolded so loudly a couple of years ago when I objected to your orders to scrub hands."

"Ah, yes—how could I forget that young man who was so unenlightened?" replied Ignác.

"'Unenlightened' isn't the word, professor," Dorfmeister shot back with an amiable laugh. "I would say 'ignorant' and 'stupid' would better describe me at that time. But let me assure you, I have learned my lesson. You were completely right, of course."

Ignác looked mollified.

"But," continued Dorfmeister, "I didn't know you were a *Marxist*! Sure, I remember you wearing this uniform sometimes when you lectured," he said, pointing to his own attire, "and also that Magyar-style suit of yours, of course, but I never for a minute imagined you to be such a revolutionary! It's so great to see you here as an admirer of Karl Marx."

"To be honest, Dorfmeister, I happened to be taking a walk to the Volksgarten. I just stopped here to see what all the commotion was about," said Ignác. "I don't know this man."

"Yeah, yeah!" responded Dorfmeister with a dismissive grin. "You want to tell me you have never read the writings of Marx? You've never even heard of him?"

With that, Dormeister grabbed Ignác s hand to shake it vigorously, and then left to catch up with some friends. From a distance he turned back, still smiling, and shouted, "Thank you, Herr Professor . . . for everything!"

Ignác didn't like the brazen student's tone at all.

In October 1848, with the Emperor and his court still in self-imposed exile, the Habsburg forces struck back against the Viennese insurgents with a vengeance. The counterrevolution was led by Prince Windischgrätz, a ruthlessly effective general who had earlier gained notoriety for crushing an uprising in Prague. By October 23, the imperial army, commanded by Windischgrätz, had surrounded the city.

Ignác left the hospital late in the evening of October 27 and started out for his apartment in Alservorstadt. But on the way he was riveted by the sight of what looked like fireworks coming from the direction of Josefstadt. As he got closer, the explosions in the area became louder. Then, looking out toward the Ottakring district, Ignác was astounded to see that the suburbs were ablaze and the night sky was lit up by grenades, shells, and rockets. Ignác walked cautiously, drawn to the sight. The mostly empty, dark expanse of heathland sloped gently upward. And when he reached the crest, he stopped in his tracks. Ahead of him was the vista of a full-scale battle in progress. The imperial troops under Prince Windischgrätz were in attack, firing on the mobile guards who appeared to be barricaded in a cemetery. The fire and rockets lit up the sign: Schmeltz cemetery.[73]

Ignác suddenly felt an inexplicable chill. He immediately ran back to his apartment just outside the city wall.

Over the next two days, the insurrection in Vienna was vanquished decisively. The Viennese revolutionaries had been hoping to be saved by Kossuth's army, which was rumored to be already in the outskirts of the city. On the last day of this final desperate insurrection, October 31, St. Stephen's Square was virtually empty while cannons thundered in the far distance.[74]

Order was soon restored in Vienna. Leaders of the uprising disappeared from view. Among them were quite a few students, especially those who were not native Austrians. They were arrested, deported, expelled from the university, escaped, or somehow silenced and reintegrated into society. The seeds of reform had been sown, but it would take some time before any tangible impact of the revolution would be recognized. This was likewise the case for academic medicine in Vienna. Many of the old-guard physicians never came back to work, to the great benefit of all. But other reactionaries, like Klein and Rosas, resumed their positions of authority, perhaps a little admonished but not at all mellowed. On the surface, life was back to normal in the imperial capital. In contrast, although Ignác didn't know it at the time, conditions were much different in Budapest.[75]

The cessation of armed combat in the streets made Ignác even more wary about his personal situation at the hospital. One encounter with Klein in the hospital, shortly after cessation of hostilities in Vienna, underscored his predicament. As they passed each other, Klein grabbed Ignác by the arm and inspected him from head to toe.

"Aaah, Semmelweis," Klein exclaimed with a sardonic smirk. "I see you are no longer in uniform."

"I don't know what you mean, Herr Professor," Ignác replied.

"That fancy native Magyar attire of yours with the ridiculous boots. And then it was the uniform of the academic legion. Politics doesn't mix with medicine, Semmelweis. We physicians rise above all that!"

We do, do we? Ignác thought to himself but didn't say it.

On March 20, 1849, Ignác's two-year term as Klein's Assistant came to an end. Despite their differences, Ignác fully expected his appointment to be extended for an additional two years, just as it had been for his predecessor, Franz Breit. After all, he had done more than just a good job, he thought. So he was stunned by Klein's decision to terminate him. There were no qualified applicants for the position, so Ignác was even more chagrined to learn that Klein had already appointed Carl Braun to be his next Assistant. Braun was an internist by training and had very little experience in obstetrics.

Skoda, Rokitansky, and Hebra protested on behalf of Ignác. But Klein stood his ground. His friend Rosas, who had by now become vice director of the hospital, firmly rejected their appeals and vociferously upheld Klein's sole authority to make such a decision.

Once again, Hebra, Skoda, and Rokitansky had to prod Ignác into action to formally protest the decision to Rosas. Ignác was extremely reluctant to do it, especially because it would mean circumventing his mentor, Klein. He still couldn't cast aside his deep feelings of inferiority and his conviction that he was unworthy of being at the University of Vienna. However, he finally went to see Rosas in his magnificent new administrator's office. Ignác was terrified, and Rosas wasted no time getting down to business.

"I can't understand what you hope to accomplish with this meeting with me. A decision is a decision, and neither Professor Klein nor I owe you an explanation. Don't you get it? You are already in a lot of trouble, you know, so why risk making it much worse?"

"I don't understand," said Ignác tremulously.

"Haven't you been told that you are under investigation for treason?"

"*What?*" Ignác replied. "I don't know what you are talking about."

"Look around you. Look at what is happening here in Vienna to your colleagues and friends, all the people who stupidly tried to challenge the authority of the emperor!"

"But I didn't . . ." Ignác was stammering: he didn't know where to begin.

"Well, you thought you could embarrass your senior professors, including Professor Klein, by brashly appearing at work and teaching in that goddamned academic legion uniform of yours. And that Magyar suit. What was *that* supposed to mean, for Christ's sake? *Who* do you think you are, boy? And *where* do you think you are?"

Rosas was now bellowing and turning frighteningly red in the face. Shaken, Ignác was about to say something about other respected faculty members, like Hebra, also wearing the uniform of the academic legion, but then he thought the better of it.

"And *this*," continued Rosas, trying to collect himself, opening the lap drawer to his desk and taking out a sheet of paper. "This tops it all off. It says here that you are an avowed *Marxist*. It says here that you have joined his fight to topple the government. You are not just a sympathizer. You are a downright militant revolutionary!"

"But, Professor Rosas, this is all a big mistake . . ."

Rosas wasn't listening; he just continued ranting. "That's why you are in so much trouble, Semmelweis!" Drawing out and accentuating the last part of Ignác's surname was quite calculated, and it came with a sneer of disgust.

"I think I know what you are referring to. I even think I know who reported this. But you must believe me. I just happened to be walking through the Volksgarten that afternoon, . . ."

"This is not intended to be a cross-examination," Rosas said, more calmly. "Not yet. We need to collect more evidence of your involvement. But you came here to appeal the decision of Professor Klein to deny you another term as Assistant, right?"

"Right."

"So I am here to affirm, in no uncertain terms, that this decision is upheld. And that's all there is to say."

Now unexpectedly unemployed, Ignác was urged by Rokitansky to apply for a position as *Privatdozent* in obstetrics. This was essentially a private practice position that also gave him privileges to teach medical students. Ignác viewed this as a heartbreaking consolation prize. However, what choice did he have but to request it? A decision would not be forthcoming for several months. In the meantime, Ignác was to have no formal responsibilities.

And then, in October, it came. Even his *Privatdozent*[76] application was turned down! No explanation was given. The shock of the decision practically paralyzed him. He felt like the world had suddenly stopped around him. His supporters were dumbfounded. But they tried to point out to him that this was a particularly inopportune time politically for Ignác as a Hungarian. It coincided with the final defeat of his homeland's uprising as well as the consolidation of counterrevolutionary power by the new Hapsburg prime minister, the virulently anti-Magyar Prince Felix of Schwarzenberg. But Ignác couldn't have cared less about politics at that moment. He knew this rejection must have been a deeply personal one, and it caused him immense pain. In the days and weeks ahead, his mind became totally preoccupied with hopelessness about his shattered future, humiliation, and absurd fantasies of revenge. He felt physically ill as waves of self-pity, indignation, and fury washed over him, virtually incapacitating him.

"A shameful setback," Hebra consoled him several days later. "No doubt political!" Hebra himself was still steaming about it but knew that it would hardly help matters to share his anger with Semmelweis in this state.

"You must apply again," Hebra said.

And Ignác did, but wasn't permitted to do so until the following February, in 1850. This time, at the urging of Rokitansky, he included in his application a special request to be exempted from the prohibition of *Privatdozents* from teaching medical students using actual cadavers in their demonstrations. *Privatdozents* were restricted to instruction with life-sized mannequins, called 'phantoms," like the midwives had to use. But after all, Ignác had become an exceptionally proficient prosector. So it was only fitting that he should be allowed to use human dissection in his demonstrations to the medical students. The re-application was accompanied by strong support, including from Carl Haller, a respected department head and hospital administrator, who had personally reviewed the obstetrical records of the hospital and verified Ignác's findings.[77] This time, the ministry promptly indicated that Ignác's application for the position of *Privatdozent* would be accepted. In fact, the new minister decried the earlier rejection and suggested that it was, indeed, probably a matter of political intrigue, for which he had no patience. Ignác was informed that a decision letter would follow. Ignác was cautiously relieved.

CHAPTER 20

MAY 1850

While awaiting formal notification of his *Privatdozent* status, Ignác finally accepted Skoda's invitation to speak in front of the distinguished assembly of the Medical Society of Vienna. He was to deliver a series of three lectures, one per month, presenting for the first time the long-awaited report of his discoveries.

He took the stage on the evening of May 15, 1850, in the surgical lecture hall that was located on the ground floor of the *Alte Universität*, home of the Medical Society of Vienna at that time.[78] The lecture hall was filled with a large gathering of eminent physicians from Vienna and other parts of the empire. Thick cigar and pipe smoke hung in the hot, stuffy air of the room. The loud chatter of the lecture hall died down as Skoda, holding his omnipresent stethoscope, got up to introduce Ignác. As he did so, only a few scattered coughs to clear throats punctured the silence of anticipation. Rokitansky, sitting in the front row, was president of the Medical Society at the time, something that should have been reassuring to Ignác. But it wasn't.

Ignác was standing right next to the podium facing the audience while Skoda was making his opening comments. He suddenly began to feel light-headed and sweaty as he looked out at the packed rows of pink-faced, whiskered, and saucer-eyed, bespectacled men, all dressed in dark grey or black frock coats. He became acutely aware that they were all professors and doctors of distinction, while he himself had failed to achieve even a simple faculty position. His heart pounding, vision dimming, perspiring and trembling, Ignác suddenly felt that he couldn't go on. He feared he would faint. Behind the haze of thick tobacco smoke that enveloped the audience, the whole room of occupied seats seemed to physically drift slowly away from him. These men began to appear indistinguishable from each other. And as they did, it curiously struck Ignác that they looked like a large pack of fat rats, all sitting on their hind legs, bruxing, boggling, and staring at him.[79]

The terror of the moment immediately receded. In this state of private amusement, he began to read his lecture in a muffled tone.

"Speak up! We can't hear you," came a shout from near the back of the auditorium. The discourteous interruption jolted Ignác to regain his poise.

To begin, he summarized the facts. Ignác said that, from the time the lying-in service of the Vienna General Hospital was founded in 1784 up to the point when the teaching of the anatomic basis of medicine became a requirement for medical students at the Vienna School of Medicine, no major epidemic of puerperal fever had occurred there. In fact, the mortality rate in Boer's earlier years as chief of obstetrics never once rose above one percent per year, whereas, under Klein, there had been periods where almost one out of two died of the complication. He concluded with his interpretation of the data that the cause of the deaths was "organic material which had become putrid" that had been introduced into the women's bodies. Furthermore, this was the case whether the material originated from a cadaver or from another living organism. The result is death from the pathologically demonstrated "exudations and metastases." Ignác also said for the first time at this meeting that unclean utensils could also be conveyers of the infection.

Ignác sensed that things had gone quite well. But his uneasiness returned when the end of his presentation was greeted by silence, followed by only scattered applause. Rokitansky stood up and announced that the second presentation in June would be mostly devoted to questions and comments from the audience. This, Ignác knew, would be the real test of his mettle.

When the meeting reconvened, the first to stand was Eduard Lumpe, the obsequious Klein protégé. Lumpe's tone was combative.

"You well know about my publications implicating harmful miasma as one of the main causes of puerperal fever. Do you not? I am surprised you didn't mention them in your lecture."

Ignác decided to not respond and just let Lumpe continue.

"It would have been important to discuss the issue of overcrowding in the First Division as an important atmospheric variable, don't you think? It is well known that there were—and there continue to be—more admissions to the First Division than to the Second Division on a regular basis."

"Yes," replied Ignác, "Dr. Lumpe is correct."

After a pause, he continued, "But there are also, as Dr. Lumpe must know, more *beds* in the First Division. So, in fact, in terms of percentage of occupied beds, the First Division has been actually the *less* crowded of the two services."

Then, as Lumpe sat back down, Ignác added, "And by the way, I do know that Dr. Lumpe has been recently scrubbing his hands in my chlorinated water before examining his patients. I am surprised that he thinks that my hand-washing routine would be an effective intervention to prevent any harm caused by those . . . atmospheric miasmas." This was greeted by chuckles from some in the audience and a smile from Ignác. Lumpe crossed his arms and legs tightly, scowled, and lowered his head.

And then came an especially vicious and cowardly attack from a certain Dr. Zipfel, who was previously an assistant in the Second Division of the Vienna General Hospital's maternity service, and had been recently appointed a *Privatdozent*. Zipfel had done a great deal of dissecting in the morgue, and the mortality rate in his division, in which deliveries were otherwise limited to midwives, had become unusually high, at 12 to 15 percent per year. Zipfel previously gave Ignác permission to use these data and had actually congratulated him in private, confiding in him that he himself had very nearly made the same discovery. But now, suddenly, and much to Ignác's bewilderment, perhaps under pressure from others, he tore into Ignác with some confusing arguments. Rather than treating the remarks of this obscure obstetrician with contempt, Ignác resisted the temptation to publicly remind Zipfel of his very different viewpoint not so long ago and just carried on with the data at hand.[80]

The next question came from Dr. Seyfert, who challenged Ignác about his statistical methods. Dr. Seyfert proclaimed that Dr. Semmelweis's data did not in any way refute the miasmal theory of disease causation.

Then a debonair blond man with a mustache stood up. "I am Professor Friedrich Wilhelm Scanzoni," he began, "from Prague. I have known about Dr. Semmelweis's findings from others, even though Dr. Semmelweis has chosen not to publish them for some reason." Ignác gulped and glanced at Skoda, who was shaking his head in agreement.

"This would be a great breakthrough," Scanzoni continued, "if it could be verified. But it can't be. It can't be verified because it is simply wrong! I have done the experiment myself in Prague."

Murmurs could be heard throughout the audience.

"Chlorine washing was first adopted in the maternity hospital in Prague in March 1848, when puerperal fever was frequent and virulent. It was used continuously through the second half of March and through all of April. During this period, we also visited the autopsy room very rarely. Since the incidence of sickness was not reduced, chlorine washings were temporarily given up as an experiment. What was not achieved with the most conscientiously undertaken and supervised washings then came about through a more favorable state of the *genius epidemicus* [natural circumstances]—the incidence of disease suddenly dropped."

Now the lecture hall was buzzing with subdued chatter. Some scattered applause even broke out. Scanzoni sat down but quickly rose again. "And I understand, Dr. Semmelweis, that your Assistant position in Vienna has not been renewed. That is regrettable."

Ignác said nothing as the commotion in the auditorium escalated. Finally, Rokitansky stood and addressed Ignác. "Dr. Semmelweis, would you like to respond to Professor Scanzoni's comments?"

"Yes," said Ignác, collecting himself. "I greatly appreciate the eminent Professor Scanzoni's report of his experiments. There could be several explanations for the discrepancies in our findings, and we must determine what they are." He said no more except, "Next question please."

A gloomy Ignác walked home alone that evening. He wondered why he should even bother to give the third lecture.

Ignác went to his third lecture to Vienna Medical Society in July with serious misgivings about how it would all end. He had a foreboding that the outcome would surely spell the end of his career. But then the tide turned. Chiari stood and directly faced Klein, who was now his father-in-law, seated at the end of the front row.

"I wish to say," Chiari started, still looking straight at Klein, "that I believe Dr. Semmelweis's discovery is a monumental achievement. Its importance is nothing less than the discovery of vaccination by Jenner. In my opinion, the detailed presentation of all the data Dr. Semmelweis so clearly wrote out on the blackboard in the course of these three lectures makes an irrefutable case for his conclusions about the cause of childbed fever."[81]

Loud applause erupted from the back of the audience. Then, one after another stood up, including Arneth, who had been Assistant in the Second Division while Semmelweis was Assistant in the First, Theodor Helm, a noted obstetrician who had pioneered the use of physical examination in pregnant women, and Anton Hayne, a scholar in comparative medicine, to praise Ignác's work and its potential of great impact for patient care.

Ignác had answered the most challenging questions with thoughtfulness, restraint, and remarkable poise. Rokitansky adjourned the general meeting.

Sweating profusely but relieved and triumphant, Ignác was swept out of the lecture hall by back-slapping colleagues and nodding physicians he had never met. Following close behind them, Hebra was grasping Skoda's arm, grinning broadly. Ignác stopped and turned around to ask the two of them a question with a troubled look on his face.

"I was going to respond to Scanzoni in detail. How can he justify 'experimenting' with alternating periods of hand washing and no hand washing, and what kinds of conclusions can he draw from doing something like that for just four to six weeks at a time? And then I was going to really take my dig and ask him where *he* has published *his* data! Nowhere, you can be sure!"

"You did the right thing, Ignác," exclaimed Hebra joyfully tousling Ignác's hair. "If there is one thing I have learned in academic medicine, it's never to get into a pissing contest with a skunk!" Hebra let out a big laugh, and Ignác thought he even detected the trace of a smile on Skoda's face. Ignác continued on with the group ahead.

"You see, Skoda, there was nothing to worry about with Semmelweis's state of mind. He was a smashing success. And weren't you impressed with how clearly he handled the questions?" Hebra asked.

"Yes, I think you are right," replied Skoda. "I was worried that he was on the verge of a nervous breakdown last year, but maybe he was just overworked. Maybe all he needed was a good rest."

Ignác was at first exhilarated by the reception of his lectures but as soon as the excitement faded, he began to brood over the attacks on him and how poorly he must have responded to them. His state of melancholy crept back. His constant indignation and rages subsided, but they were replaced by an unremitting sadness. He spent endless hours in gloomy introspection and soul-searching. And a state of inertia took over that terrified him more than anything.

He had the time now, but he still couldn't get himself to write. Skoda, Hebra, and Rokitansky had given up pestering him about publishing his work.

He couldn't get himself organized to do many of the animal experiments that needed to be done to scientifically prove his concept of puerperal fever, even though the famous physiologist Ernst Brücke had agreed to work with him on it in his laboratory, and the Academy of Sciences had offered him a research grant to support it.[82] Instead, he spent much of his waking hours walking the streets of Vienna and sitting alone in cafes, ruminating.

Ignác became aware of how utterly lonely he was. His father had died not long after his mother, and, since then, he'd kept referring to himself as ". . . an orphan . . ." He had lost all contact with his brothers and sisters in Hungary and didn't even know if they had all survived the revolution. And he had no real friends left. Marko, his roommate and guide to his new life in Vienna, had returned to Hungary. Kussmaul had gone back to Germany, Kolletschka had died, and Caroline was out of his life. His mind kept rewinding to those good old days and lamenting them. But wasn't he too young to be absorbed in nostalgia? He was no longer finding solace in the companionship of his few advocates and mentors. After all, he thought, they all had their own agendas and career ambitions. In any case, Rokitansky was really a father figure and mentor, Skoda was peculiar, and Hebra now spent all his spare time with his own family.

Ignác considered and reconsidered the facts of his own situation: out of a job, idle much of the time, aimless, and without hope for the career he had worked so hard and done so much to attain.

On October 1, Ignác received the written notification he was expecting from the ministry, finally approving his application to become *Privatdozent.*

But his heart sank when he read further that the recommended provision to teach with human cadavers had been denied. Having to resort to using only phantoms for demonstrations rendered the *Privatdozent* position virtually meaningless in his mind. But mostly, he was stung by being snubbed yet again!

Rokitansky, Skoda, and Hebra were outraged, not just for Ignác but perhaps even more for themselves. After all, this rejection undermined their growing influence and power as leaders of academic medicine at the university. Ignác's use of cadavers for dissection had been verbally approved, they were certain, several months ago, so somehow, somewhere, someone in the ministry altered it.

This last insult ate away at Ignác's soul like nothing had done in the past. Maybe it was the cumulative effect of all that had gone before. Maybe he just no longer had the energy to fight. He couldn't sleep for two days and nights. And on the third night, he tossed and turned in his bed and stared wide-eyed at the ceiling before he finally fell asleep well past midnight, emotionally spent. No sooner had he done so when he was startled awake by loud, insistent knocking on his apartment door.

CHAPTER 21

EARLY OCTOBER 1850

He saw from his window that it was still pitch dark outside. Disoriented and alarmed, he fumbled to light a candle and then lurched toward the door. He opened it without even thinking to ask who it was. The silhouette of a tall man stood in the dark hallway.

"Doctor Semmelweis, please, we need your help at once," stammered the agitated stranger. As Ignác held the candle up to the man's face, he was astonished to see Franz Siebert, the young apothecary apprentice.

"Franz!" exclaimed Ignác. "What in God's name brings you here in the middle of the night? And how did you know where . . . ?"

"I owe you a long explanation for all that's happened, but I must speak quickly now because there is a matter of great urgency."

Ignác lit an oil lamp on his table.

"It's about Caroline. I got to know her some time ago, working together with other young people. We were organizing to mobilize the poor of the city, you know, who were demanding change. And, of course, she told me all about you, and how wonderful . . . anyway, and how you broke off your relationship."

"Yes, yes. New Year's Eve," interrupted Ignác, "three years ago. That was our last time together. But what's wrong, Franz? What has happened to Caroline? Is she in trouble? Is she sick?"

"No, nothing like that," replied Franz. "You see, over time, with the revolution and all . . ."

"*What*, goddammit, just tell me!" demanded Ignác, now wide awake and himself on edge.

"Well, sir, we got married, and Caroline got pregnant, and now she is in labor. She is in terrible pain, doctor."

"Where is she, for God's sake?" Ignác raised his voice as he shook Franz by the arms.

"She is in the hospital. I took her there an hour ago. Where you work. But we couldn't find you."

"All right, let's go there right away," said Ignác, now more reassured and composed.

"Oh, how can I ever thank you, Doctor Semmelweis," Franz sighed in relief. "I was brought here in a carriage, and it's waiting for us outside. I can't tell you how grateful we are."

"Oh, shut up," yelled Ignác with a furtive smile in his eyes. "We don't have time for this. And anyway, stop calling me 'Doctor Semmelweis,' for God's sake. Call me 'Ignác.' I am already beginning to feel like part of your family!"

Ignác quickly got dressed and threw a bunch of instruments into the large black bag on his desk: delivery forceps, hooks, and speculum. Then he carefully placed some glass bottles among the instruments, each filled with clear liquids and labeled. They ran outside and jumped into the waiting carriage.

"On the double," shouted Franz to the driver. "Back to the hospital as fast as your old horse can fly!"

And they were off, their carriage careening around the corners of the empty, narrow streets, jouncing along the slick cobblestones of the main streets and muddy, rough, dirt back roads. The deserted city was blanketed with fog so dense that the sidewalk gaslights seemed suspended in midair.

Franz kept talking, but Ignác became silent and distracted. He suddenly felt a sinking feeling deep inside, in the pit of his stomach, as if it had dropped. Franz asked him what the matter was, but Ignác just glanced at him for a moment and then went back to vacantly staring straight ahead.

The speeding, rattling carriage repeatedly felt like it was about to hurtle out of control and crash. Ignác snapped back into the moment and grabbed Franz's knee to steady himself.

The carriage came to a stop at the hospital entrance on Alserstrasse. The two men vaulted out of it, raced through the courtyards of the hospital campus to the lying-in building, and up the stairs to the maternity ward, straight to Caroline's bedside.

Caroline was huffing and puffing in the middle of a contraction when they arrived. She was most assuredly in advanced labor.

"Ignác, I am so glad you are here," she said, taking his hands. "We have been so afraid of what might happen. You are the only one we would trust to deliver our baby. Will everything be all right? Is the baby all right? Do we have the childbed fever? My pains are terrible."

"I am sure everything is fine," said Ignác, placing the back of his hand on Caroline's forehead and then taking her pulse. He nodded and smiled at both of them for assurance. "But we must get to work now, my dear. And *you*," he said to Franz, "*you* must leave now. Go outside until I come to fetch you." He shooed Franz out of the ward.

A nurse came scurrying to join Ignác at the bedside, holding up a candle-lit lantern. He knew her. She was the same elderly nurse had greeted him on that first early morning of his term as Klein's Aspirant.

"How frequent are the contractions?" Ignác asked.

"They are coming every two minutes," said the nurse.

"And the water has broken?"

"Yes, hours ago," replied Caroline.

"Good. Well, let's examine you to see how far along you are. It's too dark here to inspect, so I will just palpate the cervical opening to estimate its dilation. Can I have the basin of liquid chlorine to scrub my hands, nurse?"

"Doctor Semmelweis, I haven't seen any of those basins for quite a while," she replied.

"Do you mean they have been ordered off the floor?" Ignác asked with dismay.

"Oh, I don't know if they have been 'ordered off,' exactly, sir. Some days they are here, you see, but on most days, they aren't," replied the nurse, shrugging her shoulders. "But I know they haven't been here in the past several days."

"Well, then, please get me just an empty basin. Or any kind of washbowl you can find anywhere in the hospital."

"Yes, sir. I will look," she said.

After much delay, the nurse returned with a large bowl. "I had to go over to the general wards to find one."

Ignác placed it on a table nearby. He then took the large glass bottle from his black bag and poured all its clear liquid contents into the bowl, taking care not to spill any of it in the nearly complete darkness. He also came up with a hand brush and some soap from his bag. The nurse fetched some clean towels. Removing his jacket and rolling up his sleeves, Ignác plunged into his ritual of vigorous hand and arm scrubbing. Caroline was crying with pain again, but Ignác continued to scrub and rinse until he was satisfied. Only then did he return to her bedside for the examination.

Her contractions having subsided, Caroline whispered to him, "But didn't you tell me that it had to be done only after doing autopsies?"

"You remember well, dear Caroline. But since then, we have discovered that it must be done at any time before we examine a patient or do a delivery."

"Your poor hands—it must be terribly harsh on them," she said as he began the examination.

"Not in recent months," replied Ignác.

He stood up after deftly and gently completing his examination of Caroline. "You're dilated eight centimeters," he pronounced. "I would say it may be another couple of hours. I'll go out to tell Franz, and then I'll be back to stay with you until we deliver—all right?"

"But the pain is becoming unbearable," she said as another wave of contractions started.

"Well, we can't have that," said Ignác, holding her hand and patting it. "I will give you something for it."

By tradition the Viennese obstetricians, like most others in Europe, taught that pain relief must not be administered in any form to women in labor. Labor pains were considered to be "physiological" annoyances that were nature's requirements for motherhood, and, therefore, they should not be interfered with. But Ignác had read about the recent developments in anesthesia and came to feel very differently. He was the only one, so it had become yet another source of nonconformist defiance in Klein's eyes.

"What will you give me?" pleaded Caroline.

"I have been in correspondence with a great Scottish obstetrician named James Young Simpson, who uses chloroform gas. It's very effective, and I've had quite a bit of experience with it."[83]

With that, Ignác reached into his black bag to produce a small, narrow-necked medicinal bottle. Removing the cork, he poured a small amount of clear chloroform liquid onto a piece of cloth and brought the soaked cloth to Caroline's face, pressing it against her nose and mouth.

"Don't worry—this won't cause any distress. You'll soon be asleep," he reassured her, as the chloroform turned into sweet-smelling fumes. Caroline promptly drifted into a light sleep, just enough to take the edge off the excruciating labor pains.

Ignác left the bedside to let Franz know what to expect and then returned to stay with Caroline. He watched over her, giving her small additional doses of chloroform as she needed it. An hour later, Ignác and the nurse carted Caroline into the delivery room. Expertly using his forceps, Ignác delivered a healthy, pink girl, crying her newly opened lungs out. Tears welled up in the eyes of the groggy but smiling Caroline.

Ignác told the nurse to get the expectant father, something that was a rare occurrence on these wards. Franz bumped into furniture in the darkness as he hurried to see the beaming Caroline holding their daughter. Her name would be Éva.

"I am going to see if I can take a little nap in the *Dienstzimmer*, if it's vacant," said Ignác. "It's only a few steps away from here. Franz, can I ask you to knock on the door—but not as loudly as you did on my apartment door tonight—and wake me up in about half an hour if I am not already here?" Franz nodded, without taking his eyes off his daughter.

"You wanted me to wake you," said Franz, standing over Ignác's rickety bed in the call room and gently poking him on the shoulder. "Everything is well, Herr Doktor."

Ignác sat up, shook his head as if to activate his brain circuits, and mumbled, "I told you—call me 'Ignac,' for Christ's sake."

"Can I talk to you for a few minutes in private?" Franz sat down on the chair next to the bed in the tiny room. Ignác lifted himself up, lit the single candle on his desk, and slumped back down to sit on the side of his bed.

"Are you awake enough?" asked Franz, leaning in to inspect his face. "There is something really important I must tell you."

Ignác nodded.

"So listen carefully," Franz continued. "I can't be sure of anything, but I am worried that you might be in some danger."

"Danger? Why would I be in danger?" Ignác looked up at Franz now fully awake. "I know I am not wanted here, but I've never been threatened. At least not with physical harm."

"I can only tell you what I overheard when I was still working in the hospital apothecary. And what an apprentice friend of mine there has said to me since. Just bits and pieces. I have some reason to believe that I was dismissed last year at least partly because of my connection with you."

"You were dismissed, Franz?" asked Ignác incredulously.

"Yes, I was fired."

"Hmm. And what sorts of 'connections' do you mean?"

"Just our few interactions in the pharmacy. My helpfulness to you," continued Franz. "Maybe it gave the impression that we were friends in some way."

There was a silence as Ignác tried to process all this.

"In the last year or so that I was there," resumed Franz, "I thought I noticed more people than usual coming there to talk to Director Schuster. People I hadn't seen before. People I wouldn't have expected to see in the hospital apothecary. Some would ask about you, quite casually you know, and then I would escort them to Director Schuster's back office."

"Who were these visitors?" Ignác's curiosity was aroused. He got up and paced back and forth within the narrow, dark confines of the room.

"One time it was the hospital director himself, Schiffner. Nobody in the pharmacy had ever seen him visit there before. That was before the March uprising. Then, later in 1848, while I was still there, we had a visit from Professor Rosas. He brought with him some big-deal pharmacist from Budapest. I can't remember his name. Doctor Lumpe came down once . . ." Franz paused to think.

"Who else, who else?" said the now-agitated Ignác.

"I really don't know any other names."

"So what makes you think all these visits signified danger to me?" asked Ignác. "I mean, besides the fact that these people sometimes asked about me, as you said."

"Well, one time, an older physician came in—I didn't recognize him or catch his name—and he said to Schuster as they were walking back to his office something like 'We have problems with Semmelweis again, Dietrich.' And when Schuster asked, 'Why not just dismiss him?' he responded with something I just couldn't make out. God, I wish I could be more concrete, but I can't."

"I see," said Ignác, plopping himself back onto the bed, his voice trailing off and now staring into the vacant darkness.

"And what about *your* safety, Franz, and Caroline's? You know I actually saw you once from a distance during one of the street battles. You were together on the barricades. It crossed my mind that you were a couple even then."

"We were active in the revolution," replied Franz. "But that was two years ago. Surely the authorities would have done something to me . . . to us . . . by now if we were ever going to be prosecuted. Don't you think?"

"Nothing is safe. You've got to continue to be vigilant. After all, you have a family to take care of now, you know," said Ignác, placing his hand on Franz's knee.

"Now I must see how Caroline is doing," Ignác said, standing up. "And *you* must go home for a few hours to get some sleep. Everything will be all right. You can come back refreshed tomorrow morning. Maybe even take her and the baby home soon. We no longer have to worry about that dreaded outcome!"

It was still dark when Ignác returned to the ward to look in on Caroline. She was asleep. It was obvious that she was comfortable. She didn't have a fever, and her breathing was completely normal, as was her pulse. Looking at her in the flickering candlelight, she looked more beautiful than ever. There was the appearance of real contentment on her face. He so much wanted to waken her, but he didn't. Instead, he searched the ward in the darkness and found an old, wilted nosegay of lilacs he must have left behind, and he gently placed it next to her on the bed. He bent down and ever so lightly kissed her on the forehead. And then he saw in the glow that faint but familiar smile appear.

As he had so often done in the past when he needed to clear his mind, Ignác headed straight to the Volksgarten. It was still dark, and the dense fog hadn't yet lifted. He walked briskly across the outdoor courtyards toward the hospital's main entrance off Alserstrasse. He found its great wooden doors being pulled open by the night guard at that very moment. From behind him, he heard the approaching sounds of horse hooves and the creaking wheels of carts rattling along the central path of the front courtyard on their way out of the hospital complex. Lit by the drivers' lanterns, they should have been a familiar sight to him here in the pre-dawn hours, but this time Ignác was deep in thought, and they startled him. He jumped out of their way to let them pass.

The larger, first cart was drawn by a listless old horse with a hay belly that was urged on by the bark of "hüa" from its likewise elderly driver. The open cart it pulled carried a load of several shrouded corpses piled on top of each other. They were on their way from the hospital's dead house, having been dissected in Rokitansky's morgue, to their anonymous pauper burials. Closely following was another horse-drawn cart, this one a black undertaker's hearse, carrying a solitary pine coffin. As it clattered closely by him, he could make out the large chalk markings on the coffin that presumably identified its cadaver occupant. Ignác knew this one must have belonged to a respectable working person, and it was on its way from the dead house to the funeral home to be prepared for a simple burial. He shuddered momentarily as it passed by and froze in place. He didn't know why. But then he picked up his steps to follow the pathetic procession out through the main gate.

The excitement of a job well done in delivering Caroline's baby waned, and it was replaced by that awful ache of some kind of void deep inside that overcame him in waves. He found his favorite bench in the garden. It was wet, but he didn't care; he sat on it and began to try to sort out all that was happening to him.

Methodically and dispassionately, he enumerated in his mind the circumstances of his life. It was the only way for him to try to solve problems that seemed intractable.

He had no family here.

He no longer had any real friends he could dependably turn to.

His career was at a dead end in Vienna.

His discovery was not accepted by those in command, and it wasn't even really appreciated by most of those who *did* accept it.

He had given up trying to figure out why. But he knew now that he had been outwitted by his adversaries, whoever they were. He was nothing more than a pawn in the politics of academic medicine, and to those on the inside who held all the power in Vienna, however unmerited that power might be. They had simply outmaneuvered him.

All further efforts to salvage his career here would be futile, he thought. He wasn't even sure that the few allies he thought he had were still behind him.

It was bewildering and it was rotten. But that was the way it was.

Dawn was breaking. Having whipped himself into a state of indignation, Ignác now sprung to his feet to leave. But he didn't go back to the hospital. He walked purposefully to his apartment, where he quickly packed his essential belongings in an old suitcase he had brought to medical school. He then walked back down the stairs into the cold morning light of an awakening Vienna. He was headed to the port in Nussdorf. A long walk, but there was plenty of time.

CHAPTER 22

LATE OCTOBER 1850

The metallic sound of the door knocker at the house on Iv Street became louder, with more insistent repetitions.[84] Júlia sat up in bed, startled because it was dark outside. Her husband, Peter, was sound asleep, as were all the children. The persistent knocking on the door harshly broke the silence in the house. Alarmed, Júlia bolted out of bed, lit a candle, and saw on the bedroom grandfather clock that the time was four o'clock. She hurried downstairs, and was shocked to open the door to find Ignác at the doorstep, holding his suitcase.

"Oh, my God, Ignac, my dear brother. What happened? What's wrong?" Júlia said breathlessly, her candle shaking. "I mean, why are you here in the middle of the night? Tell me!"

It took a while for Ignác to reassure his sister that he had just decided to come back to Budapest, nothing more and nothing less, and that his steamship happened to arrive at this hour after an exhausting two-day journey from Vienna. He had no other place to go.

"Would you have wanted me to walk around the dark streets until it was a more appropriate time in the morning?" he joked.

Júlia lit the lamp in the living room, and they sat there as Ignác began to explain to her the circumstances and how he'd come to this decision.

"You must have some coffee," she said, still recovering from the shock of seeing her disheveled brother so unexpectedly.

"Thank you. There is little chance that I will be sleeping any time soon," Ignác said.

Júlia agreed. "I certainly won't be able to go back to bed."

They laughed softly and hugged again in relief.

Júlia had a sad tale to tell to her brother. Their three youngest brothers, Fülöp, János, and Ágost, had fled the country. All of them had participated actively in the revolution. Although they were all seen alive after the fighting ended, they were now separately on the run from prosecution. Even their Catholic priest brother, Károly,[85] had been under arrest. Much of the family's financial fortunes had crumbled. After a brief period under arrest for his subversive activities during the revolution, Júlia's husband, Péter, was allowed to return to reopen his Tabáni Trinity Pharmacy, but only under close police surveillance. Júlia and Péter now had six children, the youngest being only one year old.

"Do you know where everyone is?" Ignác asked.

"I understand János is in London, trying to start a textile business. But I haven't heard anything about Fülöp or Ágost. I trust they are all alive and well, but they must be afraid to write to any of us."

"But surely they couldn't be traced just by sending a letter from some public post box," contended Ignác.

"Oh, Ignác, my naïve little brother," chuckled Júlia. "They aren't worried about being tracked down themselves. It's *us,* the recipients, they are worried about. Letters to Hungarians are being intercepted and opened constantly these days. And if there is anything in any of them that's even suspected of being subversive, the police will . . ."

"The police will do what?"

"Anything they want. Arrest, imprison. They are even executing people they consider to be revolutionaries."

Ignác was taken aback. He had no idea how oppressive conditions had become in vanquished Hungary

"What about Károly?" he asked.

"He was suspended from his clerical duties. He had to leave his parish, so he is back in Buda now, living with some others in one of the houses Papa bought."

"Is he all right?"

"He says he feels fortunate to not have been defrocked," replied Júlia. "A Viennese cleric saved him from a long term in prison, but he says he was interrogated brutally. He says the imperial commissioner and governor of Buda and Pest . . ."

"That's Károly Geringer," Ignác interrupted, "that sonofabitch turncoat."[86]

"Yes, Geringer. He sent a list of names of nine Catholic priests in this city who were considered to be the most troublesome 'rebel priests.' And he said our brother was at the top of that list, which went to ecclesiastic authorities and to the Hofburg. Can you imagine?"

"Oh, yes, I can imagine. Károly has always been so competitive. Always wanted to be number one in everything, ever since he graduated first in his high school class. I bet he's actually proud of this achievement, being named the top-ranked subversive priest in Hungary."

"He was charged with actively soliciting on behalf of Kossuth and with recruiting many men, including his own faithful, to join the army of the Hungarian rebels. And he was charged with being a major fundraiser for Hungary in the revolution. He apparently even gave away much of his own inheritance from our parents for the cause."[87]

Ignác shook his head.

"Do you know who else was on that list of nine?" Júlia added. "Péter's brother, József. So two of the nine most notorious 'rebel priests' in Hungary are from our family. And they are both banned from public ministerial duties for seven years. Not to mention that both have been singled out for special police surveillance."

"What about our brother József?" Ignác asked. "I heard that he has somehow managed to stay out of trouble. And he seems to be prospering!"

"Your father would have been so happy for him," said Júlia, perking up. "You know Papa didn't think József had what it would take to succeed in the family business. But look at him now. He owns the biggest and best-known grocery store in the city."

"I can't wait to see it," said Ignác.

"And with his profits, József has opened other stores, and he is now considered one of the city's most prominent merchants. He just became one of the directors of the merchant guild in Pest."[75]

"And his wife?"

"Johanna is eight months pregnant. Their first child. And she is really, really big, you know!" said Júlia. "She could deliver any day now."

"Does she have a reputable obstetrician in Pest?" asked Ignác, with a mischievous grin.

"Guess what! József and Johanna told me that if you were here in Budapest, they wouldn't *allow* anyone to do the delivery without your supervision."

Ignác told Júlia that his own savings were almost completely depleted. Having gone without salaried employment for the past two years, he was urgently in need of income. But even more importantly, he longed to restart his career as a native son who had made a momentous discovery that would now bring world fame to not only himself but also to Hungarian medicine. Here in Budapest, he planned to attain the recognition and respect so unfairly denied him in Vienna.

"Júlia, have you heard anything at all about what I have done in Vienna, my medical breakthrough?"

"Nothing," replied Júlia. "Outside this family, your name hasn't even been spoken in this city. You will have to tell us all about it."

Ignác was, at first, shocked to learn this, and then his conspiratorial thoughts rushed in. *Why should I be surprised? The spread of character assassination knows no borders.*

"I am planning to go to the St. Rochus Hospital in the morning to see what the conditions there are like and what opportunities I may have. Can I stay here for a few days until I find my own apartment?"

"Of course. Stay with us as long as you wish, and welcome home," exclaimed Júlia and gave her brother another big hug.

Nothing he had previously experienced quite prepared him for it. The beds of the ward were squeezed together and filled with women exhibiting the most gruesome signs of advanced disease. Many were writhing in agony, moaning, or screaming, others were lying completely still, and some appeared to be near death. The stench of human waste, decay, and pus was overwhelming, the stillness of the stale air suffocating. And in the midst of this cold and cavernous yet strangely claustrophobic chamber of human suffering, not a single health worker could be seen. It looked, smelled, and sounded like some kind of gigantic anteroom to the morgue, a way station to death where all hopeless souls were deposited and left to fend for themselves as they took their dying breaths.

Near its entrance, Ignác saw a woman frozen in place in her bed, eyes wide open and gaze fixed on the ceiling. She was stone-cold dead, a victim of puerperal fever, he figured. Judging by the stiffness of her ashen corpse, Ignác estimated that she had expired about eighteen to twenty-four hours ago. Not unlike the corpses he was given to dissect in Vienna. And nobody had yet come to get her. Maybe nobody had even noticed. He counted five other women in the ward who appeared to be terminally ill with puerperal fever. But Ignác also saw that there were many other women here who were obviously not in labor or postpartum, and weren't even pregnant: they were recent amputees, ones who had just had mastectomies, and others with advanced tumors and draining abscesses. Through the grimy windows of the ward, Ignác looked down over a large, overcrowded cemetery. He couldn't help but wonder how many poor souls from this ward were conveniently transferred directly there every day.

It was midday by the time he completed his own rounds, walking up and down the cluttered rows of messy beds and stopping by each one to examine the conditions of their pathetic occupants. And still no one appeared to be supervising them or even caring for them.[88]

This was Ignác Semmelweis's surreal introduction to the St. Rochus Hospital. The 600-bed city hospital was located on the Pest side of the Danube, in a complex of buildings he had often passed by in his youth and remembered for their attractive historical architecture. It was especially noted for its pretty Baroque church that served as the hospital's chapel. Even now, with its exterior façade badly damaged during the recent siege of Budapest, he never would have envisioned the horrors that lay within.

Dispirited, Ignác walked back to Júlia's house in Buda, across the floating bridge over the Danube, passing wreckages of buildings, shuttered shops, and heaps of garbage littering the streets. Even the riverbanks were thick with sewage. He had returned to his ravaged home city, leaving behind his own shattered dreams in Vienna. The Budapest to which Ignác had returned was merely a shell of the vibrant city he so fondly remembered from his visit seven years earlier. It was now the capital city of the defeated kingdom of Hungary, ruthlessly put down by the armed forces of the Habsburg Empire. Unlike Vienna, which was largely reborn, rebuilt, and liberalized after its uprising of 1848, Budapest lay in ruins and was suffering merciless retribution for its rebellion.[89] And nowhere was the devastated state of Hungary more glaringly manifest than in its medical institutions. On this morning, he had gotten a glimpse of the abominable conditions for women's care.

He found out on his first day back that twelve of the eighteen professors and department chiefs of the medical school of the University of Pest, many of whom had worked as medical officers in Kossuth's army, had been fired from their positions. One of them was the prominent young surgeon János Balassa. When Balassa and others were eventually reinstated, they came back chastened, muzzled, and submissive to Viennese authority.

Júlia explained to Ignác that most of those initially placed in key administrative, political, civil service, and military positions throughout Hungary were native Austrians who were hand-picked by the imperial government in Vienna. But with time, more and more of the appointees became so-called "reliable locals" ("*Gutgesinnte*"), native Magyars with unquestioned Habsburg allegiances. Many of the Hungarian *Gutgesinnte* were "originals," who had always had Austrian sympathies. But most were recent converts who had become collaborators, facile opportunists, chameleons of the most contemptible kind.

The academic job Ignác really wanted in Budapest was the professorship in obstetrics at the University of Pest. Surely he merited it. It was the specialty's most prestigious position in the country. But it was now occupied by Professor Ede Flórián Birly. An old-school obstetrician, Birly must have been well aware of his compatriot's discovery in Vienna, but he'd never adopted it in practice. Unlike so many others, however, Birly wasn't necessarily hostile to Semmelweis's position. He was just wholly preoccupied by his own ideas about the causation of puerperal fever, which he believed was due to "autointoxication" by the contents of unclean bowels.[90]

Since the professorship was unavailable to him, Ignác settled into a position in May as the unpaid, honorary chief obstetrician at the St. Rochus Hospital. This would at least provide him with an institution where he could implement his program to prevent puerperal fever. At the same time, he began to develop a private practice as a source of income.

Instead of the hero's welcome to his homeland's medical community he had dreamed about, there was virtually no welcome of any kind. With the exception of a couple of close personal friends, like his trusty roommate in medical school, Marko, Ignác's reception by the Hungarian medical establishment was at best chilly. Some were outright hostile, but most were simply indifferent; they just ignored him.

He was treated like an unknown, as if Budapest had never even heard of the events in obstetrics at the *Allgemeine Krankenhaus*. Or maybe the Hungarian physicians were afraid of acknowledging Ignác now that the country's revolution had been ruthlessly put down and replaced by a totalitarian police state that demanded absolute subservience to imperial Vienna. So perhaps they were just too intimidated to be seen interacting with Ignác, who was now obviously held in ill repute by medical authorities in Vienna. He imagined these would probably even include his old advocates like Rokitansky, Skoda, and Hebra. After all, he had disappeared without notice or explanation and without even bidding them farewell.

During those first days at work, Ignác walked the corridors and wards of the St. Rochus, convinced that other physicians passing by were gazing at him and then quickly turning their heads to avert his glance. Ignác felt like a pariah in his own home. As in Vienna, he couldn't imagine why.

But the young superintendent of the hospital was just glad to have Ignác's services. It was at no cost to his budget, so he wanted to be especially helpful to him. Sitting behind a simple desk in his small, littered office, he pulled a paper from its lap drawer.

"Here it is, Doctor Úr." The superintendent spoke in Hungarian as Ignác sat across the desk from him. "Chlorinated lime with corrosive sublimate. I just received this by post from Vienna. I wrote to the hospital director there to let him know about your appointment with us, and his office responded right away. God, I've never had such a fast reply from those people! Anyway, it won't be a problem at all to prepare it for you every day here at St. Rochus, just like at the Vienna General Hospital."

"But that's not correct," protested Ignác. "The corrosive sublimate was most definitively deleted from the solution several years ago! May I see it, please?"

"I am afraid I can't do that," said the St. Rochus superintendent with a nervous laugh. "These are government documents that I am not allowed to share with you. But it must have been just a little oversight. We'll leave it out. Don't worry, Doctor Úr, I'll take care of it personally. No problem. Now, do you want two fresh basins every morning, just as you had in Vienna?"

Ignác was surprised at how much the St. Rochus superintendent knew about his experience in Vienna.

As he had seen on that first shocking visit to the obstetrical ward at St. Rochus, puerperal fever was rampant. Ignác's Hungarian opponents pointed this out as proof that he was wrong. After all, they said, St. Rochus was not a teaching hospital, so there *were* no medical students here to bring contamination from cadavers to the mothers' bedsides. But these critics had obviously failed to understand the full scope of the problem. Contamination of the mothers in labor could come from many sources other than cadavers. Ignác immediately recognized that the conditions at St. Rochus didn't refute his theory; quite the contrary, they actually confirmed it in a most resounding way. The maternity patients here, whose numbers were far smaller than those at the Vienna General Hospital, didn't even have their own separate ward. They were admixed with general surgical patients whose frequently fatal operative site infections cross-contaminated them. Not only that, they were under the supervision, to use the term generously, of the hospital's chief of surgery, who had no particular expertise or even interest in obstetrics. Worse yet, individual surgeons were expected to do their own autopsies on surgical patients who died under their care, without regard for the examinations and deliveries they were also assigned to perform on women in labor afterwards.

Soon appointed head of obstetrics, Ignác was able to at least separate the obstetrical beds from those in general surgery. And he was determined to immediately institute an absolute requirement for rigorous chlorine hand washing by anyone examining his maternity patients.

This new rule caused much grousing by the patient care staff. They considered it intrusive, unnecessary, and a bureaucratic contrivance that did nothing other than waste tremendous amounts of their time. Anyway, they grumbled, who was this brazen young Dr. Semmelweis, whose first act was to increase their workload? Where did he come from? Why did he have to come here, of all places?

Enforcement of strict disinfectant hand washing at St. Rochus proved to be even more challenging for Ignác than it had been at the Vienna General Hospital. Here, Ignác was not on the payroll, so his level of authority was never really well defined; in Vienna, at least the medical students ultimately had to follow his orders. But enforce them here he did, and, almost immediately, the postpartum mortality rate plummeted to less than 1 percent.

On his solitary walks around the city, all he saw around him was the abandoned rubble of war. No accurate casualty figures had been kept, but it is estimated that about fifty thousand Hungarians had died. Pest was particularly badly damaged, as were many of the smaller cities and villages around the capital city.[91] Construction projects on new buildings and streets that must have started during those euphorically expectant days before the revolution now lay unfinished everywhere. Many stores were shuttered. The ones that were open had their signage changed back from Hungarian to German, often hand-painted in apparent haste. There was nothing left of the red-white-and-green banners and flags he had seen all over the city before the revolution—only the Austrian colors. The only park in the city, the *Városliget* (City Park), was nothing like Ignác's beloved *Volksgarten* in Vienna. It was run-down, overgrown with weeds, and largely deserted, even in good weather.

Nevertheless, Ignác felt reenergized by long walks between the *Városliget* in the outskirts of Pest and the Danube shore. He usually took a spacious, unpaved route because the only real avenue at the time, Király Street, was too congested with people and carriages, and it was either dusty or muddy, depending on the weather. His favorite times were those chilly autumn days when reddish-brown chestnuts lay scattered around him, having just dropped to the ground with soft thuds from the many horse-chestnut trees that stood along the undeveloped path. He would kick them or polish them shiny with his shirt sleeve and then throw them at imaginary targets.

It was while he was absentmindedly hurling those chestnuts one overcast fall afternoon in the *Városliget* that the horrifying images once again appeared to him of the women he saw dying in the surgical ward. He couldn't help wondering why they all had many of the symptoms and signs of puerperal fever, the same ones Ignác so often saw in the maternity wards in Vienna. But most of these women at St. Rochus weren't pregnant! They were just general surgical patients who had not even had pelvic exams performed on them.

Ignác now just stood there, alone in the park, rooted in place, and lost in his thoughts. *How did these women come to develop pyemia?*

Suddenly it clicked in his mind, as other ideas had in the past. The pieces began to fall into place, into one unifying theory. And such a simple one at that!

Why, of course! He practically shouted to himself. *The principle of pyemia must be a broad one. Pyemia can be caused by the introduction into the victim's body of any kind of contaminated substance—not just cadaveric particles. And those contaminated substances from unwashed hands can then gain entry into the victim's circulation through any kind of injury or wound—not just those caused by trauma to the birth canal.*

I had blinders on when I was first looking at those women dying of puerperal fever! It was because the only kinds of patients I was caring for were women at the time of their delivery. Hundreds of them, and nothing else! Even that woman in Vienna who had uterine cancer and started the outbreak in all the adjacent beds: she was also in labor and subjected to the same examinations and conditions as the others. But in the case of my dear friend Kolletschka, the accidental wound on his finger was the entry point.

And now in the cases of those surgical patients at St. Rochus, the wounds—the entry points—were wherever they had tumors, or abscesses, or surgical incisions. And here, even the sources of contamination were different. There were no cadavers or medical students to dissect them. The material, therefore, must have passed from one patient to another by the unclean hands of doctors and nurses, or the instruments they used.

Stirred by these ideas, Ignác quickened his pace back to the hospital.

CHAPTER 23

SEPTEMBER 1851

On Sunday, September 21, 1851, Ignác was drawn to a great commotion that was taking place around the Újépület,[92] the dreaded imperial barracks near the Danube shore, where Ignác's customary walks usually ended. Here, with much fanfare, the Austrian authorities were hanging in effigy the Hungarian heroes of the revolution, seventy-five in all, who were now in exile but had been condemned to death *in absentia* for their leadership roles in the insurrection.[93]

Gendarmes[94] were scattered amongst the noisy crowd of mostly Magyar onlookers. Ignác had often spotted them in public places, usually just observing people unobtrusively. He had never given them much thought since they so inconspicuously blended into the fabric of the populace these days. In fact, inadvertent eye contact with one of them would often elicit a courteous nod or even a fleeting smile.

Here, however, the *gendarmes* assumed an entirely different, more menacing appearance. Dozens of them were milling around the crowd. Ignác now knew that these *gendarmes* were, in fact, the ever-present eyes and ears of the imperial government throughout a conquered Budapest, invading every facet of the private lives of its citizens. But one *gendarme* in particular stood out from the rest. While all the others were facing the crowd and scanning the onlookers for possible troublemakers, this one was following only the approaching Ignác. Ignác could swear he had seen this police officer before; he recognized his extravagant handlebar mustache. *Why is he now here in Budapest?* Ignác felt his heart pounding fast.

Two years passed for Ignác with what he considered to be desperate drudgery and constant frustrations with the bureaucracy of an almost hopelessly backward medical system. He still felt estranged from his colleagues, like a *persona non grata*. He took it personally. This was the last thing he expected in his home city when he impulsively fled back to it.

At least the young superintendent at St. Rochus seemed to remain interested in Ignác's situation. Downright solicitous, in fact, Ignác sometimes thought. The only curious change that had transpired between them was that the superintendent never again talked to Ignác in Hungarian as he had done at their first meeting. Only German was spoken now.

Meanwhile, Dr. Birly, the chief obstetrician at the University of Pest, had been ailing for some time. Ignác was hearing rumors about the possibility that Birly might have to step down from his position. These rumblings fueled the flickering hope to which he had clung that he might yet be able to leave the purgatory of St. Rochus after all and get the professorship he so coveted.

One evening in late 1853, Ignác invited Júlia and her husband, Péter, to dinner. Ignác had sufficient income from his private practice by this time, and he wanted to splurge and treat them to a grand meal. He thought at first of the place in Buda, where Júlia, Péter, and that supercilious pharmacist boss of his had taken him after finishing medical school. *Just for old time's sake*, Ignác figured. But none of them really wanted to revisit that unpleasant memory.

They settled on the more intimate Kárpátia. Seated at one of the quieter tables in the back corner of the restaurant, they could easily hear each other talk, even when the four-member gypsy orchestra was whipped into its height of *csárdás* frenzy. The name of Péter's friend suddenly popped into Ignác's mind.

"By the way, Péter, whatever happened to that fellow Béla . . . Béla Esterházy?" asked Ignác.

"We never really had a falling-out," replied Péter, "but our paths just went in very separate directions. I haven't seen him recently."

"Do you know what became of him?"

"Oh, yes," said Péter. "Béla has become an extremely powerful person in Budapest. Not just as a pharmacist, mind you, but also in politics and finance. He goes to Vienna frequently. In fact, the last time I saw him, he said he had visited *your* hospital to investigate some kind of pharmacy problem there with the pharmacy director named . . . I can't remember."

"Dietrich Schuster?"

"Yes, that's it. Schuster," Péter burst out.

"Schuster is a pathetic, old, broken-down man, I am afraid. It's unlikely that he could have helped Esterházy."

As the gypsies were taking their break, Ignác heard the back-slapping joviality of a rowdy and tipsy group of men being seated nearby. One newcomer's piercing voice made Ignác's heart pound with alarm. His back was turned to the restaurant's seating area, so he couldn't see him, but the voice was unmistakably familiar. But it couldn't be! Blood drained from his head as he took a discreet glance at the new arrivals.

Yes, it was Carl Braun. He was in Budapest! And the five men with him were also familiar. They were some of the academic leaders of the University of Pest's medical school, including the esteemed head of surgery, János Balassa.[95] There was the pathologist Sándor Lumniczer. Ignác Hirschler, the famous ophthalmologist. And then, through the corners of his eyes he caught a glimpse of the internist and lung specialist Frigyes Korányi. The luminaries of academic medicine in Hungary. Ignác quickly turned back and looked down intently, fixing his gaze on the miniscule threads of the tablecloth in front of him.

"What's wrong?" Júlia asked, shaking his arm. "You look like you've seen a ghost!"

"Do I? Maybe I did," he mumbled without looking up. "Maybe I *wish* I did."

"But what is it . . ."

"Sshhh," interrupted Ignác, still staring blankly at the tablecloth. "I'm trying to listen. I'm trying to hear what they are talking about."

But he caught only a word here or there, even without the music playing. And now the gypsies were coming back, damn it. Ignác surmised that Braun was the guest of honor. *But why? What was he doing here? And what did all these Hungarian academics have to do with that snake? They weren't even obstetricians, for Christ's sake.* The three at Ignác's table hastily finished their dinner, and then Ignác tried to hide behind them, head down and turned away, as they quickly passed by the festive group of doctors on their way out.

The incident ate away at Ignác for days, recurring to intrude on his thoughts. But the explanation would come soon enough.

Recalling that Balassa was Marko Markusovsky's former mentor, Ignác went to his friend's apartment to find out what he knew about Braun's visit. He was in a highly agitated state.

Marko poured Ignác a snifter of *barack pálinka,* the traditional Hungarian apricot brandy. He trusted the strong stuff would put his old friend at ease.

"Has Balassa said anything to you about Carl Braun visiting Budapest?" Ignác wanted to get straight to the point.

"Yes he did, just this week," replied Marko. "A couple of other people also mentioned it to me. I was planning to talk to you about it. They thought they saw you in the restaurant where they were hosting Braun for dinner."

"Too bad. I thought I was able to sneak out without being noticed. In any case, what the hell was Braun doing in Budapest?"

"My dear friend, I know what you must be thinking. Old Birly hasn't been in good health for a while now, as you know," replied Marko. "And apparently there is some talk about having him retire and finding a successor."

"Braun?" Ignác's eyes opened into a wild stare.

"Yes, it looks like Braun wants to do it."

"To be Professor of Obstetrics at the University of Pest?" [96]

"Yes."

"But that sonofabitch isn't even a fully trained obstetrician!"

"I know."

"I came back here to bring the honor of my discovery to my native country," said Ignác, standing up, hyperventilating, his face now flaming red. "And that little shit Austrian worm has done nothing for obstetrics!" Ignác was now quickly pacing like a caged animal. "Except to kiss Klein's fat ass!"

"Sit down. Let's talk about this rationally."

"He doesn't even speak Hungarian, for Christ's sake!" Ignác wasn't listening. There was no way to reason with him now. "And I can't believe the bald-faced treachery of my so-called Magyar compatriots." Ignác revved up his rant. "Spineless cowards—all of them. Letting the Viennese bastards squash and spit on them, just to hold onto their own precious little positions."

"Look, I understand," said Marko. "You may be right. We are a defeated country. So many of them are running scared. And when that happens, people naturally assume a herd mentality. Even doctors. There is nothing special about us. We lose the courage of our personal convictions, and then we hide by accommodating to the enemy's party line. Some even collaborate with them."

"So I won't get the job," snapped Ignác, "will I?"

"Maybe not. You should be prepared for it. The imperial authorities in Vienna will have the final say, but they will listen to our own faculty. Our faculty will vote. And I have the feeling that the situation here is beginning to turn in your favor. There are threats of another uprising in the northern Italian territories, so the Habsburgs want reconciliation with us. They want to rebuild Hungary. They want to create a new, unified Budapest. I will try to help you as much as I can. There is hope, my friend."

Ignác walked to the window, which looked out on Gellért Hill, across the river in Buda. He pointed to the massive fortress the Habsburgs had just finished building with Hungarian forced labor. It was the Citadella, with its large garrison of imperial soldiers and its array of grand cannons aimed directly at the city below.[97]

"*Lófasz . . . !*" Ignác bellowed that most offensive of Hungarian insults.

Over the following weeks, Marko hosted several dinners in his home for Ignác to meet with small groups of Hungarian physicians, hoping to win them over to Ignác's side. On one of these occasions, two venerable private practitioners of obstetrics were the guests. They were quite obviously prosperous men, elegantly attired in perfectly tailored, pristine suits. One was short and rotund, nearly bald, with a cheerful face and a generous double chin. The other was tall and stern, with a thick head of well coiffured, snow white hair. They were also both men of considerable influence, highly respected by the city's medical community, as Marko cautioned Ignác before they arrived. They were obstetricians to the wealthy and famous, and they were well known to Ignác.

The conversation with the obstetricians turned to Birly's likely retirement and his successor as professor of obstetrics. It soon became clear to Ignác that both men had met with Braun on his recent visit to Budapest. It seemed like everybody who was of any importance in the city's medical community had met with Braun, Ignác thought. Except Ignác himself, of course. He began to wonder who had arranged all this.

"Carl would make a splendid new chief of the department here. He would absolutely revitalize it," commented the short, chubby obstetrician.

He appeared to be oblivious to Ignác's own aspirations for the same position. *Or maybe he knew everything perfectly well,* Ignác thought to himself. *Maybe they both knew.*

Of course, you idiot, they must be all in on it. The fix is in.

"That's if we can get him to come to Pest in the first place, of course," remarked the tall, dour one.

"Quite right," said the other. "He is so highly regarded in Vienna that there are already murmurs about him succeeding Klein one day. Even at such a youthful age, can you imagine?"

"A very intelligent, refined young man," continued the other. Don't you think, Semmelweis?" You must know him very well." They all turned toward Ignác for a moment.

"He is certainly . . ." said Ignác, struggling to find the right words.

"Certainly cultivated, certainly most impressive," the first one interrupted. "And I must say, he seems to be an extremely amiable, personable fellow. He would have no trouble becoming quickly accepted by our community, no matter that he isn't Hungarian."

"Accepted?" exclaimed the other. "Why, he would be *embraced*! Don't you think so, Marko?"

Marko was now squirming in his chair, increasingly anxious to change the direction of this awkward conversation. "Ignác," he said turning to his friend, "why don't you tell our distinguished guests about your work in Vienna and what you've already achieved here at the St. Rochus in just the short time since you arrived . . . I mean since you came *home*."

Ignác launched into a densely detailed, chronological presentation of the circumstances that led to his discovery of the cause of puerperal fever at the Vienna General Hospital, and then the hand scrubbing protocol that had led to the dramatic decline in deaths. He even recited the precise mortality rates and other supporting data before and after the hand washing intervention. His monologue got him more and more worked up with excitement as he related in great detail his setbacks, how he'd solved them, and how he had to overcome the indifference, the inertia, and even the resistance of the Viennese medical establishment.

He lost track of how long he had been talking without a pause before it struck him that neither of the two guests was asking any questions, neither of them seemed the least bit interested, and, in fact, both obstetricians had been sinking lower and lower into their armchairs as Ignác droned on.

Marko coughed loudly enough to startle the obstetricians into resuming their upright postures. "All right, Ignác," he said. "Now tell our honorable colleagues what you have done here at St. Rochus." Marko smiled sheepishly at his guests and then turned back to Ignác. "Make it brief, won't you, just the basics. The hour is late, and we're all tired, aren't we, gentlemen?"

Neither of them motioned any response, and both had their mouths slightly ajar.

When Ignác was finished, the tall, white-haired obstetrician cleared his throat and offered his opinion. "I admire your efforts, Dr. Semmelweis. It almost sounds like you have put your whole life and soul into this theory of yours," he said, without a trace of a smile. "But don't you see that your experience at St. Rochus actually disproves your own theory?"

"Disproves it?" Ignác was incredulous.

"Yes, it disproves it. *Negates* it. *Invalidates* it."

"How so?" Ignác began to rise to his feet, but Marko, sitting in the chair next to him, reached out to grab his arm.

"Can't you recognize it? You went to all this trouble to try to prove that it is cadaveric particles on the hands of doctors and students that transmit the disease."

"It was a reasonable hypothesis," interjected the other one.

"But Doctor, there *are* no so-called cadaveric particles at the St. Rochus. Very few autopsies are done by anybody—I am embarrassed to admit. There aren't even medical students there!"

"But it's *not* just cadaveric particles. It can be all kinds of putrid material, not just material from cadavers. The pathophysiology is generalizable. *That's* the whole point!" Ignác's voice was rising in exasperation. "I just told you how I came to deduce this," he continued gathering himself. "It came from our one patient on the ward in Vienna, the one nearest the entrance, the one who had the fungating cancer of the uterus that was discharging pus. She wasn't even being followed by our medical students. She was mostly cared for by the nurses . . . who had never even seen a cadaver, much less dissected one. And yet this solitary patient caused an outbreak of puerperal fever in the women who occupied the sequentially adjacent beds to hers. It was transmitted by the nurse*s* tending to her, who weren't washing their hands between examining patients."

"I guess I must have missed that little story," muttered the short, cherubic one.

"I have explained all this very clearly," protested Ignác, barely able to contain his frustration. "And then I told you about my observations here at St. Rochus, where the general surgical patients had all sorts of draining lesions, which I could directly link to puerperal fever in the obstetrical patients placed next to them."

Ignác stopped, and all were quiet.

The tall, humorless physician now sat forward with an expression of complete befuddlement on his face, eyes darting from one to another, as if he had been suddenly seized by hopeless disorientation.

"Surgical patients?" he stammered. "I don't understand. What surgery? Why? I thought . . . I thought we were talking about obstetrics. Am I . . . am I mistaken? I am not a surgeon, you know. Why are you telling me this?

I am an obstetrician." He sat back, straightening his collar. "A very well-known obstetrician at that."

Ignác and Marko looked at each other, desperately trying to remain collected. But Ignác couldn't contain himself any longer and stood up, looming over the obstetricians.

"If it's misunderstood, it must be because someone is intentionally spreading misinformation to discredit me," he yelled, "and I think I know who that is."

"Ignác!" Marko held up a hand to quiet him.

"But we haven't read a single paper you have ever written on the subject, Dr. Semmelweis," said the other obstetrician. "Dr. Braun reminded us of that when he was here."

Ignác sat back down, now seething.

"But I have lectured on it. And the transcripts of those lectures *were* published."

"Not the transcripts, Doctor, just some brief summaries of your lectures. There haven't been any original papers written by you that I am aware of, I am afraid."

The tone of the conversation was becoming contentious. "Well, gentlemen," Marko said, clearing his throat, "several of us have urged our brilliant young Hungarian colleague here to write it all up for publication in a major medical journal. But there is a lot of material to report, and as we all know, conditions over the past few years have made it difficult to do scholarly work. The situation was hardly in his control. But you are writing now, aren't you, Ignác?" Marko knew that his defense was a feeble one.

Ignác just nodded and turned the palms of his hands upward.

"Well, tell us what you think these *putrid* materials contain that cause such a terrible disease to be transmitted from one to another by our unwashed hands." Marko was giving Ignác another opening to expound on his theory, rather than getting further bogged down in a semantic dispute about "cadaveric" versus "putrid."

"Hah!" Ignác's face now lit up. "That's the next big question we must study. Frankly, I am not sure Doctor Braun would agree with that direction." He glanced at Marko's guests, whose expressions remained frozen. "But can you imagine, gentlemen, if a visionary new professor of obstetrics at the University of Pest could lead this line of research? Why, it might put Hungary right into the forefront of medicine in Europe!"

"Let's not get carried away, Doctor Semmelweis," said the somber white-haired obstetrician. "Have you considered Dr. Markusovszky's question? Do you have any idea at all about the nature of the harmful component in your cadaveric . . . I mean *putrid* material?"

"I think it may be those *animalcules* Leeuwenhoek saw with his microscopes," replied Ignác.[98]

Both obstetricians now let out loud barks of unamused laughter. "Oh yes, those *amazing little animalcules* Leeuwenhoek drew pictures of," the tall one said with a smirk. "What was it, more than 150 years ago? *Animalcules,* he called them! Well, why not?"

Ignác stayed behind after the obstetricians left.

"I am at a loss," he despaired. "How can so many intelligent people so completely misunderstand my theory?"

"It's partly your fault, Ignác. Many of us have been trying to tell you that for years. You have simply failed to *communicate* it properly."

"But it's . . ."

"But it's *nothing,*" Marko interrupted, noticeably irritated by his friend's obstinacy. "It's nothing until you have written and published your own definitive paper on it. You can lecture all you want, you can have people like Skoda lecture about it on your behalf . . ."

"Maybe it wasn't on my behalf, after all."[99]

Marko continued as if he hadn't heard that. "Others can write about it for you, like Hebra, and spread the word for you throughout Europe, like Kussmaul. You can have summaries of your talks published by others in Viennese journals. But it will continue to be misunderstood until you publish your work in your own words, for all of your peers throughout the world to judge. It's the way all medical progress is communicated. It's the accepted convention—not only throughout Europe, but even in more backward places like America."

"I *will* do it, I swear. But it still seems like there's a conspiracy of intentional misunderstanding!"

"I think you are greatly exaggerating it," said Marko.

"I mean you have to admit it; the medical establishment is out to discredit me. There is something rotten going on out there. Something *personally* hostile. And I think I know exactly where it's coming from. It's that sonofabitch Klein and his sycophant Braun. And now Braun is after the job I was meant to have. He has stepped up his smear campaign against me, even in my own home city!"

Marko hung his head and said softly, "It's not Braun."

"So who is it then? Marko, for God's sake, you are my best friend and you are well connected here. You must hear everything. You've got to tell me who has been spreading the dirt around here, if it isn't Braun himself."

"Späth is probably the most vocal one, from what I can tell speaking to our Hungarian colleagues," replied Marko, still looking at the floor uneasily, turned away from his friend.

"I should have known," said Ignác, his eyes now flashing with fury. "I knew he was a bad apple from the moment I met the arrogant bastard. He was Chiari's privileged student." Ignác was practically snarling as he slowly and sarcastically enunciated the word "privileged."

"Did you know he is director of the midwives' clinic now?" asked Marko.

"What a *verfickte Sheiße.* He is going nowhere in his career, so he is sucking up to Braun and serving him as his mouthpiece."

"Of course, there is Rosas, too. He has been talking about you to people in Budapest."

"Who has *he* been talking to?"

"I don't know, but I suspect it must be those hospital administrators. The bureaucrats. Remember he is an ophthalmologist, so most of the obstetrics community in Budapest wouldn't even recognize his name. So I doubt that he would be talking to them."

"The bigot!" Ignác exclaimed. "Klein's good friend. Birds of a feather. He must still be convinced that I am a closet Jew."[48]

"Maybe," said Marko, "but he is also now the Vice Director of the *Allgemeine Krankenhaus,* and he has become a powerful man."

"Are you saying he even pulls weight with our hospital administrators here in Budapest?"

"Yes, indeed," replied Marko. "I'm sure he does. As did that fellow Schiffner before him in the director's office in Vienna."

"Schiffner. Well now, there's another man I managed to piss off. Don't you remember? He caught me nosing around the hospital records for mortality statistics on the maternity wards when I first needed them to formulate my ideas." Ignác sighed, turning his eyes up to the ceiling. "And I actually thought I wouldn't be hearing *his* name again after he was dumped . . ." Ignác feigned a cough. "I mean after he was *retired,* following the revolution."

"The Viennese medical establishment has always been a very small and closed one, I am afraid," said Marko. "And now our little establishment here in Budapest has become even more beholden to the one in Vienna since 1848."

Marko stood to see his friend to the door. "Listen, whatever campaign you think the Viennese are waging on behalf of Braun to damage your reputation, I really think your Hungarian colleagues will rally to support you for the professorship at the University of Pest. When the chips are down, national solidarity will always win the day."

Ignác despaired. *National solidarity, my damned foot. It's every man for himself in this city.*

CHAPTER 24

FEBRUARY 1855

On a gloriously clear, frigid February day in 1855, along Vienna's ancient city wall, the steam locomotive of the *Emperor Ferdinand Northern Railway* was approaching the *Westbahnhof.* Vienna's West Station was just a small building next to dirt paths alongside the tracks. But the main hall of a grand new *Westbahnhof* was already under construction at the same site to accommodate the empire's rapidly growing steam rail system. On the next arriving train was Carl Braun. He was returning to Vienna from Budapest. Waiting to greet him at the station were Lumpe, Klein's deferential former Assistant, Späth, and Gustave Braun, Carl's younger brother, who was himself an aspiring obstetrician.

Birly had died suddenly in November of 1854. Six candidates for his position were to be expeditiously considered, including Braun and Semmelweis. And Braun was now returning home after his series of interviews with the most influential faculty members of the University of Pest's medical school.

The great steam engine of the train was now in the sight of those waiting at the station. Its *chuffa-chuffa-chuffa* sound, emitted by the heated steam exhausted through the engine's tall smokestack, was getting ever louder and slower. The train's welcoming bell and whistle sounded repeatedly. As it chugged alongside the small station building, the engine's pistons connecting its massive wheels labored to a screeching stop. Lumpe, Späth, and brother Gustave hurried to surround the steps leading down from the side door compartment of the wooden first-class passenger carriage.

"You must be utterly exhausted, Carl," said his brother, giving Braun a hug as soon as he stepped off onto the ground. The other two men excitedly shook Braun's hand.

"Yes, but every minute was worth it. I feel quite energized." Braun looked composed and somber.

"When will you know the outcome?" Späth jumped in.

"I already know it. The faculty has already voted. A messenger caught me with the news just as I was boarding my first train to Vác at the Nyugati Station."

"Well, don't torture us!" shouted Gustave, playfully elbowing his brother.

Braun almost seemed to smile. "They voted for me," he said as the others started whooping and cheering, pounding him on the back. "It was a split vote apparently, but I was told it was a decisive one."

"Congratulations, Carl," said the beaming Späth. "So you are going to leave us to become the professor at the University of Pest. I'll be damned. We are so proud of you!"

"Not so fast," cautioned Braun. "Remember it's just the recommendation of the faculty. Our Minister of Education must formally confirm it."

"Yes, yes, but come now—just look at the facts," replied Späth. "The ruling authority is in Vienna, and now even the defeated Magyar faculty wants you. Why, it's a win in every way for the imperial government, don't you see?"

Lumpe carried Braun's luggage as the jubilant group of men pranced through the station building. Späth shouted, "Let's celebrate!"

In Marko's apartment, Ignác looked devastated. And his stunned friend couldn't console him this time. Neither of them could explain the cruel turn of events.

"I honestly didn't expect this," Marko began, but his words trailed off.

Ignác was too dazed to even say anything about how terribly betrayed he felt by his compatriot physicians. He couldn't even mutter anything about how unjust it was, voting for Braun—*a younger man of virtually no accomplishment, who wasn't trained in obstetrics, and wasn't even Hungarian.*

What was unspoken between the two men was that they both knew this was more a repudiation of Ignác than a victory for Braun.

Before they got drunk on Marko's sweet apricot brandy, Marko tried to tell Ignác that he should now just seize whatever opportunity would come his way by continuing to work at the St. Rochus Hospital. He should use his position there, however less prominent and prestigious it was compared to the university professorship he so coveted, to make more great contributions to the field of obstetrics.

Ignác dropped his head, shaking it slowly in resignation.

The weeks leading up to the formal announcement of Braun's appointment was a new low point in Ignác's career—indeed, his whole life. He was tormented by the heartache of personal rejection. He succumbed to uncontrollable surges of jealousy toward Braun and blinding rage at his fellow Hungarian physicians who had betrayed him. And, in between, he spent hours awake in his room, incapacitated by suffocating rumination about the end of his career. His few friends in Budapest were seriously concerned that this would finally break him. His coworkers at the St. Rochus Hospital and his private patients became troubled by his long and unexplained absences. And on those rare occasions when he did appear in public, he looked like a disheveled ghost.

But then a remarkable transformation began to occur. Ignác seemed to come to peace with himself. He earnestly immersed himself in his work at both the hospital and in his thriving private practice on the fashionable Váci utca. Even his hospital superintendent admitted how much he admired Ignác's professionalism and equanimity in the face of such bitter disappointment. At nights he quietly threw himself into the long-delayed task of writing up the results of his theory and doctrine, his so-called *Lehre.*

And to everyone's amazement, he roused himself to appear at a few social functions. Hesitantly and uneasily at first, but then he began to actually enjoy them, and his charming, funny, charismatic old self began to slowly reemerge. He was regaining his swagger. He even began to flirt again with the young ladies, something he had eschewed since his medical student days.

CHAPTER 25
JUNE 1855

It happened on a hot, sultry June night. Ignác was in his apartment, deeply absorbed in labored writing of his *Lehre*, papers strewn all over his desk and on the floor, windows thrown wide open to try to catch a passing breeze. He was startled by an urgent knock on his door. When he opened it, he saw in the flickering light from his candle his landlady, standing there in a highly agitated state.

"Doktor úr," she said in her rustic *csángós* accent. "There is an imperial military man here to see you. All dressed up in his uniform, he is. And he insists he is here on a very urgent matter."

"Well, send him up right away, Mrs. Popa," Ignác replied nonchalantly. "I can't imagine what he has on me . . . at this hour of the night."

But, as he returned to his desk, he was immediately filled with dread. The worst possible thoughts flooded his mind. Was he being arrested on some trumped-up charge? Was Braun already having him sacked from his position at St. Rochus? Or was he having him barred from practicing medicine altogether? Having him deported maybe? But before he could conceive of any reasonable scenario, there appeared in front of him a young man dressed in full military regalia, standing ramrod straight, feet together and arms at his sides, practically at attention.

"Herr Professor . . ." he began.

"Just Herr *Doktor*, I am afraid," Ignác corrected him, "not Professor."

"My name is Lieutenant Christoph von Bechtold, and I have a letter of great importance to deliver to you from the Imperial Ministry of Education . . ."

"So late?" Ignác smiled nervously.

"Yes, it's urgent," said the lieutenant. "I have just arrived directly from Vienna."

"All right, let's have it then."

Passing it to Ignác across the desk, the lieutenant straightened up even more stiffly while Ignác read it.[100]

"Sehr geehrter Herr Professor Doktor Semmelweis:

In the name of His Imperial Majesty, Emperor Franz Joseph, I hereby appoint you to the position of Professor of Obstetrics at the University of Pest, effective July 18, 1855, with all the rights, privileges, and responsibilties attached thereto.

Leopold, Count von Thun und Hohenstein
Imperial Minister of Religion and Education"

Ignác slumped back in his chair, utterly speechless, as the young lieutenant stood motionless in front of him. On the one hand, he was overjoyed beyond belief, but, on the other hand, he couldn't help wondering why this had transpired, and if the explanation might be sinister. And who the hell was Count von Thun? The name seemed vaguely familiar.

The lieutenant broke the silence by asking Ignác to write a note formally accepting the appointment, which he immediately did in great haste and with a trembling hand. Returning it to the young man, Ignác at last saw him smile as he clicked his heels and said "*Guten Abend*, Herr . . . *Professor*," and turned to leave.

Ignác looked down to the street from behind the curtains of his window and waited until the Viennese officer stepped into a carriage to leave. He then snatched the letter from his desk and bolted from his room just the way he was, sleeves rolled up and shirt tails untucked. He hurtled down the stairs, almost falling at the feet of the petrified Mrs. Popa, who stood there agape.

"*Istenem, Doktor úr! Mi történt itt?*" Mrs. Popa screeched. "Are you going to be arrested?"

Ignác stopped in his tracks and then turned back to his hysterical landlady.

"Arrested?" he laughed. "Why, my dear Mrs. Popa, not arrested. *Appointed!*" Then he clutched Mrs. Popa's head with both hands and planted full kisses on both her cheeks. "Appointed!" Out the door the beaming Semmelweis dashed before the landlady could recover her senses.

Ignác bounded through the dimly gaslit streets of Pest, heading straight to Marko's apartment. When he found the lights out in his window, he knew he must be at the nearby *Erzsébet kávéház*, his favorite coffee house.

There Ignác found Marko sitting at his usual table, deep in conversation with the lean, stately, and stone-faced János Balassa. As Ignác approached them, Marko sprung to his feet at seeing his discombobulated friend so unexpectedly. Balassa remained sitting, impassively.

"Ignác, for God's sake, what the hell is the matter? Sit down, sit down. You know Professor Balassa, I presume."

"Hello, Semmelweis," Balassa added coolly.

"Hello, Professor. It's such a privilege to finally meet you formally. I only regret the circumstances . . ." And then, turning back to his friend,he continued breathlessly: "You won't believe it, Marko! An imperial officer from Vienna just came to my apartment tonight to deliver a letter . . . from the honorable Minister himself . . . appointing me to the professorship in Pest!"

Marko knocked over his own chair in his haste to embrace the perspiring and shaking Ignác.

"Justice has been served, my dear friend!" he shouted. "I am so happy for you!"

When Marko finally released him from his hug, Ignác saw the inscrutable Balassa standing up behind him, half-heartedly extending a hand to Ignác.

"Congratulations." Balassa stepped forward. "Why don't you join us?" As Ignác fumbled to draw up a chair, Balassa sat while Marko waved to a waiter to come over.

"I knew it was the right decision," Balassa said, looking indifferently at Ignác, his hands folded on the table in front of him.

"*Knew*?" Marko injected. "How the hell did you know, Jancsi?"

Balassa seemed to ignore the question and continued to address Ignác with a tinge of sarcasm. "Why, you must have friends in very high places, Semmelweis!"

"You mean in Vienna, Professor Balassa? Hardly. The few I thought I had there haven't even replied to my letters to them since I came back to Hungary. It even crossed my mind tonight that this is all some kind of diabolical scheme hatched up by Carl Braun and his circle to . . ."

"To do *what*?" Balassa snapped. He now looked annoyed. "Don't be a fool. There is nothing they can do. The decision is final. It's all just part of the politics of academic medicine, young man."

"Ignác does have a point though, Jancsi," said Marko. "The politics of academic medicine are just as dirty as the politics of . . . well, politics. The politics of government and big business. Our medical colleagues can be just as conniving, bullying, and mean-spirited as those others."

Ignác's demeanor abruptly turned serious. "Yes, but our petty politics are even more pernicious, because we hide them behind the façade of a noble profession."

"I am afraid you have lost your innocence much too early in your career, Semmelweis." Balassa sighed, with his hand gripping Ignác's shoulder, looking away from him. "But for tonight, let's not be philosophical. Let's just celebrate."

Stumbling through the unlit streets of Pest, Ignác didn't return to his apartment until well after 2 a.m. He fell into a fitful sleep, tossing and turning in his bed as his mind raced through all sorts of fleeting fears and fantasies. But mostly fears. Terrifying fears about what this turn of events could *really* mean. His mind was restively searching for what exactly it was that was unsettling him. It should have been a moment of vindication and fulfillment. But his years of growing cynicism about the machinery of academic medicine had made him wary about being entrapped in a snake pit full of enemies out to get him, and for reasons he didn't even comprehend. Some of those adversaries were unconcealed ones, he now suspected, maybe even some of those he had trusted so much.

One fleeting image kept coming back to him this night, and he had no idea what it meant. He was back on the maternity ward of the *Allgemeine Krankenhaus* as Klein's young Aspirant. It was during that visit by the hospital inspectors. Ignác saw himself tending to a new mother, when a shadowy figure appeared at the foot of the bed, just standing there and silently observing him. He was tall and lanky, with a courtly bearing, leaning on a cane in one hand. But he couldn't make out his face except for what was probably a prominent moustache. Utterly exhausted, he finally fell asleep at the break of dawn.

Ignác awoke with a startle to the bright sun blazing through his window. His heart was beating furiously, and he was drenched with sweat.

"Thun!" he shouted to no one, suddenly sitting bolt upright. "Count Thun. Leopold, Count von Thun und Hohenstein. Christ! The imperial minister of religion and education!"

Ignác quickly got dressed. He was struck by the possibility that the Count Thun he had briefly encountered years ago at the maternity ward inspection, and the Count Thun who had now signed the letter of appointment to be the new professor of obstetrics at the University of Pest, were one and the same.[101] The Count Thun who had told Ignác how impressed he was with the compassionate care he was providing to his frightened young patient.

Ignác hurried to meet the superintendent of St. Rochus to inform him about his appointment. After Ignác told him the story of the commission visit in Vienna many years ago, the young hospital superintendent sat back in his chair, hands clasped behind his head, and smiled.

"He must be the same one," he said. "Count von Thun came from an aristocratic Bohemian family, and he did a lot of charitable work to help the disadvantaged. Like the prostitutes of Vienna. And then, yes, after the revolution, he was appointed the Imperial Minister of Education. I guess it was because of his high social standing and his connections to the court. His reputation for being an upstanding character didn't hurt him, either." He laughed.

"What a coincidence," said Ignác.

"But it's *not* a coincidence," replied the superintendent. "Yes, academic medicine is a cruel business today. Everyone seems to be out for only himself. It will be different in the future. But it's heartening to know that every now and then a simple, unrehearsed act of kindness to a patient gets noticed and isn't forgotten. So, no—it wasn't a coincidence. You have been justly rewarded!"

"And all this time I was sure it was Professor Balassa who interceded on my behalf."

"Balassa?" The superintendent looked incredulous. "I don't know why you would think it was Balassa. You must surely know that he hasn't been exactly one of your big supporters since you came back to Budapest."

Ignác's heart sank hearing this. *You never know where your enemies are lurking in friendly disguise*, he thought to himself.

Ignác finally had the position of authority and influence he had so fervently sought. It was the platform he needed to enable him to widely apply his great discovery, and perhaps guide his homeland from being a backwater of medicine to a center of enlightened obstetrical practice. And he still had his directorship position at St. Rochus, which provided him with many more patients and larger facilities to demonstrate the validity of his ideas. He had grasped victory and vindication at the very moment he was despairing about its prospects forever eluding him.

His elation was to be short-lived. In fact, his appointment would be grudgingly—if at all—acknowledged by the medical community, even in his native country. There were no celebrations. There were no standing ovations at public meetings. No toasts. No letters of congratulations. Not even an invitation to meet the university provost, which was customary with professorial appointments.

The first blow came even before his official start date as chief of obstetrics at the university. It was his removal from the directorship of the obstetrics service at St. Rochus. His heavy-handed enforcement of hand scrubbing prior to each patient exam there, this time supported by the hospital superintendent, had once again resulted in a precipitous decline in the postpartum mortality rate, just as in Vienna. In fact, during the previous year, it had dropped to an astonishing 0.89 percent, while at the same time it was back up to fifteen percent in Vienna, only five years after his departure, and was comparably rampant in other European capitals. The reason for forcing him out was that one of the losing candidates for the university professorship, an obstetrician of no special distinction named Ignác Rott, had vigorously protested to the government that no man should be allowed to hold both positions at the same time. The Hungarian officials agreed, so Ignác had to resign from the St. Rochus job. And it just so happened that his successor was the enterprising Dr. Ignác Rott.

Ignác felt compelled to inspect the university's obstetrics service even before his official professorship appointment there started in July 1855.

Located on the second floor of a dilapidated city building on the corner of Hatváni and Újvilág streets,[102] the small maternity ward was arranged haphazardly in absurdly cramped quarters. There was practically no ventilation. It had barely enough space for patients, doctors, nurses, and orderlies to squeeze between beds, much less allow any kind of bedside teaching of students. Like the ward at St. Rochus, a single small window overlooked a cemetery, making Ignác wonder if these entities were co-located in this fashion by coincidence or by convenience. Indeed, the mortality rate from puerperal fever here was much higher than the rate at St. Rochus.

The superintendent of the hospital was an ambitious young man named von Tandler. *Statthaltereirat* von Tandler came from an aristocratic Viennese family.[103] He spoke fluent Hungarian but with a thick German accent. Von Tandler was marked by the Habsburg Imperial Ministry from very early in his career as an up-and-coming hospital administrator destined for a high-level bureaucratic position. As such, he was installed in his current post in the aftermath of the failed Revolution of 1848, as part of General Haynau's Austrian police state. Part of his job was to monitor and ferret out subversive and dissident elements within the medical establishment of Budapest, many of whom were suspected to be doctors. The position would be an ideal audition for the ambitious young man.

Ushered into von Tandler's office for his introductory meeting, Ignác was struck by its elegance and spaciousness. It was in stark contrast to the suffocating gloominess of the rest of the hospital. In his mind's eye he estimated it could even accommodate a whole additional maternity ward. The superintendent greeted him with a bone-crunching handshake.

"Herr Professor," he said. "I suppose I can call you that now, can't I? It's such a *pleasure* to meet you." The word "pleasure" was enunciated slowly and emphatically.

"Likewise, Herr Statthaltereirat von Tandler," replied Ignác.

"Congratulations on your appointment. I have many friends and colleagues at the Allgemeine Krankenhaus, and they've told me *so much* about your accomplishments there. The former Herr Direktor Schiffner was my *mentor*, you know," he said puffing out his chest.

Ignác thought it would be important to appear impressed with von Tandler's connections, so he raised his eyebrows as high as they would go, in mock awe.

"And Professor von Rosas, of course, you must know him. I have known those two especially well since even before those unfortunate events of 1848. By the way, in case you haven't heard, Professor Rosas is in poor health now. One of the great physicians of our era, you know. Anyway, I trust that you will be able to promptly reproduce for us the same miraculous results you had in Vienna."

"Yes," replied Ignác, adding "I hope we can do that together, you and I."

God only knows what they really told him about me. Tandler probably researched my entire past when he heard about my appointment, thought Ignác as he left von Tandler's office. *They are all colluding against me, these bastards. I didn't escape the persecution when I fled Vienna.*

From the outset, Ignác knew that the cards were stacked against him in his quest to control puerperal fever at the university hospital. He had to cope with dreadfully crowded and poorly maintained, old facilities, downright unsanitary conditions, serious shortages of essential supplies, and an obstinately unresponsive faculty, midwifery, and nursing staff. But he never imagined that the obstacles here could be even greater than those he had encountered in the past. After all, he was now finally in charge.

What he found most bewildering was the intensity of pervasive hostility toward him personally. Was it a function of a deep-seated culture of professional backwardness? Or was the defamation Ignác suffered in Vienna now infiltrating a subdued and cowed medical establishment in Budapest? Under the ever-present police state of surveillance of post-revolutionary Hungarians, there was widespread fear among the people for their jobs if they did anything out of the routine. Rumors had, in fact, begun to percolate throughout the hospital that the new boss had been sacked in Vienna and was now out of favor with the medical establishments of both Austria and Hungary because of his insubordination and his radical, disruptive medical practices.

The orderlies and nurses were apathetic, inattentive, and often downright neglectful. When Ignác tried to provide what he considered to be constructive and judiciously worded criticism, it was met with passive-aggressive silence. At first he tried to reason with the staff and get them to understand the rationale for his policies. He even sat down with the head nurse to show her the actual data supporting the favorable results he had amassed during his terms in Vienna and at the St. Rochus Hospital. It was intended to be a gesture of collegiality with subordinates. But all to no avail.

Never long-suffering when it came to his personal expectations for rigor in patient care, Ignác soon began to be more and more insistent about adherence to his hand-scrubbing protocol and improvement of the existing unsanitary conditions. Confronted by obtuse resistance to what he considered to be simple rules, his frustration began to boil over at times.

Apathy and passive aggression by the ward staff toward Ignác now turned into intense dislike of him. All except perhaps the old orderly who brought the prescribed bowls of chlorinated lime solution to the ward every morning, to whom Ignác had been unfailingly courteous and thankful. He affectionately called him "Tamás Bácsi," Uncle Thomas.

The more notes Semmelweis sent to von Tandler about lapses in patient care, the more annoyed the superintendent became. And whenever they saw each other, von Tandler would greet him with increasing chilliness. In his new position, Ignác was becoming keenly aware of the need to exercise much greater restraint with von Tandler than he had in the past. But he was at a complete loss to understand why there was so much antagonism to his dictates, which were, after all, in the best interest of their patients.

With the start of the academic year in September came the deluge of regular medical students and pupil-midwives, all returning from their summer break. They arrived one day, unannounced, like a swarm of locusts, occupying seemingly every square inch of floor space where one could possibly still stand. Not infrequently, their overflow would spill into the outlying corridors. For Ignác, it made bedside teaching practically impossible. For the already miserable patients, the suffocating conditions became almost barbaric.

The situation was treated with indifference by the hospital staff and administration. It was the way it had been for as long as they could remember, so there wasn't a pressing need to change things now. Exactly the same attitude he had encountered in Vienna. So Ignác recognized that these conditions would make it formidable for him to reproduce the favorable results he had achieved in Vienna and at St. Rochus. His protests fell on deaf ears, especially since he had already become such an irritant to so many people.

Ignác figured there was no way he was going to get von Tandler, comfortably ensconced in his palatial administrative suite, to initiate any improvements. So he decided to do it himself. He sent a lengthy petition to the government authorities in Budapest, which included the following excerpts.

"The (obstetrical) clinic is situated on the second floor, and indeed in the furthermost part of the rear of the whole building, so that the poor women in labor must not only travel considerable distances from one part or the other of the city but are compelled to drag themselves up two flights of stairs and through a long corridor, so that it happens

that births on the stairs are not a rarity . . . The windows on the one side open on the dead-house, while the others are directly over the dissecting room. As if that were not enough, there are to be found in one wall of the actual sick-ward about three, well-drawing chimney flues of the chemical laboratory on the first floor directly underneath the obstetrical clinic, which in the middle of the summer turn the wall into a veritable giant oven. If one does not believe this, let him place his hand on the wall: I know for a fact that he will not do so a second time . . .

". . . The windows open onto the northern shaft. The lavatories for the first three floors are in this light well. On the ground floor, next to the lavatory, is the building garbage pit. This decaying mass exudes a penetrating stench. Facilities for pathological anatomy are on the first floor. Drains from these facilities, through which all liquid wastes are discharged, are immediately below the windows of the maternity clinic . . . One should now picture a busy clinic, attended this semester by 93 pupil-midwives and 27 medical or surgical students, with the thermometer at 26°R[104] *in the shade . . .*

". . . There lay on the diagonally placed bed a truly pitiable creature; instructor, assistant, and a dense throng of pupil midwives and medical students stand around it; even in the third room beyond, they are closely packed head to head, able only to hear the patient's screams, without being able to see; heat that was rather more capable of forcing one out of the world than attracting one into it . . . The air becomes so stale that it is dangerous to the patients . . . the temperature in these rooms becomes unbearable.

". . . The honorable college of professors can well imagine the undesirable position of a professor of obstetrics who is obliged to choose either to have the windows hermetically sealed, and so to allow his patients to grow worse by breathing air befouled by throngs

of (sweating) students, or to leave the windows open and to admit air saturated with corrupted organic matter."[105]

When von Tandler found out about this this petition, he immediately sent Semmelweis a stern letter admonishing him for going behind his back to a higher authority. He warned him of dire consequences should something like this happen again. Enraged, Ignác felt like walking straight into von Tandler's office with his letter of resignation. *That would fix him!* But as he started writing the letter, it occurred to him that von Tandler might accept the resignation and just bid him farewell.

He fantasized repeatedly about von Tandler begging him to stay. At the same time, Ignác was becoming aware of his increasing tendency to ruminate and obsess for long periods about thoughts of revenge and conspiracy.

But whatever lack of respect he was experiencing professionally, his standing in the social circles of Budapest seemed to be on an upswing. He was invited to gatherings, dinners, and even to gala affairs. He attributed this to the public profile of his new prestigious position, and he found some respite in it.

Then Ignác received an invitation to the formal ball the university sponsored every year, one of the annual highlights of Pest's high society calendar. His sister Júlia took on the task of getting him properly attired for the event. He was fitted for a new dark tailcoat and trousers, which he would wear over a white linen shirt with an upturned stiff collar and a white cravat. Júlia also told him that a wealthy merchant named Weidenhoffer, a former friend of their father József, had been asking around about Ignác since his professorship was announced. He wanted to introduce him to his daughter, Maria.[106] The Weidenhoffers, including Maria, would be attending the university's gala ball, and it seemed to be an ideal occasion for them to meet. Júlia also tried to give Ignác a crash course in etiquette for these kinds of events, but this was clearly a futile undertaking. Decorum was not among Ignác's God-given gifts.

The university ball was held in a temporary but sufficiently decorated building, on the site of the former Redoute Hall of the Pesti Vigadó, which had been destroyed during the battles of 1848.[107] As usual, ballroom dancing floor managers were appointed from among the ball's planning committee. The assignment for these formally attired individuals was to ensure the smooth flow of rotating dancing partners, the appropriate mix of dance music played by the quadrille band, and, above all, enforcement of proper protocol at all times. There was to be no display of Hungarian nationalism, as there had been before the revolution. But every now and then, the band broke into a traditional *czárdás*, which was immediately greeted by a burst of applause.

When Ignác approached the Weidenhoffers' table, which he had put off doing until well into the evening—and even then, only at the relentless hectoring of his companions—he was instantly entranced by Maria. She wore a very low-necked, light blue, floor-length evening gown that fell off her shoulders, short sleeves, and perfectly fitted, long white gloves. Her bountiful golden-brown hair was parted in the middle and in a braid wound at the back, puffed out over the ears and decorated with a single flower on one side. After acknowledging her parents, Ignác bowed to Maria, introduced himself, and asked her for the honor of the next dance. Maria demurely smiled—he thought he could see her even blush in the dim light—and almost inaudibly said that she was engaged.

Without saying another word, the horrified Ignác turned and fled from the scene. Maria's father promptly pursued him through the crowd and finally found him cowering in a corner of the ballroom. With an expansive greeting, he shook Ignác's hand with a firm grip and a grin, and introduced himself as a friend of his deceased father. When Ignác tried to offer his apologies for offending his daughter by not knowing she was engaged, Mr. Weidenhoffer let out a roaring laugh. "She is not engaged to be *married*, Semmelweis," he bellowed. "She is just engaged for the *next dance.* Come back and ask her again!"

"But how will I know . . ."

"How will you know when she is available?" Weidenhoffer was still chuckling. "You have to sign up on her card."

Ignác haltingly returned to Maria's table, his arm firmly pulled by Weidenhoffer through the jostling crowd. She greeted him with a girlish giggle, gloved hand to her mouth, and pushed her card on the table toward Ignác. When the time came, Ignác found that his old dancing skills hadn't abandoned him. He twirled her around the floor to a Strauss waltz with great abandon as other dancing couples parted to give them a clear path around the floor.

When Ignác held onto her hand for the next dance, a polka, one of the alert floor managers discreetly walked over to whisper to Ignác that Maria was engaged with someone else for the next dance. He would have to wait to take her again when she was next available, this time for a Circle Dance. Ignác wanted to have a chance to talk with her, so he surreptitiously led her to one of the side rooms as soon as the Circle Dance was over. But the same obtrusive floor manager materialized there to break them up and escort Maria back to her table. It was only later that he learned from his sister that this kind of private conversation during a ball was considered to be a serious violation of the rules of conduct. But Ignác didn't mind because their mutual attraction to each other had been sealed.

Although he appeared to be alienating everyone he worked with on the obstetrics unit, the results of Ignác's policies were beginning to yield favorable outcomes during the first year. Ignác and his hard-working young assistant,

József Fleischer, begged, pleaded, cajoled, flattered, and then eventually threatened, bullied, and intimidated—whatever it took to get the staff of the ward to comply with the new hand scrubbing rules. At the end of the 1855–1856 academic year, Ignác's first as chief, there were only two deaths among 514 deliveries, for an astonishing mortality rate of 0.39 percent.

Fleischer promptly wrote up these remarkable results, and his paper was published later in 1856 in the widely read Viennese medical journal, *Wiener medizinische Wochenschrift.* But an anonymous editorial note was appended to the article, which concluded, "It would be well that our readers should not allow themselves to be misled by this theory . . . we thought that the theory of chlorine disinfection had died out long ago." It was never determined who authored this caustic comment.[108] Perhaps not coincidentally, it appeared right after the sudden death of Johannes Klein and the not-unexpected appointment of his favorite pupil, Carl Braun, to the most influential position in Viennese obstetrics.

Even as the impressive outcomes of the first year were being published in Vienna, serious setbacks began to happen. There were several consecutive postpartum deaths, and by the end of the first quarter of Ignác's second year in charge, one-third of the women had succumbed to puerperal fever. Ignác and Fleischer were stumped. They were quite certain that there had not been any major lapses in the hand scrubbing protocol, even though the grumbling among the ward staff had escalated to outright anger over the intrusive new rules. The notion of sabotage was unthinkable even to Ignác. And although the putrid stench of the labor ward hadn't changed, Ignác had successfully browbeaten von Tandler into allocating more hospital funds to improving the cleaning of instruments between their use in different patients, and even to contracting for the first time with a daily laundry service to wash the bed sheets for use between patients.

As in times of crisis in the past, Ignác systematically checked off all the various conditions on the service, no matter how trivial, that might have changed in any way in recent months and could give him clues. But then he remembered the admonitions of Rokitansky and Skoda that systematic reasoning wasn't enough for solving the most challenging problems. They had taught him the powers of keen listening and observation. So, as the situation escalated, he spent entire evenings making his own private rounds, when the ward was quieter and the frantic activity of daytime had subsided. There was no longer enough space between the beds for him to carefully inspect every patient, so instead he would sit on a stool at the foot of each bed, talking to the patients one by one to absorb everything he could about their circumstances. If one was sleeping or in too much distress with labor pains, he would just sit there and watch her for a while.

On one such occasion, he sat with a young woman who was in the early stages of labor. Her amniotic sac hadn't broken yet. He learned that she was a single mother of two toddlers, whom she often had to leave in the care of her neighbors so that she could work to support them. Her own parents had disowned her. The young woman was undoubtedly one of the anonymous multitude of Budapest's wretched prostitutes, Ignác thought to himself, but she was too proud to admit it.

Ignác wondered. His eyes were blankly fixed on the patient's bed sheet when he was startled by something he had been staring at but now actually saw. There was a large, faded stain on the sheet where it was tucked into the corner of the mattress. He asked the young woman to sit up and then ripped the sheet out, turning it over. And there it was!

The underside of the sheet was covered with foul-smelling stains of old pus, lochia, mucus, blood, and even a few fragments of what appeared to be crusted uterine tissue firmly stuck to the linen. In a fit of rage, he now went from bed to bed, throwing open the covers and pulling out the sheets with little regard at that moment for the conditions of the beds' occupants.

Sure enough, everywhere he looked, but previously hidden from plain view, the sheets and covers were full of intentionally concealed, putrefied filth and waste.

Ignác practically accosted the elderly night-shift nurse, who was cowering in a corner of the ward, worrying about what this madman might do next. But, of course, the poor nurse really knew nothing about the matter. She had been just given some folded sheets with instructions to place them on the beds with the "clean side up" before any new patient arrived.

Ignác was determined to confront the head nurse, as soon as she arrived for work the next morning, which was usually at sunrise. He was much too agitated to go home, so he stayed overnight in his small hospital office, with its window overlooking the cobblestone inner courtyard of the building. He had dozed off in his chair and was awakened at dawn by sounds of the slow, labored clip-clop of a horse and the wheels of a wobbly carriage it was pulling into the courtyard. Parting the curtain and looking down, he could barely make out the sign on the side of the cart indicating that it was from a cleaning service: *"Királyi Tisztító"* he thought it read.

An old man stepped slowly from the cart and was met halfway to the main door by the head nurse herself, who was carrying a big pile of white sheets in both hands, which she then dumped into the cart with his help. Several more piles were then brought out, filling the cart, before the man stepped back up to his seat to take the reins again, turning the horse around to lumber out of the courtyard. The head nurse suddenly glanced up to Ignác's window, perhaps spotted him there, and then quickly walked out of sight, back into the building. So there really *was* a laundry service now, after all. But it didn't take long for Ignác to catch on to the reason why filthy sheets were still being used for the patient beds.

The same old man with his horse and cart reappeared in the courtyard not more than half an hour later. This time, one of the hospital orderlies came out and picked up armloads full of neatly folded white sheets. They were placed in tidy piles on a table in the hospital lobby. When Ignác came down from his office to inspect them, they were indeed perfectly folded. But they were also still deeply creased from previous use. And they were sickeningly foul-smelling at close range. Opening one of the sheets on top, he saw that it was covered with stains of all kinds of excrement, blood, and bodily discharge. What kind of scam was this? A laundry service that picks up soiled sheets and then immediately returns them folded but uncleaned! And who was on the take? Who was getting the kickbacks from this racket?

With uncontrolled fury, he grabbed a large armload of the stinking, filthy sheets. He stormed across the courtyard to von Tandler's administrative suite, dropping some along the way in his haste, and barged into the inner office, where von Tandler was presiding over the morning meeting of his executive staff. Without acknowledging any of the dumbstruck men in the room, he ran straight to von Tandler's enormous, ornate desk behind which he was sitting and dumped all the sheets on it.

"What the hell?" remonstrated von Tandler.

Ignác's face was flushed, his eyes were wide open in a mad stare, and he was sweating profusely.

"There!!" he shouted at von Tandler, spitting saliva, the veins of his red temples bulging. "There are your goddamned laundered sheets! You are killing my patients!"

Then picking up one of the sheets and splaying it in front of von Tandler's nose with a large, dark blood stain in the center, he finished his tirade: "Here, this blood is on your hands!" Flinging the sheet on top of the others that were now covering the desk, Ignác stomped out, slamming the door behind him, before anyone could say anything.[109]

Their relationship was now irreparably damaged. Semmelweis was convinced that von Tandler was a crook, and all but said so; von Tandler, in turn, had been publicly humiliated. They still had to communicate about hospital business, but hereafter they did it through intermediaries, or by scribbling terse, rude notes to each other.

In the aftermath of the affair of the sham laundry service, some changes did take place. The head nurse was dismissed and replaced with someone who at least initially seemed more responsive to Ignác's directives. And the bed sheets were being well laundered now, subjected every morning to a military-style inspection by Ignác. But at the same time, old Tamás Bácsi, who brought up the freshly constituted bowls of chlorinated lime wash from the pharmacy every morning, one bowl always clearly labeled for Semmelweis himself, quietly disappeared. Some said he had become ill; some said von Tandler fired him out of spite. In any case, the task now fell to an unlikely individual. He was a well-dressed, articulate, but strait-laced young man with a thick German accent who was unfailingly courteous but laconic. His name was von Lakai. Nobody knew his first name, so he was called just "Lakai." Lakai seemed ill suited for this job. Ignác was quite sure he was actually one of the administrators he'd seen when he burst into von Tandler's office on that infamous morning. It did cross his mind: *Why would von Tandler want to put one of his trusted administrators into a job like this? He was so obviously overqualified.*

Trying to ignore the tense atmosphere, Ignác applied himself harder than ever to reversing the recent uptick in maternal mortality. The changes did seem to be working from the outset. Much to the chagrin of the staff, he intensified the hand scrubbing requirements for everyone who was permitted to touch a patient, as well as the cleanliness of instruments and other possible sources of contamination.

At the beginning of 1855, it was announced that the antisemitic Anton von Rosas would be at the University of Pest to give a lecture on ophthalmology. At the age of 64, Rosas was frail and ailing but still powerful in the medical community. Ignác wanted to see him, partly because he was curious about what was happening in Vienna, but mostly to flaunt his new position. He could never forgive Rosas' contempt for him.

Ignác approached Rosas after his lecture, as he was being helped off the podium by some students. He had given his talk in German even though he was in Budapest, evidently still quite ashamed of his Hungarian roots. Ignác pushed his way through the small crowd of jostling physicians who had quickly converged around Rosas as he tried to leave the hall.

"Welcome to Budapest, Herr Professor," Ignác called out. Rosas looked flustered, his eyes darting around, searching for the voice that called him.

Only when Ignác came face to face with him did the old man recognize him. "Why Semmelweis," he stammered. "I am surprised to see you."

"I was hoping to speak with you, Herr Professor," said Ignác.

"Well, as you can see, this is not the best time. I have to join my hosts for lunch."

Rosas tried to move on through the crowd, but Ignác gently grabbed his arm. "As you may have heard, Professor Rosas, I was recently appointed to the professorship in obstetrics at the University of Pest. I am . . ."

"Yes, yes, I know," Rosas interrupted. "Good for you." He stopped for a moment. "It must be quite a bit *easier* for you here, I am sure. Not as much competition as in Vienna, eh? Expectations aren't as high in this city, don't you think?"

"Well, there are problems to be solved here also," replied Ignác.

"Aaah, yes—problems. Always trying to solve problems, aren't you? Herr Direktor von Tandler told me you are stirring up trouble here, too!"

Ignác was dumbfounded.

"But that's alright," continued Rosas with a smirk and a derisive guffaw. "These Hungarians need some stirring!"

Just then von Tandler appeared to whisk Rosas away, accompanied by the young Hungarian ophthalmologist, Ignác Hirschler.[110] On their way out, none of them acknowledged Ignác.

The brief encounter with Rosas was deeply upsetting to Ignác. It was a sobering reminder that he was still just an outsider, even here in his homeland. A slap in the face to remind this bumbling, simpleton Hungarian that he would never be allowed to break into the inner circle of the Empire's medical elite. No matter how hard he worked, and no matter how important he thought his contributions were.

He began to distance himself from his colleagues and staff. He started missing more and more meetings and functions of the medical school's physician faculty. But, curiously, he wasn't staying away from them as a form of protest. He was staying away because he had become gradually aware of an odd feeling of nervousness whenever he found himself in public in the company of people he knew. He realized this angst was irrational, and he was mad at himself for allowing it to creep into his psyche. Maybe he considered himself unworthy. This curious feeling of overwhelming shyness wasn't new, he realized. He experienced it to a lesser extent in Vienna, like the time he ran away from the reception in Klein's home. But he thought he had gotten over his social anxiety. Now it was back again, worse than ever, and he felt helpless to control it.

At work, he found himself walking out of his way to avoid running into other doctors and having to talk to them. When he spotted even one of the more amiable faculty members approaching him down the corridor, reflexively he popped into a stairwell or a closet until he passed.

For the first time, Ignác began to feel nervous even about teaching medical students and midwifery students. He had never before felt inhibited in the classroom or at the bedside, and he should have been even more comfortable in his present environment because now he was speaking to them in Hungarian. He told colleagues he was feeling increasingly claustrophobic in the overcrowded facilities. But in reality, he was feeling self-conscious about his Hungarian speech now being laced with a German accent. As he talked, he thought he saw students silently glancing at each other with furtive smiles, and he was sure they were making fun of him.

Ignác became keenly aware of his increasingly odd reclusiveness, which, in turn, further fueled his social insecurity. He made excuses not to attend communal activities of the medical school. He almost always dined by himself at lunch. If someone he recognized did approach him during a meal, he would quickly rise, wipe his mouth with a napkin, and pretend he had just finished dining and was on his way out to something urgent. Once an extroverted, affable young man with *joie de vivre*, he was now deeply troubled by his loss of sociability and his need to withdraw from contact even with old friends. He knew there was something very wrong.

CHAPTER 26

SUMMER 1856

At the same time, his courtship of Maria was blossoming, even though Maria's mother appeared to be none too pleased by their ninteen-year age difference. Maria's father, on the other hand, seemed more supportive than ever. Weidenhoffer saw Ignác as a great match for his daughter, and having a prominent physician as his son-in-law would be surely advantageous to the family's social standing.

Ignác called on Maria to invite her for walks on weekends whenever the weather permitted, often on the promenade along the Buda bank of the Danube—and always in the vigilant company of Maria's perpetually frowning mother. Notwithstanding her hovering, these were cheerful respites from the pressures of his work.

Mr. Weidenhoffer owned a successful business in marketing ribbons and provided his family with a very comfortable way of life. But Maria's mother came from a different social stratum altogether, born into the immensely wealthy and prominent Walthier family. She was the only daughter of Ferenc Walthier's five children. Her father was a renowned master glazier, making decorative glassware for some of Europe's finest palaces and public buildings. He then parlayed the wealth he accumulated from this craft to build glassmaking workshops and factories. He also invested well in real estate.

So Maria's mother grew up in a milieu of affluence and privilege. Moreover, she was adored and pampered by her four brothers, Ferenc junior, Antal, Alajos, and Ágost. All of the brothers themselves became enormously successful in business and commerce and independently became prosperous, multiplying the Walthier fortune and creating a family that was archetypical of the ambitious urban German bourgeoisie of that time.

If Maria's mother was frosty at the prospect of her daughter marrying Ignác Semmelweis, the others on her side of the family, the Walthiers, were outright antagonistic from the outset, especially her mother's four brothers and their father. No one knew exactly why.

As Ignác's courtship of Maria progressed, Mrs. Weidenhoffer's oldest brother, Ferenc, invited him to his home to become better acquainted. Ignác assumed it was for dinner, so he got dressed in an evening suit, picked up flowers for Ferenc's wife, whom he had never met, and took a carriage to their villa in a prestigious enclave of grand homes in the outskirts of Pest. But there was to be no dinner. And, instead of Ferenc's wife, Semmelweis found Ferenc's three brothers gathered there. He awkwardly handed the flowers to Ferenc.

"Welcome, Professor Semmelweis. It's so good of you to come," Ferenc said with a slight bow. "Please join us over here." With an outstretched arm, he directed Ignác to a stately door off the foyer.

Ferenc ushered Ignác into a softly lit, magnificently furnished library, with bookshelves filled to its soaring ceiling. An exquisite Turkish carpet covered most of the fine wood floor. Sitting in armchairs around an ornate coffee table were the other brothers, Antol, Alajos, and Ágost.

"Well, boys, here is Professor Semmelweis," said Ferenc, scanning the room without success for a place to put the flowers. So he held them up like a whimsical trophy. "Look what he brought. A beautiful bouquet! Isn't that thoughtful?"

The brothers all stood in unison to shake hands with Ignác, each with a regimented nod of the head.

"Please, Professor, we have left the couch all for you," Ferenc continued. He pointed to a golden-yellow-upholstered, Biedermeier-style sofa on the other side of the coffee table. Ignác situated himself in the middle of it. He now found himself facing the four brothers in their armchairs arrayed in a semicircle around the marble coffee table.

Cigar smoke hung thick in the air, but Ignác courteously declined the offer to take one. However, he did gladly accept a glass of Tokaji wine, which Ágost poured for him.

"Tokaji Aszú, the finest. Five puttonyos," said Ferenc. "We have bottles of the Tokaji Eszencia in the cellar, but I think that would be too sweet for this early in the evening, don't you think? When in Rome, do as the Romans do," he said holding up his own glass of the white wine. "So, when in Hungary, do as the Hungarians do, I say. *Egészségedre! Prost!*"

The brothers hoisted their glasses of Tokaji, fixing their gazes on Ignác, who, in turn, meekly raised his with a nervous smile.

"So, Professor . . ." Ferenc started.

"Please. Call me Ignác."

"All right, *Ignác*," Ferenc repeated. "I regret that our father couldn't be here this evening. He very much wanted to join us, but he is ill in bed."

"I hope nothing serious," said Ignác.

"Probably not. But you never know for sure at his age. We haven't had a chance to get to know each other, so I thought it would be time to do so. Just informally, you understand, like this. After all, Ignác, we may become your *uncles* in the future," Ferenc said with a pretentious laugh.

"My God, Ferenc," added Antal in mock horror, "that really sounds awful. *Uncles*? I picture uncles as old men. But we're all around the same age as you, Ignác, aren't we? I can't bear to even think of a day when you would call me 'Uncle Antal.' Can you?"

"Impossible," asserted Alajos. "I would deny my identity if someone called me 'Uncle Alajos.'"

They all chuckled, sipping the sweet Tokaji.

Ferenc stretched out his legs and crossed them at the ankles, sitting back to take a long puff of his cigar, resting his head on the back of the chair. He exhaled the smoke slowly to form rings in the air. "Seriously, that's one of our questions, Ignác." The smile vanished from his face. "You are almost twenty years older than our niece Maria. Don't you think that might cause problems in the future?"

"What kinds of problems?" Ignác asked.

"Well, you know, later, *much* later, of course, there is always the possibility . . . this is not pleasant to even contemplate now, but we must . . . that you might leave her a widow. Maybe even a widow for many years. What is to happen to Maria in that case?"

Ignác laughed. "Well, yes, it's possible. But I am in good health now. And by the time I plan to die, Maria will have grown children, maybe even grandchildren, to take care of her and keep her happy. And while I don't think I'll ever be *this* wealthy," Ignác said, looking around the library and spreading his arms, "I am sure I will have left her a sizable sum of securely accumulated income from my practice as a doctor."

"All right, but I must say our father has expressed deep concerns about the age difference, and he wanted us to convey that to you."

Now Ágost, the youngest, spoke up. "Are you Jewish, Ignác?"

"No, I am a devout Catholic, as is everyone in my family. One of my brothers is actually a priest."

"We know all that," Ágost replied. "We have had it extensively investigated, believe me. I am asking about your ancestors. 'Semmelweis' sounds like a Jewish family name."

Ágost flapped the cigar smoke from in front of his face and continued. "And you know you do have some subtle facial features that suggest a Jewish heritage."

Ignác now felt like a gnome swallowed up by the vast sofa he had sunk into. Looking around at the four brothers, all staring at him from their higher seats, he was now struck by their handsome Nordic features. They were all quite a bit taller than him. That was glaringly obvious from the moment they'd all stood to shake hands with him at the beginning. They all had luxuriant, neatly combed-back, blond hair, with clear, glowing complexions that only long periods of outdoor leisure could create. He self-consciously brushed back his own thinning and graying hair.

"No. None of my ancestors, as far as I know," replied Ignác. "There are parish baptismal records going back several generations."

"But not *complete* records," said Ferenc. "We have looked."

"Well, then, I confess—I don't have absolute proof. Maybe there *was* someone in the Middle Ages who had Ashkenazi ancestors and slipped into the family tree somehow while no one was looking," said Ignác with a sarcastic smirk.

"But this is a serious matter," said Ágost, uncrossing his legs, sitting forward, and putting his wine glass on the table.

"You know," replied Ignác, "I grew up in the Tabán district in Buda, where my friends came from all sorts of nationalities and cultures. Yes, most of us were Catholics, but there *were* quite a few Jews . . . and Protestants and Greek Orthodox and Islam. As boys, we didn't even know who was what. And I don't think our parents cared much, either, who they socialized with."

"I say," Antal said, standing up. "We must have some more Tokaji."

Antal refilled everyone's glass and then opened another bottle.

"But let me get to the problem that has us *most* concerned, Ignác, if I may be completely candid with you."

"Of course, we must be completely candid with each other," said Ignác, asking himself *what the hell are these snots going to grill me about now?*

"We have deep unease about your political . . . position," Ferenc continued. "And your family's. We have been told that three of your brothers fought in the revolution and are now on the run from prosecution, hiding out in unknown places. We also know that your brother Károly was a notorious activist and agitator and that he used his priest's holy pulpit to recruit Hungarians into Kossuth's army. He even collaborated with Kossuth directly."

"I don't know about that last one, the one about the relationship between Károly and Kossuth," said Ignác. "But please, do go on. I didn't mean to interrupt." *You son of a bitch*, he added to himself.

"Even your sister's husband and her in-laws were active participants," continued Ferenc. "We know the Ráth family well. My father used to do business with their father. So we know very well what their political views are. They are overtly liberal reformists and nationalists. And they are in positions where they can still do much damage."

Ferenc now sat back in his armchair, relit his cigar, and took a couple of slow puffs while the others remained silent.

"So what do you say to all that?" Ferenc continued, stretching out his legs again.

"Well, I think each person has his own beliefs and his own reasons for what they say and do. There's nothing I can do to change those personal matters of the mind and heart, but . . ."

"But yes, you can," blurted out Ágost in an agitated state. "You can lock them up in a prison or even eliminate them if necessary!"

Everyone was startled, but Ferenc quickly interceded.

"Shut up, Ágost! We are not arguing here. And you interrupted the professor," he said glaring at his young brother. "Ignác, please go on, and I apologize. That outburst was very . . . imprudent."

"As I was saying," continued Ignác, trying mightily to maintain a cool façade, "each man had to do whatever his conscience dictated during the revolution. But we were all patriots, for goodness' sake. Hungarian patriots."

"Please don't misunderstand. The Walthier family has been patriotic also. We even consider ourselves to be *Hungarian* patriots, despite our Germanic roots. But we have felt that the situation in this country demanded a much different course of action. Not rebellion. You must also respect that different point of view."

"Certainly . . ." started Ignác.

"And please allow me to add something to what Ferenc just said, if I may," said Antal. "Look at this family, Ignác. We have been successful in our lives. And, yes, we are grateful to Hungary for giving us the opportunity to be that. My father and brothers have worked hard, and, no question about it, we've been fortunate to amass great wealth. But our successful businesses have also enriched this country. We have given back. This idiotic war for independence was a bloody fiasco. It was invented for amusement by idle young men. Shallow hooligans, like that poseur poet Petőfi. We ourselves have suffered losses, you know. Some of the Walthier houses and factories have been damaged. One of them may even have to be torn down and rebuilt. And for two years, while the revolution raged, our businesses took big hits. As you can imagine, demand for our glassware almost stopped. We are just now beginning to recover . . ."

Bullshit, Ignác thought, *you bastards probably figured out a way to profit from the war.*

". . . so we think Hungary must now pull itself together, reintegrate into the Empire, reassure Vienna that we will be loyal partners. That means we have to continue to crack down on dissidents. We must restore law and order."

"*This,*" picked up Antal, "is why our family is so concerned about being linked to yours. It's not you personally, you understand? It's the damage that might come to our businesses and our reputations from just the suspicion that the Walthiers are connected in any way to subversive elements."

"Frankly, you yourself *were* a member of the Academic Legion in Vienna. And we know that you protested by wearing traditional Magyar attire while teaching medical students," said Ferenc.

"How do you know all this?" Ignác asked incredulously.

"Let's just say the Walthiers are well connected," Ferenc replied.

"But I *never* spoke out for rebellion, I *never* carried any weapons, and I *never* killed or even hurt anybody," remonstrated Ignác. "I did quite the opposite. I worked day and night to save lives. So how could anyone possibly say that Maria Walthier Weidenhoffer would be married to a seditious, treasonous agitator?"

They parted on politely strained terms. Ignác felt he had been ambushed. It was a completely unexpected interrogation. He bitterly resented being caught off guard. Once again, he found himself seething with humiliation about his naiveté and ineptitude in his interactions with powerful people. Ignác was determined to marry Maria anyway. They both wanted it, and Maria's father certainly wanted it. But as he walked home that night, foregoing a carriage ride, he could not see how he would ever be able to trust, much less respect, his future in-laws. And he was still hungry for dinner.

CHAPTER 27

NOVEMBER 1856

Finally, at the end of 1856, Ignác summoned the courage to ask Mr. Weidenhoffer for Maria's hand in marriage. His nervousness was unnecessary. Maria's father immediately responded with a suffocating bear hug from which Ignác was finally released only when he threw up his arms in submission.

The wedding took place in June of 1857. The Weidenhoffers and their friends greatly outnumbered the Semmelweis party. A solitary, red-uniformed *gendarme* stood silently at the back of the church. To Ignác's delight, but perhaps much to the chagrin of the Walthiers, the ceremony was officiated by his Catholic priest brother, Károly. Ignác and Maria moved into a modest apartment on the third floor of a house on Váci utca, a busy shopping street. Its location was a convenient walk for Ignác to the hospital, and the apartment's windows overlooked a lovely, small inner courtyard.

It was where the new couple started their family.[111] And it was where Ignác now found his nighttime sanctuary from the escalating turmoil and hostility of his workplace.

Over the next six years, Maria gave birth to five children. The couple experienced boundless joy, but also despair and heartbreak, because two of the children died in infancy. Though he often came home bone-tired, the solace of his growing family revived his spirits. Ignác began to realize that the only way to fight back professionally, to beat down the forces of ignorance in the medical establishment, was to do what his friends had been pleading with him to do for so many years. Maybe his book would be regarded as inelegant, unsophisticated, even ridiculed by all those haughty, pretentious medical "scholars" of Europe. But he had to put pen to paper and document the details of his great discovery for all the world to read. The raw data, the pure facts, he assumed, would speak for themselves.

And so, in the late hours of the night, Ignác began to apply himself to the labor of completing his definitive book, *Die Aetiologie, der Begriff und die Prophylaxis des Kindbettfiebers* (*The Etiology, the Concept, and the Prophylaxis of Childbed Fever*). It was a painfully slow process. Some nights he would sit at his desk for what seemed like hours without creating a single properly structured sentence. But then, ever so slowly, night after night, in the dead silence and stillness, his writer's block began to evaporate. With growing confidence, he began to pour out the story of his discovery and its aftermath. Attempts at sticking to scientific writing conventions, style, and format succumbed to an increasingly passionate exposé of events as he saw them. The text was often rambling, unstructured, even repetitious, written like a man driven. Facts were decorated with Semmelweis's free-wheeling commentaries, including vitriolic criticisms of the medical establishment, personal insinuations and accusations directed at named individuals, and a general baring of his tortured soul.

The *Etiology* was finally finished in October 1860 and published the following year.[112] He expected the public reaction to it to be controversial, but at least the book would vindicate his personal struggles for acceptance of the unassailable truth. Whatever professional hostilities the work would likely provoke, its ultimate effect would be the saving of millions of lives of mothers and their babies in the generations ahead.

So he waited for the reactions.

But there was practically none. Maybe, he thought, there had been a problem with the book's printing, its dissemination, or its publicity. But after many months, the only response Ignác received was a mere trickle of critiques and even less praise from mostly unknown physicians.

Semmelweis was bewildered by the silence. And then he became increasingly resentful. Worse than being criticized was being ignored. At least he could rationally rebut criticism, but what could he do about silence?

In utter frustration, Ignác now took matters into his own hands and launched a campaign of personal letter writing to the most prominent and influential obstetricians in Europe, especially those he understood to be the most outspoken opponents of his theories. Even more than in the book, he blasted his adversaries with unfiltered, self-righteous indignation, fury, and indictments. He spared no one, including former colleagues in Vienna like Späth. And to rub salt into the wounds his words inflicted, he impulsively made his individual letters public, copying them to all he considered to be of any stature in the field in the great universities of Europe.

In many cases, there were still no responses. Undoubtedly the recipients of the letters were sometimes too shocked to reply, or considered any response to be beneath their dignity. But in other cases, the counterattacks were swift and devastatingly toxic. Just as he had polarized the medical establishments where he worked in Vienna and Budapest, Semmelweis now found himself in the center of a professional storm that he alone had created, the brunt of which was to become irreparably destructive to his reputation.

The ensuing years were characterized by an ever-increasing compulsion to work, with obsessive attention to detail and micromanaged control. His periods of self-imposed social isolation and dread of being among people intensified, even as puerperal fever remained pervasive in other countries. He was tortured by his awareness that most of Europe continued to ignore or downright reject his findings. His ever-present consternation about it erupted into periods of unfettered rage with increasing frequency. *Why, God, is the world denying or renouncing my discovery?* Ignác would storm. *It can't be just personal animosity. And it can't be just lack of enlightenment, now that my data and my book are published for all to see! I know now that there is a deep-rooted inclination of mankind to combat new ideas,*[113] *but it surely can't be sheer obstinacy!! Even if they don't like me, they are all doctors, aren't they? If they don't believe my data, they can at least try to reproduce them conscientiously. Can't they? What would be the harm?*

And, with time, his growing self-righteous resentment gradually yielded to an inexorable disintegration of personality.

CHAPTER 28

JULY 1864

On Saturday, July 2, 1864, Ignác awoke at an uncharacteristically late hour for him. He hadn't slept well, but that was happening often these days. He threw open the windows to the back courtyard. It was already a hot and hazy summer morning. In the distance, he could hear the clip-clopping of horse-drawn carriages passing by the front of the house and the stirring of street life on Váci utca. Maria and the children were still asleep.

The day before had been Ignác's forty-sixth birthday, but it had passed unnoticed. Even Maria had forgotten about it, but Ignác didn't mind. She had her hands full with the children, and their days of mutual infatuation for each other had long ago receded behind the daily struggles and heartbreaks of family life. But when Ignác looked in the mirror over his washbasin this morning, he was startled. He couldn't take his eyes off the visage that stared back at him.

He glimpsed at himself in the same mirror every day, but what alarmed him this time was the apparition of an old man. He gazed at the wrinkles and furrows, the dark circles and bags under the eyes, the jowls and sagging neck, and the appearance of a double chin. Turning away from the mirror and glancing at his portrait on the wall that had been painted only a few years earlier, he saw a shockingly changed person. He had stopped trying to brush his dark hair across his balding forehead, but what little remained of it over the back of the head and sideburns, as well as his mustache, had now turned a drab grey. His eyes had narrowed and become deeply set.[114]

By now there were practically no remnants of his eccentric charm left to redeem his likability for anyone who worked with him. For those who hadn't known Ignác for long, he was just a wretchedly bitter, spiteful, prematurely old man. Some of his colleagues, even those who had always admired and supported him, openly worried that he was losing his mind.[115] Was he turning into a raving lunatic?

And yet, at the same time, Ignác remained unfailingly kind to his patients. He had never been more indulgent and empathetic toward them. He still gave lilacs, picked in the spring and summer months from the hills of Buda, to the new mothers and their newborns. He twirled them in front of the babies with great delight before he pinned them on their dresses. He remained uncompromising in his insistence on the mothers' welfare and even comfort. He spent endless hours listening to their complaints, tending to their ailments, and getting to know them as people.

Ignác's own hand scrubbing routine assumed practically fanatical dimensions. He would scrub his hands and arms like a man possessed, sometimes repeatedly after drying them. It was almost as if it was to make up for the deficiencies of others. Or he sometimes forgot that he had just scrubbed his hands, so he did it again in case he hadn't. His hands and arms were constantly red and raw, as Maria pointed out to him; the skin sometimes sloughed and blisters appeared. But Ignác carried on, more strenuously than ever. And he didn't try to hide his unsightly skin condition. In fact, he viewed it as a badge of his determination, something he wanted his students to see and emulate.

In the late fall, Ignác was in an especially foul mood on the morning of a scheduled meeting with von Tandler. The very idea of being summoned by anyone, particularly a bureaucrat like von Tandler, annoyed him immensely. But at the appointed hour, he completed his patient rounds, scrubbed his hands, slicked down the unruly sides of his thinning hair, and started to walk toward von Tandler's office. Lakai, the young hospital administrative assistant who had been bringing Ignác his basins of chlorinated lime every morning since Tamás Bácsi disappeared, intercepted Ignác at the door. Lakai was more formally attired than usual this morning and looked uncharacteristically somber. He said he'd been assigned to escort Ignác to the meeting. After crossing the courtyard, Lakai made a sharp left turn instead of walking straight into von Tandler's office suite. He ushered the now puzzled Ignác up the warped marble staircase to the board conference room, where he was asked to take a seat outside its massive, closed door until he was called in. Ignác noticed that a *gendarme* was standing silently near the staircase. *Was it him again? Who assigned him? Why do I keep seeing him? What does he want?*

"What's this all about, Lakai?" asked Ignác.

"Herr Direktor will come out when they are ready."

"What do you mean *they*?"

Lakai just shrugged his shoulders and walked away, leaving Ignác to ponder this unexpected situation. He heard some men's voices from behind the closed door but couldn't make out who they were or what they were saying. Finally, after what seemed like an eternity, the door was flung open by an orderly, who beckoned Ignác in.

Arrayed around three sides of the massive board table were several men he instantly recognized but was shocked to see here. A lone, vacant chair at one end was clearly reserved for him.[116] Directly across from him sat von Tandler at the head of the table. Ignác had never been inside this room. It was poorly lit, with heavy curtains drawn to block the sunlight from entering the large windows. The air was heavy with dust. On the walls were large portraits of older men who must have been important at one time. A dim chandelier was the centerpiece of the ceiling.

Each of the men rose, tentatively, to sheepishly acknowledge Ignác. He suddenly felt faint. Not only had he expected this to be an informal private meeting of no special gravity with von Tandler, but he was now at a loss to figure out what each of the others was doing here. Späth was there from Vienna: they greeted each other stiffly and with mutual wariness. There was a man he instantly recognized despite his much-changed appearance since they last saw each other before the revolution: it was the pharmacist Béla Esterházy, that overbearing Habsburg loyalist. The young ophthalmologist Ignác Hirschler was there: Ignác had last seen him with von Tandler, escorting the old Anton von Rosas during his last visit to Budapest. And there was the surgeon Balassa, impassive and inscrutable as usual, barely lifting himself out of his chair.

Ignác was asked to take his seat. As if on cue, Lakai reappeared to bring Ignác a glass of water he hadn't asked for, and then took a seat nearby against the wall.

As von Tandler began in a tone of excruciating formality, Ignác's apprehension turned to alarm. The feeling of being trapped swept over him like a wave. Blood seemed to rush to his head, his face felt red hot, his heart was pounding, and he was getting lightheaded. The men around the table began to appear faceless and otherworldly. *What the hell was going on here?*

He took a sip of water.

"I want to explain, Dr. Semmelweis, why I have asked these gentlemen to join us today," began von Tandler. "Professor Späth, to my left, was recently appointed professor of obstetrics at the University of Vienna. I think you know each other well. I understand that he and you trained together under Professor Klein."

Ignác just sat there, dazed and silent.

"Dr. Semmelweis," called out von Tandler. "Professor Späth here . . ."

"No," muttered Ignác, blankly staring into the distance.

"No?" von Tandler thundered insistently.

Ignác now snapped back into focus. "No!" he asserted. "He was actually an Assistant to my colleague and friend, Johann Chiari, not Professor Klein."

"I beg your pardon," continued von Tandler. "I stand corrected. Next to Professor Späth is Herr Béla Esterházy. I know the two of you met several years ago. Herr Esterházy is now the Deputy Minister of Public Education for Hungary."

"Well, Herr Esterházy, you have certainly done well for yourself since the revolution. My congratulations to you," Ignác said with a sarcastic bow of his head.

"Thank you, Semmelweis."

"So this means you must be working under my friend, the Count von Thun, the imperial minister who appointed me. He and I . . ."

"The Count hasn't been in that position for more than two years now," von Tandler interrupted. "He committed suicide; don't you know?"

Seeing Ignác's distress, Lakai stepped to his side and whispered in his ear. "He didn't really commit suicide. He meant *career* suicide. He was just replaced."

"This is Doktor Ignác Hirschler," von Tandler continued, "who you also know well as your colleague and a former pupil of the late Professor von Rosas. And then sitting next to Hirschler is, of course, our eminent Herr Professor János Balassa. And back there against the wall is my administrative aide Lakai, who I had *personally* assigned you—as you well know, Professor—to prepare and deliver those basins of water with your chemicals for your hand-washing . . . ritual." Lakai stood up and then quickly sat back down again.

"With a special basin prepared and labeled for your exclusive use only. Just like you ordered in Vienna," von Tandler added, now shuffling some papers in front of him. "We are meeting with you here today because of our deep disappointment with your lack of progress in eradicating puerperal fever on our maternity ward at the University of Pest," von Tandler began. "It was because we thought you could do something about it that we brought you here to oversee the service in the first place."

His heart and head began to pound again. It took all his powers of self-control to keep from jumping out of his seat to berate von Tandler. But von Tandler continued calmly and deliberately.

"Beginning with the year after I agreed to provide you with considerable additional funds to contract for a daily laundry service, provided you with a paid assistant, daily service to prepare that chlorinated lime concoction for you, as well as many other support services, the annual mortality rate in maternity has essentially doubled each year. Yes, *doubled*," he repeated as he scanned his colleagues around the table. "For the current year, you are on track for a mortality rate of almost five percent."

Ignác was dumbfounded. He couldn't believe what he was hearing. But he knew he had to collect his thoughts quickly to give a rational response to an irrational attack.

"First of all, that's just incorrect," he snapped. "I don't know where the hell you are getting those numbers from . . ."

"They are from our government records," injected Balassa.

"Horse's ass! I have kept unassailably accurate numbers—and you know that damned well, von Tandler," he now shouted, pointing his finger directly at the director. "You know that because you get my monthly reports, which you are invited to challenge any time if you disagree. But you've never bothered to do so."

"Calm down, Herr Professor," warned von Tandler. "The numbers I have were verified by the ministry. We even have burial records. Here, pass this paper around to him!"

"Whatever that paper states, the numbers are obviously cooked," snapped back Ignác before the paper even reached him.

"What do you mean 'cooked'?" Hirschler now joined in.

"Cooked . . . inflated . . . padded . . . fabricated, damn it," Ignác shot back. "But even if they were correct, which I repeat they aren't, they would be infinitely superior to the death rates in Vienna, *after* my departure that is, or in Prague, or Berlin, or any other major city in Europe!" He took a gulp of water. "What is this all about, anyway?" Ignác said, looking around the table with darting glances at his stone-faced interrogators.

"I don't wish to get into an argument," Späth now spoke up quietly, "but in Vienna the numbers have been going in the *opposite* direction to what is happening here. Improving every year for the past three years."

"What the hell are you talking about, Späth? Your mortality rate shot up to more than fifteen percent right after I left because Klein and Braun and all their ignorant sycophants stopped washing hands. Our baseline in Pest following just my first year here was 0.39 percent in 1855–1856! Do you understand what that means? That's about as close to eradication as you can get!" thundered Semmelweis. He was now unable to stop himself from standing up.

No one spoke.

"There must be something else behind this meeting!" he shouted and then sat down.

"Honorable Herr Esterhäzy, now please tell the professor the concerns of the ministry," resumed von Tandler.

"Well, not only has your performance deteriorated . . ."

"Deteriorated bullshit!" bellowed Ignác. "Haven't you been listening?" Lakai's hand on his shoulder stopped him there.

Esterházy continued in a controlled tone. "Not only has your performance deteriorated, but you have created a serious budget deficit for your service, which is now near crisis levels unless you can fix it immediately." Esterházy picked up a paper from his own file and held it up, reading from it. "Just in the past year alone, your operating deficit was 314,000 gulden and 40 kreuzer."

"That's close to catastrophic," exclaimed von Tandler, accompanied by a collective gasp from around the table.

"But that's . . ." Ignác now found himself unable to get a word in edgewise.

"Just for comparison," interrupted Hirschler, "our ophthalmology service made an almost 30,000 gulden profit last year."

"Your patients are not all destitute like ours! How can you . . ."

"Well, what do you have to say?" added Balassa.

"I am trying to explain if you give me a chance . . ." But yet again Ignác couldn't finish a sentence. He was feeling ambushed.

"This is sheer fiscal irresponsibility," exclaimed Esterházy.

"What do you want me to do about it? I am not even allowed access to these numbers. For all I know . . ."

"You don't seem to know very much, do you? This was supposed to be your *job* when you were appointed chief of the service."

"We also have that matter of your involvement with Herr Marx several years ago," von Tandler interrupted. "There have been grave concerns for quite some time, as you well know, about your Marxist sympathies. Where do you stand now, insofar as your loyalties are concerned, to the present government?"

Ignác felt as if his head was about to explode. He asked Lakai for another glass of water.

"I can't answer several questions at the same time! Is this a firing squad?"

"Well, let's just pause here so that you can gather yourself together, Semmelweis," suggested von Tandler, "because there are even more serious matters we must attend to."

"*What* matters?" Ignác was aware that he was beginning to lose his grip.

Turning to Balassa, von Tandler asked him to present the other problems.

"Simply stated, you have antagonized most of the people you have been working with, whether they be your physician colleagues, your staff, or your administrators. You make unreasonable demands, your attitude is supercilious, and from everything we know about your time in Vienna, this pattern of behavior is a continuation, and it's getting much, much worse. You are frankly becoming an embarrassment to this institution and to our medical community in Budapest."

Balassa's comments were made calmly, barely audibly, without ever making eye contact with Ignác. He almost seemed to be reading them from a script. When he finished, Balassa didn't look up.

"Professor Späth," said von Tandler, turning to the visitor from Vienna, "you yourself have been the recipient of one of those defamatory letters, haven't you?"

Späth nodded and now read out *verbatim* the public letter Semmelweis had recently written to him personally:

> *"Herr Professor,*
>
> *You have convinced me that the Puerperal Sun which arose in Vienna in the year 1847 has not enlightened your mind, even though it shone so near to you. This arrogant ignoring of my doctrine, this arrogant boasting about your errors, demands that I make the following declaration:*
>
> *Within myself, I bear the knowledge that since the year 1847 thousands and thousands of puerperal women and infants who have died would not have died had I not kept silent, instead of providing the necessary correction to every error which has been spread about puerperal fever.*
>
> *And you, Herr Professor, have been a partner in this massacre. The murder must cease, and in order that the murder ceases, I will keep watch, and anyone who dares to propagate dangerous errors about childbed fever will find in me an eager adversary . . ."*

Späth paused to look around the room and then, locking eyes with Semmelweis, he read the conclusion of the letter in a raised voice, quavering with barely contained anger:

"In order to put an end to these murders, I have no resort but to mercilessly expose my adversaries, and no one whose heart is in the right place will criticize me for seizing this expedient."[117]

There was a murmur around the room. Individuals around the table glanced knowingly at each other. Then there was a lengthy, awkward silence.

"So what do you want from me?" Ignác asked. "What's the bottom line here?"

"I think that's all we need from you, at least for now," sighed von Tandler as he stood to signal the end of the meeting to everyone. The others remained seated and started chatting with each other, expecting Ignác to leave the room. But he didn't. In fact, he sat back in his chair, his legs outstretched, hands behind his head, patiently waiting for everyone's attention. As one by one they all stopped talking and turned to see him still in his place, he finally spoke up, looking straight at von Tandler.

"So let me try to understand, Herr von Tandler, why exactly you convened this distinguished group of gentlemen." Von Tandler sat back down tentatively. "Was this intended to be a tribunal of some kind? And what was the intended outcome? Some sort of disciplinary action directed at me?"

There was no immediate response. Several of the men around the table began to squirm and fidget uncomfortably. Finally, von Tandler leaned forward to address Semmelweis.

"I think you have the gist of it, Herr Professor," he said. "Now if you don't mind, I would ask you to leave the room. Lakai will escort you. My office will notify you in due time if and when any further action is deemed indicated. Thank you for your time."

Von Tandler was scribbling a note as he said this. When Lakai passed by him as he was following Ignác out of the room, von Tandler held him up and gave him the note. Lakai read it, nodded to von Tandler, folded it neatly, and put it in his pocket.

Ignác left the boardroom shell-shocked. His gait had become noticeably wobbly and shuffling, his shoes sliding like slippers along the waxed wooden floor of the corridor. He gripped the wrought-iron balustrades as he walked down the warped marble staircase step by step. He stumbled out into the courtyard, breathing rapidly and feeling dizzy again. Lakai ran up behind him and grabbed his arm before he could fall.

"Are you all right, Professor?" he asked, but Ignác didn't hear him. His ears were ringing.

Lakai walked away. Ignác finally pulled himself together and got back on his feet slowly, holding onto the arm of the bench. He looked around suspiciously to make sure no one else had seen him, and then he walked out of the courtyard into the street.

He instinctively found himself briskly walking toward his favorite spot in the City Park, a good distance away but an opportunity to clear his head in the fresh air. His customary trail through the park had been recently paved with gravel, and there were now some horse-drawn carriages to look out for, but there was no foot traffic. And it still had those great chestnut trees that were almost bare now.

He sat on a park bench to think. Just like in Vienna, at a time that now seemed so long ago, when he used to escape to the Volksgarten to wrestle with his private anguish in solitude. At a distance, he thought he saw the *gendarme* sitting on a bench, dressed in the traditional red tunic uniform and plumage-decorated black hat. The *gendarme* was looking down at the ground, but when he raised his head, Ignác immediately recognized that damned black, twirled, handlebar mustache. *Oh, God,* thought Ignác, now shivering intensely. *It's him again! Who is that man? What does he want from me?* Ignác looked the other way. Maybe he hadn't noticed him.

He kept replaying certain parts of the meeting in his mind, feeling the waves of indignation sweeping over him. He never saw what was coming at him when he walked into that room. He was enraged about having been blindsided like that. And even more so about all those people ganging up on him. *It was orchestrated, no question about it,* he thought. But what was he to make of this assault? It was obviously a conspiracy, but a conspiracy to do *what*? To discredit him? To fire him? To get rid of him altogether? There was no question in his mind that these people were out to get him! And how wide was this net of conspiracy? Why couldn't he learn to be more skillful in navigating the indecent politics of academic medicine? Why couldn't he scheme better? Why couldn't he plot and collude and maneuver with more cunning? His gullibility always left him exposed. No, it did more than that; it *invited* attack.

Ignác nodded off on the bench. He was exhausted from the interrogation and even more so by the conspiracy theories and self-reproach that now filled his mind. Not much time passed before he was awakened by a carriage rolling past him filled with merrymaking passengers laughing and shouting out of its open windows. The solitary *gendarme* was gone now.

He felt refreshed. He took a walk along familiar paths. It was late for chestnuts, but he searched for some old ones that might have been left on the ground nonetheless. He found a few on the gravel path that were squashed, undoubtedly by the carriages. He picked one up and held it in his palm. The brilliant, shiny color was gone, but as Ignác stared at its peculiarly flattened configuration, its shape appeared strangely familiar. He stood transfixed at this squished chestnut, and it transported him back to that New Year's Eve in Vienna, his last time with Caroline, when the old gypsy woman poured molten lead for *das Bleigiessen.* Yes, that's what it looked like, he thought with his heart now pounding; it looked like *das Kreuz* . . . . a cross! The gypsy woman had told him what it signified: death.

CHAPTER 29

FEBRUARY 1865

Ignác began to descend into the darkest depths of insanity at the beginning of 1865. Even the few who had remained close to him, like his wife and Marko, could no longer deny it. They could no longer attribute his increasingly bizarre behavior to just his old eccentricities. His forgetfulness was now pervasive, and it was evident to all around him. No longer were his fits of temper and inconsolable melancholy interspersed with long periods of reason and amiability. The disintegration of personality was now virtually complete.

Passing by István Bathory, his current Assistant, in the corridor one day, he stopped him and casually said:

"Oh, Bathory. I think I forgot to tell you. I am not renewing your appointment for another term."

Bathory looked dumbfounded. "I don't know what to say," he stammered. "I mean, things have been going quite well, don't you think? I thought you were pleased with my work. At least you haven't said anything . . ."

Ignác just looked at him vacantly with unchanged expression. "Well, that's it, then," he said.

"That's it?" Bathory was practically speechless.

"Yes, it's done," replied Ignác flatly. "I have hired someone else."

"But . . . Why? . . . Is it because you were also allowed to do only one term in Vienna when you were in my position? I am sorry. I didn't mean it that way, sir."

"All right, then. Have a good day." With that, Ignác walked on, leaving Bathory frozen in place.

At other times, Ignác even raged at his best friend, Marko, as if he were a complete stranger, one of those incompetent hospital employees. When Maria took him to the countryside with the young children to try to lift his spirits, he wandered off by himself without saying a word, as if he had come alone.[118] And his conduct began to assume ever more frightening and even perverse qualities. He was now unable to sleep most nights and found himself aimlessly roaming the dark, deserted streets of Pest, sometimes for hours at a time, in the middle of the night. He often wandered into seedy neighborhoods, where he encountered only prostitutes and drunks. His inhibitions now crumbled, Ignác had no compunction about approaching some of these denizens.[119] What he said was stereotypical and idiosyncratic babble only about puerperal fever and his discovery. People quickly moved on in utter bewilderment. To Semmelweis, the topic of hand scrubbing to prevent puerperal fever had now become an *idée fixe*.[120]

In the daytime, sleep deprived as he was, he roamed the congested streets of Pest carrying a stack of page prints from his book to hand out to any passerby who would take one. He stood in place on street corners and repeated the same phrases over and over again, warning young women against the dangers of maternity wards. He repeatedly recited the same sentences about childbed fever and unclean hands. Practically no one stopped to listen, but many glanced at him and wondered who this raving lunatic was. The very same mind that had been so open to observation and discovery was now closed to the opinions of others and the concern of his friends.

I

In the Spring of 1865, the perennial fragrance of lilacs swept down from the Buda hills with the warm June breeze. People in the streets looked more cheerful than they had been in a long time. And it wasn't just because of the promise of summer. This time there was also a sense of refreshed freedom in the air as the Viennese authorities finally began to loosen the viselike grip of spying and censorship they had imposed since Hungary's failed revolution seventeen years earlier. Women could again be spotted in public daring to wear traditional Magyar costumes. It was said that the Ruszwurm café in Buda even flew the red-white-and-green flag alongside the Austrian one.

But for Maria, these were the gloomiest days of her life. She was overcome with a sense of total helplessness as she tried to deal with her husband's deteriorating mental state, all the while fully occupied with raising their children. Her mother's brothers, the Walthiers, had repeatedly tried to persuade her to move out of the house with the children and come to live with one or another of them. Ágost even outright told her to leave that madman to rot away by himself. Out of desperation, she visited Marko in his medical office, bringing with her little Antonia while her mother looked after the others. There she tearfully described Ignác's rapidly progressive forgetfulness.

"You know he has been that way for years," Marko tried to reassure her, empathetically smiling as he sat cross-legged in his armchair across from Maria and the baby, trying to appear at ease.

"Yes, Marko, I know," she replied. "But this is very different. He doesn't seem to remember things he said just a few minutes earlier. He will forget where he placed his pocket watch or his glasses the night before—and then he'll shout at me the next morning, accusing me of intentionally moving them. And he has completely lost track of our finances. He'll buy all sorts of extravagant things . . ." Maria choked up, sobbing.

"For you?" interrupted Marko.

"Yes, sometimes for me. An expensive necklace or a bracelet . . ."

"Well, isn't he just like the old charmer!" Marko tried to make light of Ignác's profligacy.

". . . but also, all kinds of odd things for himself that he then tends to misplace or never use at all."

"Here, have some coffee, Maria." Marko stood up to pour her a cup, handed it to her, and gently patted the smiling Antonia's head.

"He is spending all the money we have," said Maria. "I've even had to cover his tracks and sometimes give merchants promissory notes. I haven't told him any of this. But you know what's especially troubling? I don't even know *where* most of our money is disappearing."

Marko listened intently as Maria continued. "And then there are the nights he can't sleep. He sometimes paces around the bedroom in the dark, loudly bumping into things. But more and more I see him, through one open eye, getting dressed and quietly leaving the house. I don't know where he goes, Marko, but sometimes he doesn't come home till daybreak. And then when he does, he smells awful . . . stale cigarette smoke and liquor. Even vomit and urine sometimes. When I try to ask him if he is all right, he starts to shout at me, tells me it's none of my business. Then he climbs back into bed and abruptly pulls the cover over his head."

"My dear Maria, he is just passing through a troubled time," said Marko unconvincingly, staring into the distance. "We have all noticed that he looks a bit disheveled these days—that's all."

"Disheveled?" Maria raised her voice. "You have no idea! There are mornings when I have to help him get dressed properly. The other day I overslept and opened my eyes in time to see him trying to leave without his trousers on."

Marko walked over to place a reassuring arm around the distraught woman's shoulders and squeezed them. She stood to embrace him, quietly sobbing on his shoulder.

"Maria, believe me that we will help you and Ignác get through this together. You're not alone, my dear."

With that, Maria picked up little Antonia and left Marko's office, sniffling, with a forced smile behind the teardrops pouring down her cheeks. As the door closed behind her, Marko slumped into his armchair, leaned forward with elbows on knees, and buried his head into his hands.

On Friday afternoon, July 21, 1865, Ignác arrived late for the monthly meeting of the medical school faculty. Someone else was already presenting a report, but many in the room turned to look at Ignác as he shuffled to his chair. The scant hair above his ears was sticking out, and his black cravat was partly untied and askew around his neck. He was noticeably more agitated and preoccupied than usual, and didn't make eye contact with anyone around the large table as he took his seat with an uninhibited grunt. Nor did he look up at all as the meeting proceeded. His mind was miles away.

"Professor Semmelweis!" called out Professor Balassa, who was chairing the meeting. Ignác's body jolted to attention. "You are next on the agenda. Please give us your report on the status of the search for a gynecologist to fill the vacancy on your faculty."

Unsteadily, Ignác rose to his feet. Gripping the back of his chair as he positioned himself behind it, he bent forward at the waist and lowered his head as if he were about to faint. Then, gathering himself, he finally looked up, his face ashen and his eyes scanning the room in befuddlement. He rubbed his furrowed forehead and then frantically reached into his trouser pockets, pulling out a crumpled piece of paper. He held it up close to his squinting eyes with trembling hands and began to read it silently, as if it were the first time he had seen it. Finally, he cleared his throat and began:

"You shall swear first that you will be diligent and faithful and ready to help every woman laboring of child, as well the poor as the rich; and that in time of necessity, you shall not forsake the poor woman to go to the rich . . ."

Several around the table looked befuddled at their colleagues.

"... You shall neither cause nor suffer any woman to name, or put any other father to the child, but only him which is the very true father thereof..."

A growing murmur arose within the room, as many began to whisper to each other or cough uncomfortably.

"... You shall not suffer any woman or her child to be murdered, maimed, or otherwise hurt..."[121]

Balassa slowly stood up and walked over to Ignác, gently placing a hand on his shoulder. He was soon joined by József Fleischer, Ignác's former Assistant, István Bathory, his current one, and then Marko. Ignác uttered a few more words and then slumped back into his chair, appearing exhausted.

The crumpled piece of paper from which he had been struggling to read fell onto the table in front of him. It was impossible to read the practically illegible scribbling on most of the sheet. But the heading, written in large but tremulous capital letters was The Midwife's Oath.[122]

As the room now filled with loud conversation, Marko leaned over to say something to Fleischer, and the two men gently lifted Ignác up and slowly escorted him out the door, one on each arm. Bathory had run out ahead of them to hail a carriage, into which Ignác was then helped. Accompanied by his friends, he was taken home. Maria opened the door and cupped her hand over her mouth in fright as they supported him into the house.

"He became very tired," Marko said to Maria. "I think he will feel much better after he gets some sleep."

They looked at each other knowingly, both understanding that something was awfully wrong, as the men assisted the dazed Ignác into his bedroom, followed by Maria and then little Antonia[123] crawling after them.

Maria helped Ignác undress and put him to bed. Fleischer and Bathory left, but Marko waited for her in the living room. It was a long wait. When Maria finally emerged, she broke down sobbing. Marko sat her down next to him and placed his arm around her shoulder. She was convulsed in tears.

"What am I going to do now? What is to become of us?"

Ignác awoke completely confused on Monday morning. He tried to go to work, but Maria convinced him to stay at home to get more rest. In the meantime, arrangements were being hastily made at the hospital under János Balassa's directions to have Ignác committed to an insane asylum. A friend of Ignác's, the pediatrician János Bókai, was assigned to write up the medical letter of referral to the new public asylum in Vienna. Maria was right: with Ignác's profligacy, they didn't have the money to place him in a private clinic. And she was too proud to ask her family for money. Bókai went to Ignác's home under the pretext of paying him a social visit, examined him in only the most unobtrusive and cursory fashion possible, and then wrote a detailed history based entirely on Maria's account of what had transpired. The referral letter was promptly co-signed by an internist named János Wagner, and by Balassa.[124]

In Maria's presence, Ignác's Assistant, Bathory, was summoned by Balassa and enlisted to accompany his chief on the train journey to Vienna. As Balassa prescribed it, Ignác would be told by Maria and Bathory that they were traveling to the famous spa of Gräfenberg in Bavaria. They would say that they had arranged for Ignác to take a much-needed vacation, to take the waters in the natural springs for a health cure. At the same time, Balassa enlisted the complicity of Hebra, Ignác's old friend and colleague in Vienna, to intercept him at the train station in Vienna and then help spirit him off to the asylum under a false pretext, in Ignác's best interest. Bathory wondered whether someone other than him should be chosen to go with Ignác.

"As you probably know, Professor Semmelweis won't be renewing my position as his Assistant after this year. If that means he doesn't trust me, he could become suspicious about what I am doing traveling with him to a spa," Bathory protested.

"Not at all, my boy," replied Balassa. "The professor is a very ill man, and we want him to get the care he needs in a most expeditious way. In his delusional state, he would never agree to it. But you are his current Assistant, and you probably know his state of mind these days better than anyone."

"But I think his best friend, Professor Markusovszky, would be surely a better person to do this. I know Professor Semmelweis would respond to him much more willingly than to me," said Bathory.

Balassa shook his head. "No, no, not Markusovszky! We are not going to get him involved in this at all. It would be too complicated. Semmelweis would immediately suspect something was up."

And after a long pause, Balassa declared firmly, "This is the way we are going to do it. Do you understand?"

"Yes, sir. And what about Professor Semmelweis's family?" Bathory asked.

"Well," exhaled Balassa, "*this* is his family right here," he said, extending his arm towards Maria. "His dear wife is in complete agreement with the plan, as you can see, and she will be with you on the trip along with one of her uncles for support."

"But the professor also has brothers and sisters, and surely they would help . . ."

"Absolutely not," Balassa replied, raising his voice. "We don't expect this to be a lengthy hospitalization, and the last thing we want to do is create needless anxiety for everyone in his family. Now if you don't mind, we have no time for argument. So go along now; I know I can trust you to do your part to help your professor."

On Saturday evening, July 29, Ignác, Maria, little Antonia, who was still being breastfed, Maria's uncle, Antal Walthier, and Bathory arrived at the *Keleti* station in Pest to take the overnight train to Vienna. From there, Ignác was told he would be taking a reserved carriage on his own directly to the spa at Gräfenberg. Ignác didn't appear to even recognize Antal Walthier, or at least didn't care that he came along. Antal was coming on this journey ostensibly just to support Maria, so he constantly sat next to her, often holding her hand.

"I still don't know why there is all this fuss about accompanying me on the train," he said to the others as they walked together to the westbound platform of the station. "I'm not a child," he chuckled, "and I'm certainly not royalty. So I don't know why I need to be escorted."

The platform was crowded with passengers and well-wishers. They made their way to their reserved compartment. Ignác insisted on sitting by the window. While everyone else was busy settling in and putting away their suitcases and other belongings, Ignác plopped down in his seat and sat motionless, looking out the window as the train pulled away. It was as if he knew he would never see Budapest again. Those remaining on the platform were waving goodbye to their friends and relatives, and many were walking alongside the train trying to keep up with it as it gained speed. Everyone on the platform was in motion, except for a solitary man Ignác thought he saw in red uniform standing at attention. It was the *gendarme*.

CHAPTER 30

JULY 1865

Ignác wasn't tipped off to Hebra awaiting him at the *Westbanhof* station in Vienna the next morning. So when he stepped down from the train onto the platform and spotted the searching Hebra at a distance, he let out a hearty whoop of delight. The two old friends embraced, leaning tearfully on each other's shoulders for what seemed like an eternity.

"It's been more than fifteen years, you son of a gun!" roared Hebra affectionately. "Why the hell haven't you written?"

"I thought you and Skoda and Professor Rokitansky would be angry with me . . . you know, with the way I snuck out of Vienna that night."

"We were all very disappointed by how you left, without even telling us about it or saying goodbye. But eventually we came to understand what must have been your feelings at that time. Skoda took it the worst, I must say. He was really hurt by it and remained quite resentful. From what I understand, he hasn't even spoken your name since the day you left."

Hebra pulled away but held his grip on Ignác's shoulders to inspect his old friend. "Well, you have gotten bald, and look at you," he said, glancing down at Ignác's waistline, "you've gotten fat!"

"You should talk! You look like a damned walrus. Life must be good for you."

"Yes, it has been that . . . mostly. But, of course, the political intrigues at the university never cease. You know that better than anyone, heh?"

"I wish I could say it's different in Pest," replied Ignác.

"But never mind that, my old friend. I know you're on your way to get some rest in Gräfenberg, and I wanted to arrange for you to make a little detour here to come to our home for some coffee and pastries, and to see Frau Hebra!!"

"And little . . . ?"

"Ah, yes, and *little* Hans," replied Hebra with a guffaw.

Introductions were made all around. Hebra hugged Maria and muttered something in her ear that was inaudible; then he bent down to the baby stroller to kiss little Antonia on the head.

Hebra had hired two carriages to take the party from the station to his home. In the first carriage sat Ignác, flanked on either side by Hebra and Bathory. In the other sat Maria, holding Antonia, with her uncle, Antal Walthier. It wasn't even noon yet, but it was already a sweltering, hot day. The men took off their jackets and rolled up their shirt sleeves. Ignác was struck by how much more advanced Vienna's *Westbanhof* train station appeared than the little hut that served as Budapest's station. And the hustle and bustle and traffic of carriages and pedestrians outside was a sight to behold.

Hebra and Ignác continued to chat nonstop on the way to Hebra's house. Bathory was heartened to see how revived his chief appeared. He seemed almost back to his old self, rejuvenated by memories of his Vienna days long ago.

"I am so glad to see you, Hebra," said Ignác. "But where are the others? Where are Skoda and Rokitansky and . . . ?"

Hebra appeared not to hear the question, but he looked intently into Ignác's eyes without responding. He then turned abruptly toward the street and called out, "Look, the Volksgarten. Your favorite old spot!"

"And there is that beautiful gazebo," Ignác said, excitedly pointing ahead. Again he was taken aback by the striking contrast in the opulence and affluence of Vienna compared to Budapest. From the carriage behind them, Maria was happy to see that Ignác appeared more animated than he had been in many weeks.

But as Ignác was extending his arm to point to another site, Hebra grabbed it forcefully and pulled it closer to his bespectacled eyes.

"What the hell is this?" he blurted out, assuming an entirely more serious tone of voice. "What's wrong with your arm?" he said. Then, unfolding Ignác's hand, "and your hand, too?" He took Ignác's other arm and abruptly extended both of them in front of him. "For Christ's sake, what is the problem?" Both upper extremities appeared like they had been burned and disfigured.[125]

Ignác tried to make light of it. "Oh, it's nothing. It's just clean hands. And clean arms. Maybe I scrub them too frequently in the chlorinated lime wash I use between seeing my patients."

"Chlorinated lime, my ass!" barked Hebra. "Chlorinated lime doesn't do *this* to you, my friend!"

"Well then what else could it be?" chuckled the nonchalant Ignác.

"It's some kind of advanced dermatitis," Hebra replied, now scanning Ignác's arms and hands up close so that he could examine them intently in the rattling carriage. "Maybe some form of eczema." He looked even more closely. "No, it's some kind of chemical agent."

Ignác now became silent and somber. "What kind of chemical agent?" he asked.

"Hmmm. I have seen something like this before." And then he said, "Like a heavy metal. Ignác, you don't have mercury in your hand-wash solution, do you?"

"Of course not," replied Ignác. "I did include it at the outset when I began the work here in Vienna. But then Kussmaul warned me to remove it because it could cause side effects." Ignác's mind flashed back to that café, Gerstner's, where he and the young visiting student Kussmaul had gone many years ago. He was pleased with himself at how vividly he could recall the details of that afternoon, even as he struggled these days to remember what happened just a few hours earlier.

"Well, have you talked to Kussmaul since then?"

"No, I've lost touch with him. But now I remember him telling me to go and see you about it because you were already an authority on skin diseases by then."

"So why didn't you?"

"I actually thought I had," said Ignác. "But it doesn't matter really because it resolved after I ordered the mercury to be taken out of the solution."

"And is this the same now?"

"I don't know," Ignác replied, taken aback by Hebra's forcefulness.

"Well, damn it, take a good look at them," Hebra shouted, thrusting Ignác's hands practically into his face.

For a little while, Ignác examined his hands.

"I suppose so," he said meekly.

"Well, Kussmaul should have known what he was talking about to you. As you probably know, he has since become an eminent physician, known throughout his native Germany and all over Europe. But he must have been already thinking about mercury toxicity when he was just a student visiting us in Vienna. At that time, most of us thought the symptoms of syphilis and the side effects of the mercury we have been using for ages to *treat* the syphilis were pretty much the same. But our boy Kussmaul has now published the definitive research on the subject.[126] He meticulously studied and then cataloged all the symptoms and signs of a population of men living in the towns of Erlangen and Fürth. And he found that he was able to clearly distinguish between those who were chronically exposed to toxic mercury in the mirror plating shops where they worked but *didn't* have syphilis, and the men who *had* syphilis but hadn't yet been exposed to mercury. It's a brilliant piece of work!"

Then, still holding Ignác's hands, he added, "What you have here, my friend, is, I think, a bad case of what Kussmaul called *dermatitis mercurialis*."

Before they could discuss Ignác's problem further, the carriages arrived at Hebra's house. Frau Hebra came running out to embrace Ignác and bid everyone in the party to come in for some *café mit schlag* and her warm Apfelstrudel.

As they sat around the homey living room Ignác remembered so well, a slightly built, studious-looking young man walked in carrying a large book, walked over to Frau Hebra, and bent down to ask her quietly, "*Mutter, kann ich einen strudel?*"

"*Ach mein Gott!*" exclaimed Ignác. "Can it be? Can it be my *little* Hans? You don't recognize me, but I recognize *you*! In fact, I was the very first person in the whole world to lay eyes on you!"

Hebra walked over to his son and put an arm around him. "This is my old friend, Professor Semmelweis. He delivered you, Hans, eighteen years ago."

"*Eighteen?*" Ignác put down his coffee and strudel. "You know, you are just about the same age I was when I came to Vienna. What are your aspirations in life?"

"I will be a doctor," Hans replied decisively. "A dermatologist."[127]

Later in the morning, Hebra pulled Ignác aside, and the two old friends chatted about affairs in Vienna and Budapest. Hebra must have noticed that Ignác looked so much older, at least a decade beyond his actual age.[111]

"Listen, my friend, I'll tell you what. Your carriage to Gräfenberg doesn't leave till this afternoon. Why don't you come with me to pass the time and let me show you one of our new institutes? It's a new building, quite impressive as you'll see, and it's a good example of the kind of progressive medicine in Vienna I was talking about."

"A new lying-in hospital?" Ignác asked.

"Nah!" Hebra brushed that off with a laugh. "That'll be the last thing to change, now that Braun has succeeded Klein as chief. No, this is an institute for mental hygiene. The first of its kind in Europe. We were able to recruit the leading psychiatrist from Prague, Dr. Josef Riedl, to become its first superintendent. He'll be there to show you around."

"Well, I don't know much about that, Hebra."

"Nonsense! It will be an enlightening experience. In any case, Riedl wants your advice about how to maintain the best sanitary conditions there. It's part of his overall plan. He has heard about what you've accomplished in the maternity wards, and he wants to make this a state-of-the-art facility in every way. We'll bring Bathory with us and leave all the non-medical folks back here for a while so they can continue their chit-chat."

Before Ignác could say anything more, Hebra summoned Bathory from the living room and whisked his two physician guests out the front door and into a carriage which happened to be waiting there.

On the way to the *Niederösterreichische Landes-Irrenstadt,* as the new asylum was named, Hebra and Bathory engaged in a spirited conversation about the future of enlightened psychiatry, something neither of them was expert in. They talked about Riedl's revolutionary practices of doing away with chains and straitjackets for all but the most violent patients, and instead providing them with paid work therapy, music therapy, structured recreation, and vigorous physical exercise.[128] Bathory even suggested that a facility like this could be more effective than Europe's famous spas to relieve anxiety and stress. They simultaneously looked over at Ignác, who hadn't said a word throughout the ride. But he wasn't listening: he seemed to be elsewhere, gazing out at the familiar sights of the old city.

As they passed by the *Allgemeine Krankenhaus*, Hebra tapped Ignác on the shoulder. In case Ignác hadn't heard about it, Hebra said, a young physician scientist named Carl Mayrhofer[129] was working—quite possibly at this very moment—in Braun's laboratory. Ignác shook his head but was listening intently. Hebra said it was his understanding that Mayrhofer had successfully reproduced puerperal fever in experimental rabbits, intentionally inoculating their reproductive tracts with secretions from infected women. And, Hebra said with a devious smile, the young Mayrhofer was apparently getting results that supported Semmelweis's theories about causality and contagion.

"Much to Braun's chagrin, undoubtedly," said Ignác. "If that's what the young man is doing, I doubt if he will be there for much longer."

The carriage had arrived. It brought them around a lovely garden with its large, ornate fountain, right up to the portico of the elegant white building.

Ignác finally spoke. "It looks grand. Much different from what I envisioned when you told me about it. I kept thinking only of that medieval Tower of Fools, the *Narrenturm,* the one we all used to pass by every morning on our way across the courtyards from Rokitansky's autopsy lab to the maternity ward. It looked so spooky from the outside that I never got up the nerve to look inside. I hope they're going to tear it down now. Just think of the tortures those wretched lunatics must have endured there!"

A voice answered the bell at the locked front door, and Hebra shouted out, "I am Professor Hebra. We have arrived with Dr. Semmelweis."

The massive door opened slowly to reveal a windowless and darkened foyer. They were led up the staircase and then through a maze of narrow, bare corridors. The moisture-laden air was stifling, and it was permeated by the pungent smells of stale urine and chlorine bleach, not something one would expect for a new building.

They arrived at a door on which a sign announced "Dr. Riedl, Superintendent." A clerk led them into the spartan office. Dr. Riedl sprang from the chair behind his desk and greeted the visitors with outstretched arms and an effusive welcome.

"So which of you is the eminent Dr. Semmelweis?" Dr. Riedl asked.

Ignác hesitantly stepped forward and shook hands with the superintendent, followed by introductions of the others.

"Come, let's take a brief tour," Riedl beckoned without even asking them to sit, "and I'll tell you about how things work here as we walk along. We really need your suggestions, Dr. Semmelweis, about how best to maintain absolute . . . cleanliness."

Riedl stuck his head into a side door leading to another room and called for his two assistants to join them.

"These are Wilhelm and Fritz," Dr. Riedl introduced them, as the earnest young men stood at attention and bowed slightly to the visitors. They were dressed in grey uniform suits and wore black field caps with stiff, rounded visors and flat tops.

The group started down the cramped hallways, with Ignác and Dr. Riedl leading the way, already absorbed in animated conversation, followed by the two strapping assistants, who remained silent, and Hebra and Bathory bringing up the rear. The corridor opened up into a busy lobby that looked like a reception area, and here the group paused as Dr. Riedl pointed out some things to Ignác.

While Ignác was engaged in conversation with Dr. Riedl about the conditions in the new facility, with the superintendent's assistants now standing very close to them, Hebra and Bathory quietly snuck away unnoticed. They found their way back to the asylum's entrance. And then they stepped into the glaring sunlight of midday. They could hardly have known that it was a sun Ignác Semmelweis would never see again.

The next day, Maria insisted on going to the asylum to see her husband. Her uncle, Antal, accompanied her. When they arrived, Antal told Maria to stay in the carriage while he went to inquire about visiting Ignác. He returned a few minutes later with a security guard and shook his head when Maria stood up.

"I am afraid you are not allowed to visit Ignác today. This man says he is no condition to have visitors now."

"Is he all right?" Maria asked, alarmed.

"Oh, yes, Frau Semmelweis," the security guard said, "physically he is all right. He is very hungry, and they are feeding him well; don't worry about that. But mentally?" He turned to go back, shaking his lowered head and making circles with his index finger pointed to it.

"Maria," said Antal, taking her hand, "I am afraid he is not rational right now. Let's return to Budapest and maybe in a few days you can come back to see him."

Antal Walthier approached the guard again at the main door and handed him an envelope. They exchanged some words and shook hands. He then got back into the carriage to hold the tearful Maria as they departed.

As the carriage rattled through the streets of the old city, the sobbing Maria turned to Antal. "I am going to have to tell his sister Júlia and his brothers. They probably don't even know what's happening."

"No you don't," said Antal, dabbing the tears from her eyes with his handkerchief. "We will tell them for you. Don't worry yourself about it now. You need to go into seclusion for a while to calm your nerves. Your mother will look after the children until you feel better. We'll make sure you have an ample supply of your tincture of laudanum at home so that you can sleep well and feel less sorrowful when you are awake. Everything will be all right."

Two weeks later, Maria and her uncle Antal were notified that Ignác Semmelweis had unexpectedly died. The letter stated that, at the insistence of a doctor named Josef Skoda, who had been his only visitor at the asylum, he would be taken for an autopsy prior to his burial.

Semmelweis's body was removed from the asylum to the Vienna General Hospital's dead house, and the next day it was autopsied in Rokitansky's institute, in the very same dissection room where Semmelweis had himself conducted hundreds of postmortem examinations. In the dark, silent pre-dawn hours of the next day, his remains were placed in a plain coffin made of pine, the most inexpensive wood available. The coffin, without drapes, flowers, or other frills, was then transported in a shabby, lantern-lit, one-horse hearse across the courtyards of the Allgemeine Krankenhaus, and out through the hospital's main entrance on Alserstrasse.

EPILOGUE

The lightning and thunder were now directly overhead. The doctors and the priest scattered from the graveside, sloshing through the mire in the driving rain. Marko grabbed Rokitansky's arm.

They had known each other in passing when they were colleagues at the Allgemeine Krankenhaus, but they'd lost contact after the 1848 revolution when Marko returned home to Budapest. What they had in common here was their admiration for Ignác and their unwavering loyalty to him even through his adversities and descent into insanity.

"Come on, Herr Professor, let's find some shelter until this storm passes," shouted Marko.

The doctors were unfamiliar with the outskirts of Vienna, where the Schmelz cemetery was located. It was a notoriously downtrodden neighborhood, and now the deluge was making visibility almost impossible.

Clutching broken and practically useless umbrellas over their heads, they found themselves on a desolate street lined with dilapidated buildings. One of them looked like an inn, and its front doors were secured wide open under an awning. They dashed inside into a dark, cavernous room that appeared to be empty, filled with long wooden tables with benches. The smell of stale beer permeated the dank air. As uninviting as the place was, it was at least a shelter, so Rokitansky and Marko brushed the rain from their drenched suits and took seats across from each other near the open door. As their vision accommodated to the dark, they saw a solitary figure at the very back who was sleeping on a bench. The muffled rumble of fiercely pelting rain on the rooftop above them was unnerving.

"I was surprised to see the Braun brothers at the cemetery," began Marko. "I know Carl was always such an outspoken adversary, and I presume his younger brother Gustav couldn't have liked Semmelweis, either."

"Yes, I was taken aback as well. But our friend was a polarizing personality," replied Rokitansky. "He had a lot of enemies, but he wasn't just an innocent victim of their animosity, you know. He certainly didn't make things easy on himself, especially as his madness deepened."

"Yes, and I saw the worst of it in Budapest. All the more reason it seemed so curious to see his most contentious opponents there. I wonder why they came."

"Who knows?" Rokitansky replied.

The rain, thunder, and lightning weren't letting up. Conversation naturally turned to Semmelweis's death. Marko asked Rokitansky if he knew anything about the circumstances.

"I do," replied the professor. "As you know, he died unexpectedly two weeks after he was admitted to the asylum. My assistant, Gustav Scheutauer, performed his autopsy at the institute, and I supervised it. I have to say, it was, emotionally, the most difficult one I've ever done."[130]

"And . . . ?"

"And the immediate cause of death was almost certainly the severe trauma inflicted on him by his wardens in the asylum. At autopsy we found his body covered with fresh bruises and deep hematomas. His left chest had been perforated by a fist-sized hole that tore right through his ribs and intercostal muscles. When we probed that site, it drained a large amount of stinking yellow-green pus. The beatings and kicks the poor man sustained must have been savage!"

Marko slammed his fist on the table, his jaw clenched. "Damn it! Those bastards did this to Semmelweis? Didn't they know who he was? Didn't they know he wasn't just some common lunatic? He was Ignác Semmelweis! People called him the savior of mothers!" And then, composing himself, he quietly added, "I am sorry, Herr Professor."

Rokitansky just shook his head. "Nothing to be sorry about. I am just as horrified as you are at the indignity of it all."

"And how sad it was to see the absence of so many people who should have been at the funeral," added Marko.

"Did you know that both Hebra and Skoda saw him during the past two weeks?"

"No!" Marko replied, shocked. "Where?"

"Right here. In Vienna."

"Where in Vienna?" Marko leaned forward to make sure he caught every word.

"Curiously, each of them separately brought to my attention that Ignác was back in Vienna," said Rokitansky. "So, as soon as I heard from Skoda that Ignác had died in the asylum, I asked for a meeting of the three of us to get as much information as I could before we did the autopsy."

"So?"

"So it turns out Hebra was personally involved in bringing Ignác to the asylum."

"I'll be damned. How was that?"

"By subterfuge, I am afraid. The way Hebra described it to us," Rokitansky continued, "Ignác had become progressively more insane in Budapest until nobody, including his own family, could reason with him any longer. He had essentially lost all touch with reality. He was doing things in public that embarrassed everyone around him and, most of all, himself. Hebra told me it was a very rapid decline."

"But it wasn't so rapid, you know," Marko interrupted. "I saw him as frequently as anyone after he returned to Budapest, and I can tell you without doubt that he had been exhibiting symptoms of mental illness for years. Certainly since he came back to Hungary and likely earlier in Vienna."

"Really?"

"In fact," Marko said, "we all know that Ignác had periods of instability even back when he was still here in Vienna."

"Well, he was eccentric."

"Yes, but don't you remember those periods of insane rage when he became spitting mad, often without any kind of provocation?"

"Of course," Rokitansky replied. "I saw it myself only once or twice. But several of you were becoming concerned for his well-being. To be honest, I just thought it was part of his fiery Hungarian persona."

"But how did Hebra get involved? In the end, I mean."

"Quite odd, now that I think of it," Rokitansky replied. "Balassa contacted him from Budapest . . ."

"Balassa!" Marko blurted out. "Why in God's name Balassa?"

"Balassa wrote to Hebra that poor Ignác had become totally unhinged and that they had to get him into an asylum as soon as possible. He said there weren't any that were good enough for Ignác in Budapest, so they were going to have him committed to one in Vienna. There was going to be no way Ignác would go willingly, so Balassa asked Hebra, who he knew Ignác still trusted unconditionally, to facilitate an intricate ploy here in Vienna to divert Ignác to the asylum instead of where Ignác thought he was going, a spa for rest."

"And Hebra agreed to do it? Just like that?" Marko asked incredulously.

"Balassa can be very persuasive, as you surely know better than me, Marko."

"And what about *me*?" Marko exclaimed. "Why not have *me* do it? Balassa knows very well that Ignác and I have been close friends from our days in medical school. And Balassa didn't even tell me about it! This is the first I've heard of this so-called 'arrangement.' I wonder why Balassa wanted to keep me in the dark!"

"That's a good question," replied Rokitansky. "Needless to say, Hebra is now crushed by the outcome. He feels like he was an unwitting accomplice to Ignác's death. I am sure that's why Hebra wasn't here today. Ignác was his son's godfather. He delivered him!"

"And what about Skoda, then?"

"Skoda had essentially expunged Ignác from his life and never even spoke his name again. But when he found out from Hebra last week that his life had fallen apart, he couldn't ignore it. So he went to visit him in the asylum."[131]

"So what happened at that meeting?"

"According to Skoda himself," said Rokitansky, "it was dreadful."

"Did he even recognize Skoda?"

Oh, yes, he did. In fact, he spewed venomous accusations in Skoda's face. He said some fantastical things. He charged Skoda with being one of the masterminds of an international conspiracy to slowly poison him to death. He named a long list of co-conspirators. And he said this was the last step, 'the execution' as he called it, luring him into this prison. He was in a straitjacket when Skoda saw him."

"And why do you think none of Ignác's family came today?" Marko asked.

"His wife, Maria, apparently tried to visit him in the asylum the morning after he was committed there but wasn't allowed in. I suspect he was in no condition to see anyone from the outside at that point, not even his wife. She was accompanied by one of her uncles, a rich merchant named Antal Walthier."

"So Walthier just took her back to Budapest?"

"I suppose so. Not what you would normally expect."

"So, what about the rest of the autopsy? His brain. Was that dissected also? Did you find anything that could tell us what drove him mad?"

"There were some abnormalities," replied Rokitansky. "But I am not sure what to make of them right now. The brain showed shrunken convolutions, especially in the anterior lobe of the cerebrum."

Rokitansky reached into his inside breast pocket and took out a leather wallet that contained several folded sheets of paper. "This is the draft of the autopsy report. We just finished it yesterday."[117]

Turning to the last page and holding it up to face the light emanating through the door, he read the summary to Marko. "It says here that our final diagnosis of the brain was '*hyperemia and atrophy of the cerebrum with chronic hydrocephalus.*' It's something we often see in patients with syphilis even after attempts to treat that disease with mercury. But we can also sometimes see it in much older non-syphilitics. So I am afraid we don't have a conclusive diagnosis for the cause of his madness. His brain was certainly not normal pathologically. Maybe future generations will understand it better."

The storm was now passing. With only the pitter-patter of slowing raindrops on the roof barely audible, the dark, empty interior of the tavern became forebodingly silent. But at once Rokitansky and Marko both sensed the presence of someone else with them in the room. They looked up and turned toward the door.

Silhouetted against the steamy sunlight that was now emerging outside in the haze was the figure of a caped man with a top hat, carrying an umbrella and a briefcase. He stood motionless in the doorway, facing them. They couldn't tell how long he had been there.

As Marko began to rise to his feet, the man stepped forward into the darkness of the room, and his features came into view. It was Joseph Späth, the fifth man at the graveside. He was dripping wet.

Rokitansky and Marko both stood to greet him, albeit guardedly, and invited him to sit with them.

"I am afraid there is nothing to drink or eat here, Späth," Marko said. "The doors were wide open when we ran this way, so we ducked in for shelter."

"Oh, I don't need anything—thanks," Späth replied. "I ran after the two of you. I tried to follow you from the cemetery but lost track of you in that downpour."

"Take off that drenched coat of yours and that dripping hat," said Rokitansky.

"I wanted to talk to both of you. I need to explain . . ." Späth stopped.

"Explain? Explain what?" Marko demanded.

Späth sat down.

"I believe Ignác Semmelweis was a great man. I am now completely convinced that he was entirely right," he began. "He made a discovery that will, in due time, change the way everyone in the world will practice obstetrics. Not just obstetrics, but also surgery, and I think maybe all of medicine. His death at such a young age is a tragedy for all of us."

Rokitansky and Marko looked at each other, flabbergasted.

"It's a little too late for that, isn't it?" Marko said derisively. "You've even published your opposition to him."

"Yes, I know. But my views have completely changed. Not just privately. I have admitted I have been wrong and will continue to do so in all future publications. You may not have seen the article I published last year in the *Medizinische Jahrbücker*," Späth said, opening and reaching into his briefcase to pull out a copy of the medical journal. He turned to the page he had bookmarked and read them a passage he had written:

"I also venture to state unreservedly that there is no longer any obstetrician who is not most deeply convinced of the correctness of Semmelweis's views, even though he may still talk very much against them." [119]

"I dearly hope Ignác read this when . . . when he was still lucid," Späth continued. "And then look at this." Späth lifted a hefty textbook from his briefcase, placed it on the table, and opened it to a page he had also bookmarked. "This is the textbook I wrote with Johnann Chiari and Carl Braun. It was published just a few months ago. It's the *Klinik der Geburtschülfe und Gynäkologies*, our new textbook of obstetrics and gynecology. Right here," Späth said, pointing to the corresponding text, "we acknowledge Semmelweis! You see, Chiari and I just outnumbered Braun as the authors, so he *had* to agree to include it."[132]

"God rest Chiari's soul," said Rokitansky. Chiari had died of cholera two years earlier, at the age of thirty-seven.

"And how he liked and respected Semmelweis," added Marko. "Ignác was sure that Chiari would turn against him when he announced that he would be marrying Klein's daughter. But Chiari remained steadfastly loyal to him. I'll never forget how he stood up in his defense at the last of those three lectures Ignác gave at the Medical Society."

"I was sitting in the front row," said Rokitansky, "and saw how that courageous young man defied his own father-in-law, who was also sitting right there in front of him. He literally looked directly at Klein as he spoke in support of Semmelweis that night."

Späth became subdued as he stared down at the table in front of him. "Gentlemen, I can't describe to you how remorseful I feel for how I treated Semmelweis. That's why I ran here after the burial; to find you and to confess to you. I have already taken the sacrament of penance from a priest. I have confessed and repented my sins in this matter."

"Come, come, Spath. Don't you think you are overreacting to all this?" Rokitansky asked. "We can't forget how personally accusatory Semmelweis was toward you in his public letters . . ."

"But he was a sick man," Späth interrupted.

". . . calling you a partner in the massacre of women."

"He was very ill," Späth repeated, shaking his head and still looking down. "We know that now."

"But how does that excuse him for what he said about you?" Rokitansky asked, looking perplexed.

"Because, you see, I was . . . I think I may have been an accomplice to making him ill," said Späth, covering his face with a hand.

There was stunned silence. Marko and Rokitansky gazed into the distance, trying to assimilate what Späth was saying.

The rain let up. The setting sun emerged, shrouded by haze. Steam rose from the ground outside, as densely humid air poured into the cool darkness of the tavern.

The silence was broken by an approaching clamor of women and children shouting and laughing outside. And then they appeared at the tavern's open doorstep. There were five pretty young women, all heavily made up with red rouge and lipstick, dressed in wildly colorful, low-cut dresses, smoking cigarettes, giggling, and laughing. They sauntered to sit at a nearby table, engaged in boisterous, raunchy-tongued conversation. The children followed. They looked like urchins in their tattered and dirty clothes, dripping wet. They ran around in circles and jumped onto and down from the benches as if they belonged here. Then a more mature woman appeared, her face still lovely but the rest of her covered in drab work clothes. She was carrying two babies, one in each arm. A space was cleared on a bench among the other women to let her sit there with her back to the wall, giving her a view of the entire room. The physicians thought she must be the caregiver or nanny to these children, maybe a grandmother.

The sleeping man in the back finally awoke to the noise. As if on cue, he sprang to his feet to greet the ladies and offered them drinks and an early dinner that had already been prepared for them. They were, evidently, regular customers.

"I don't understand, Späth. When you start using words like 'accomplice,' you make it sound like there was some kind of criminal plot," Marko continued.

"Just tell us the facts you *know*," added Rokitansky with uncharacteristic impatience.

"No, no," replied Späth. "I don't think there was any kind of grand plot to get rid of Semmelweis. There wasn't a single, coordinated plan, as far as I know. But there were cabals . . ."

"Cabals?" exclaimed Marko. "What do you mean by 'cabals'? If there were conspirators, there must have been a conspiracy. No?"

"Let's just say 'networks' then," Späth stammered. "Connections among academic physicians, pharmacists, administrators, maybe his own in-laws, and others, working across the border over the years to try to remove Semmelweis from positions where he could cause these people more damage."

"Damage? What damage? He was saving the lives of women, for goodness sake," Marko snapped back.

"I suppose the people in power who felt threatened by Semmelweis and his discovery must have each had their own personal stakes to protect," replied Späth. "Some thought their reputations might become damaged; others worried that they would lose their jobs if the truth was uncovered. For self-serving men, you know, the profession of academic medicine is no different from other pursuits. It's quite simple, really. It all comes down to money, power, or control. Or all of these. For personal interests, you know."

"And which of those was *you*, Späth?" Marko sneered.

"Come on now, Marko," Rokitansky chided.

"But I owe Marko an answer. He is right to ask that question," said Späth. "I have agonized over it endlessly. What was my own motive? I am still not sure, but, at least initially, it was to please my superiors. I wanted to ingratiate myself to those who I stupidly thought were in the best positions to advance my career. Later? Well maybe later I became blinded by ambition and convinced myself that Semmelweis's conclusions really *had* to be flawed."

"But what was it exactly that people were hoping to do to remove Semmelweis, as you put it?"

"If they couldn't make him disappear altogether, they wanted to at least *discredit* him. I was with Klein many years ago at a reception in his home when he actually used that very word among a few of us."

"And how were these people going to discredit him?" Marko wondered.

"They were going to drive him insane. By whatever means necessary."

"By whatever means necessary," repeated Rokitansky very slowly, gazing into the distance.

"And what was your role in all this?" Marko followed up.

"I was just *in on it.* I insinuated myself into the inner sanctum of academic medical politics. I found safety for myself by being in a position to abet those with more malicious designs," replied Späth. "Isn't that enough, for God's sake?"

"But what exactly . . ." Marko insisted.

"There was chatter about mercury. Vienna is, after all, where corrosive sublimate was introduced as a disinfectant. As the only effective treatment for syphilis. It was Kussmaul who unwittingly talked to people here about his ideas just before he went back to Heidelberg. He said he thought most people with syphilis go insane because of the mercury treatment, not because of the disease itself. And then, as you know, he proved and published it."

"But how?" Rokitansky asked.

"It's readily soluble in water for handwashing. It's invisible. And it has no odor."

"My God, Späth!" Marko exclaimed. "I just can't believe it!"

"The rain has stopped, and the sun is setting, gentlemen. I propose we repair to a more appropriate restaurant than this rathole for a quick supper," suggested Rokitansky.

But as they rose to leave, a little girl of not more than four appeared in front of them. She had wandered away from her group. She spotted the big textbook on the table, which Späth was about to put back into his briefcase, and thrust her arm out straight to point to it.

"What's that?" she asked with earnest inquisitiveness.

"That's a medical book," replied Späth. "To teach doctors how to make sick people better."

The men looked at the blond, curly-haired little girl standing there in an oversized, threadbare dress. Not even her dirt-smudged cheeks and runny nose could mask her saucer-eyed, adorable face. She reached up to try to pick up the book with both hands, but it was too heavy to even move.

"Are you a doctor?" she now asked Späth, as she gazed up to him.

"Yes," Späth replied. "All three of us are doctors."

"My mommy told me all about doctors like you. About how kind they are sometimes."

The girl's mother hurried over to fetch her daughter.

"I am sorry, gents. Is she is bothering you? I told you not to be so nosy with people you don't know." The mother bent down to the girl, angrily wagging her finger.

The young woman then grabbed her daughter's arm to lead her away. But the little girl pulled back.

"What is that called?" she asked.

"*Obstetrics and Gynecology,*" replied Späth.[132]

"Well, most of 'em could care less about us poor women, you know, sir," the mother said, turning to Späth, "excepting yourself, of course, I'm sure. Why, you look like a very respectable gentleman, you do. Here you are, sir. God bless you . . ."

She reached into her frock pocket and pulled out a flattened lilac. Gently brushing it back to its full form, she handed the revived flower to the perplexed Späth.

Marko nodded and beamed a knowing smile. "Ah, so it's a lilac," he said.

"But mine was quite special, you know," the woman continued. "I owe my daughter's life to that kind gentleman, and my own life, too."

"*I* want to be a doctor too, you know," the little girl declared, tugging at Späth's coat.

Marko took the purple lilac out of Späth's hand and carefully placed it into the little girl's hair.

At this, Späth stared down at her, covering his mouth with his hand, momentarily speechless, and then erupted with a restrained belly laugh.

"Girls can't be doctors," he said, trying to hold back his chuckling. "But you can do many *other* good things to help sick people." He patted her head.

Rokitansky frowned. With some difficulty, he lowered himself to a squatting position in order to meet the little girl's wide, blue eyes at her level, and then clasped her shoulders to get her full attention. He whispered into her ear loudly enough for the others to hear, very slowly and very clearly.

"Well, then, go tell your mommy here," pointing to the girl's mother, "that a doctor is *exactly* what you are going to be. Why not! And what a very fine one you will make."

The three men then walked out and disappeared into the steamy late afternoon.

HISTORICAL POSTSCRIPT

It is known that only five people attended Semmelweis's burial at the Schmelz cemetery in the suburbs of Vienna, on Tuesday, August 15, 1865. Why were they there and why not others? These questions shall forever remain unanswered.

Josef Späth's presence at the funeral was perhaps the most enigmatic of all. After the abrupt departure of Semmelweis from Vienna, Späth assumed the directorship of the midwives' Second Division in 1861. There he escalated his position of being one of Semmelweis's most outspoken opponents, culminating in the personally vituperative letter to him from Semmelweis in which he publicly accused Späth of being a "partner in this massacre." However, Späth himself, unbeknown to Semmelweis, subsequently validated Semmelweis's original findings. He found that after Semmelweis left, the incidence of puerperal fever at the university was back up to 22.6% compared to only 1.1% in women who gave birth in the streets during the same period. To his credit, Späth refused to disregard these data and summoned the moral courage to openly retract his own position on Semmelweis. Shortly after Semmelweis's death, he wrote that "in my opinion there is no longer a reputable teacher in midwifery who is not in his own heart convinced of the truth of the doctrine of Semmelweis, even when he still professes to be opposed to it," and he paid "a tribute to Semmelweis." Späth died at the age of seventy-three.

Carl Braun, who followed Klein as the chief of obstetrics at the Allgemeine Krankenhaus, went on to a quite distinguished career. He has been credited in part with giving identity to the field of gynecology as a distinct specialty. He later became dean of the medical faculty and then Rector of the University of Vienna. Nevertheless, he publicly remained Semmelweis's hostile and obstinate adversary for the rest of his life. As late as 1881, he was still enumerating long lists of conjectural factors as possible causes of puerperal fever, either placing human transmission of a disease agent near the end of lists of up to thirty different causes or not at all. He never once mentioned Semmelweis's name in in his writings and lectures.

Carl Braun's younger brother, Gustav, followed the same dogmatic position as Carl in opposing Semmelweis. He followed his brother as Klein's assistant in the First Division. Then he followed Späth in his positions at the Josephs Academy and then as director of the midwives' service at the general hospital. Other than advocating for the use of a decapitation hook at the time of delivery in cases of fetal malformations, Gustav is not remembered for any special contributions to the field, dying in 1911 at the age of eighty-two.

Carl von Rokitansky became a giant in medical history. His original contributions to the field of pathology were extraordinary. They included the first descriptions of numerous diseases, syndromes, anatomical identifications, and clinical findings, at least eight of which now bear his name. Rokitansky also became a leader of medicine, a noted philosopher, and a politician. He was a pioneer of medical ethics, a founder of the school of Austrian high liberalism, and a leading force in the movement for academic freedom.

Lajos Markusovszky steadfastly remained Semmelweis's lifelong best friend and sometimes his virtually lone advocate in both life and death. He became one of Hungary's most distinguished surgeons in his time, as well as the founding editor and publisher of the Hungarian medical journal, *Orvosi Hetilap*, which continues to be widely read today, 150 years later.

IN THE AFTERMATH

At each institution Semmelweis worked, the mortality rate from puerperal fever spiked after his departure, almost back to the same shamefully high levels he had found upon his arrival. A physician named János Diescher, rather than one of Semmelweis's assistants, was appointed to his position at the University of Pest after his death. As soon as Diescher took over, the hand hygiene protocols and other sanitary policies Semmelweis had established in the face of so much institutional resistance became neglected. Between 1865 and 1875, in the first decade after Semmelweis's death, the mortality from puerperal fever rose to nearly six percent. Semmelweis's discovery likewise failed to penetrate obstetrical practice in most other countries in continental Europe. For example, during the period of 1873–75 in Paris, maternal mortality rates were reported to be: 4.5% in general hospital maternity departments; 4.7% in maternity hospitals; but only 0.07% in home deliveries by clinic-employed midwives; and 0.1% in home deliveries by other midwives.

While Semmelweis was struggling at the University of Pest to convince the world of the importance of his findings, a young chemist in northern France, who had no medical background, was assigned to solve the problem of spoiling in the making of alcoholic beverages. He demonstrated through microscopy that living microbes were causing the souring of wine and beer, as well as milk. And in the year of Semmelweis's death, the same Louis Pasteur saved France's silk industry by proving that different microbes were infecting healthy silkworm eggs and that the disease could be prevented by eliminating those microbes. It wasn't long before Pasteur was extending his germ theory of infection to human diseases. In 1879 he began to investigate the presence of bacteria in the discharge of recently delivered mothers. At a now-fabled meeting of the Académie Française in Paris, Pasteur found himself forced to prematurely announce his finding. His principal opponent, Jacques-Francois-Édouard Hervieux, the powerful chief obstetrician at Maternité, the premiere lying-in hospital in the country, an inveterate non-believer in the germ theory, imperiously lectured on and on about the various possible causes of puerperal fever, not unlike Carl Braun. Hervieux concluded, looking directly at the clinically unqualified Pasteur sitting in the audience, "I am afraid I will die before I have seen the 'microbe' that produces this fever." With that, Pasteur jumped to his feet, strode up the blackboard, and quickly drew with chalk a picture of what looked like a string of beads, and declared, "There that is what it looks like." The string of beads depicted the microscopic appearance of what are now termed "streptococci," the predominant pathogenic cause of puerperal fever at that time.

Across the English Channel, also at the time of Semmelweis's death, a young British surgeon named Joseph Lister was avidly reading about Pasteur's microscopic discovery of living microbes invading silkworm eggs. He made the conceptual leap that something like that must be causing the foul-smelling pus draining from the amputation sites of patients who died after surgery at the Glasgow Royal Infirmary, where he was operating. Lister was already an expert microscopist, so he readily identified microbes consistently infiltrating the healthy tissues of these patients and changing them into necrotic, purulent debris. Reasoning like Semmelweis probably did and would have done, he washed and dressed these wounds with solutions of carbolic acid until he could no longer smell them. In so doing, he promptly reduced the postoperative mortality rates by almost two-thirds. As Lister subsequently refined and improved his antiseptic methods, he, too, encountered fierce opposition and even hostility from established surgeons. But, unlike Semmelweis, this English Quaker maintained his emotional equilibrium and remained visibly unperturbed in the face of repeated verbal attacks by ignorant and intractable colleagues. Lister's serene temperament, as well as his ability to promptly and persuasively publish his findings, made it easier for him than for Semmelweis to ultimately have his principles of surgical antisepsis widely accepted. Lister was knighted, followed by his investiture as a Baron. He then served as Queen Victoria's personal surgeon and lived to enjoy worldwide fame.

Pasteur and Lister, amongst others in this next generation, thus validated the long-ridiculed microscopic observations of "animalcules" by van Leeuwenhoek more than 150 years earlier, work that Semmelweis undoubtedly knew about. Their research also placed Semmelweis's discoveries onto a practically unassailable scientific foundation.

Neither Pasteur nor Lister crossed paths with Semmelweis in their lifetimes, as far as we know. Pasteur, in fact, never mentioned his name in his writings and lectures. Lister claimed that he had not even heard of Semmelweis until much later in his career. When, in 1906, he was confronted with allegations that he actually owed his ideas to Semmelweis, he responded resolutely:

"When, in 1865, I first applied the antiseptic principle to wounds, I had not heard the name of Semmelweis and knew nothing of his work. When, twenty years later I visited (Budapest), where I was received with extraordinary kindness by the medical profession and the students, Semmelweis's name was never mentioned, having been, as it seems, as entirely forgotten in his native city as in the world at large," and went on to state that "while Semmelweis had no influence on my work, I greatly admire his labours and rejoice that his memory will be at length duly honoured."

Nevertheless, Semmelweis's biographer, K. Codell Carter, has argued that Lister must have heard of Semmelweis much earlier, or at least had ample opportunities to do so. Even though he wasn't recognized throughout much of the continent of Europe, Semmelweis's name did appear often in the British medical literature during Lister's years of medical training there. In addition, Lister and his wife spent two weeks in Vienna as guests in Rokitansky's home. Also, during Lister's visit to Budapest in 1883, he spent a long evening at a meeting in the company of Lajos ("Marko") Markusovszky. Following that visit, there is evidence that Markusovszky probably sent a signed copy of Semmelweis's "*Etiology* . . ." to Lister.

FROM THE DARKNESS TO LIGHT

Posthumous recognition of Semmelweis and the impact of his discoveries was extremely slow to materialize throughout most of Europe and the rest of the world. But nowhere was the complete silence after his death more appalling than in his own homeland. Except for a lengthy obituary by his friend Lajos Markusovszky in the *Orvosi Hetilap*, which he himself edited and published, there was barely a brief notice about it in newspapers. Carter and Carter describe an annual retreat of the Hungarian Association of Physicians and Natural Scientists, led by János Balassa, that took place as scheduled two weeks after Semmelweis's death. The bylaws of the society specifically required that a commemorative address be delivered in honor of each member who died during the preceding year. As documented in the minutes of that association meeting, Semmelweis's death was not even mentioned. No doubt, many in the physician community had considered Semmelweis's behavior in his last years a public and national embarrassment. Even Semmelweis's widow and children changed the family name to Szemerényi in 1879, presumably out of shame over his insanity and the manner of his death.

It took the passage of a whole new generation for Semmelweis's monumental achievements to be recognized as such. The power of overwhelming evidence, which continued to accumulate in support of his principles after his death, simply couldn't be ignored for very long. Nor could the dawning of the germ theory of disease, which provided a sound scientific basis for his observations and, ultimately, irrefutable proof of it. Finally, in

1891, Semmelweis's remains were transferred from the neglected Schmelz cemetery in Vienna to the Kerepesi cemetery in Budapest. Money was raised to commission Hungary's foremost sculptor, Alajos Strobel, to create the life-size statue of Semmelweis that is now situated in a small, leafy park next to the St. Rochus Hospital. Semmelweis stands on the pedestal holding a book; at the base of the statue sits a breastfeeding mother gazing up at Semmelweis, who is surrounded by three angelic babies. A smaller statue of Semmelweis was unveiled at the medical University of Vienna in 2018. In 1964 his remains were transferred to their current resting place in a space in the garden wall of the house where Semmelweis was born on the Buda banks of the Danube River. And in 1969 the medical school where he worked in Budapest was renamed Semmelweis University of Medicine, today one of the great medical schools of Europe.

As for the disease that was the mission of his lifework, its victims continued to fester and die in great numbers because of the stubborn ignorance of the medical establishment throughout most of the world for the next two decades. But then the tide turned as a more enlightened generation of physicians assumed control, so that by the 1890s the mortality rates in hospitals in Europe and the United States had declined to levels seen with home deliveries. With microbiological identification of the primary organism that caused it and the advent of antibiotics in the first half of the twentieth century, even those women who contracted the disease could be treated and cured. The terms "puerperal fever" and "childbed fever" are obsolete today. Infectious complications of delivery are now most commonly called "postpartum infection" or "postpartum sepsis." Statistics for its incidence and mortality are actually less clear today because of disagreements about a strict definition of the disease. But worldwide rates for "maternal sepsis" in the year 2000, broken down by epidemiological subregions of the world by the World Health Organization (WHO), are reported to be as follows. The highest rates are in different parts of Africa, with an incidence of approximately 7 per 1,000 women and a mortality of approximately 25 to 28 per 100,000. In Austria and Hungary, these rates are 0.9 to 1.5 per 1,000 and 0.01 to 0.15 per 100,000, respectively. And in North America, they are approximately 1.4 and 0.01, respectively.

Once embraced in his home country as a hero and a martyr, the adulation for Semmelweis seemed to have no bounds. The glorification and veneration afforded him, with appellations like "the savior of mothers," have been attributed by some to the Hungarian character's tendencies to the melodramatic, sensational, and histrionic. Perhaps so. But, in fact, not many of even the greatest physician investigators in the history of medicine can lay claim to discoveries that directly saved as many lives as did Ignác Semmelweis.

ENDNOTES

1. Following the autopsy, the body of Semmelweis was taken to the Schmelz cemetery. It is today an abandoned site in the depressed area of Langmaisgasse, Vienna's 15th district. Only seventeen years prior to the Semmelweis burial there, in October 1848, the imperial forces of Prince Windischgratz crushed one the last remaining revolutionary outposts of Vienna in brutal hand-to-hand combat with mobile guards barricaded in the Schmelz cemetery. (See Mike Rapport, *1848. Year of Revolution* [Basic Books, New York, 2008], p. 285; and Wolfgang Maderthaner & Lutz Musner, *Unruly Masses. The Other Side of Fin-de-Siecle Vienna* [Berghahn Books, New York, 2008], p.103.) In the decades following the Semmelweis burial, the mostly uncultivated heathland around the Schmelz became the site of suburban construction of tenements to accommodate Vienna's rapidly growing impoverished and immigrant population, settlements that "soon became a byword for social squalor, desperation, immorality, and criminality" (Maderthaner & Musner, p. 104) which lasted well into the second half of the twentieth century.

2. The only individuals who are known to have attended the funeral service were the Braun brothers, Späth, Markusovsky, and Rokitansky. "Apparently, not one family member, not one in-law, not one colleague from the University of Pest was in attendance. Semmelweis's wife later explained her own absence on the grounds that . . . she had become so ill that she had been confined to her bed for six weeks" (from K. Codell

Carter, Scott Abbott, and James L. Siebach, Five Documents Relating to the Final Illness and Death of Ignaz Semmelweis, *Bull. Hist. Med.* 1995, 69:255–270; K. Codell Carter and Barbara R. Carter, *Childbed Fever. A Scientific Biography of Ignaz Semmelweis* [Transaction Publishers, New Brunswick, 2005], p.78; a notice of Semmelweis's death that appeared in *Orvosi Hetilap,* 1865, 8:554.)

3. The *Franz I.* was the first steamboat of the Erste Donau-Dampfschiffahrtsgesellschafet (First Danube Steamboat Company), which made its first voyage in 1830. The upstream travel time, from Budapest to Vienna, was two days (although it was much shorter along the fast-flowing Danube in the other direction, downstream from Vienna to Budapest). Even today's hydrofoil takes six to seven hours to complete the upstream trip.

4. Christian Joseph Berres (1796–1844) was a surgeon who became a pioneer of microphotography. He invented the process of etching daguerreotype plates, transforming the teaching of anatomy. He was able to visualize cells that were first discovered by Robert Hooke through the development of microscopy and later identified by Schwann, Schleiden, and Virchow as the fundamental units of structure and function in all living organisms. Original microphotographs by Berres can be found in Joseph Berres, *Anatomie der Mikroskopischen Gebilde des Menschlichen Körpers,* First Edition, Wien, 1837. Also https://hagstromelibrary.ki.se

5. There is no evidence that this incident occurred. However, it is known that Semmelweis enrolled in the University of Vienna's law school in 1837 in accordance with his father's wishes but transferred to its medical school the following year after attending an anatomy class with a medical student friend. See: Sir William J. Sinclair, *Semmelweis. His Life and his Doctrine. A Chapter in the History of Medicine.* (Chapter 10: University Education). Manchester: University of Manchester Press, 1909.

6. The University of Vienna Medical School's curriculum at this time and the reforms in it that took place after 1848 are described in detail in Erna Lesky, *The Vienna Medical School of the 19th Century,* The Johns Hopkins University Press, 1976, pp. 96–106.

7. Joseph Skoda (1805–1881) was only a year younger than Rokitansky but was already recognized as the premier internist of Vienna. Ignác had learned earlier that Skoda was born in Bohemia to the wife of a poor locksmith. He was apparently always an ambitious young man and was said to have walked six days from Pilsen to Vienna to gain entrance to its famous medical school. Formally trained in acoustics, he became an innovative master of percussion and auscultation in the physical examination of patients. He gained universal renown as a diagnostician. This somewhat eccentric man also became a devoted medical educator and one of Semmelweis's most influential mentors. Skoda was contemptuous of the efficacy and safety of the therapeutic methods used during his time, mostly consisting of bloodletting, leeches, sweating, catharsis, and untested polypharmacy. He thereby undeservedly developed a reputation for being a "therapeutic nihilist." (Sakula A. Josef Skoda 1805–81: a centenary tribute to a pioneer of thoracic medicine. *Thorax* 1981; 36:404–411.) Skoda's "program of therapeutic nihilism" was at first met with a storm in Vienna, angering practitioners, conservative professors, and pharmacists. (see Erna Lesky, *The Vienna Medical School of the 19th Century,* Baltimore: The Johns Hopkins University Press, 1976, p.122.)

8. Carl von Rokitansky (1804–1878) came from humble German roots in Bohemia and rose to attain stature as one of the titanic figures of nineteenth-century medicine. He pioneered the field of forensic pathology. Many diseases and morphologic features of disease were named after him. He later revolutionized the curriculum of the Vienna medical school, placing it firmly on a scientific foundation. He was also a philosopher and politician who was instrumental in shaping the new era of Austrian high liberalism.

9. Some years earlier, through Rokitansky's efforts, Emperor Francis I had decreed that all who died in the Allgemeine Krankenhaus would be subject to autopsies. It was this edict that allowed Rokitansky to oversee and in many cases perform more than 60,000 post mortem examinations.

10. The Rokitansky home was suffused with the love of music. His wife, Marie Pauline, nee Weis, was a noted soprano who was known for her singing Schubert lieder, often accompanied by the composer himself. One son, later to become Baron Hans von Rokitansky (1835–1909), was an operatic bass who sang for decades in concerts and operas throughout Europe. Another son, Victor (1836-1896), became a composer.

11. Ferdinand Ritter von Hebra (1816–1888) was the youngest of the three Bohemian–Moravian physicians who became most influential in Semmelweis's medical education. He later became the founder of the New Vienna School of Dermatology. At this point in his career, he was well on his way to laying the foundations of modern dermatology. His personality was strikingly unlike that of his older colleagues Rokitansky and Skoda. Merely two years Semmelweis's senior, Hebra was witty, charming, cheerful, and flamboyant. In those youthful days, the dapper Hebra was a handsome, trim man with dark hair. With his keen intellect, Hebra did not suffer fools gladly. He was not afraid to make stinging, caustic comments to those who irritated him. But the great mutual respect he and Semmelweis developed for each other that day in the lecture room turned into a lasting friendship.

By this time, Hebra had already discovered the pathogenesis of scabies, considered then the most commonplace of all diseases and the prototype of an infectious skin disease. He experimented and infected himself and others with a minute mite, the scab mite. As he related, "then I inserted into the inner surface of the middle finger of my left hand a live scab mite which I had previously observed under the microscope, and after eight days, during which time I was plagued by a strong itch that spread over my entire body, the first scabies manifestations appeared almost simultaneously on both my hands. In order to study precisely the progress of the disease, I applied no treatment for two months . . ." See Erna Lesky, *The Vienna Medical School of the 19th Century*. Baltimore: The Johns Hopkins University Press, 1976, page 129.

12. Obstetrics was one of the least desirable specialties of medicine at that time. It was widely disdained as a practice that was more suitable for midwives than for physicians. In fact, the clinical student clerkship in obstetrics was offered only as an elective course in the medical school, in contrast to mandatory curriculum requirements like internal medicine, surgery, and even more highly specialized areas like ophthalmology, otorhinolaryngology, and urology.

13. Chiari (1817–1854) had been Assistant to Klein from 1842 to 1844. He later became Klein's son-in-law. His original description, with the German gynecologist Richard Frommel, of the syndrome of postpartum galactorrhea and amenorrhea is still referred to today as the "Chiari-Frommel Syndrome." Chiari's illustrious career was cut short when he died of cholera at the age of thirty-seven.

14. Inspired by news of the uprisings in France and Poland, Hungarians agitated for their constitutionally guaranteed autonomy. Winning over and assimilating the lower classes and peasantry, radical Hungarian reformers, led by Lajos Kossuth, began to advocate forcefully for a modern and powerful new nation. The dashing, fearless, and charismatic Kossuth was also a brilliant orator. Coming himself from lesser nobility, he was poised to become the ideal leader for the time and place.

15. The only living Semmelweis sister, Júlia (1815–1910), was married in 1836 to the promising pharmacist Péter Ráth (1812–1873). They had six children. Péter took over the family-owned Tabáni Trinity Pharmacy and later became the founding President of Hungary's National Pharmacy Association. (From Károly Kapronczay, *A Semmelweis Család Története,* Semmelweis Kiadó, Budapest, 2008; also, Károly Kapronczay, "The roots and history of the Family Semmelweis," in *Kaleidoscope; Journal of History of Culture, Science and Medicine.* ISSN:2062-2597, 2010/1, vol. 1/no. 1, pp. 47–73.) http://www.kaleidoscopehistory.hu/index.php.)

16. Alservorstadt was an independent municipality at that time. Like the Allgemeine Krankenhaus, it was located just outside the Inner City of Vienna. Semmelweis's third-floor window looked out over the glacis, a wide green space that was often used as military parade grounds, surrounding the old city walls. By this time, the city walls were left standing less for the purpose of keeping invaders out of Vienna and more to separate the Inner City from the suburbs, where the undesirable lower classes lived. Not long after Semmelweis's time here, the old walls would be torn down and today's magnificent gothic City Hall of Vienna, the Wiener Rathaus, would be built within a couple of blocks of Wickenburggasse 2.

Vienna's medieval city walls had been reconstructed in 1548 as defensive fortifications against Turkish sieges. With industrialization in the first half of the nineteenth century, the working class and immigrant poor became concentrated outside the city wall, along with factories and relocated graveyards, in miserably crowded suburbs like Neulerchenfeld. In 1858, the wall was finally demolished, and the Ringstraβe, the magnificent wide boulevard that still encircles the Inner City of Vienna today, was built in its place.

17. Franz Breit (1817–1868) was an obstetrician who studied medicine in Padua, Prague, as well as Vienna, and then served as Assistant to Johann Klein at the Allgemeine Krankenhaus. When he was subsequently appointed to a professorship at the University of Tübingen, his position as assistant was filled by Semmelweis. Breit became a notable academic obstetrician in the course of his career.

18. Autopsies were mandated by Rokitansky to be performed on every patient who died in the hospital. It has been estimated that Rokitansky himself supervised 70,000 of them and personally performed more than 30,000 in the course of his career. (Jay V. The legacy of Karl Rokitansky. *Arch Pathol Lab Med* 2000;124: 345–346.)

19. Jakob Kolletschka (1803–1847), born in Bohemia, became Professor of Forensic Medicine in Vienna. His tragic death provided his friend Semmelweis with the key clue to unraveling the cause of puerperal fever.

20. The Vienna Foundling and Orphans Home was located on Alser Strasse, just across the street from the hospital's main entrance. It was established decades earlier to reduce the high rate of infanticide of illegitimate, abandoned, and orphaned newborns in the city, which comprised up to one-third of all children born in Vienna at that time. Care in the foundlings' home was provided by so-called "board women" from lower-class and peasant backgrounds who were paid nominal but much-needed allowances. However, the conditions and level of care were so poor that infanticide outside was essentially replaced by a mortality rate of more than two-thirds inside the Foundlings Home, mainly as a result of rampant infectious and digestive diseases.

21. Data cited by Semmelweis. (From Ignaz Semmelweis, translated by K. Codell Carter, *The Etiology, Concept, and Prophylaxis of Childbed Fever* [The University of Wisconsin Press, Madison, 1983], Table 8.)

22. Eduard Lumpe (1813–1876) was Assistant to Johann Klein from 1840 to 1842. He is best known today for compiling a list of possible causes of puerperal fever, including harmful miasma, cold, diet, shame, and fear of death. These were mainstream views at that time. Later, he tempered his opposition to Semmelweis by adopting a "wait and wash" philosophy. (Eduard Lumpe. *Die Leistungen der neuesten Zeit in der Gynaekolgie.* Zt. K. k. Ges. Aerzte zu Wien, 1845, I:341–371.)

23. Franz Xaver Bartsch (1800–1861) was described by Erna Lesky as "a timid pupil of Klein's." (Erna Lesky, *The Vienna Medical School of the 19th Century,* The Johns Hopkins University Press, Baltimore, 1976, p. 58.) Thomas Dormandy described him as "a somewhat withdrawn scholarly individual whose main interest was in Byzantine church architecture." (Thomas Dormandy, *Moments of Truth.* Chichester, West Sussex: John Wiley & Sons, Ltd., 2003, p. 177.)

24. Semmelweis wrote in his autobiography: "The patients really do fear the first clinic. Frequently one must witness moving scenes in which patients, kneeling and wringing their hands, beg to be released in order to seek admission to the second clinic." Ignaz Semmelweis, translated by K. Codell Carter, *The Etiology, Concept, and Prophylaxis of Childbed Fever.* Madison: The University of Wisconsin Press, 1983, p. 70.

25. Johann Christian Schiffner (1779–1857) received his medical doctorate from the University of Vienna. He became Director of the Allgemeine

Krankenhaus in 1830, shortly after which he played an important role in containing the 1831–1832 cholera epidemic in Vienna. He was named Honorary Citizen of Vienna on September 22, 1834, following the likes of Haydn, Beethoven, and, later, Rokitansky.

26. Women were first admitted to the University of Vienna in 1897 and to its medical school in 1900, well behind almost every other country in Europe.

27. The Haskalah movement started amongst Jews in central and eastern Europe in the early 19th century. Also known as the Jewish Enlightenment, it was in many ways an extension of the eighteenth-century European Enlightenment. As an ideological and social movement, Haskalah advocated acculturation and promoted the social, economic, and cultural integration of Jews into mainstream society.

28. Semmelweis had many female companions during his Vienna years. But the only love interest we know today by name was identified as "Charlinchen" in a letter written by Semmelweis on June 24, 1850, to his best friend Markusovszky ("Marko"). "Charlinchen" must have been the affectionate diminutive form Semmelweis used for "Karolinka," or "Caroline" in English. The letter wasn't discovered until the mid-20th century, and it includes the following passage: "My dear Marko, seeing my letter will probably puzzle your brain as to what happened to your laziest correspondent . . . there is a trifling affair I would like to discuss with you . . . Oh, Caroline, it will be your fault if my friend Marko is struck by astonishment. You will probably remember that I brought with me from Pest among other things a small locket, made from Hungarian revolutionary six-krajcár coins linked together. As a matter of fact, it turned out: First, the locket made out of the coins is too small for the purpose. Second, the locket is not enough, there should be at least two of the same. Third, let me ask you, my dear Marko, to have two lockets made, this time of larger twenty-krajcár coins. Sorry to hurry you, but they should be here, without fail, in ten days at the latest. You will be refunded by cable, to be not too quick, with my thanks. *But Marko, this is top secret!*" (From Claudius F. Mayer, Two Unpublished Letters

of Semmelweis, *Bull. Med. Libr. Assoc.* 1942, 30(3):233–236. Translated in: Gy. Gortvay and I Zoltán. *Semmelweis. His Life and Work.* Budapest: Akadémiai Kiadó, 1968; p. 71. Also see: József Antall, Viola R. Harkó, Tivada Vida, "Semmelweis Ignác Összegyüjtött Kéziratai" in *Orvostörténeti Közlemények*, Communicationes de Historia Artis Medicinae, Budapest, 1968, pp. 202–213.) The author took the liberty of expanding Caroline's role in this book without factual support, mainly using her character as a narrator to Semmelweis about the political and sociologic conditions in Vienna outside the hospital and outside the city wall.

29. As Dormandy indicates, "Count Thun [was] much loved for his charitable work among the prostitutes of Vienna . . ." (From Thomas Dormandy. *Moments of Truth.* West Sussex: John Wiley & Sons, Ltd. 2013, p. 181.)

30. "Starting in December 1846, the hospital excluded foreign students." (From Herbert F. Spirer and Louise Spirer, "Death and Numbers: Semmelweis the Statistician," *PSR Quarterly* 1991, 1:43–52.)

31. These data are directly extracted from Semmelweis's own later report in his book, *The Etiology, Concept, and Prophylaxis of Childbed Fever* (translated by K. Codell Carter), The University of Wisconsin Press, Madison, 1983.

32. Carl Braun (1822–1891) was born in Zisterdorf, a town located in the northeastern corner of present-day Austria. He studied at Vienna's medical school, but according to his obituary in the *Medical Record* (May 2, 1891), he never trained in obstetrics: ". . . graduated in Vienna in 1847, and after a short time spent in the pathological laboratory became assistant in obstetrics under Klein." Braun was a lifelong, bitter adversary of Semmelweis. Even though he eventually quietly adopted Semmelweis's hand scrubbing routine following Semmelweis's departure, preventing the mortality statistics from regressing to their historical baseline, Braun steadfastly refused to acknowledge Semmelweis's contributions. Nevertheless, he attained academic distinction later in his career, establishing the first gynecology clinic and serving as dean of the medical faculty and rector of the university. In 1877, he was named Hofrat, a title reserved for the most eminent professors.

33. Karoline von Perin-Gradenstein (1806–1888) came from a wealthy, aristocratic family and was the widow of a baron. She became a solitary pioneer of women's rights and in 1848 founded the Viennese Democratic Women's Association. She sacrificed her fortune for the causes of women's rights and other democratic ideals of the revolution, and died in Vienna at the age of eighty-two, alone, unhappy, and in near poverty. (From Francisca de Haan, Krasimira Daskalova and Anna Loutfi, *Biographical Dictionary pf Women's Movements and Feminisms in Central, Eastern, and South Eastern Europe: 19th and 20th Centuries,* Budapest: Central European University Press, 2006, pp. 424–426.)

34. Several scholarly books provide a comprehensive social, political, and economic analysis of the factors that converged to create the 1848 revolutions in Europe, including the following: Jonathan Sperber, *The European Revolutions, 1848–1851.* Cambridge: Cambridge University Press, 2005; Priscilla Robertson, *Revolutions of 1848. A Social History.* Princeton, New Jersey: Princeton University Press, 1971; Mike Rapport, *1848. Year of Revolution.* New York: Basic Books, 2008.

35. Joseph Späth (1823–1896) was born in Bozen, which was then in the Austrian province of South Tyrol. Today it is called Bolzano, a mostly German-speaking province in Northern Italy that is part of the autonomous region of Trentino-Alto Adige/Südtriol.

36. Semmelweis had been scheduled to begin his two-year term as Klein's Assistant in July 1846. However, this was postponed for several months when Breit requested and was granted an extension of his term. It is not clear if Breit actually needed the job or if Klein was having increasing misgivings about Semmelweis assuming the position and therefore persuaded Breit to continue for a while longer. During this period, Semmelweis was called a Provisional Assistant and was rescheduled to begin as actual Assistant in March 1847.

37. Semmelweis himself elaborates on Kolletschka's autopsy findings in Ignaz Semmelweis, *The Etiology, Concept, and Prophylaxis of Childbed Fever*

(translated by K. Codell Carter). Madison: The University of Wisconsin Press, 1983, pp. 87–88.

38. The words "disinfectant" and "antiseptic" first appeared in the English language in the early 17th and mid-18th centuries, respectively, well before the germ theory of disease was understood decades after Semmelweis's discovery. It had been believed that unidentified "effluvia" existed in the air and on surfaces, and that they communicated certain diseases. Hence, they had to be removed or destroyed. The word "antiseptic" derives from the Greek words "*anti*," meaning "against," and "*septikos*," meaning "putrefactive" or "rotting." Without any notion of the existence of microorganisms, it was not known at that time how putrefaction and decay were produced. (Patterson AM. Meaning of "antiseptic," "disinfectant" and related words. *Am. J. Public Health* 1932; 22:465–472.)

39. It has been pointed out by several biographers that Semmelweis's name could be easily taken for Jewish, a stigma in the Vienna of that time of which, as Nuland has commented, he may have been "only too painfully aware." (Sherwin B. Nuland, *The Doctors' Plague. Germs, Childbed Fever, and the Strange Story of Ignàc Semmelweis,* W. W. Norton & Company, New York, 2003, p. 173.) Controversy and misunderstanding about the matter continues even today (see *The New York Review of Books. "The Fool of Pest": An Exchange; Sherwin B. Nuland, reply by Richard Horton,* March 25, 2004). In fact, the Semmelweis name is Swabian, not Jewish, and the identities of Semmelweis's direct forebears are traceable to the birth and baptism of his great-great-grandfather, György Semmelweis, in 1670. One of Semmelweis's brothers was an ordained priest, although he had found it important in 1844 to change his surname to Szemerényi, which sounded more Hungarian. Like his ancestors, Semmelweis was born and died a Roman Catholic.

40. Franz Schneider (1812–1897) was working at that time at the medical-surgical Joseph's Academy, the second-most prominent medical training center in Vienna. Among his important contributions to medical chemistry research was his development of the first useful method for the detection of trace amounts of mercury; this would become relevant in the long-standing debate on whether the manifestations of secondary syphilis were due to the disease or its treatment with mercury. Wenzel Bernatzik (1821–1903) was only twenty-six years old at this time, likewise working at Joseph's Academy, and touted to become the future chair of pharmacology and pharmacognosy at the University of Vienna; however, when the time came in 1874, he was passed over for the position in favor of the younger August Emil Vogl. Joseph Redtenbacher (1810–1870) was a chemist not at the medical school but at the Faculty of Philosophy of the university. One of his many illustrious students was Ernst Brücke, one of the giants of 19th-century chemistry who was later to establish Vienna's school of chemistry.

41. In fact, a study published in Germany just three decades later, shortly after the discovery of bacteria, demonstrated that *corrosive sublimate* and *chlorine liquida* (in that order) were the two most potent antibacterial antiseptics. The maximum dilutions of *corrosive sublimate* and *chlorine liquida* required to "prevent the development of bacteria which are conveyed directly to broth" were found to be 1:25250 and 1:20208, respectively. (By contrast, some other antiseptics included carbolic acid, which was first used for surgical antisepsis by Joseph Lister in 1865, and its maximum dilution was 1:669.) (Dr. Nicolai Jalan de la Croix, Das Verhalten der Bacterien des Fleischwassers gegen einige Antiseptica, *Archiv für experimentelle Pathologie,* 20 janvier, 1881, t. XIII, p. 175 à 225. Cited in Paul Bar, *The Principles of Antiseptic Methods Applied to Obstetric Practice,* Philadelphia: P. Blakiston, Son & Co., 1887, pp. 36–37.)

42. Gerard van Swieten (1700–1772), one of the towering figures of 18th-century medicine in Europe, was a Dutch Roman Catholic who trained to be a physician at the University of Leiden but, because of his religion, was denied an opportunity for a professorship there. The Empress Maria Theresa of Austria, however, invited van Swieten to become court physician in Vienna. And here he had a transformative influence on reforming health care in Austria, establishing the great Vienna medical school and organizing its faculty, and developing libraries, chemical laboratories, and botanical gardens. He died in the Schönbrunn Palace.

43. *Corrosive sublimate* is bichloride of mercury ($HgCl_2$). Mercury and its salts are among the most potent antiseptics known, but also among the potentially most toxic. As described in Dr. Paul Bar's 1887 book on obstetric practice (see citation 44), "the employment of corrosive sublimate presents a series of advantages and disadvantages. The advantages are as follows: the great antiseptic power of the agent, the low price of the solutions employed, the complete absence of odor, and the easy preparation of the solutions. The disadvantages are: its actions upon the skin, which becomes hard and slightly tanned . . . The true disadvantage is, without doubt, its toxic power." Mercuric chloride was used to prevent sepsis in wounds by Arabian physicians in the Middle Ages. For the treatment of syphilis, prior to the advent of antibiotics, mercuric chloride was ingested (in the form of *Liquor Van Swieten,* consisting of one part mercuric chloride, one part sodium chloride, and 1000 parts water), injected, applied topically, and even inhaled (in the form of "mercurial vapor baths," using various contraptions like a metal housing chamber for the patient receiving treatment). (Richard M. Swiderski, *Quicksilver. A History of the Use, Lore and Effects of Mercury,* Jefferson, North Carolina: McFarland & Co., Inc., Publishers, 2008, pp. 113–115.) As discussed later, the signs of chronic mercury toxicity could resemble those of the late stages of syphilis for which it was intended as the treatment.

44. Dr. Paul Bar's 1887 treatise on the principles of antiseptic methods in obstetrics describes the practice of using *van Swieten's solution* of corrosive sublimate (bichloride of mercury) at the Paris Maternity just a decade after Semmelweis's discovery. "You will observe that from 1859 the general curve of mortality at this institution gradually declined . . . When pupils come into this apartment (*sic*), they are compelled to wash the hands, using a nail-brush, with a solution of corrosive sublimate 1 to 1000. They are not allowed to examine different women without repeating the disinfection of the hands with van Swieten's solution. The pupils have never experienced the least inconvenience from this practice . . . It is useless to say that the operator and his assistants have previously disinfected their hands and forearms with the same solution." (Dr. Paul Bar, translated by Henry D. Fry, M.D., *The Principles of Antiseptic Methods Applied to Obstetric Practice,* Philadelphia: P. Blakiston, Son & Co., 1887.)

45. It is known that Semmelweis did experiment with various disinfectant solutions. (Kadar N, Romero R, Papp Z. Ignaz Semmelweis: the "Savior of Mothers." On the 200th anniversary of his birth. *American Journal of Obstetrics & Gynecology [AJOG]* 2018; 219:519–522). However, it should be stated here that there is no direct evidence that Semmelweis ever used bichloride of mercury. Its well-established antiseptic properties by this time, its introduction into medical practice by topical application by Vienna's renowned Gerard van Swieten a century earlier, its use in the treatment of syphilis, and its well-documented use for obstetrical antisepsis elsewhere in Europe, including the Paris Maternity, make this highly plausible. Its use in obstetrics was generally accepted even in the U.S: "Before examining the patient, the physician, after careful washing of his hands with soap and hot water, should immerse them for several minutes in a 1:2000 solution of mercuric bichloride." (Montgomery EE. *Some Points in the Management of Normal Labor. Maryland Medical J,* Jan. 2, 1886, p.182.) For a discussion of Joseph Lister's (1827–1912) antisepsis in surgical and obstetrical practice, and whether or not it was influenced by Semmelweis, see: "Lister and Antisepsis," in *The Tragedy of Childbed Fever,* by Irvine Loudon (Oxford: Oxford University Press, 2000), pp. 130–150.

46. At this time (and beginning in the 18th century) in Austria, a young man (as no women were allowed) wishing to become an apothecary had to complete a five-year apprenticeship in a pharmacy. Following this training, he would typically seek work for a period as a "journeyman" in different pharmacies in order to expand his experience. He was finally required to pass an examination administered by the Medical Faculty of the University of Vienna before he could acquire his own pharmacy. Also by this time, pharmacy apprentices and journeymen were required to attend lectures at the university in areas like chemistry and botany; this had been mandated by van Swieten, who was himself a fully trained apothecary as well as a physician. (Kletter C. Austrian pharmacy in the eighteenth and nineteenth century. *Sci. Pharm.* 2010; 78:397–409.)

47. Semmelweis's own wash basin is on display today in Vienna in the Josephenum collections of the Medical University of Vienna (www.josephenum.ac.at)

48. Anton von Rosas was an outspoken anti-Semite. He openly advocated for exclusion of Jews from the medical profession. As cited by Katz (Jacob Katz, *From Prejudice to Destruction: Anti-Semitism, 1700–1933.* Cambridge: Harvard University Press, 1980, p. 225), Rosas published his opinion "On the Sources of Present Medical Discontent" in the *Medizinische Jahrbücker des kais. königlichen österreichischen Staates* (Vienna, 1842, pp. 1–19) that the disproportionate increase in Jewish physicians was the major cause of the general deterioration of the medical profession. He stated that Jewish doctors were "inclined to charlatanism," and that, having for two thousand years embraced material gain as their guideline for action, Jews could not be expected to rise to the ethical standards required for medical practice. Rosas concluded that "the Israelite as he is may and should become peasant, artisan, artist, indeed anything in the world rather than doctor, . . ." As noted by Katz, Rosas's preconceived notion of Jewish mentality served as an ideological weapon in defense of the exclusive right of Christians to certain professions then endangered by Jewish competition.

49. Semmelweis himself couldn't remember the exact date.

50. Hans was the name by which Hebra's first son, Johannes, who was delivered by Semmelweis in 1847, would be known throughout his life. Hans von Hebra would become, like his father, a professor of dermatology. In fact, the Hebras belonged to an extended "royal family" of Austro-Hungarian dermatologists in the 19th century because Hans's younger sister, Martha, married Moritz Kaposi, the dermatologist who described Kaposi's sarcoma. (From: Holubar K. Ferdinand von Hebra 1816–1880: On the occasion of the centenary of his death. *International Journal of Dermatology.* 1981; 20:291–295.)

51. Gustav Adolf Michaelis (1798–1848) was the director of the obstetrical department in Kiel. Michaelis was a pioneer in scientific obstetrics, best remembered today for his work in the field of pelvimetry, such as the role of a "narrow pelvis" in complications associated with childbirth. The "rhombus of Michaelis," a contour in the region of the coccyx and sacrum is named after him. (Neitzke G. Gustav Adolph Michaelis—Artz, Forscher, Lehrer. Eine Würdigung zum Jubiläumsjahr 1998. *Gynäkologe* 1999; 32:660–664.)

52. The actual letter is reproduced in Ignaz Semmelweis, *The Etiology, Concept, and Prophylaxis of Childbed Fever,* translated by L. Codell Carter, The University of Wisconsin Press, Madison, 1983. The letter from Schwartz to Michaelis, which Michaelis then forwarded to Professor Karl Edouard Marius Levy in Copenhagen, was published along with a commentary by Levy in: "De nyeste Forsög I Födselsstiftelsen I Wien til Oplysning om Barselfeberens Aetologie," *Hospitals-Meddelelser* 1848;1:199–211 in K. Codell Carter's "Translator's Introduction" to Semmelweis's book.

53. Adolf Kussmaul (1822–1902) became one of the leading clinicians of his time, still known today for important physical examination findings that have been named for him: "Kussmaul breathing," a distinctive type of labored breathing seen in diseases like diabetic ketoacidosis; and "Kussmaul's sign," a diagnostic pattern of changes in jugular venous pressure that can be observed in the patient's neck and is found in constrictive pericarditis. He was also the first to describe medical disorders such as aphasia, polyarteritis nodosa, and mesenteric embolism.

54. Even at this young age, Hebra was already editor of the prestigious journal, *Übertagungen der Kaiserlichen und Königlichen Gesellschaft der Ærtze zu Wien.* Finally, in January 1848, after repeatedly pleading in vain to Semmelweis to submit a paper, Hebra himself published an editorial in his journal touting Semmelweis's great discovery and, of course, giving him complete credit for it. He wrote: "This most important discovery, worthy of being placed beside Jenner's discovery of cowpox inoculations, has been completely confirmed in the local maternity hospital, and supporting testimonials have been received from foreign countries."

55. Gerstner opened on April 24, 1847. Its founder, Anton, was appointed Imperial Court Confectioner in 1873. The small pastry shop on Kärntner Straβe in the heart of the old city remains open today as a popular café.

56. Hebra's pioneering work in classifying skin diseases, elucidating their pathogenesis (also see reference 11), and developing treatments for them laid the groundwork for the modern discipline of dermatology. Erna Lesky has described in detail Hebra's pivotal role in the development of this field of medicine and the resistance that it initially met, in her book *The Vienna Medical School of the 19th Century*, Baltimore: The Johns Hopkins University Press, 1976, pages 128–133.

57. Later, in the 1860s, Adolf Kussmaul himself published his definitive description of the distinctive symptoms of mercury toxicity, based on his own direct observations of mirror workers who were required to use it regularly for their occupation. Kussmaul also differentiated the symptoms of syphilis and mercury poisoning, defining them as two entirely different diseases. (Theodore H. Bast. *The Life and Time of Adolf Kussmaul.* New York: Paul B. Hoeber Inc, 1926, p. 101. Originally in "Untersuchungen über den constitutionellen Mercurialismus und sein Verhältniss zur constitutionellen Syphilis." Würzburg. 433 pp.). Symptoms of chronic mercury toxicity, including excessive salivation, skin eruptions, mouth ulcerations, tremor, anorexia, and personality changes, were well known before 1847. In fact, they were first recognized by ancient Greek and Roman doctors, something Kussmaul would have undoubtedly known because of his strong appreciation of medical history. As mercury in all kinds of preparations (such as topical ointments, syrups and pills) became popularly prescribed for syphilis during this period, theories became widely accepted that the symptoms of syphilis and mercury toxicity, for which it was used, were actually indistinguishable, even though the notion of a specific "mercurial disease" was described by the prominent British physician Andrew Mathias, in 1811. (From Richard M. Swiderski, *Quicksilver. A History of the Use, Lore and Effects of Mercury,* McFarland & Company, Inc. Publishers, Jefferson, North Carolina, 2008.)

58. This anecdote was related by Kussmaul himself. As his biographer, Theodore Bast, described it, Kussmaul's Professor Tiedmann "never gave illustrations on the board but illustrated his lectures with demonstrations which his attendant, Jacob, brought at the proper moment. One of these demonstrations to the medical students was to show the rapidity with which certain substances rubbed into the skin are excreted by the kidney." And Kussmaul never forgot the turpentine experiment. (From Theodore H. Bast, *The Life and Time of Adolf Kussmaul,* Paul B. Hoeber, Inc., New York, 1926.)

59. Semmelweis wrote in his autobiography: "In consequence of my conviction I must affirm that only God knows the number of patients who went prematurely to their graves because of me. I have examined corpses to an extent equaled by few other obstetricians. If I say this also of another physician, my intention is only to bring to consciousness a truth that, to humanity's great misfortune, has remained unknown through so many centuries." (From Ignaz Semmelweis, *The Etiology, Concept, and Prophylaxis of Childbed Fever.* Translated by K. Codell Carter, Madison: The University of Wisconsin Press, 1983, p. 98.)

60. In retirement and near his death at the turn of the century, Adolf Kussmaul wrote in his "Youthful Memoirs of an Old Physician" the following memories of his experience in Vienna at the time of Semmelweis's discovery: "In Austria a revolting system of favoritism dominated everywhere; there were incompetent professors and chief physicians who owed their appointments to the patronage of distinguished petticoats and influential cowls." (Adolf Kussmaul, *Jungenderinnerungen eines alten Arztes.* Stuttgart: A. Bonz und Co., 1899. Also in William J. Sinclair. *Semmelweis. His Life and His Doctrine.* Manchester: At the University Press, 1909, pp. 113–114.)

61. Neitzke G, Hoffmann S. Gustav Adolph Michaelis—Physician, Researcher, Teacher. *Gynäkologe* 1999; 32:660–664.

62. Hebra was editor of the journal "*Übertagungen der Kaiserlichen und Königlichen Gesellschaft der Ärtze zu Wien*" and his editorial about Semmelweis's discovery was published in the January 1848 issue. In it,

Hebra stated "Dr. Semmelweis [note: without mention of Klein] . . . for the last two years has devoted special attention to the causes at the root of the prevailing epidemic of puerperal fever. On this subject he has left nothing untested and everything that could exercise an injurious influence was systematically eliminated . . . These and other observations aroused in him the thought that perhaps in lying-in hospitals pregnant and parturient women might be inoculated by the *obstetrician himself* [Hebra's italics] . . . In order to test his opinion, he ordered that everyone in the First Clinic should wash their hands in an aqueous solution of chloride of lime . . . The result was both surprising and gratifying . . . Therefore, *the conveyance of a foul exudation from a living organism may be the main cause of puerperal fever* [Hebra's italics]." (Abstracted from Thomas Dormandy, *Moments of Truth,* John Wiley & Sons, Ltd., Chichester, West Sussex, England, 2003, pp. 199–20.)

63. Anton Füster (1808–1881) was born in what is today Slovenia. He was ordained into the Roman Catholic priesthood at the age of twenty-four. He became a noted theologian, teacher, and political activist. Only one year earlier, in 1847, he had been appointed professor of philosophy at the University of Vienna. Following the outbreak of revolution in Vienna, Füster became a passionate revolutionary and fought alongside the students on the barricades. After the revolution was crushed in 1849, he emigrated first to England and then to the U.S., where he lived in Philadelphia. Toward the end of his life, he returned to Vienna, where he died at the age of seventy-three. (Walter Sauer. Anton Füster: Priester der Wiener Revolution. *Zeitgeschichte.* 2.Jahr [1975] Heft 1–12, pp. 249–256.)

64. What transpired in the great hall was the mass signing of a petition to the imperial government demanding freedom of the press, speech, religion, and teaching, as well as radical educational reform. It was decided that the students of the university, including the medical students, would march early next morning to the opening of the Landhaus to present the petition to the Lower Austrian Estates. At nightfall, many of the students got through the guarded city wall gates into the dilapidated tenements of the working-class suburbs, where they tried to rouse the citizenry to join their uprising the next day.

65. Adolf Fischof (1816–1893) was born to Moravian and Hungarian Jewish parents. He grew up in Budapest and, like Semmelweis, studied medicine at the University of Vienna, becoming an obstetrician in 1846. While continuing to practice medicine in Vienna, Fischof immersed himself much more in in politics, writing, and government. He made his political debut with his famous speech in the courtyard of the Landhaus of Lower Austrian estates on the morning of March 13, 1848, helping to ignite the 1848 revolution in Vienna. After the abolition of the Reichstag in 1849, where he had served, Fischof was arrested and convicted of high treason for being an accomplice in the murder of Foreign Minister Theodor Baillet Latour (see later). He was exonerated and released nine months later. However, financial difficulties resulting from the Vienna stock market crash and poor health led him to move to Emmersdorf, where he died. (Michael Graetz. *Adolf Fischof. Ein jüdischer Akademiker an der Spitze der Revolution von 1848.* In: *Zwischen Wissenschraft und Politik. Studien zur deutschen Universitätsgeschichte. Festschrift für Eike Wolgast zum 65. Geburtstag. Hg. von Armin Kohnle und Frank Engehausen.* Stuttgart: Steiner 2001, S. 126–137. Also: https://www.habsburger.net/en/chapter/citi)

66. On March 3, 1848, Kossuth addressed the Lower House of the Hungarian Diet and delivered the speech that contained this passage and led directly to the upheavals in Vienna and Hungary. It has been called the "inaugural address of the revolution." It was quickly translated by sympathizers into German the next day and distributed in Vienna, creating extraordinary excitement upon its public reading by the journalist Franz Putz. (In: Istvan Deak. *The Lawful Revolution. Louis Kossuth and the Hungarians 1848–1849.* London: Phoenix Press, 1979, p. 66.)

67. An excellent and more detailed narrative of the events of the first days' uprising is in: Mike Rapport. *1848. Year of Revolution.* New York: Basic Books, 2008, pp. 61–66.

68. On the night of Monday, March 14, 1848, the old Chancellor Klemens von Metternich and his wife slipped out of Vienna in a carriage that took them to a train. The train then transported them across Europe to The Hague in the Netherlands, where they spent two weeks before boarding a steamer to London, their destination. (Mike Rapport. *1848. Year of Revolution.* New York: Basic Books, 2008, p 64. Also, von Hügel C. *The Story of the Escape of Prince von Metternich.* National Review, vol. 1 [1883], pp. 590–601, and Palmer AW. *Metternich.* New York: Harper & Row, 1972, p.310.)

69. The Academic Legion, the so-called *Burschengarde*, was formed with 3,000–4,000 student members. It included five divisions: (1) medical students, (2) law students, (3) arts students, (4) technical students, (5) college students, as well as faculty members, with a total membership of about 6,000. The members of the legion wore a uniform of gray trousers, a tight navy-blue jacket with black buttons and a wide-brimmed hat with black feathers. It was disbanded on May 15, 1848, but the members of the Academic Legion continued to play an important role in revolutionary activities. (György Gortvay and Imre Zoltán. *Semmelweis. His Life and Work.* Budapest: Akadémiai Kiadó, 1968, pp. 62–63.) Not all biographers agree that Semmelweis actually did join the Academic Legion. (See Thomas Dormandy. *Moments of Truth*, Chichester: Wiley, p. 503, footnote 137.) However, an early photograph does exist showing Semmelweis in uniform. Other biographers have indicated that Semmelweis was much more actively involved in the revolution, even stating that "Semmelweis was one of the most passionate and active revolutionary fighters." ("Semmelweis gehörte zu den begeisterten, glühendsten Freiheitskämpfer." Cf Schürer von Waldheim. Semmelweis Sein Leben und Wirken. Urteil der Nachwelt. [Wien, 1905], p. 90. Translation in Gy. Gortvay and I. Zoltán. *Semmelweis. His Life and Work.* Budapest: Akadémiai Kiadó. 1968. p. 63.)

70. The barricades on Michaeler Platz in May were painted in oil by Anton Ziegler in 1848. (Historisches Museum der Stadt Wien)

71. The historic roles of insurgent barricades, and specifically their widespread use in insurrections throughout the Habsburg Empire and elsewhere in Europe in 1848, has been thoroughly researched and described in detail in Mark Traugott. *The Insurgent Barricade,* University of California Press, Berkeley, 2010. The three major outbreaks of barricade events in Vienna in 1848 occurred during March, May, and October. Also see Jill Harsin. *Barricades: The War of the Streets in Revolutionary Paris, 1830–1848,* New York: Palgrave (formerly Macmillan Press Ltd.). 2002.

72. Karl Marx (1818–1883) was the Prussian-born economist, philosopher, and journalist who became a revolutionary socialist and developed what is today known as the *Marxist theory,* the economic model of labor as it relates to capital. A prolific writer, he authored *The Communist Manifesto* (with Friedrich Engels [1820–1895]) and *Das Kapital.* His works are among the most influential in the modern history of the world. As documented in the *Neue Rheinische Zeitung,* the newspaper Marx edited and frequently wrote for, Marx was actually in Vienna on August 28, 1848, to deliver a speech to the recently formed Vienna Democratic Association. The Viennese newspaper reports about this event related that "Herr Marx was of the opinion that it was a matter of indifference *who* was Minister, for here too—as in Paris—it was now a question of the struggle between the bourgeoisie and the proletariat. His speech was very witty, trenchant, and instructive . . ." He went on to say in this speech: "*Up to now the speakers mentioned only two great powers, the Imperial Diet and the Emperor . . . but the greatest power, the people, has been forgotten! We must appeal to the people and must try to influence it employing every possible means. We must raise a storm against the Government, and must work towards this end in every possible way . . .*" [*sic*] (*Der Radikale* No. 64, August 31, 1848, and *Wiener Zeitung* No. 252 [supplement], September 17, 1848.) Julius Fröbel (1805–1893) was a noted journalist, author, and publisher at that time.

73. Wolfgang Maderthaner and Lutz Musner, *Unruly Masses: The Other Side of Fin-de-Siècle Vienna*, Berghahn Books, New York, 2008, chapter 10. This is the same Schmelz cemetery where Semmelweis himself was to be buried seventeen years later.

74. More than 2,000 revolutionaries lost their lives in this final siege.

75. Although fighting in Hungary continued through the next year, the country's fate was sealed by the crushing of Vienna's last insurrection in October 1848. It was just a matter of time before the country fell next. The revolution in Hungary ended a year later with the invasion of 200,000 Russian troops crossing the Carpathian Mountains into Hungary, sent by the Tsar at the invitation of the Habsburg Emperor.

76. *Privatdozent* was an academic title conferred by universities, mainly in German-speaking European countries in the 19th century, upon individuals deemed qualified to lecture and teach but who were not salaried by the university. They would typically collect teaching fees from their students directly and were free to spend their remaining time pursuing other jobs, including private practice.

77. Carl Haller (1809–1887) had read the following before the Vienna Medical Society on February 23, 1849, referring to Semmelweis's work. "The importance of this practical knowledge for lying-in hospitals, *for hospitals in general, for the surgical wards in particular,* [my italics] is such an incalculable one, that it appears worthy of the most serious attention of all men of Science and certainly ought to be worthy of suitable recognition by the high authorities of the State." Haller's words, in alluding to antiseptic surgery, remained unheeded until several decades later, when Lister successfully brought into practice what Haller foresaw would someday confer inestimable benefits to humanity. (Duka T. Childbed fever: its causes and prevention: a life's history. *Lancet* 1886; 206–208.ii.) (Translated by Frank P. Murphy, *Ignaz Philipp Semmelweis [1818–1865], an Annotated Bibliography.* Bulletin of the History of Medicine; vol. 20, no. 5, Baltimore: The Johns Hopkins Press, 1946, p. 656.)

78. Between May 15 and July 15, 1850, Semmelweis delivered a series of three lectures to the Medical Society of Vienna. The lectures were not published in full but do appear in the secretary's minutes. However, the discussions following the lectures were recorded. (See: K. Codell Carter, *Translator's Introduction* to Ignaz Semmelweis, *The Etiology, Concept, and Prophylaxis*

of Childbed Fever. Madison: The University of Wisconsin Press, 1983, p. 23 [footnote 68] and p. 32.)

Exactly who was in attendance and spoke at these Semmelweis lectures in 1850 at the Medical Society of Vienna (also named the Imperial Society of Physicians) is open to some question. There is little doubt that Rokitansky, the society's president, Skoda, Hebra, and Klein were among the many in attendance. The minutes of the meetings were reported by Dr. Heinrich Herzfelder, the first secretary of the society. They were abstracted by Sir William Sinclair, *Semmelweis. His Life and his Doctrine. A Chapter in the History of Medicine.* Manchester: University of Manchester Press, 1909. Sinclair's work was notably the first English-language biography of Semmelweis.

According to the minutes of the July 15 meeting, "Doctors Zipfl and Lumpe provided powerful and praiseworthy opposition to this view of the origin of the disease; they sought to vindicate the miasmatic origin of this evil by the use of statistical data. In the discussion, however . . . this conception of the disease, most warmly defended by Doctors Arneth, Chiari, Helm, and . . . by Professor Hayne, can be recognized as a true triumph of medical discovery." (Heinrich Herzfelder, "Bericht über die Leistungen der k. k. Gesellschaft der Ärzte in Wien während des Jahres 1850," [*Zeitschrift der k. k. Gesellschaft der Ärzte zu Wien* 8 (1851): vii; author's note], translated by K. Codell Carter, in Semmelweis, p. 210.) Elsewhere, it was suggested that discussion ensued in which Scanzoni, Kiwisch, and Seyfert also took part (Duka T. Childbed fever; its causes and prevention: a life's history. *Lancet* 1886, vol. 2 [August 7]; 2:246.)

79. Bruxing is the act of rats rapidly grinding their teeth together. It is thought to promote the growth of sharp teeth. Boggling is a sign of especially enthusiastic bruxing; it is expressed by their eyeballs disturbingly bulging out of their sockets.

80. The nature of Zipfel's startling and unexpected personal assault on Semmelweis was graphically described by Sir William Sinclair in his original English-language biography of Semmelweis. He suggested that Zipfel "attacked Semmelweis in a violent and offensive manner" and that this illustrated the "length and depth to which some of the mercenaries of debate were willing to go in order to curry favor with their seniors, but could not understand and therefore must treat" Semmelweis "disingenuously and spitefully." Sinclair goes on to comment that "it was natural, considering his own record, that Zipfel would not willingly admit that cadaveric poison was a cause of infection in childbed fever." (Sir William J. Sinclair. *Semmelweis. His Life and His Doctrine. A Chapter in the History of Medicine.* Manchester: University of Manchester Press, 1909.)

81. In: William J. Sinclair. *Semmelweis. His Life and His Doctrine.* Manchester: At the University Press, 1909.

82. "In order to confirm my views directly, I felt it was necessary to conduct animal experiments. With my friend, Dr. [George Maria] Lautner, assistant to Professor Rokitansky, I carried out experiments on rabbits . . ." (In: Ignaz Semmelweis. *The Etiology, Concept, and Prophylaxis of Childbed Fever.* Translated by K. Codell Carter. Madison: The University of Wisconsin Press, 1983, p. 105.)

83. Chloroform was introduced in 1847 for pain management in labor and delivery by the eminent Scottish obstetrician, James Young Simpson of Edinburgh. It was found to be significantly more effective and safer than ether, which it therefore quickly replaced. However, its use in obstetrical practice at first met with powerful medical, moral, and religious opposition. As physician to Queen Victoria, Simpson used chloroform during her delivery of Prince Leopold in 1853, much to the queen's great gratitude. After that, the use of chloroform in childbirth expanded rapidly throughout Europe. Simpson was among the first to learn of Semmelweis's findings in Vienna, and it is known that they corresponded through Semmelweis's Viennese friend, Franz von Arneth, who was fluent in English. Mainly because of misinterpretation of Semmelweis's conclusions, Simpson initially dismissed the findings as being nothing new to obstetricians in England; however, he later grew to appreciate the importance and novelty of Semmelweis's contributions. (Grant GJ, Grant AH, Lockwood CJ. Simpson, Semmelweis, and transformational change.

Obstetrics & Gynecology 2005; 106:384–387.) As K. Codell Carter has noted, Semmelweis considered Simpson to be "the most famous obstetrician of our time." In turn, after the death of Semmelweis, Simpson paid tribute to him by being one of the planners of the monument to Semmelweis in Budapest. (No author. International monument to Semmelweis. *BMJ* 1892 Nov 5;2[1662]:1026–1027.)

84. Semmelweis's sister Júlia lived in a spacious house on Iv Street, one of the houses her affluent merchant father, József, owned and gave to her as her wedding dowry. It was located just behind the family's original home on Apród Street in Buda. Buda and Pest were separate cities at that time, with Buda lying on the western bank of the Danube and Pest on the other. The merger into Budapest occurred in 1873, after the Chain Bridge (Lánchíd) was built in 1849 to connect them. (In this book, the city name of Budapest is used throughout.)

85. Kapronczay Károly, Semmelweis/Szemerényi/Károly/Fülöp in: *A Semmelweis Család Története*. Budapest: Semmelweis Kiadó, 2008, pp. 26–29.

86. The Hungarian Károly Geringer was appointed imperial commissioner of Hungary during the country's brutal suppression by Vienna following the 1848 revolution and reported directly to the Habsburg imperial government.

87. Kapronczay Károly, Semmelweis József in: *A Semmelweis Család Története.* Budapest: Semmelweis Kiadó, 2008, pp. 23–25.

88. In the words of Semmelweis: "On the following morning [after returning to Budapest], in order to convince myself, I visited the maternity hospital. There I found a corpse, not yet removed, of a person who had just died of puerperal fever, another patient in severe agony, and four others seriously ill with the disease . . . The air becomes so stale that it is dangerous to the patients . . . On the ground floor, next to the lavatory, is the building garbage pit. This decaying mass exudes a penetrating stench . . . linen that is still befouled with the blood of earlier deceased patients is spread under newly admitted patients." (*Ignaz Semmelweis. The Etiology, Concept, and Prophylaxis of Childbed Fever.* Translated by K. Codell Carter. Madison: The University of Wisconsin Press, 1983.)

89. The reign of terror the Habsburg Empire had imposed on the Magyar people was supervised at first by General Baron Ludwig Haynau, who was appointed commander-in-chief for Hungary by the new Emperor Franz Joseph and his prime minister, Schwarzenberg. Haynau was an imposing, aristocratic soldier whose actions had brought him notoriety for his devious and sadistic nature. Moreover, Haynau had a visceral hatred for Hungarians. Hundreds were executed for complicity with the revolution. They even included Hungary's constitutional prime minister, Count Louis Batthyányi, who was shot by an Austrian firing squad in Pest on the same day thirteen Hungarian honvéd generals met the same fate or were executed by hanging in the city of Arad. Countless others were imprisoned and tortured. An ever-present police state descended over life in Budapest. Censorship and police surveillance became pervasive. Vienna was bent on humbling the seditious Hungarians and teaching them a bitter lesson, creating a so-called "neo-absolutist" state of subjugation that was to continue for fifteen years. See: Robert Nemes. *The Once and Future Budapest.* DeKalb: Northern Illinois University Press. 2005. Chapter 7 ("The Road to Budapest"), pp. 152–180.

90. Birly was a fervent proponent of purging. He prescribed purging in all kinds of forms before and after delivery. It was to be done in the most vigorous ways possible to cleanse the bowels and flush out the bodily toxins he felt caused the fatal disease. He purged with cathartics, he purged with enemas, he purged by colonic irrigation. It was not uncommon to see Birly's expectant mothers lying on their sides in the clinics with lubricated nozzles inserted into their rectum to infuse enema fluids from bags suspended above their beds. And he especially advocated the use of large amounts of calomel, a solution of mercury chloride that he prescribed to be taken internally to disinfect the gastrointestinal tract and the birth canal. Birly was fond of referring to the eminent American physician, Benjamin Rush, who also recommended the use of calomel mercury purging at doses high enough to cause excessive salivation, a well-known sign of mercury toxicity.

91. On August 11, 1849, the National Assembly of Hungary met for the last time and declared the War for Independence lost. On the morning of August 13, Hungary surrendered to the Russian army invading the country and occupying Pest from the East at the invitation of the Habsburg Emperor, while Baron Julius Jacob von Haynau, the Austrian commander-in-chief in Hungary, occupied Buda. Kossuth abdicated and fled into exile. Haynau didn't even acknowledge the Russians in his victory speech on August 18: "The triumphant Imperial-Royal Arms have smashed the thousand-headed hydra of the Hungarian Revolution . . . The whole of Hungary has now been occupied by the Imperial Royal armies." (Istvan Deak. *The Lawful Revolution. Louis Kossuth and the Hungarians 1848–1849.* London: Phoenix Press. 1979.)

92. The Újépület (*Neues Gebäude* in German) barracks were built in 1786. They became a symbol of Austrian terror after the 1848 Revolution but were not demolished until the end of the nineteenth century. Today the site has been replaced by *Szabadság tér* (Liberty Square), one of the most beautiful squares in Budapest, surrounded by grand and important buildings. Andrássy (1823–1890) was to become a leading architect of the city's reconstruction and its development into a great metropolis. The walking path Semmelweis took to and from the City Park (*Városliget*) was built into one of Europe's most impressive avenues and was named Andrássy út. The author grew up at number 66, Andrássy út.

93. In September, 1851, an army executioner in Budapest ceremonially posted the names of 75 prominent Hungarians who had escaped but were now found guilty of treason *in absentia* on the individual gallows where they were hung in effigy. They included Kossuth himself, Batthyány, Count Gyula Andrássy, and others whose names were listed in the September 23 1851 edition of Budapest's leading newspaper, the *Magyar Hirlap*. In: Istvan Deak. *The Lawful Revolution. Louis Kossuth and the Hungarians 1848–1849.* London: Phoenix Press, 1979, pp. 336–337 and 383 (ref. 35).

94. The *gendarmerie* originated from the 1848 revolution as a military force charged with police duties. It was a component of the k.k. Army, but its operational control was later (in 1860) assumed by the Austrian Ministry for the Interior. Police (*gendarmes*) and non-uniformed "censors" were assigned to closely monitor schools and other institutions, public events, social gatherings, marketplaces, the media, religious services, voluntary associations, coffeehouses, youth organizations, and other potential forums of public opinion for signs of unrest and to identify agitators and other possible subversives.

95. János Balassa (1814–1868) was one of the great surgeons in Hungarian medical history. He was a pioneer of cardiac resuscitation and plastic and reconstructive surgery. He introduced ether anesthesia into Hungary in 1847 and was a leader in adopting antiseptic surgery, using hypochlorite solution to wash the hands and disinfect wounds. (From: Husveti S, Ellis H. Janos Balassa, pioneer of cardiac resuscitation. *Anaesthesia.* 1969; 24:113–115.)

96. Carl Braun did in fact throw his hat in the ring to apply for Birly's position in Budapest. He was one of the six finalist candidates selected.

97. The Citadella, planned in 1851 in the aftermath of the Hungarian uprising and completed in 1854 during the reign of Emperor Franz Josef, was designed by the Habsburgs not to protect the city but rather to intimidate the Hungarian citizenry as a permanent reminder of the repercussion of insurgency. Its sixty cannons were never actually fired with hostile intent. During the 1956 Hungarian revolution, however, Soviet troops occupied the remnants of the Citadella and fired their tanks down upon the rebellious city. Today, sitting atop the Gellért Hill in Buda, it provides arguably the most stunning views of Budapest. (See: Géza Buzinkay. *An Illustrated History of Budapest.* Budapest: Corvina Books Ltd, 1998.)

98. Antonie van Leeuwenhoek (1632–1723) is now referred to as the "Father of Microbiology." A tradesman from Delft, in the Netherlands, he had no higher education and was not the inventor of the microscope, but his skill at grinding lenses and ability to greatly improve lighting allowed him

to build microscopes that magnified over two hundred times. He used these to become the first to observe microscopic single-celled organisms, the existence of which was previously unknown. Among these was the discovery and meticulous drawings of bacteria that he observed on plaque between his own teeth. He reported to the Royal Society of London that he saw "many very little living animalcules, very prettily a-moving" in various ways of locomotion and in various shapes. He often referred to them as those "*amazing little animalcules.*" Their relationship to the causation of infectious diseases, however, was not even speculated at that time.

99. Although Skoda has been historically portrayed as one of Semmelweis's most influential supporters, more recently questions have arisen about his personal motives. Did Skoda sincerely admire Semmelweis's revolutionary theory, or was his support for it used by him as ammunition for his own agenda to liberate the Vienna Medical School from the orthodoxy of reactionary physician administrators who were appointed through patronage by the imperial government? Did Skoda intentionally misrepresent Semmelweis's views about the cause of puerperal fever being entirely the result of cadaveric poison, which in subsequent years became an unyielding point of attack on Semmelweis by his critics? Skoda also conspicuously remained silent after the first of three lectures he gave on May 15, 1850, in Vienna, after which Semmelweis was malevolently attacked. While many historians would argue with this, Kadar has recently concluded that the most likely reason Semmelweis left Vienna as abruptly as he did was his realization that Skoda had never really agreed with his theory and had merely used it for his own political ends, costing Semmelweis the extension of his assistantship. (Kadar N. Rediscovering Ignaz Philipp Semmelweis [1818–1865]. *American Journal of Obstetrics & Gynecology* 2019; 220:26–39.)

100. A photograph of this letter is in: Georg Silló-Seidl. *Die Wahrheit über Semmelweis. Das Wirken des gro⌧en Arzt-Forschers und sein tragischer Tod.* Genf: Ariston Verlag, 1978 (Figure 18).

101. Count Leopold von Thun (1811–1888) came from an aristocratic family and studied law and philosophy at the University of Prague. He traveled extensively throughout Europe, including England, where he became heavily influenced by the Tractarian Party, a romantic movement, and the Ultramontane revival. These experiences led to his interest in prison reform, as well as philanthropic and charitable work. In 1849 (until 1860) he was appointed the Imperial Minister of Education, where his paths with Semmelweis would cross again indirectly.

102. These intersecting streets in Budapest today are named Kossuth Lajos utca and Semmelweis utca, respectively. The Medical Faculty of Budapest opened in 1770 and was originally located in the small town of Nagyszombat. It subsequently moved to Buda, which proved to be an unsuitable location for the university, and finally to Pest in 1784. This is the location where the Medical Faculty had established its home at the time of Semmelweis's arrival. Some modernization did take place during the reactionary period immediately following the 1848 Revolution, but it was still a "miserable and crowded Medical Faculty." The practical part of medical education continued to be regarded as inferior mainly because of the lack of availability of a large public teaching hospital comparable to the Allgemeine Krankenhaus for the University of Vienna. (http://semmelweis.hu/english/the-university/history/detailed-history) A photograph-based drawing of the hospital of the University of Pest at that time is shown in: Georg Silló-Seidl, *Die Wahrheit über Semmelweis. Das Wirken des groẞen Arzt-Forschers und sein tragischer Tod.* Genf: Ariston Verlag, 1978 (Figure 19).

103. Although the name of the superintendent is documented, little else can be found on von Tandler. *Statthaltereirat* was a title given to a high-ranking official in the Habsburg Empire.

104. 26°R refers to the Réaumur scale, in which the thermometer contains diluted alcohol. It was widely used in many parts of Europe from the 18th century through the mid-19th century, when it was gradually replaced by the Celsius scale. 26°R converts to approximately 95°F.

105. These actual personal accounts, translated by Slaughter and Carter, provide a good contemporary description of the conditions Semmelweis encountered in the university maternity wards of Pest. (From: Frank

G. Slaughter. *Immortal Magyar: Semmelweis, Conqueror of Childbed Fever.* New York: Henry Schuman, 1950, pp. 143–147 and 171–172. Also from: Ignaz Semmelweis. *The Etiology, Concept, and Prophylaxis of Childbed Fever.* Translated by K. Codell Carter. Madison: The University of Wisconsin Press, 1983, pp. 108–110. Also from: William J. Sinclair. *Semmelweis. His Life and His Doctrine.* Manchester: At the University Press, 1909, p. 140–141.)

106. Even in the late-19th century, most marriages in Hungary, except within the working classes, were still arranged between families. "It was unlikely that an engagement would take place without the family of the bride having some connection with, or at least substantial information about, the family of the groom," and "it was difficult, nay almost impossible, for a young girl to meet a young man outside the social circles arranged by her family, and outside acceptable places . . . like balls of the various university faculties." (From John Lukacs. *Budapest 1900: A Historical Portrait of a City and Its Culture.* New York: Weidenfeld & Nicolson, 1988, pp. 104–105.)

107. Reconstruction of the Pesti Vigadó was completed in 1865, and today the palatial concert hall is still situated on the Danube river promenade. (Also see: Robert Nemes. *The Once and Future Budapest.* DeKalb: Northern Illinois University Press, 2005, pp. 93–101.)

108. József Fleischer: Statisticher Bericht der Gebärklinik an der k. k. Universität zu Pest in Schuljahre 1855–56. Wiener medizinische Wochenschrift 1856, pp. 534–536.

109. This scene is described in more detail by Semmelweis's earliest notable biographer: "He found that the patients in labor were laid upon filthy sheets which actually stank of decomposed blood and lochia. These had been received and accepted as clean by the head-nurse from the laundry contractor, who had accepted the contract at an especially low rate. All the circumstances pointed to corrupt practices from the superintendent to the pupil-midwife. So, with his whole heart and soul filled to overflowing with his aspirations to save from suffering and death the poor creatures consigned to his care, Semmelweis had to look after the washing! Meeting with official apathy and procrastination while the unhappy women were perishing, [Semmelweis] one day bundled together some of the evil-smelling "Wasche" just as they were taken from the beds of new patients and went straight to the chief official person, von Tandler . . . and demonstrated the urgent call for improvement to his eyes and nostrils . . . It was not to be expected that Semmelweis could with impunity offend the dignity of such a high and mighty official as Statthaltereirath von Tandler, under whose nose he had thrust the vile-smelling napkins snatched from the bed of a lying-in patient." (From: William J. Sinclair, *Semmelweis. His Life and His Doctrine.* Manchester: At the University Press, 1909, pp. 129–130 and p. 136.)

110. Ignác Hirschler (1823–1891), Hungarian ophthalmologist, Rosas' specialty.

111. Photographs and paintings of Ignác Semmelweis, his wife Maria (née Weidenhoffer), and their family can be found in: Kapronczay Károly, *A Semmelweis család története.* Budapest: Semmelweis Kiadó, 2008, pp. 8–9 and pp. 55–60.

112. Ignaz Semmelweis, *The Etiology, Concept, and Prophylaxis of Childbed Fever,* translated by K. Codell Carter. Madison: The University of Wisconsin Press, 1983.

113. Misocainia in medicine (author unknown). New York: Achilles Rose. *The Medical News,* 1904, vol. 85, pp. 1077–1078.

114. One of the most striking series of portraits of Semmelweis that highlights his alarmingly premature graying and aging was published by József Antall. It includes one oil painting, an aquarelle, a lithograph, and six photos, the last taken in 1864 and showing "a completely broken, aged Semmelweis." (Antall J. *The Contemporary Portraits of Ignác Semmelweis.* In Orvostörténeti Közlemények. (67–68) Budapest: Hungaria, 1968, pp. 159–164.)

115. Semmelweis's abnormal behavior was first noted by his first biographer, Theodore Duka, who thought early symptoms of it were apparent even in 1850 or before. Duka T. Childbed fever, its causes and prevention: a life's history. *Lancet*, 1886, ii. 206–208 (July 31, 1886) and pp. 246–248 (August 7, 1886).

116. The meeting described here is fictional. However, von Tandler's continued harassment of Semmelweis is not. Nor were his entirely unjustified charges directed at Semmelweis that had been already communicated to imperial government officials. (Frank Slaughter. *Immortal Magyar.* New York: Henry Schuman, 1950, pp. 162–164.) The charges depicted here against Semmelweis were essentially factual. The scene is intended to fictionally portray the plausible positions taken by the characters at this point, as well as Semmelweis's reactions to them.

117. This is the best English translation of Semmelweis's actual letter to Späth, as it was published for the public to read. Letters to other noted obstetricians were comparably incendiary. (Sherwin B. Nuland. *The Doctors' Plague. Germs, Childbed Fever, and the Strange Story of Ignác Semmelweis.* New York: W.W. Norton & Company, 2003, pp. 159–160.)

118. This was recalled by Semmelweis's widow in her old age when she was interviewed for a newspaper in 1906. (Interview with Semmelweis's widow. *Magyar Hirlap*, October 2, 1906. Also see Gortvay Gy, Zoltán I. *Semmelweis. His Life and Work.* Budapest: Akadémiai Kiadó, 1968, p. 186.)

119. Semmelweis's biographers have provided detailed descriptions of his bizarre behavior at this time, including his hectoring of strangers on the streets about his theory, his perseveration about hand scrubbing, abusive language, insomnia, memory loss, unrestrained eating, irrational spending, and even hypersexuality. (See: Obenchain TG. *Genius Belabored.* Tuscaloosa: The University of Alabama Press, 2016, pp. 179–185; Gortvay Gy, Zoltány I. *Semmelweis. His Life and Work.* Budapest: Akadémiai Kiadó, 1968, pp. 182–187; Nuland SB. *The Doctors' Plague.* New York: Atlas Books, 2003, pp. 162–163.)

120. The term *idée fixe* is no longer used in psychology and psychiatry. In its pathological form, it is an obsessive preoccupation of the mind, a form of monomania, that comes to dominate completely an individual's thinking. It is still used today as a descriptive term.

121. This passage is abstracted from an earlier, 17th-century midwives' oath. (Robert Baker. *Before Bioethics*. Oxford: University Press, 2013, pp. 19–35.)

122. Described in Duka T. Childbed fever, its cause and prevention: a life's history. *Lancet*, 1886, ii. 206–208 and 246–248.

123. Antonia was undoubtedly Semmelweis's favorite, even in the depths of his madness. A photograph of her as an attractive young woman is found in: Kapronczay Károly, *A Semmelweis Család Története*. Budapest: Semmelweis Kiadó, 2008, p. 56.

124. Hospital policy at that time in Budapest required that referrals for commitment to a psychiatric institution be signed by three physicians. However, it did not specify any required qualifications of those physicians. As Carter and Carter have noted, no evidence exists that any of the three physicians who signed Semmelweis's commitment referral letter had ever actually examined him or had any training in psychiatry. Although there were respected psychiatrists in Budapest at that time, not one of them was consulted. (K. Codell Carter and Barbara R. Carter. *Childbed Fever: A Scientific Biography of Ignaz Semmelweis*. New Brunswick: Transaction Publishers, 2005, p. 75.)

125. Published reports of chemical burns of the skin from contact with mercury include: Ross WD, Sholiton MC. Specificity of psychiatric manifestations in relation to neurotoxic chemicals. *Acta Psychiat Scand* 1983;67 (Suppl 303):100–104.

126. Theodore H. Bast and William Snow Miller. *The Life and Time of Adolf Kussmaul*. Paul B. Hoeber, Inc., New York, 1926, p. 101, referring to Kussmaul's work, "*Untersuchungen über den constitutionallen mercurialismus und sein verhältniss zur constitutionellen syphilis.*" Würzburg, 1861. Richard M. Swiderski. *Quicksilver. The History of the Use, Lore and Effects of Mercury*. McFarland & Company, Inc. Publishers, Jefferson,

North Carolina, pp. 104–112. Also see Abramowitz EW. Historical points of interest on the mode of action and ill effects of mercury. Bull NY Acad Med 1934;10(2):695–705.

127. And indeed he did. Hans von Hebra (1847–1902) became a highly respected Professor of Dermatology at the University of Vienna, wrote an important textbook on skin diseases, and was admired for his impassioned public advocacy for legislation to promote sanitation.

128. Josef Gottfried Riedl (1803–1870) had made the insane asylum in Prague the most progressive in Europe. In recognition of this, he was recruited to the imperial capital to become the first superintendent of the new Vienna Asylum (*Niederösterreichische Landes-Irrenanstalt*), also known as the Imperial Royal Institution for the Treatment and Care of the Insane, which opened in 1852 in an impressive new building at Lazarettgasse, 14 (today Am Alserbach 26), in the city's suburbs. It was built on an open hill, surrounded by extensive grounds, with space for 700 patients. (The asylum was demolished in 1974 to create space for expansion of the Vienna General Hospital.) Riedl advocated a much more liberal policy for the use of restraints than were traditionally used for the seriously mentally ill. These progressive practices included a type of straitjacket, called a camisole, which allowed patients to ambulate rather than resorting to the exclusive use of chains and straps by which patients were confined to their cells. Amongst the innovations introduced by the enlightened Riedl were work therapy, including paying the patients for the work they produced, recreational treatment, music therapy, and encouragement of physical exercise. Riedl later founded the Association of Austrian Psychiatrists, was named "emperor counsellor," and was widely consulted by dignitaries and royalty throughout the continent.

Prior to Riedl, psychiatry in Austria was a largely neglected medical specialty and the care of mentally ill patients lagged badly behind other European countries like England and Germany. Psychiatric patients were institutionalized, or more aptly imprisoned, in the *Narrenturm* ("Tower of Fools"), a gloomy and menacing, five-story round, bare brick structure on the grounds of the Vienna General Hospital (*Allgemeine Krankenhaus*), which can be still visited today. One exception was a private hospital in Döbling, the first private psychiatric institution in Austria, where the "mentally ill" could be treated in accordance with their personal "hobbies." The private hospital was very expensive, however, requiring the relatives of a patient to pay up to 5 florins daily, something Semmelweis clearly couldn't afford in his current financial condition. (Erna Lesky, *The Vienna Medical School of the 19th Century,* The Johns Hopkins University Press, Baltimore, 1976, pp. 149–151.) The treatment of mental illness in Riedl's new public Vienna Asylum was in sharp contrast to what were by then notoriously primitive conditions under which the insane had been confined to their cells in the only other option, the state-run Narrenturm. Nevertheless, the use of restraints even by violent force, if necessary, was still frequently employed. (*Guestbook: The story of the psychiatric ward in Prague with portraits of famous people.* Gasset, 2007.)

129. The story of Carl Mayrhofer is a sad one and in many ways parallels Semmelweis's, as told in *Childbed Fever: A Scientific Biography of Ignaz Semmelweis* (by K. Codell Carter and Barbara R. Carter, Transaction Publishers, New Brunswick, 2005, chapter 5; and also Carter KC. Ignaz Semmelweis, Carl Mayrhofer, and the rise of germ theory. *Medical History* 1985; 29:33–53.). In 1860 he was awarded his M.D. degree and in 1862 was appointed second assistant to Carl Braun, who by then had succeeded the deceased Johannes Klein as chief of obstetrics in Vienna, the same facility where Semmelweis had instituted his hand scrubbing protocol fifteen years earlier. Braun was still intensely interested in disproving Semmelweis's theory and proving his own. To that end, Braun instructed Mayrhofer to do the appropriate experiments and generously supported his work with whatever resources he needed. Louis Pasteur by this time had demonstrated microorganisms in the process of fermentation. Using an expensive new microscope Braun bought for him, Mayrhofer readily demonstrated the presence of many types of microbes (which he called "vibrions") in uterine discharges from numerous living and dead women with childbed fever. To prove causation, he sprayed these discharges—and later the isolated microbes cultured and filtered from those discharges—into the vagina of newly delivered rabbits. He found that most of them became ill, died, and showed many of the same findings on autopsy as those seen in human victims.

At first, Braun interpreted these findings as supporting his own theories about airborne germs causing puerperal fever, which Semmelweis had ridiculed. Feeling vindicated, Braun ensured that Mayrhofer's first lecture about the findings was enthusiastically received, and then persuaded the Viennese authorities to install an expensive new ventilation system in the maternity wards. But as he continued his research, Mayrhofer became more and more convinced that Semmelweis was completely right. So, despite his dependence on Braun's financial support, Mayrhofer delivered a second lecture in 1864 explaining his conclusions that postpartum infection was in fact usually caused by the contaminated hands of examining personnel (in both rabbits and humans). This lecture was published in 1865, probably around exactly the same time Semmelweis was riding in a carriage past the *Allgemeine Krankenhaus* on his way to the insane asylum. Soon after this, Mayrhofer was forced out of his position by Braun and, leaving Vienna, found a job in private practice. A number of personal misfortunes ensued, he contracted tuberculosis, became addicted to morphine, and died, unrecognized, in 1882 at the age of forty-five.

130. Carter KC, Abbott S, Siebach JL. Five documents relating to the final illness and death of Ignaz Semmelweis. *Bull Hist Med*; 1996:69:255–270.

131. Skoda reportedly visited Semmelweis in the asylum on August 5, nine days before his death. From: Obenchain TG. Genius Belabored. Tuscaloosa: The University of Alabama Press, 2016, pp. 192–193.

132. As written by Dormandy (Thomas Dormandy, *Moments of Truth,* Chichester: John Wiley & Sons, 2003, p. 235) and from Benedek (István Benedek, *Semmelweis és Kora,* Budapest, 1967, p.432), few had the moral courage of Späth, for long one of Semmelweis's most determined adversaries and the target of Semmelweis's first vitriolic open letter, when he wrote soon after Semmelweis's death: "I venture to state as clearly as I can that in my opinion there is no longer a reputable teacher of midwifery who is not in his own heart convinced of the truth of the doctrine of Semmelweis, even when he still professes to be opposed to it . . . It is all a tribute to Semmelweis."

133. Johann Baptist Chiari, Carl Braun, Joseph Spaeth, *Klinik der Geburtshilfe und Gynaekologie*. Verlag von Ferdinand Enke, 1855.

AUTHOR'S NOTE

The inspiration to write this book must have germinated from the earliest memories of my childhood in Budapest. My mother had a chronic illness that required prolonged hospitalizations at the institution where Ignác Semmelweis first worked upon his return to Hungary, the St. Rochus Hospital. I would often visit her with my father, walking past a grand marble Semmelweis monument in front of the hospital entrance. My father and his best friend, Dr. Imre Magyar, with whose children I used to play, told me all about this persecuted, young Hungarian doctor who made a great medical discovery that would save the lives of countless mothers in labor. I was fascinated by his story. Perhaps it even contributed to my early ambition to become a physician. When I was 9 years old, we escaped from Hungary in the wake of the 1956 revolution (which bore some uncanny parallels to the 1848 revolution described in this book). As I grew up and became a doctor, the story of Semmelweis disappeared into the deepest recesses of my mind.

Then it suddenly and unexpectedly reappeared. Several years ago, when I served as physician-in-chief at a world-renowned medical center, one of my responsibilities was to oversee the program of constant quality improvements in patient care. Specific quality metrics were and continue to be used to measure the performance of our attending physicians and trainees compared to those at other hospitals and to nationally established benchmarks. One of these metrics has been for many years the rate of compliance with hand washing. That is, how frequently physicians and medical trainees wash their hands before they enter a patient's room and upon leaving it. At my first formal presentation to the understandably demanding hospital board, I had to report with trepidation that, during the previous year, my medical service had fallen short of the 92% threshold level for compliance with hand washing. We came in at 89%. I was excoriated for it. Returning to my office to lick my wounds, I thought long and hard about what had just happened. I realized that, of course, the board was completely justified to publicly admonish me. And that's when the Semmelweis story resurfaced. Not only was the board right, but I wondered why the benchmark threshold was only 92%. Why not 100%? After all, didn't Ignác Semmelweis demonstrate to the world 150 years earlier, well before the discovery of the germ theory of disease, that handwashing in hospitals was nothing less than life-saving?

It was at that moment that I decided to learn everything I could about Semmelweis and his personally tragic but ultimately, for the world, triumphant work in Vienna. As I began to write this book, I read practically every detail of his life and times I could find. I finally went to Vienna and back to Budapest to do some primary research in the medical archives of their medical schools. The director of the Josephenum at the University of Vienna wasn't very helpful in advance and in fact didn't even tell me that the building would be closed for gut renovations when I planned to be in Vienna. In fact, it was temporarily surrounded by barbed wire. I therefore had to use a less than ideal way to gain access to the library and archives in that historic building. The situation in Budapest was quite the opposite. The director of the Semmelweis Library and Archives is a man named Lászlo András Magyar and he offered his personal help in searching for pertinent material. His family name is a very common one in Hungary, so I didn't at first make much of it until we discovered that his father was Dr.

Imre Magyar, my father's best friend, whose children I played with more than 60 years earlier.

This is a work of fiction. It has to be that by definition because almost all the dialog was written by me and many of the scenes were created as ones that would be plausible given the known facts, but not documented. However, almost all of the major characters were real. Two notable exceptions were women. Caroline did actually exist because she is named as a love interest of Semmelweis in a recently found letter from him to his friend Marko. But nothing else is known about her. I have introduced her into the story mainly to serve as Semmelweis's narrator to the realities of the outside world in Vienna at that time. His almost single-minded immersion in his work within the physical confines of the hospital likely precluded any meaningful understanding of the social, economic, and political climate that surrounded him. An entirely fictionalized character was Erzsike, Semmelweis's patient in the maternity ward. The intent here was to humanize the suffering of the women afflicted with puerperal fever. For readers with a special interest in the historical details that form the foundation of this story, I have added detailed Endnotes that document them.

There are many people to whom I owe a debt of gratitude for making this book happen. For critically reviewing or editing the book, I thank Stuart Horwitz, Andrea Cumbo-Floyd, Leslie Wells, Richard Rosen, Drs. Brendan Reilly and Steve Greenberg, and my copy editor, Elisabeth Kauffman. For coming up with the cleverly ambiguous title late one night in a Chinese restaurant, I recognize Charlie Greenberg. I am grateful to Michele DeFilippo at 1106 Design, LLC for guiding me through the publishing process. And finally I am so thankful for the forbearance of my wife, Pauline, and my children, Eric, Pamela, and Kate, as well as the inspiration of my grandchildren, Evan, Samantha, Nathaniel, Patrick, Caroline, and Meghan.

ABOUT THE AUTHOR

Andrew Schafer was born in Budapest and at the age of nine escaped with his family to the west following the defeat of the 1956 Hungarian Revolution. Educated in medicine at the Universities of Pennsylvania and Chicago, he became a distinguished hematologist at Harvard Medical School. He was later elected to the presidency of the American Society of Hematology and also served as chairman of the departments of medicine and chief of medicine at Baylor College of Medicine in Houston, the University of Pennsylvania, and Cornell. Elected to the National Academy of Medicine and to leadership in other prominent medical organizations, he continues to be an active clinical practitioner, researcher, and medical educator at Weill Cornell Medical College and the New York-Presbyterian Hospital. An editor and author of major medical textbooks as well as hundreds of original research articles in medicine, this is his first foray into historical fiction. He lives in New York City with his wife, Pauline, and is the proud father of three children and grandfather of six grandchildren.

BUDAPEST, HUNGARY—SEPTEMBER 20, 2017: This beautiful marble monument of Ignaz Semmelweis was sculpted in 1906 by Hungarian sculptor Alojs Stróbl. It can be seen in front of Szent Rókus hospital in Budapest where Semmelweis worked for a few years and introduced his methods for the prevention of puerperal fever.

Made in United States
North Haven, CT
12 March 2023

33963526R00225